ANNE STUART

has written over sixty novels in her twenty-five-plus years as a romance novelist. She's won every major award in the business, including three RITA® Awards from Romance Writers of America, as well as their Lifetime Achievement Award. Anne's books have made various bestseller lists, and she has been quoted in *People, USA TODAY* and *Vogue*. She has also appeared on *Entertainment Tonight,* and according to her, done her best to cause trouble! When she's not writing or traveling around the country speaking to various writer's groups, she can be found at home in northern Vermont with her husband, two children, a dog and three cats.

DEBRA WEBB

was born in Scottsboro, Alabama, to parents who taught her that anything is possible if you want it badly enough. She began writing at age nine. Eventually she met and married the man of her dreams, and tried some other occupations, including selling vacuum cleaners, and working in a factory, a day-care center, a hospital and a department store. When her husband joined the military, they moved to Berlin, Germany, and Debra became a secretary in the commanding general's office. By 1985 they were back in the States, and finally moved to Tennessee, to a small town where everyone knows everyone else. With the support of her daughters, Debra took up writing again, looking to mystery and movies for inspiration. In 1998 her dream of writing for Harlequin came true. Now multipublished, Debra writes spine-tingling romantic suspense for Harlequin Intrigue and heartfelt love stories for Harlequin American Romance.

ANNE STUART

DEBRA WEBB

A STRANGER'S KISS

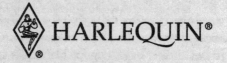

HARLEQUIN®

TORONTO • NEW YORK • LONDON
AMSTERDAM • PARIS • SYDNEY • HAMBURG
STOCKHOLM • ATHENS • TOKYO • MILAN • MADRID
PRAGUE • WARSAW • BUDAPEST • AUCKLAND

ISBN 0-373-83546-9

A STRANGER'S KISS

Copyright © 2003 by Harlequin Books S.A.

The publisher acknowledges the copyright holders
of the individual works as follows:

WINTER'S EDGE
Copyright © 1995 by Anne Kristine Stuart Ohlrogge

SAFE BY HIS SIDE
Copyright © 2000 by Debra Webb

Visit us at www.eHarlequin.com

Printed in U.S.A.

CONTENTS

WINTER'S EDGE

Anne Stuart

For Julianne Moore.
I couldn't have done it without her.
And maybe I shouldn't have.

Prologue

She was coming back. The cunning little tart had managed to fool them all. She'd survived the blow on the head, the coma. So far she hadn't said a word, but there was no counting on that happy state of affairs to continue.

She had a reason for her silence, there was little doubt of that.

She would have to die. Sooner or later. Before she decided to start talking. Before she decided to turn the tables, and try her delicate hands at a little extortion. She would have to die.

The only problem was how to arrange it. Make it look like an accident? Or make it look like someone else had murdered her...

That would be the most delicious of all. Kill two birds with one stone. She would die. And he would be blamed.

Ah, life could be very sweet indeed.

SHE WAS COMING BACK. He had no choice in the matter, Patrick Winters thought as he slammed around the empty kitchen. She'd been hurt, she needed time to recover. She'd been implicated in a suspicious death, and she'd refused to answer questions. The police wanted her readily available, and he was the logical person to provide her a place to live.

He leaned back against the kitchen counter. It was just past dawn, and if he was a decent, caring man he'd be preparing to drive across the river to New Jersey, to the hospital, and fetch her back to Winter's Edge, the only home she'd ever known. She'd lived there for seven years, and she had no place else to go.

If she had, he'd gladly send her there. He never wanted to see her again, not if he could help it. She'd caused too much harm, destroyed too much, with her willful anger and childish spite. He wanted her away from here, out of his life.

Before he made the mistake of thinking there might be something else, some faint glimmer of hope.

He'd been a fool in the past. He wasn't about to let her make a fool of him again. She'd come back, spin her persecution fantasies, and then, once the police or someone was able to force the truth out of her, he'd send her away.

He had no responsibility for her. She had more than enough money, more than enough self-absorption to handle life. She could go, and he'd never think of her again.

Until he signed the divorce papers.

He wasn't going to waste his time, his day, going after her. There were plenty of other ways to get her safely transported back to the sprawling estate in Bucks County. Someone else could do it.

In the meantime, he was getting the hell out of there. And he wasn't sure when he'd bother to come back.

Not until he could look at her, at her pale, innocent face with the green-blue cat's eyes, at her soft mouth, and not think about the past.

And how much he'd wanted her, once, long ago.

And damn it, how much he still wanted her.

SHE WAS GOING BACK. She knew it; the thought danced through her befogged mind as she drifted in and out of sleep. She felt both frightened and excited, reluctant and eager. Yet she wasn't sure where she was going, or why.

She didn't know what she'd find when she got there.

She only knew she was returning to where she belonged. Whether they wanted her or not.

Chapter One

It was very still in the room, still and warm. Maybe that should have reassured her, but it had the opposite effect. She fought her way out of the cocooning sleep, the too familiar feelings of panic beating about her like the dark wings of a thousand bats. She opened her eyes to face the sterile whiteness of a hospital room, and she remembered nothing. Except that she was afraid.

Without moving a muscle she slowly began taking in her surroundings. Her head pounded like a sledgehammer, and she reached a tentative hand out to touch it, finding a tender scalp beneath a surprisingly heavy mane of hair. Drawing back her shaking hand, she looked at it closely. It appeared neither foreign nor familiar, a tanned, capable hand with long fingers, short nails and no rings. And her panic grew.

"You're finally awake then." A voice broke through her tangled thoughts, and her eyes met the warm, friendly ones of a young nurse. "I thought you'd sleep forever after that last shot we gave you. You were pretty upset." She moved closer, her eyes cheerfully curious behind the wire-rimmed glasses. "How are you feeling, hon?"

She hated being called hon. That little she could remember. "Where am I?" she demanded finally in a faintly husky voice that was equally startling. She didn't dare ask the more important question—*who* am I?

"Riverview Medical Center," the nurse answered, watching her closely. "Is something wrong?"

"How long have I been here?"

"Two weeks," the nurse answered. "Don't you remember?"

She shook her head numbly, and the wicked pounding increased. "Not a thing."

The nurse clucked with professional sympathy, her brown eyes troubled. "Take a deep breath and try to relax. You've had several of these blank spells before—with any luck this one won't last too long. They often follow a bad concussion like you've had. Do you remember anything at all this time?" she asked curiously, making a small notation on the chart in her capable looking hands.

"Nothing. How long have these blank periods usually lasted?" She clasped her unfamiliar hands together in an effort to hide the tremor.

The nurse shrugged. "They come and go. A few hours, at the most. Once it went on for several days. You just lie back and rest and I'll get the doctor to answer any more questions you might have. This is such a shame—they were planning to discharge you today if it was all right with Lieutenant Ryker."

"Lieutenant Ryker?" she echoed. "Is he in the army?" It was a stupid question and she knew it. She might not have any concrete memories, but she knew she was in trouble. Deep trouble.

"He's with the police. You've forgotten how you got in here, haven't you?" She leaned over, taking her pulse.

The woman in the bed nodded miserably.

The nurse hesitated, glancing toward the door as if expecting help. "You were in a serious car accident, Mrs. Winters."

The name meant nothing to her. She glanced down at her hands, but there was no ring. No telltale mark of one recently discarded. "How serious?" She managed to keep her voice reasonably calm.

Once more the nurse hesitated. "The passenger in your car was dead, and you had sustained a severe concussion and some unpleasant bruising. You were unconscious for several days, but since then you've been healing very rapidly. Except for your occasional bouts of amnesia."

"And what does this Lieutenant Ryker have to do with all this? Did I commit a crime? Is there some question of negligence?"

The nurse busied herself with the pillows. "You've refused to give us the name of the man who was with you. That, combined with the $350 thousand in cash that they found in the trunk of the car has raised a lot of questions. Questions you won't answer." She dropped her wrist lightly on the starched white sheet. "If you'd just cooperate and answer the police's questions, I'm sure they would let you go home and recover at your own pace. Sometimes it just takes time."

She stared at the nurse blankly. "I wish I could. I only wish I could."

She clucked sympathetically, patting her hand with a reassuring gesture. "Try not to worry. I'll go find Dr. Hobson. In the meantime you just rest and think about your husband."

"My husband?"

"You mean to say you don't remember him either?" she demanded, astonished. "I would have said he was almost impossible to forget."

"Is he…nice?"

"Nice?" She considered the notion. "Somehow I don't think so. As a matter of fact, the two of you don't seem to get along so well. But God, is he beautiful! I wouldn't kick him out of bed for eating crackers."

"I beg your pardon?"

"Just a figure of speech," the nurse said hastily. "I'll get the doctor."

She lay back against the starched white sheets, trying to put a tight control on the panic that was sweeping over her. She knew nothing, absolutely nothing about who and what she was, and the few little tidbits the talkative nurse had dropped made things even worse. A strange man dead? A fortune in cash? A handsome husband who hated her?

This must all be some hideous nightmare. In another moment she would wake in her own bed in… The blankness that met her probing mind filled her with more horror than the thought of a dead man sitting beside her in her car, and she felt the burn of frightened tears stinging her eyes. *But I never cry,* she thought, blinking the tears back with a sort of wonder.

She pulled herself slowly out of bed, marveling at the exhaustion that suffused her unknown body, at the weakness in her legs. She moved across the cool, tiled floor to the small mirror above the washstand and examined herself carefully. It was a complete stranger staring back at her.

No, perhaps not complete. It was like looking at a picture of a distant relative. She didn't know the person in the mirror. But she looked vaguely familiar.

She surveyed the various parts of her. Long, honey-blond hair that could do with a thorough washing, slanted green-blue eyes, a nose too small and a mouth too large. High cheekbones and a determined chin completed the picture, yet she felt neither strangeness nor recognition. She looked to be in her early twenties, far younger than she felt. She turned away from that lost face and moved slowly back to the bed. She'd lost more than twenty years someplace. Twenty-some years, and a husband she hated.

"There you are, my dear. Feeling a bit dodgy this morning?" She could only assume this elderly gentleman in the rumpled white lab coat was her doctor, but she eyed him with patent distrust and disapproval. "I don't know whether you should be out of bed quite yet," he continued.

She sat back on the side of the mattress, watching him with a distrust that seemed natural to her. "I thought I was leaving today," she said shortly. "Surely I'll have to be able to walk?"

He raised an eyebrow. "The nurse says you've had another memory loss. I guess you've forgotten that you trust me just a tiny bit."

She stared at him. He looked more like an elderly David Letterman than a doctor, she thought vaguely. And then the realization struck her—how did she know what David Letterman looked like, when she didn't know her own face?

"How much is missing this time?" he asked.

"Everything," she said wearily. "I have no idea who I am."

He frowned. "Amnesia isn't usually like that. There should be some patches of memory, some faint traces. While you've had intermittent memory loss, there hasn't been anything this severe. You have no pressure building on your brain, no sign of any trauma other than the concussion, but perhaps another CAT scan might be in order."

"No!" she protested. "No more prodding. I just want a few answers."

"Are you certain you just don't want to go home to your husband?" he asked shrewdly.

"Of course I don't want to go home to a husband I can't

even remember," she said, the anger building inside her oddly familiar. She must have spent a lot of time being angry. "Do you think that's enough to frighten me into remembering again? Maybe I'm just looking for an excuse not to have to identify the dead man in the car I wrecked."

"You remember that?"

"No. The nurse told me. I remember absolutely nothing." Her voice quavered slightly—another sign of weakness that she fought back with fierce determination. She couldn't afford to show any sign of vulnerability. That certainty stayed with her.

Dr. Hobson looked at her curiously. "What happened to that fiendish temper of yours?" he asked mildly. "You've already terrified two of the toughest professionals on this floor."

"I'm frightened," she said in a tight little voice. "I can't be strong all the time."

"Of course you can't," he said soothingly. "No one expects you to be but yourself."

"Well, I expect too much," she said in a muffled voice.

He patted her hand. "You do, indeed. Do you think you're ready to go home? I'm worried about this recent blank spot. Chances are it will pass as swiftly as the others, but still, it concerns me."

"If I put it off I may never be able to go back," she said in a quiet voice, steeling herself. "The sooner I face up to it the better off I'll be. The nurse says these blank spells don't last long. I'll probably remember everything by the time I reach home. Wherever that is," she added with an attempt at humor that sounded just a bit bitter.

"Out in the country, in a small horse-farming community. Bucks County, I gather. We're just on the other side of the river in New Jersey—it shouldn't take you more than an hour to get home. Depending on the traffic." He took a step back, surveying her. "It's probably a wise decision," he added. "Despite the memory lapse, you're perfectly well, and we try to get people out of the hospital as soon as we can. The insurance companies don't like paying bills any more than the rest of us."

She tried to smile at his attempt at humor, but it fell flat. "A wise decision," she repeated doubtfully, half to herself.

He was already moving toward the door. "I've given your husband instructions, but I'll repeat them to you. Don't drink alcohol, don't take drugs, don't do anything too strenuous for a while. Try not to start smoking again if you can help it—it'll kill you sooner or later."

"I smoke?"

"Not for the past two weeks. Fortunately you've gone cold turkey already, so you shouldn't even miss them. Just take it easy and give yourself time to mend."

"There…there wasn't any brain damage, was there?" she questioned nervously.

"None," he said, his voice firm. "We'll give it about a week. If the amnesia continues, or you have dizzy spells, anything at all after that, I want you to come straight back here. All right?"

She summoned up her coolest smile. "Of course," she lied.

He hesitated. "You might as well get dressed, then. I'll send the nurse in to help you. Your clothes should be in the locker behind the door."

She dressed quickly, surprised by the clothing they insisted was hers. The raw silk suit, the ridiculously high-heeled shoes, the leather purse. They were hers—and yet she had no sense of recognition. They felt both familiar and alien to her, as if they belonged to a different sort of person. To that stranger who bore a distant resemblance to the woman in the mirror.

She tied the silk scarf around her neck with the ease of long practice, just as the nurse returned. "Is it cold outside?" she asked in a deliberately nonchalant voice.

The nurse shrugged. "About usual for the end of March." She eyed her curiously. "You *did* know it was the end of March, didn't you?"

She smiled at her. "I do now." She glanced back at her reflection. She was Mrs. Winters, tall and leggy and well dressed, suspected of God knows what, on her way to meet her handsome husband whom she apparently hated, on a day in late winter. And she was leaving behind the only people she knew in the world.

"You know, things could be a lot worse," the nurse broke into her troubled thoughts.

"I beg your pardon?"

"You've got money. You've got your health, even if your memory's a bit patchy. Even though he's a bit older than you, your husband has to be one of the most gorgeous creatures I've seen in centuries. A few nights with him should put the color back in your cheeks."

"I thought you said we hated each other," she protested faintly.

"Well, sometimes it's awfully hard to tell the difference between hate and love," the nurse said. "Maybe you can spend the next few weeks finding out which one it is."

"Maybe. I just hope it turns out to be the right one." She was unable to make her voice sound overly optimistic.

"If it's not, I'll give you my address and you can send your husband to me," the nurse said, straight-faced.

She finally found she could smile. "I'll be happy to."

"Oh, I nearly forgot. Lieutenant Ryker would like the pleasure of your company," she said, her voice heavy with sarcasm, picking up the discarded hospital robe and heading for the door. "Don't let him scare you—he's all bark and no bite. Dr. Hobson's told him to go easy on you, but I wouldn't count on it. Just don't let him browbeat you." She smiled. "Good luck to you."

And then she was alone once more, staring down at the shiny green vinyl floor and wondering what ghastly crimes she had committed.

None. She knew that with an instinct both sure and comforting. Unfortunately she had no memory, no way to refute any accusations.

Maybe she wasn't suspected of anything. Maybe she was just being paranoid. She looked down at her elegant clothes and considered her absent husband. Somehow she didn't think paranoia was a major part of her difficulties.

Lieutenant Ryker was more than happy to inform her what her difficulties were. He was a middle-aged man, with sandy hair, sandy eyes, and a tense manner that was slightly intimidating. Not the ogre that the nurse had painted, but no charmer either. She sat across from him in the private lounge and crossed her ankles with a casual disdain that seemed to come naturally.

"Mrs. Winters, we're releasing you into your husband's custody today—against my better judgment, I might add. You must remember that you have given your oath that you'll remain in his care until this matter is cleared up." His eyes were faintly contemptuous.

"What matter?"

"Dr. Hobson told me you have a temporary memory loss." He looked skeptical. "How very convenient for you. To summarize briefly, Mrs. Winters, you were found in a wrecked car near the Jersey coast with a dead man beside you in the passenger seat. We finally got an ID on him, no thanks to you. George Andrews. You had a concussion that may or may not have been caused by the accident, and the autopsy showed that rather than dying from injuries sustained in the accident, your companion had been strangled. Now obviously you haven't the strength to strangle a man of Andrews's height and weight. Obviously, also, you must have a good idea who did it."

"Why do you say that?" she countered swiftly. "How do you know that man didn't knock me unconscious before someone showed up and strangled him?"

"Highly unlikely, Mrs. Winters. There were signs of a struggle—you had bloodied and broken fingernails, and there was no blood on Andrews's body."

"Blood? What about DNA testing...?" From somewhere in the recesses of her knowledge came the question.

"It was your blood, Mrs. Winters," he said wearily. "And the dead man isn't your only problem. There's also the question of $350 thousand found in the trunk of your car. Your fingerprints are all over that money, Mrs. Winters. Yours and Andrews's." His voice was hard, implacable and furious. "You have refused to cooperate with the police from the first moment you regained consciousness, telling us absolutely nothing, and you still refuse to do so. We know several of your companion's aliases from a fingerprint check, but after that the trail gets cold. We know he was a criminal, Mrs. Winters. A petty, blackmailing criminal." He shook his head angrily. "Maybe your husband will be able to convince you to do the honorable thing."

And maybe you can go to hell, she thought silently, maintaining an impassive countenance. "What was I doing with this man? Where was my husband?"

"I think you can answer that far better than we can, if you wanted to. All we know of your movements is that you left your husband five weeks ago, two weeks before you turned up in that wrecked car. Perhaps you've changed your mind and feel like enlightening us?" He didn't look hopeful.

She shook her head. "I'm afraid I can't." Despite the man's hostility she wanted the same answers that he did, and she made an effort to smile politely. "I simply don't remember. Not right now, at least. I should before long, or at least that's what the doctor assures me."

He snorted, his contempt obvious. He must have thought she was a spoiled, frivolous creature, and yet she didn't feel very frivolous, except for this silk suit she was wearing. Had she got it from her handsome husband, she wondered, the one she'd run away from? Or from her dead lover?

"Is my husband here yet?" she asked, dreading the moment when she had to meet the stranger who would have so much control over her life, the stranger she had run from. There seemed no way to avoid it much longer.

Apparently there was. "He's not coming," Lieutenant Ryker said shortly. "He's gotten a friend of his to come and get you. I don't imagine his feelings toward you are any too charitable right now."

"I imagine not," she agreed faintly, wondering desperately what, besides a husband she hated, would await her when she arrived at her forgotten home.

The answers were there. The answers she needed, the reason she'd run.

But more than answers might await her. She couldn't picture a place, or a person. But she recognized the familiar feelings that swept over her as she contemplated her return.

Longing.

And fear.

Chapter Two

The car sped across the endless stretch of crowded highway, the landscape brown, dead and dreary. What an awful
time of year, she thought gloomily. Everything dead from
winter, the spring teasingly out of sight. She wondered
dismally where she was going. Bucks County, they'd told
her. Somehow that didn't sound promising.

"Excuse me, Officer Stroup." She leaned forward and
spoke to the thickset shoulders in front of her. "Where is
it exactly that we're headed?"

He permitted himself a stare of incredulity before returning his stolid gaze to the fog-shrouded highway.
"Come off it, Mrs. Winters. You know as well as I do
where we're going. To Winter's Edge, your husband's
farm in Belltown, Pennsylvania. In Bucks County, where
you've lived for the past seven years."

She leaned back with a languor that came easily to her,
a languor she didn't like. She sat back up stiffly. "Do I
know you?" she asked suddenly. She hadn't registered any
sense of familiarity when she'd been introduced to the sullen hulk of her husband's errand boy, one of the local
policemen, apparently.

"Your husband and I have been friends for years," he
said, but there was an undercurrent in his voice she

couldn't quite define. "We could have been friends too, if you know what I mean. If you weren't so picky."

She could guess what he meant, and she shuddered. "Why didn't he come and get me?" She finally voiced the question that had been eating away inside her. There was no reason it should bother her—she didn't remember the man, so why should he have the ability to hurt her? But he did. Perhaps it was no wonder that she hated him.

"I don't imagine he wants to have any more to do with you than he can help," Stroup shot back, his thick red neck mottled with irritation. "I owed him a favor or two, so I offered to take this little chore off his hands for him. Besides, I thought you might be feeling a little less uppity after getting involved in a murder."

Her eyes met his in the rearview mirror, and there was no mistaking the meaning in them. Another shudder washed over her.

"I'm feeling as uppity as ever," she said sharply, leaning back against the seat. Her head was throbbing again, and she longed for a room hidden away from everyone. Which was just what she'd get if they proved she had anything to do with the mysterious George Andrews's murder. "And you're hardly acting like my husband's friend," she added belatedly.

He laughed, a fat, wheezy chuckle. "You should realize by now that your husband doesn't give a damn what you do and who you do it with. You made sure of that a long time ago."

She turned away, trying to shut out the sight of him in the front seat, trying to shut out the sound of his voice. Anything to still the pain in her head. Obviously Stroup believed her capable of adultery as well as murder. She wondered what she could have possibly done to alienate everyone so completely. Particularly her handsome husband.

She tried to picture him. Older, the nurse had said. Very handsome. She summoned up the image of someone gentle, smiling down at her, with faded eyes and a fatherly manner. Gray hair, slightly stooped. But the comforting image shifted, almost immediately, and the man in front of her had midnight black hair, winter blue eyes, and a cool, mocking smile that held no warmth whatsoever.

Suddenly her hands were cold and sweating, her heart was pounding beneath the silk suit, and the hairpins were digging into her scalp. Her eyes shot open, and she stared determinedly at the brown, blurred landscape. She wasn't going to let them destroy her. She hadn't before, and she wouldn't this time.

The stray memory flitted through her brain like a wisp of fog, gone before she could snatch it back. Who had tried to destroy her? And why? The past remained stubbornly, painfully blank, with only the tantalizing memory to further claw at her nerves.

The sun was setting as they pulled into a small, old-worldly town somewhere over the Pennsylvania border. The gloom of the day had worked itself up to the tangible expression of pouring rain, and she watched the dead countryside fly by the windows with unabated gloom. Heaven only knew what sort of man she was about to meet. Her husband, they told her, but how did she know whether she could believe them or not? Maybe this was all some conspiracy—maybe they were trying to make her doubt who and what she was.

If only she could believe that. She felt bone tired, her head pounding. More than anything she wanted to sink into a soft, warm bed and sleep for hours and days until this nightmare had passed. But would she be sleeping alone, or with a hostile stranger who didn't even care enough to pick her up at the hospital?

She felt the sudden sting of tears in her eyes, and she opened her expensive leather handbag, searching for a tissue. The lining of the purse still smelled of the cigarettes she'd tossed, and there was no doubt she'd once been a smoker. The smell of it made her ill.

Tucked inside were two handkerchiefs, linen and expensive. The first was very plain and masculine, and the initials, embroidered so carefully on the scrap of material, were *P.A.W.* There were pale orange streaks across the white linen, too pale to be the blood she had first suspected.

Panic filled her, swift and unreasoning, and she shoved the scraps of cloth back into the purse, no longer eager to open the Pandora's box in her lap. *M.A.W.* the other handkerchief had read. If Winters was her last name, then her first must be Mary or Magdalene or something of that sort. Though why the image of Mary Magdalene, the great whore, would have come to mind when she was looking for an identity was something she didn't want to think about. She only knew she wasn't going to let strangers convince her she was something that she wasn't.

The weather didn't choose to improve. She shivered slightly as the car pulled away through the deep troughs of water, out across the rain-swept highway, then leaned back, eyes shut, heart pounding. She didn't want to watch where he was taking her. She simply wanted to arrive, and face up to it when she had to.

It was far too easy to drift into a strangely altered state. She had no idea whether it was the result of her head injury, or whatever drugs they'd given her, or just stress and exhaustion. But as she closed her eyes she could see him, through a mist of anger and desire. His eyes, winter blue, staring at her with frustration and contempt. His mouth, wide, sexual, set in a thin line of anger.

She wanted to lift her hand, to touch him. To brush a strand of inky black hair away from his face, to soothe away the fierceness as he looked at her. If she could just explain...

But it was too late for that, she knew it. Too late for second chances, too late for the truth. She let herself sink back, into the darkness, into the forgetfulness that was a mixed blessing.

The sudden bumpiness of the road jarred her into reluctant alertness, and she sat up straight, guessing by the unevenness that they must be crossing a wooden bridge. She looked out the streaming windows at the long low building as they drove by. An old stone farmhouse loomed beside it, wet and forbidding in the glare of the headlights through the pelting rain. Stroup brought the sedan to an abrupt halt, the jolt flinging her body against the back of the seat.

"Shoulda worn your seat belt, Mrs. Winters," he said with a malicious chuckle. "Or did you *forget* that it was the law nowadays?"

Her nerves had reached fever pitch. "So arrest me," she snapped back.

"Don't I wish I could," he replied, and she had no doubt he meant it. "Maybe I'll get my chance later on. In the meantime, we're here. Home sweet home, Mrs. Winters." He leaned over the back seat. "It looks pretty deserted. You want I should see you inside?" The leer was back in his thick face.

She controlled the shiver of disgust. "I don't think so, thank you. Do I have any luggage?"

"You know that as well as I do," he answered shortly, leaning back against the seat. He smelled like stale cigarettes and yesterday's beer. "You were found in the clothes you're wearing and no sign of where you'd come from. I'm sure your husband will have plenty of other stuff waiting for you. Both of you can afford it.''

She stared back at his pugnacious face, struggling to think of something suitably devastating, something that would make him flinch as he'd made her flinch. Her tired mind remained a blank. She could be cruel and cutting, she knew it with a perverse pride. At least she wasn't totally defenseless. But right now she was too exhausted and tense to find the words.

''Thank you,'' she murmured inanely, reaching out and opening the door into the torrent of rain.

''I'll be seeing you around,'' he said, before driving off and splashing her liberally with mud and water. His last words echoed unpleasantly as she stood there, and for a moment she considered running.

But where would she run to? They hadn't passed another house or a car for miles; she was out in the middle of nowhere, and the rain was like tiny pellets of ice pelting against her skin. She'd been running away when they found her. Maybe it was time to stop running. Time to face the truth, no matter how unpleasant it might be.

She moved toward the back door of the house with an instinct she didn't stop to consider, her head held low against the driving rain. Pulling at the knocker, she huddled under the tiny porch roof. There was no answer.

She knocked again, this time more loudly. The strain of the day, the wetness of her clothes and the pain in her head were all joining to make her furiously angry with a fate and a husband who had put her in such a miserable situation. She stared out at the rain-soaked landscape, sorely tempted to take off into the late afternoon downpour, never to be heard from again. But cowardice and discomfort were too much for her, she thought bitterly, and feeling like a fool she turned back and knocked one last time. "The hell with it," she muttered, as she pushed open the door and stumbled in.

It took her a moment to get her bearings. The interior was warm and dark, with the scent of lemon oil and wood smoke in the air, and there wasn't a sound other than the steady tick of a grandfather clock gracing the stone-floored hallway. Her high-heeled shoes were wet and slippery, and she kicked them off with a sigh of relief before moving down the strange hallway in her damp stocking feet. Her total lack of recognition should have disturbed her. They had told her this was her home—she had no choice but to take their word for it. For the time being all she wanted was to find someplace warm and sit down.

She found her haven at the end of the hall—a warm, cozy living room with a fire crackling in the fieldstone fireplace, sending out delicious waves of heat. There was no one in sight, and for the first time she thought to announce her presence.

"Hello!" she called out, softly at first. Then, gaining courage, she shouted louder. "Is anyone home?" There was no answer, just the hiss and pop of the fire. Sighing, she sank down in one of the overstuffed armchairs by the fire and took stock of her surroundings.

She'd never been here before, she told herself incredulously. If she had, how could she have forgotten it, how could she ever have left it? Even with the gloom of the lashing rain outside, it was surely the most beautiful room she'd ever seen in her life. The walls were of an old and mellow oak panelling, the ceiling low and comforting, with shelves of books all around. The furniture around her was old, a wonderful mix of antiques and overstuffed comfort. To her right was a gateleg table with a Chinese porcelain bowl of fresh flowers on it; across the room was a Chippendale highboy that made her ache with covetousness. And yet there was no need for envy, she realized suddenly. This was her home.

She lost track of the time, staring absently into the fire. It could have been five minutes, or an hour, before she became aware of her damp, uncomfortable condition. Her silk suit was ruined, and her entire body felt clammy and stiff despite the warmth of the fire. She decided then she couldn't wait any longer for her phantom husband—she simply had to get into more comfortable clothing.

Making her way into the back hall, she turned on the lights against the late afternoon gloom. It was an eerie feeling, wandering around this vast, strange yet familiar house. At any moment she expected some stranger to pop out of a hidden doorway, to denounce her as an imposter.

But no one appeared. She climbed slowly up the curved wooden staircase with its lovely oak planks polished to a mirror shine. At the top she stopped in confusion. There were six or seven doors leading from the long, narrow hallway, and the passage itself took a sharp turn and went down two steps into another section. She had no idea which was her room.

She explored slowly, noisily, so as to alert any possible inhabitants. But all the room were deserted. Four of the bedrooms were apparently occupied, three were just as obviously guest rooms.

It was hard to decide which room could have been hers. The first contained clothes rather like the ones she was wearing: elegant, expensive, sophisticated and very uncomfortable looking. Yet they simply weren't the sort of thing that the young woman in the mirror would really want to wear, especially at her age.

But the other bedroom's closet revealed even less likely apparel. In it were dresses belonging to an obviously elegant, well-dressed matron of indeterminate age, wearing a stylishly stout size 24.

She wandered back into the other bedroom, with no choice but to accept the fact that everything was fitting in with the unattractive picture she was building of Mrs. Winters. While the other bedrooms had beautiful old flooring covered sparingly with antique hooked rugs, hers was awash with puffy white wall-to-wall carpeting. The other rooms boasted lovely old furniture, with gleaming woods lovingly tended. Her room had a matched set of expensive ugly modern furniture, all chrome and glass at screaming odds with the lines of the old room. The drapes and bedspread were satin, and the entire effect was one of tasteless opulence. She sat down at the mirrored dressing table and stared at herself over the rows of silver-topped bottles of perfumes and creams. That slightly tanned creature with the splash of freckles across her nose didn't belong in this room, did she? Somehow she had the uneasy feeling that she did.

She got up quickly, with an air of decision. Before she could begin to fathom what was going on, she needed a shower and clean, dry clothes. Searching through the many drawers of the ugly-elegant dresser, she finally discovered one pair of ancient and faded jeans among all the silk. There was a warm turtleneck, and heavy cotton sweater, stuck at the back of the drawer, and she carted them into the bathroom, stripping off her clothes as she went. The discarded suit went into the trash can. Never again would she wear one—those suits symbolized what surely must have been the most awful day of her life. If there were any worse in the lost past, she didn't want to remember them.

It wasn't until she was scrubbing her hair that realization struck her. She had gone straight to the bathroom without a moment's hesitation. She had known where it was.

Trembling slightly, she rinsed her hair and stepped out of the shower, no longer able to deny that she had been there before. No longer could she clutch at straws, hoping they'd mistaken her for someone else. She'd just wrecked that theory by coming straight to the pink-and-white bathroom that matched the fussy tastes of the sybaritic bedroom.

She dressed quickly in the chill air, towelling her long hair dry. She grabbed a pair of heavy wool socks before she ran back down to the living room and that cozy fire, the only warm room in this vast house, it seemed. It must be the stone walls, she thought. Or perhaps her husband was a miser, or an energy freak. The temperature seemed a little extreme, even for that, but then, the lady of the pink-and-white bedroom was nothing if not pampered. Maybe the creature she used to be couldn't survive those temperatures, but the new woman she was determined to become could grin and bear it.

Her hair was almost completely dry when she heard the back door slam. It took all her self-control not to jump up in panic, and she forced herself to stay still. Her elderly husband couldn't be bothered to drive to the hospital to pick her up. Well, he could at least make his way into the living room. She was damned if she was going to go to him.

She leaned back, trying to still the sudden panicked racing of her heart. Her life was about to change. She knew it, with a bleak, desperate certainty. She heard a noise by the entrance, and she looked up, a deceptively cool expression on her face.

Chapter Three

It wasn't who, or what, she'd been steeling herself for. A giant black animal ambled into the room. He stared at her from large, mournful eyes, and from the recesses of her memory she came up with a name. He was a Newfoundland dog, large and friendly. Though the look he gave her was just a bit wary.

"Hello, boy," she said softly, holding out a hand for him to snuffle. He lumbered over, his dark eyes suspicious, and with great caution he allowed her to pat his massive, leonine head, going so far as to honor her with a lick from his large and lolling tongue.

"So you're back." A high-pitched voice, soft and unfriendly, came from the door of the room, and she jumped guiltily. He was an indistinct, shadowy figure in the half light of the doorway, and she felt no pang of recognition. An older man. He could only be her husband.

She couldn't imagine what to say to him, so she was silent. He moved into the room, his paunchy figure staggering slightly, his receding chin thrust out aggressively. He was middle-aged and flabby, with a few strands of orangeish hair combed carefully over his shiny pink scalp, and his mouth had a petulant, spoiled look about it. The nurse must have had a decidedly odd sense of humor to consider this man handsome.

His eyes were small and shrewd and light-colored in his puffy red face, looking as if they could see through all her pretenses. She had no pretenses, she wanted to cry. But she never cried, she thought, staring at him silently.

"What's this new act, Molly?" he said, lounging with what he obviously considered a lazy grace in one of the comfortable, overstuffed armchairs. She hoped, perversely, that it was still damp from her sojourn in it. "This country girl look isn't quite your style, is it? You've always been more Neiman Marcus than Eddie Bauer. Maybe you're hoping to appease Patrick with your newfound docility. It won't wash, my dear, I promise you that." There was an ill-concealed malice in his slurred voice, combined with an odd wariness on his part, a watchfulness just under the slightly drunken surface.

She edged closer to the fire, away from him. "Patrick?" she questioned innocently. Her name was Molly, then. Not bad. At least it was better than Mary Magdalene.

"Oh, come off it. You needn't play games with your old pal Willy. Haven't I always been on your side?"

From the look of him she doubted it. "Who's Patrick?" Molly questioned again, stubbornly.

Willy smirked. "Why don't you go into the kitchen and find out?" he suggested amiably. "I'm sure he's dying to see you after five long weeks."

Molly rose, reluctantly, and headed out to the hall, keeping well out of old friend Willy's reach. He looked like the type who pinches. The dog lumbered after her, obviously preferring her company to Willy's. Dogs are more discerning than humans, she thought.

She found the kitchen after only one false foray into a clothes closet. The room was huge and dark, and reaching out, she switched on the light. And then realized that although she hadn't known where the room was, she'd found the light switch without the slightest hesitation.

He'd just come in the door. He stood there, staring at her, cold, implacable anger emanating from him. The dog sensed something in the air, and he whined and moved closer to Molly, nearly knocking her over in the process. She looked up at the man across the room, and felt those familiar-unfamiliar emotions rushing through her. Longing. And fear.

He was the man from her dreams, her brief flashes of memory. Now she could see him clearly, without the fog of time, and she wasn't sure she liked what she saw.

He was handsome enough, despite his unfriendly expression. He was dressed in faded jeans and an old, torn sweater. His cold blue eyes were bitter, his mouth tight-lipped and angry. He wore his black hair long, tied at the back to get it out of his way, and drops of rain glittered in the dark mane. He looked to be in his midthirties, about ten years older than she purportedly was, and he stared at her out of those wintry eyes, an angry, beautiful man. Despite his animosity she felt a stirring inside her, a stirring she knew she hadn't felt for many men. She knew who he had to be. But she wasn't ready to accept the disturbing truth.

"So you're back," he said, echoing the words of Willy. "I never thought my wife would care to grace this—now what did you call it?—this miserable old pile of stone again."

"Your wife?" Molly echoed faintly. The word was spoken—there was no way she could avoid it any longer.

"My wife," he said, his voice like ice, cold and hard. He moved closer to her with a totally unconscious grace that was somehow sinuous and unnerving at the same time.

"I gather you didn't save me the trouble and get a quickie divorce during your...vacation."

He was quite close to her by now, towering over her, and she clamped down the sudden spurt of nervousness. She was afraid of this man, and she couldn't remember why. "I...I don't know," she said, determined not to back away.

His black eyebrows shot up in disbelief, giving his cool, handsome face a harsh look. "No," he said shortly. "You would have sent the decree off to me as fast as you could. I guess you'll have to cool your heels around here until we can do something about ending this ridiculous farce of a marriage." His eyes flicked over her body contemptuously. "Why have you got those clothes on?"

"I...I was cold." She controlled the chattering of her teeth with an extreme effort, knowing that her shivering was caused by nerves as much as the chill in the air. The man in front of her, her dearly beloved husband, terrified her. And that knowledge made her angry.

"You always are," he mocked, and there was no missing the double meaning. "Why didn't you turn up the thermostat?"

"I didn't know where it was."

Those cold blue eyes looked askance at that. "You've lived in this house for seven years, dear Molly. You should have learned where it is by now."

"Seven years?" she echoed, shocked. "Have we been married that long?" It was out before she could stop it. She hadn't looked old enough to have been married for so long, but then, with all those creams and potions on her dresser upstairs, maybe she was simply extraordinarily well preserved.

His eyes narrowed in surprise for a moment. "That's right, I forgot you were playing the amnesiac. No, we have not been married for seven years. I would have killed you long ago if we had. We've been married ten months, almost to the day."

"Then why did I live here?"

"You know as well as I do," he snapped, moving away from her as if he couldn't bear to be that close. "My father adopted you when you were sixteen. He always had a habit of picking up stray relatives like you and Willy. He found his only child a major annoyance. I'd never do what he wanted, so he had to settle for other people he could control."

"We're related?" She wasn't sure that made the whole situation any more palatable.

"We're fifth cousins, something like that." He dismissed it. "Look, I'm not really interested in playing games with you tonight, Molly. It's Mrs. Morse's day off and I've got to get dinner. Why don't you go back into the living room until it's ready? Keep Willy company—you'd like that, I'm sure."

That was just about the last thing she wanted to do. She took a deep breath, deciding an attempt at cordiality might not be a bad idea. "Wouldn't you like some help with dinner?" she offered tentatively.

He stared at her with amazement. "You hate to cook," he responded flatly. "Now get out of here and leave me alone."

There was no way she could refute his statement. For all she knew she could be the worst cook in the world, so she simply left him without another word. There had to be a reason behind his rampant hostility, just as there had to be a reason why he frightened her. He didn't look as if he were in the mood to answer her questions, and she wasn't in the mood to ask.

The Newfoundland followed her back into the cozy living room, deserting his taciturn master. To her relief, Willy had departed, and she seated herself on the floor by the fireplace with the huge dog beside her, her brain whirling. Nowhere had she found any sense of recognition, any feeling of familiarity. Not to mention any sense of welcome. She almost wished she hadn't had those two moments of knowledge, when she'd found the bathroom and the light switch without conscious effort. It seemed to be no more than a vain hope that everyone was mistaken, that she didn't belong with that angry man in the kitchen, with the leering Willy.

She leaned back against the seat of the chair and sighed. At least she was happy in this room. She was Molly Winters, age about twenty-three. She sighed, and the dog moved closer, nuzzling his lion's head under her unresisting hand. Ringless, she noticed absently, shutting her eyes.

If only she could just relax, let things come out on their own accord. But she couldn't. There was danger all around. Paranoia, she thought again, trying to dismiss the fear that clawed away at her. But it clung with iron talons.

She didn't know much about her life, but she knew one thing. She really was in danger.

And she needed answers. Fast.

She must have dozed off. The next thing she knew she was being called for dinner, and she awoke with a start, disoriented, suddenly panicked. When full consciousness came it wasn't much of an improvement, and she rose from her uncomfortable position on the floor, hurrying out to the kitchen. Her stranger-husband glowered at her from his place at the kitchen table. He gestured to a seat opposite him and the plate of unappetizing, overcooked beef.

''Willy's gone into town for dinner,'' he offered shortly, sawing away at his overdone steak with a vengeance. She toyed with some lumpy mashed potatoes, obviously instant from the paper taste of them, and she nearly muttered that she didn't blame him. The vegetables were bland and tasteless, the company was hostile, and she had to force herself to eat. If this was Patrick's idea of cooking she would clearly have to remedy the lack in her education. Maybe she wasn't quite as disinterested a cook as he thought.

The silence stretched and grew, while he ate and she watched. When he was finished he got up, poured himself a cup of coffee from the pot on the back of the stove before he stalked out of the room. She stared after his tall, lean form for a long, thoughtful moment. Either her husband was an incredible pig, or she'd done something totally unforgivable. She didn't remember whether he was the forgiving type, but she wasn't sure she was ready to find out.

She cleared the table, loaded the dishwasher and poured herself a cup of coffee that resembled black sludge. For a moment she hesitated, trying to decide whether to drink it in the safe, solitary confines of the kitchen or brave the lion in his den. She was learning a lot about herself fast, and one thing she'd discovered for certain—she wasn't a coward. She followed Patrick into the living room.

He was staring moodily into the fire, one tanned, long-fingered hand stroking the dog's head, the other wrapped around his empty coffee cup. He barely glanced up when she entered, and paid no attention when she sat down in the chair opposite him.

She took a sip and shuddered, then felt his eyes on her.

"You take milk and sugar in your coffee," he said in a bored voice.

"I don't know if it would help. This coffee is a lost cause."

"Maybe you could learn to make something other than instant," he snapped back at her.

She bit back her annoyed response. "Maybe I could," she said in a neutral voice. "What's the dog's name?"

"Beastie," her husband answered, staring into the fire. Upon hearing his name the dog raised his head and looked at Molly from his soulful eyes for a moment before dropping back down with a deep, doggy sigh.

She sat back in silence, sipping on the rancid brew, before making another attempt at polite conversation. "Patrick."

He looked up, startled. "Why did you call me that?" he demanded. "You usually call me Pat. When you aren't using nastier terms."

"Do I?" she murmured absently, determined not to let him goad her. "Well, if you prefer it, I'll call you Pat."

"No, I don't prefer it." He gave her his full attention. "Listen, I think we'd better come to an understanding if we're forced to share each other's company for the next few months."

"Few months?" she echoed in a hollow voice.

He nodded grimly. "It will take that long for our divorce to go through, and I promised the police I'd be responsible for you till then. I'm a man who pays attention to my responsibilities, even the unpleasant ones, but I won't have you dragging my name into the gutter any more. You will stay on this farm with no long-term visits to any so-called friends from school. If you behave reasonably well I'll give you use of one of the cars to go shopping on occasion. I know how you love to spend money," he added bitterly, the fire lighting up his cold, handsome face. "Willy will be around to entertain you, as will Aunt Ermy. You're simply going to have to curb your jet set tendencies for a while, until I'm free of you. There are the horses, as you well know, and you might even have Mrs. Morse teach you a bit about cooking if you've decided to put on a housewifely act. But don't think for a moment that you'll fool me again. Most of all, you're to keep out of my way and out of my business. Is that understood?''

She had a temper. Dr. Hobson had warned her of it, but she hadn't seen much of it in the short time her memory had been active. During the last twelve or so hours she'd been alternately frightened and uneasy.

But right now her anger overrode any lingering nervousness that might be plaguing her. She looked at the cold, handsome man who insisted he was her husband, the man who'd just dismissed her so cavalierly, and her last attempt at polite behavior vanished.

''You'd love that, wouldn't you?'' she said. ''You want me to go away, keep my mouth shut, leave you alone and stop asking questions. Sorry, I won't do that. You can't dismiss me like a good little girl and expect me to be seen and not heard.''

''You've never been a good little girl in your entire life,'' he snapped. ''I didn't expect you to start now. Your so-called amnesia is only supposed to cause memory loss, not total personality change.''

''My supposed amnesia?'' she echoed.

''You don't think I buy that for a moment, do you? It's a little too convenient, Molly dearest. You don't usually underestimate me—I suggest you don't start now. I don't believe in your amnesia, I don't believe in your lost little girl act, and I don't believe in your country girl look either. If you want to reinvent yourself, wait till you have a more appreciative audience. You lost me years ago.''

''I thought we'd only been married ten months?''

It silenced him, effectively, if only for a moment. ''Get out of here, Molly.''

''I'm not that easy to get rid of.''

"No, you aren't," he said in a faintly menacing voice. "That doesn't mean I won't try."

"Is that a threat?"

"Take it whatever way you want."

"What I want are some answers. You can give me that much, can't you? Just a few answers to a few simple questions? That shouldn't be too much of a strain on your good nature."

He stared at her for a long moment. There was no warmth, no caring in his cold face, but a certain angry resignation. "I'll answer your questions," he said, "if you promise to leave me the hell alone once I do."

Molly sat back, an equally chilly smile on her own face. This, at least, was familiar. She'd fought with this man before. The familiarity, unfortunately, was far from comforting.

"Okay," she said. "Question number one. Why do you hate me?"

"I don't hate you, Molly," he said in a cold, weary voice. "I don't give a damn about you one way or another."

"Why not? I'm your wife."

"What makes you think marriage makes people get along? We used to be better friends before we made the stupid mistake of getting married."

"Why did we get married?"

"Youthful passion," he snapped.

"I thought you were going to answer my questions."

"Those I feel like answering. I'm not in the mood to do a postmortem on our tangled relationship."

She stared at him, frustrated. Memory might fail her, but instinct told her she wouldn't get any farther with that line of questioning.

"What is it you think I've done? What is it the police

think I've done? Lieutenant Ryker said he didn't think I could have killed that man. Do they think I was an accessory? If so, does someone want to kill me? Do they think I stole that money…?''

''You had no need to steal any money,'' Patrick said. ''You have plenty of your own.''

That startled her more than anything. ''You mean I'm rich?'' she gasped, wondering why that notion felt so alien to her.

''Very. Why do you think I married you?''

It was a stunning blow, the effect of which she tried to hide. ''How noble of you,'' she said lightly. ''What was I doing with this strange man in the first place? Why had I run away from you?''

''I guess love's young dream had faded,'' he said with something close to a snarl. ''You always liked older men—I presume you just decided a ten-year age difference wasn't enough. You wanted someone more mature.''

''That shouldn't have been hard to find,'' she snapped.

She had managed to startle him. There was a light in his eyes that was almost appreciative. ''Be that as it may, our marriage was effectively over. You decided to take off, and it didn't really concern me why or where you were going. I was too busy dealing with the mess you left behind.''

''What mess was that?''

''I'm getting a little weary of this, Molly. Besides, you may be independently wealthy, but I have work to do.''

''You don't have money?''

''This is an expensive place to maintain. I'm always in debt.''

''And who inherits my money if I die?'' The initials on the handkerchief were his. Why was it one of the few things in her possession? It hardly seemed as if it were a love token, given their acrimonious relationship.

His smile was cool and deceptively sweet. "Why, I do, Molly. Why do you ask?"

He knew perfectly well why she was asking, and the notion amused him. Had he tried to kill her? Had he driven her away from this place that, despite the strangeness and the hostility, still felt like home, and then followed her, murdering her lover and trying to kill her as well? He had the clear motive.

"Where were you the night of my accident?"

He laughed then, and the sound wasn't reassuring. "I have an alibi, Molly. Ironclad. I didn't try to kill you, and the police believe me. You should as well."

"Why should I?"

"Because if I tried to kill you, I wouldn't make a mistake. You'd be dead. And I'd be a very wealthy man."

"Then why don't you? It seems the logical thing to do, and you appear to be a very logical man."

"Don't tempt me," he said, but his voice was like silk, and he reached out and slid his hand along the side of her neck, up under her hair. "I could break your neck, and make it look like a fall. The stairs are winding, the floor is slate, and you're recovering from a concussion. Not to mention that convenient amnesia. It wouldn't take much to arrange."

She swallowed. His skin was warm, rough and oddly erotic against her neck. "Wouldn't the police get suspicious?"

"I imagine I could handle them," he said in a dreamy voice. "No one likes you very much, you know."

"Why not?" She swallowed, and his thumb stroked the front of her throat, gently, with only the faintest hint of pressure.

"They don't like the way you treat me."

"And what about the way you treat me?" she countered, fighting the need to bat his hand away. Fighting the need to sway closer to him.

"They don't care, Molly."

She was too close to him. She looked at him then, directly into his dark, stormy blue eyes, and a little frisson of fear danced down her spine. Followed by something else.

He could kill. She believed that of him. He could have killed the man she'd supposedly run away with, out of jealousy or something else. He could have tried to kill her, but something stopped him from making the blow fatal. Or maybe he'd run them off the road, she'd been knocked unconscious by the accident, and he'd quickly and efficiently killed his rival.

But why hadn't he finished her? Did he still want her? Or just her money?

He was stroking her, slowly, with erotic intent. His head dipped toward hers, blotting out the light. He was going to kiss her, she knew it. He had every right to kiss her—he was her husband.

So why did it feel as if it were going to be her first kiss?

She held herself very still, waiting for the touch of his mouth against hers, letting her eyes drift shut, aware of the danger, the draw of the man, and no longer caring if she was playing with fire.

And then he pulled back, abruptly. "That's enough questions for now, Molly," he said in a bored drawl. "This marital togetherness wears thin pretty damned fast. Go away."

She opened her eyes and stared at him in confusion. He wanted her. She knew that, with a sudden sureness that left her curiously triumphant. He wanted her, but he was half afraid of her.

It was a small consolation. He scared the hell out of her. She didn't bother arguing with him. She simply rose, taking her mug of undrinkable black sludge. "Pleasant dreams," she said sweetly.

His response was a growled obscenity. The dog lifted his head, looking at the two of them questioningly before lumbering to his feet, preparing to follow her.

"Beastie!" Patrick spoke sharply, and with an air of reluctance the dog returned to his side. Molly went slowly up the stairs, feeling oddly, doubly forsaken.

SHE LAY AWAKE for hours, listening to the rain beat down on the slate roof. The queen-size bed with its voluptuous satin sheets was too soft, and before an hour of tossing and turning had passed her back began to ache. The clinging nightgown, so revealing and provocative for a nonexistent lover, was obviously made to be discarded early in the night. It made her itch.

The room was stuffy and suffocating, and the heavy formal drapes kept out any trace of moonlight. She lay there and hated that room, hated it with a passion. If she was going to be a prisoner there she would have to change it, despite her husband's likely objections. Surely he couldn't approve of the lavish style of it. How had he managed to put up with it when he used to visit his wife?

Or had she gone to his room?

She stiffened uncontrollably. Slow, measured footsteps were mounting the stairs, and she could hear the clicking of the dog's nails as he followed his master up to bed. She lay there, tense and unmoving, scarcely breathing, as she waited for him.

She hadn't imagined the look in his eyes earlier, the

slow, sensual heat that he'd deliberately banked. He wanted her. And he seemed to be a man who took what he wanted.

He stopped in the hall, and she could almost hear his breathing. After a moment he went into his own room and closed the door.

She felt a stinging dampness in her eyes, and she wiped it away angrily. Molly Winters, who never cried, had wept three times in one day. She wasn't going to keep giving in to some maudlin weakness, she told herself firmly. She was glad he hadn't come to her room, that cool, angry stranger, she was absolutely delighted. As a matter of fact, the nurse had been right.

She hated Patrick Winters with his cold heart and his cold blue eyes, hated him more than she had hated any person in her entire life. She knew that hurt and hatred—it was a familiar companion in the old stone house.

PATRICK WASN'T QUITE SURE how he was going to stand this. He told himself there was no way he could hear her breathing through the thick old walls, no way he could smell the faint trace of perfume that clung to her hair.

But he could. The scent, the sound, the feel of her followed him into his bedroom, teased him unmercifully. The last few weeks had been the first peace he'd known in more than a year. He hadn't wanted her back, and he didn't want her sleeping two doors away from him, totally immune to him.

He wanted to be immune to her. Oblivious. To be able to ignore her, and the way she crawled beneath his skin, danced in his blood. His feelings for her should have been over long ago. They were never very sensible—she was a decade younger than he was, a sixteen-year-old child when he'd first seen her, a twenty-three-year-old child when he'd made the very dire mistake of marrying her.

And he couldn't blame anyone but himself. Sure, his damned autocratic father had set things in motion, determined to get his way, even beyond the grave. But Patrick had never danced to his tune. And marrying Jared Winters's chosen one should have been the last thing he'd do.

But the problem was damnably simple. His father had always known him far too well, for all they'd fought like cats and dogs. He'd chosen Molly for him, for the simple reason that he knew Patrick wanted her. Wanted her desperately.

Well, he'd gotten her. And desperation as well. He'd made his bed, and he'd lie in it alone. Until Molly was out of his house, out of his life, for good.

And then, maybe he'd be able to get her out of his soul as well.

Chapter Four

The room was dark and still when she awoke the next morning, alone in the wide, uncomfortable bed. She was sweating all over, and her hands were trembling. Shaking herself slightly, she rolled out of bed. A nightmare, she told herself, as she pushed open the heavy drapes and stared out into the early Pennsylvania morning. The sky was a sullen blue, not unlike Patrick's eyes, and she felt as weighted down as the weather. She pushed open the window, hoping for a soft breeze, but she was rewarded with an icy blast of cold. She slammed it shut quickly.

The tiny gilt clock beside the massive bed said six-thirty, and she wondered whether she usually rose at such an early hour. She was in no mood to tempt fate with another nightmare—besides, she had too much she needed to learn. Maybe today was the day she'd begin to find out the answers to some of the thousands of questions plaguing her.

She went through the connecting door to the tiny bathroom and scrubbed at her face fiercely with hot water and the designer soap in the gold soap dish. Looking into the mirror, she wondered once again at the oddness of her surroundings: the cold, modern luxury everywhere in her rooms. A luxury that was both unnatural and stifling. But the reflection of that long oval face with the slanted green-blue eyes was that of a stranger, and could give her no answers.

She dressed swiftly in the same clothes she'd worn the night before—from what she'd seen of the overstuffed contents of the closet and dresser there was nothing else even remotely suitable for an early spring day on a farm. Though Molly had the feeling this was no ordinary farm.

The old kitchen was even more attractive in daylight. An old-fashioned brick hearth and oven took up one wall, and a small fire was crackling cheerfully, bringing a warmth to the room that was spiritual as well as physical. The gleaming wooden counter, the copper pots hanging from the whitewashed walls, the massive old cookstove and the harvest table created a feeling of simple needs and pleasures, and she found herself slightly, dangerously at peace for the first time since she'd arrived in Bucks County. For the first time since she'd woken up in that hospital room, just one short day ago.

"My goodness, Mrs. Winters, what in the world are you doing up so early?" an amazed voice demanded from the pantry door. "I was planning on bringing you your breakfast in bed, same as I always did." A starched, comfortable figure stood in the doorway, another unnerving sign of normalcy.

"Good morning," Molly greeted her hesitantly, taking in the woman's graying hair, curious black eyes and general air of motherliness. "I decided it was too nice a day to stay in bed."

The woman turned to peer out the window, then looked back at Molly in surprise. "Well, it's not exactly the day I'd pick for a picnic, but it's well enough, I suppose, especially after last night. And of course, you so long in the hospital, poor girl. Now you go and sit yourself down in the dining room and I'll set you a place in two shakes.''

"If you don't mind I'd rather eat in here.''

She looked even more startled. "Well, certainly, if that's what you want. I will admit it's warmer and cozier in here. Pat always eats his breakfast in here with me, and that's a fact. Says it warms him up.'' She kept a steady flow of chatter while she deftly set a place at the table, poured her a cup of coffee with just the right amount of cream and sugar, and started some toast. "What'll you have for breakfast, Mrs. Winters? The usual?''

Molly could feel an odd blush of color rise to her cheeks. "I'm afraid I...that is...''

"Oh, heavens, what a fool I am, jabbering away at you. Pat explained your little problem, but I forgot all about it. You probably don't even know who I am, do you? I'm Fran Morse, the housekeeper, and you usually have two slices of toast and orange juice. But maybe I could tempt you with something a bit more substantial this morning?''

Molly sipped at the wonderful coffee. "Well, my... Patrick made dinner last night,'' she said carefully, oddly unwilling to call Patrick her husband.

"Then you must be starving,'' the woman said with a friendly smile. "That man can't cook to save his life.''

"I *am* a bit hungry,'' she admitted. "I'd love some eggs and bacon if it's not too much trouble. And some of your poppy seed muffins.''

The woman beamed fondly. "Well, it's a treat to see you've got some appetite. These last few months you were eating like a bird. And you remembered my muffins, bless your heart!'' She deposited some in front of Molly, kindly ignoring her sudden start.

She'd have to get used to remembering, Molly told herself shakily. Things are bound to come back like that, a bit at a time. She took a bite out of the muffin, and the familiar-unfamiliar taste warmed her tongue. Slowly she began to relax. For the first time since she arrived she felt comfortable and comparatively happy. Here was one person who didn't seem to blame her for a thousand anonymous crimes. Molly watched Mrs. Morse bustle around the kitchen with a sense of quiet gratitude, and she wished that feeling could last forever.

By the time she devoured her breakfast and had seconds of muffins and coffee she was ready to face the day. "Would you like some help washing up?" she offered, bringing her dishes over to the sink.

Mrs. Morse stared at her strangely. "Well, I never thought to hear such words from your mouth again," she said frankly. "But there, I always said you weren't so bad underneath. No, dearie, I can manage these myself. After all, it's what I'm paid for."

Molly nodded, trying to ignore those words that kept repeating themselves, around and around in her brain. *I always said you weren't so bad underneath.* Who did she say it to?

There wasn't much she could say in response. She plastered a cool smile on her face. "Well, if you need any help with lunch or anything just call me."

It was just past seven o'clock when she wandered out of the kitchen, more troubled than she cared to admit. She didn't know where to start. Her life was an Agatha Christie novel—full of clues and question marks, suspects and red herrings, and the thought of sorting them out was daunting. It didn't sound as if there was anyone she could turn to for help or answers—from the impression she'd gotten from Patrick and company she had no friends in the area, and it was unlikely that anyone would want to have anything to do with her.

She ended up back in the opulent bedroom, staring at the walls. Patrick had gotten up and left early, Willy apparently didn't make an appearance until past noon if he could help it, and Molly was doomed to her own frustrating company.

She went to the closet, looking through her wardrobe. Within minutes her disgust was even stronger. Those expensive clothes were absolutely lovely, but they were as ill-suited for her as gold lamé on a child. She went out on the landing and called to Mrs. Morse.

"Have we got an old trunk anywhere?"

"What in the world are you doing, Mrs. Winters?" She appeared at the bottom of the stairs, a dust rag in one capable hand.

"Cleaning house, just like you," she replied smartly. "Have we got a trunk anywhere?"

"Should be one in the back of your closet," Mrs. Morse answered, curiosity alight in her face. "Do you need any help?"

"I can handle it," she said, heading back in to discover an old-fashioned steamer trunk, large enough to hold even Molly Winters's extensive wardrobe. Working at a leisurely pace, she loaded it with almost every conceivable piece of elegant clothing. Patrick must have been using understatement when he said she loved to spend money. It was a good thing she apparently had plenty of it. The stuff in the closets and drawers must have cost a fortune. Sudden guilt swamped her. Surely there was some deserving charity in town that would love something a bit better than rags.

She kept very little: a number of subdued cotton sweaters, a blessed second pair of worn jeans. Out went the gold-threaded caftan, the black satin sheath with the neckline down to there, the turquoise silk lounging pajamas.

Whether she liked it or not, she was really a T-shirt and jeans type, and dressing up in sophisticated clothes would only make her look more ridiculous. And make the situation that much worse.

What situation? she asked herself suddenly. There was no answer. Only the instinctive knowledge that she wanted to be beautiful. Was she fool enough to care what her bad-tempered husband thought? If she harbored any warm emotions in that direction she would be wise to forget them quickly. Her life was a tangled mess, and she had absolutely no idea how things had gotten that way. She sighed as she shut the trunk on the expensive, unsuitable clothes.

There wasn't much left. Several drawers full of lace underwear that she'd lost her heart to, those itchy nightgowns, and the sweaters and shirts. And one very beautiful eyelet and cotton dress of pure white. The woman Molly had begun to think of as her predecessor didn't seem to go in for simple things like this, and she wondered if it had actually belonged to someone else. For the time being she could wear it if the occasion demanded a dress, which seemed unlikely. From what Patrick had said, it seemed as if she were to be kept in total seclusion. Until her memory returned, Molly thought she might prefer it that way.

She glanced down at her clothes. Sooner or later she would find out how to get hold of her money. She'd need to buy at least a few new things—she couldn't spend all her time in two pairs of faded jeans and a few sweaters. Then again, maybe she could. After all, who was she trying to impress? If it was Patrick Winters, it was obviously a lost cause.

"I've got a trunk full of clothes up there." Molly walked into the kitchen. "Have you any idea where I could send it?"

Mrs. Morse looked up from her luncheon fixings in surprise. "Send it?" she repeated blankly.

"Yes." Molly reached out and snatched a piece of sliced carrot. "I don't want them anymore. They're not at all my style."

"I was wondering if you'd ever learn that." She offered her another carrot. "I'll have Ben take care of it for you when he comes in for lunch."

"Ben?"

She looked at her oddly. "My husband," she said after an uncomfortable silence. "You've only known him since you were sixteen."

Molly shrugged with embarrassment. "Will lunch be ready soon? I'm starving."

She nodded, an even more uncomfortable look passing over her face. "Mrs. Winters, I don't know if it's my place to say this, but..."

"Have you always called me Mrs. Winters?" Molly interrupted, snatching one more carrot.

"Since you've been married. Before that you were Molly to me and Ben."

"Then I think I should be Molly again." She smiled warmly at her. "Mrs. Winters doesn't seem like me at all. Molly at least seems a little closer to who I feel like."

"All right. If that's what you want." She glanced uneasily toward the door. "I think I'd better tell you something before they come in for lunch."

It was there, a tiny fluttering of anxiety in the pit of her stomach. She managed a calm smile. "Tell me what, Mrs. Morse?" She leaned against the counter, hoping she looked nonchalant.

"It's common knowledge around here that they're going to be married as soon as the divorce is final." She said it all in a rush, clearly eager to get it over with.

Molly looked at her blankly. "Who's going to marry whom?"

"Patrick. It looks like he's going to marry Mrs. Canning. Her husband passed away the day you left here and it looked like they started making their plans right away." She looked miserable. "I thought you'd better know, in case you started getting...well, getting ideas."

"What kind of ideas would those be? That my husband shouldn't be getting ready for wife number two before he's gotten rid of wife number one?" She couldn't keep the trace of bitterness out of her voice. "Who's Mrs. Canning? Do I know her?"

"You and Lisa Canning used to be thick as thieves," Mrs. Morse replied grimly. "She and Patrick are out riding now. I'm expecting them in for lunch any minute now. If you want I can give you a tray in your room. It couldn't be very pleasant for you, dearie. It's always been that way between Patrick and her, ever since she married old Fred Canning and moved here five years ago. Though I used to think it was more on her side than his."

"Then why did he marry me? For the money? He told me I was rich."

"I was never really sure of why he married you, honey. I guess I hoped that he loved you."

"But he didn't. Did he?"

She wouldn't answer, busying herself with the dishes. Then she looked up. "All I know is that Pat wouldn't have done something like that. If he'd wanted that money there were other ways he could have gotten it."

Like killing me, she thought, unable to hide from the chilling notion.

At that moment there was a commotion in the yard, and with a false calm Molly moved to the window and looked out. And some of the pieces fell together in the puzzle.

At first her attention was drawn to the man who was still, ostensibly, her husband. He looked as if he were born in the saddle. He was tall and gorgeous in the bright sunlight, his long, muscled legs easily controlling the spirited bay, and Molly had no doubts at all as to why she had married him. By his side was her erstwhile friend Mrs. Canning, a well-preserved beauty of indeterminate age, her white blond hair expertly tinted and coiffed, her face youthful, her figure opulent and desirable. Everything Molly was not. She laughed and put one hand on Patrick's arm, and the look he gave her was one that sent such a flashing wave of jealousy through Molly that she felt sick. She might not remember Patrick or the woman, but that emotion was an old and comfortable foe.

The woman dismounted from the horse in one lithe movement, and suddenly Molly realized why she looked vaguely familiar. She belonged in that bedroom upstairs, with the pink-tinted satins, in those sophisticated and expensive clothes. They were made for a woman like her, and Molly wondered who had decorated that bedroom and chosen those clothes. Had it been Patrick? Or the helpful Mrs. Canning? Or had Molly tried to turn herself into a clone of the woman Patrick loved?

They were already seated when she walked into the dining room. "Molly, darling!" Mrs. Canning rose and enveloped her in a warm and highly scented embrace. Poison, Molly decided, a fitting enough scent, and then cursed herself for knowing the names of perfumes and not of her closest friends.

"We missed you so much," the woman continued, her heavy gold bangles digging into Molly's back. She drew away and looked into her face, frowning. "You don't look at all well, my dear. And where did you get those awful clothes?"

"From my room," she answered lightly, drawing away as unobtrusively as she could manage. "It's good to see you again."

Her luminous eyes were warm and friendly and just ever so slightly assessing. "Darling, it's so good to see *you!* We were paralyzed when you ran off like that, absolutely paralyzed." She moved back to the table and put one possessive hand on Patrick's arm. "Weren't we, darling?"

Molly half expected to see painted fingernails like red claws. Wasn't the Other Woman always supposed to have red fingernails? The hand on Patrick's forearm was well-shaped, with pale, well-manicured nails. And not nearly as interesting as the tanned, muscular forearm beneath it, Molly thought hopelessly.

Patrick had risen. He simply looked at her, an unwelcoming expression on his face. Molly thought of her room with a faint trace of longing, then steeled herself.

He didn't look like a man who could kill. He simply looked like a man surrounded by too many women.

Another motive, though. If Molly died, Patrick would have her money and revenge for her running away with another man. He'd also have the beautiful Mrs. Canning, and Molly had to admit that most men would have found that incentive indeed.

"Wouldn't you rather have a tray in your room, Molly?" he asked in a cool voice. "You've just gotten out of the hospital, and you look tired."

"Heavens, no!" she said so brightly she wanted to wince. "I need to get back in the swing of things. I need to spend time with friends and family. Loved ones," she added with a pointed, saccharine look at Patrick.

She might have pushed him too far. He shoved back from the table, but once more Lisa put a restraining hand on his arm, and he subsided with a glare in Molly's direction.

"Pat says you have amnesia," Lisa murmured. "How fascinating. It sounds like something out of a bad novel."

"It is," Patrick growled.

"I'm surprised he told you," Molly said, ignoring him. "I get the impression that my husband doesn't quite believe me."

His response was a disbelieving snort. Lisa's hand tightened warningly on his arm, and Molly couldn't tear her gaze away from that possessive clasp.

"Of course he believes you, Molly. Why else would you have run off without a word to me, your dearest friend? Or to your husband, or anyone? You must have had a reason, and if you could only remember I'm sure you'd tell us everything."

Molly looked at them both. The dearest friend, with her phony, cooing concern and her possessive grip. The husband, watching her with stony distrust.

They could have been in it together, Molly thought. Her disappearance benefited everyone. It was no wonder she'd run.

"Of course," she said calmly, helping herself to the plate of delicate sandwiches Mrs. Morse had provided. She was famished, and she didn't care if her abstemious so-called friend watched as she devoured her lunch.

Molly shoved a sandwich into her mouth, then reached for another. "So tell me," she said in a conversational voice, "what's been happening with you two while I've been away?"

Patrick promptly choked on his coffee.

IT HAD BEEN an illuminating meal, Molly thought several hours later as she sat cross-legged on her bed, staring down at the telltale handkerchief. Lisa was obviously adept at awkward social situations, Patrick had been totally uninterested in putting a smooth front on anything. Clearly everyone knew about Lisa and Patrick—just as clearly, it was supposed to be ignored.

Molly played the game very well. She made all the right responses, slipping easily into the role of younger friend. So easily that she suspected that was how it used to be with the three of them.

Lisa and Patrick, tolerant of the exuberant teenager who followed them around. She could almost see it, almost remember it.

Why hadn't he married Lisa? Belatedly, she remembered Lisa's elderly husband. Mrs. Morse said he'd died recently, yet Lisa hardly seemed the grieving widow. It was too bad the old man hadn't died ten months ago and saved everyone a great deal of trouble. Patrick could have married Lisa instead of settling for his wealthy fifth cousin twice removed or whatever she was.

She stared down at the scrap of cloth in her hand. Those orange streaks looked oddly familiar, yet she couldn't trace them. They were neither rust nor blood stains, and she wondered why the police hadn't taken it for evidence. Had she hidden it from them? If so, why?

So many questions. She was still hungry, and she was exhausted. Patrick had left the table abruptly, Lisa vanished soon after, and Molly could only imagine where they were and what they were doing.

She didn't want to.

She lay back on her bed, tucking the handkerchief beneath her pillow. She wasn't ready to have anyone see it. She wasn't certain what it signified, but right now it was the only clue, the only advantage she had. She wasn't about to let anyone else get a look at it until she was good and ready.

Chapter Five

Amnesia. What a crock! Who did Molly think she was, expecting them to believe such a cock-and-bull story? Maybe in romance novels, maybe in TV movies, but not in real life.

It was just a little too damned convenient. As long as she pretended not to remember anything, she was buying herself time.

But she couldn't keep it up forever. Sure, her eyes looked wide and guileless as she looked at each of them in turn, but she could be acting. She'd gotten damned good at it.

If she wasn't faking, then things were even more dangerous. If that too convenient amnesia was the real McCoy, it could disappear as quickly as it came. Leaving her with a clear memory of what had happened to her just a few short weeks ago.

And what had happened to the man known as George Andrews.

That couldn't be allowed to happen. She was going to have to die. Sooner or later.

And sooner would be a much more acceptable alternative.

MOLLY WOKE UP in darkness, disoriented, panicked. It took her a moment to remember where she was. She sat up in bed, switching on the light, trying to still the fear that washed over her. She was just feeling stir crazy—she hadn't wanted to go outside for fear she'd run into Patrick and Lisa. An hour of their company had been about all she could handle. She knew she wouldn't be allowed to take the car anywhere until she'd proven her *trustworthiness* to that self-righteous, adulterous pig of a husband, even though the car might very well belong to her. Willy had disappeared as soon as he got up, and she didn't even have his doubtful company to distract her. There was a stack of mysteries in the bookcase, but to her disgust once more her memory failed her. She may not have known her own face, name, or even how she drank her coffee, but all she had to do was read the opening paragraph to remember whodunit.

She still hadn't met the other occupant of the old stone farmhouse. Cousin Ermintrude White, known to her as Aunt Ermy, said Mrs. Morse, was off on one of her incessant rounds of visits. Molly could tell from the housekeeper's look of disdain that Ermintrude White was not looked upon with affection in this household. Indeed, most of Mrs. Morse's approval seemed reserved for Patrick, despite his lapse in taste when it came to Mrs. Canning, and for Molly, a fact which surprised her. Here was one person who didn't hold her previous bad behavior against her. Perhaps if one dug deep enough there were excuses, but at that point Molly couldn't begin to fathom what they could be.

Nor was she particularly interested in hearing the details of all the evil she had done, at least, not from the one person who seemed to like her. Molly was simply glad to bask in the sudden affection. She was a good woman, Mrs. Morse, and it felt oddly encouraging to have her approval.

She heard the heavy footsteps first, followed by the peremptory knocking on her door. She leaned back, waiting, knowing perfectly well who was coming upstairs in such a towering rage. She had no intention of reacting if she could help it.

The door flew open and Patrick stood there, tall and lean against the doorway, and for a moment she felt a little clutching sense of longing. One that disappeared when she realized this wasn't a friendly visit.

"I would have thought," he said, his voice cold and cutting, "that you would have the common courtesy to abide by the schedule in this house. I should have known it would be too much to ask, but nevertheless I not only ask it, I demand it. You will come downstairs for drinks right now and be polite to our guests. I suppose even you are capable of that much." The withering contempt cut through her as she lay there motionless. "Now!" He moved into the room menacingly, and she sprang from the bed before she could stop herself.

He laughed then, and it wasn't a pleasant sound. "I'm glad to see I'm at least able to frighten you into decent behavior. We'll be in the library." He started out the door, stopped and turned. "By the way, in case you've forgotten, you usually dress for dinner."

Molly could see from the faint light in the hall that he was still wearing his faded jeans, and she shrugged with a fine show of bravado. "I have no clothes," she said simply. "These will have to do."

"By that I assume you mean that your extravagant wardrobe no longer interests you and you wish to go out and spend a similar sum or more." He shrugged. "Be my guest. Mrs. Morse can accompany you if you insist. After all, it's your money.''

"How much money is there?'' she demanded, scrambling off the bed.

"I wondered when you'd get around to asking,'' he said with an unpleasant laugh. "As a matter of fact, it was your seeming disinterest in money that almost had me believing your cock-and-bull story about amnesia. I should have known you couldn't keep it up.''

"I merely wanted to know,'' she said in a cool voice, "if I have enough to buy you off. If I give it to you would you let me go?''

She'd managed to startle him. "I don't want your damned money,'' he said bitterly.

"Then what do you want from me? Why did you marry me?'' She scrambled off the bed, starting toward him. She was deliberately trying to goad him, and she told herself she was simply wanting to get the truth from him. And she knew she was lying.

She was trying to goad him into touching her again. She wanted to see if his touch still made her tremble, as it had last night.

He backed away, not bothering to hide his uneasiness. "Be down in five minutes, Molly. Or I'll come back to get you.''

It was supposed to be a threat. It sounded more like a temptation to Molly.

She waited just long enough before leaving the room, running down the curving stairs swiftly, two at a time, knowing if she hesitated she would lose her courage. Stopping before the living room door, she heard the noise of glasses and ice, quiet laughter and camaraderie that would vanish the moment she appeared. But appear she must—

her husband had so decreed. Taking a deep breath, she ambled into the room with studied unconcern.

Patrick ignored her when she entered the room, busying himself at the bar.

"There you are, darling!" Lisa greeted her. She was curled up on the sofa like a contented cat. "Did you have a nice afternoon?"

"Lovely," she replied politely. "And you?"

Lisa cast a meaningful glance at Patrick's back, and her smile was unbearably smug. "Very stimulating."

Molly gritted her teeth, glancing around the room to see Willy, who seemed to be viewing the proceedings with a great deal of faintly drunken amusement.

"How are you tonight, Willy?" she greeted him, desperate to remove herself from Lisa's arch glances. She didn't need her far from subtle reminder of what she'd been doing with Molly's husband.

"Good enough, m'dear," Willy answered, raising a dark amber drink in greeting. "Glad to see you decided to join us after all."

She felt a sudden spurt of anger at all of them. They must have discussed poor little Molly in their various condescending tones, conspiring to torment and embarrass her. Well, she wouldn't let them down, she decided suddenly, throwing herself down into the most comfortable chair in the room and glowering at them all like a spoiled teenager.

Patrick stalked over to her to thrust a tall glass of bright red liquid at her. "Here you are," he said with false solicitude, and she controlled the urge to throw the drink back in his face.

"What is it?" she demanded suspiciously.

He raised an eyebrow. "Your usual. Cranberry juice, just as Aunt Ermy ordered for you, though tonight without the vodka. I assume you aren't allowed to drink after your supposed blow on the head.'' His voice was cool and disbelieving, and she barely controlled an equally snappish answer.

Instead she took a small, ladylike sip of it and wondered absently if among her myriad other faults she had been a drunk as well. She took a second, larger sip and leaned back further into the protective recesses of the chair to watch her family and friends.

Her participation was not missed. Willy, Patrick and Lisa were deeply involved in a discussion of horse breeding, a subject as foreign to her as mountain climbing. Though of course, she thought ruefully, she could very well have dabbled in both. She was the first one to notice the arrival of another guest, walking quietly along the stone-floored hallway. He was above medium height, though shorter than the lanky Patrick, with curly brown hair and a quiet intensity about his eyes. He looked handsome, shy, and out of place, and quite friendly in a quiet, gentle way, so far removed from the tightly leashed violence she sensed in her husband. She suddenly felt a little more optimistic. Maybe she'd finally found an ally among all these enemies.

''Hello, there.'' He cleared his throat at the door and they turned to greet him with enthusiasm.

''Toby!'' Patrick's sudden, friendly grin was a revelation. ''We were just discussing Arab's points. We'll forgive you for being late if you can clear something up.''

Molly stared at Patrick, shocked into momentary silence. Remembering, almost remembering, with the sight of that sudden, devastating smile...

And then Toby stepped between them, and his eyes were warm and sympathetic. ''How are you, Molly? We missed you.''

The others were staring at him with silent disapproval,

as if they suddenly discovered they had a traitor in their midst, but Toby didn't seem to notice. For the first time someone seemed sincerely glad to have her back, and Molly's eyes threatened to fill with those unwanted tears again.

"Thank you, Toby," she said softly, smiling up at him.

"Let's go in to dinner," Patrick said abruptly, breaking the moment. He took Lisa's silk-clad arm and led her toward the dining room. "I could eat a horse. Next time I invite you for dinner you come on time, boy," he said with mock seriousness, and Toby laughed.

"I was held up, Pat," he said, following Willy's beefy form. "Miss Molly's just about to foal and I didn't know whether I dared come at all."

By the time Molly entered the dining room she noticed with a grimace that Lisa had taken the traditional seat for the woman of the household, at the foot of the table opposite Patrick, and she was relegated to a seat next to Willy. She sank down with sullen grace, wondering once more what she could have possibly done to have turned her family and friends against her. And what further insults would she have to bear while she remained a prisoner in this house. At least there was Toby, looking across at her with undisguised admiration. She tried to concentrate on that, shutting out the sound of Lisa's arch laughter as she flirted with Patrick.

"Molly, darling." Lisa turned to her in a coaxing voice. "Pat says you want to do some clothes shopping. I'd be delighted to come with you, give you a few pointers on style." Her expression told Molly that she badly needed all the help she could get.

"No, thank you, Lisa." She managed to control the faintly homicidal urge that was building up in her. "Mrs.

Morse will come with me—I wouldn't think of bothering you.''

"But darling, it's no bother," she protested prettily. "Remember what fun we had, picking all your other clothes? I've always helped you choose; you know I love to do it."

So she had Lisa to thank for that closet full of unsuitable clothes, Molly thought. *And I bet she did it on purpose.* "No, I don't think so, Lisa. I prefer to choose my own clothes." Her voice was cool and firm, and there was nothing Lisa could do but shrug her elegant shoulders and exchange a look with Patrick as if to say, what can I do?

Toby tried to smooth over the moment of tension by expressing a sudden interest in the weather, but Molly had finally had enough of the strained atmosphere and subtle sniping. Of the secrets that no one was supposed to mention. "Tell me, Lisa," she said in a casual voice, flashing her as false a smile as she'd been given. "When is it that you and Patrick plan to marry?"

"I beg your pardon?" Lisa demanded in frosty tones.

Molly took a bite out of the rich chocolate cake Mrs. Morse had provided for dessert, revelling in the shocked expressions of all those around the table. She looked up with innocent eyes. "I just thought it would be easier if I knew what your schedule was. Your husband's been dead…how long? I think I was told it was five weeks, is that right? And I gather you've both been planning this for years, so I'd hate to make you drag out any role-playing as a grieving widow." Molly's eyes drifted down Lisa's seductive apparel with a faint smile. "Perhaps you could persuade my husband to get an apartment somewhere while we wait for the divorce to go through. I wouldn't want to cramp your style, and you *are* so good at persuading my husband."

"Get out of here," Patrick said quietly. Molly turned her blandly innocent smile in his direction, wanting to lash out and hurt him.

"But why are you so mad, darling?" She mimicked Lisa's tone of voice perfectly. "You shouldn't let the fact that her husband's barely cold in the ground get in the way of your plans. After all, you only married me because you couldn't have her. And now you've got her. Happy happy, joy joy." She rose and stalked out of the room, anger finally taking control. She was halfway up the stairs when she heard him coming after her. Stifling a sudden, panic-stricken desire to run and lock herself in that sybaritic room, she turned at the top of the stairs and waited for him with spurious calm.

He caught her wrist in a grip that was almost painful, his blue eyes dark with anger. "What the hell did you mean by that little scene in there?" he demanded.

"Isn't it true?" she asked quietly. "Isn't every word I said true?"

"You have no right to criticize anybody. Not when you're dealing with gossip and suppositions and half-truths," he said in a furious undertone. "I didn't run off in the middle of the night, I didn't set fire to the east barn and kill three horses, I didn't crack old Ben on the head and leave him bleeding in the middle of the yard. I wasn't found unconscious with a murdered man beside me."

Molly felt sick and shaken. "And you're saying I did these things?" she asked in a hoarse whisper.

His voice came towards her, cold and distant with what she now knew was a justifiable rage. "No one else could have. Either you or the man you ran away with. Half our breeding stock went in that fire. Have you ever seen a barn fire, Molly? Do you know what it's like, listening to the screams of the horses, smelling the charred flesh, knowing there's nothing you can do to save them?''

She shook her head and tried to pull away, but he was inexorable.

"The house nearly went too. Did you know that? Not that you'd care. You're just a spoiled, vicious child who lashes out and destroys without thinking when she doesn't get her own way!''

"And what was my own way?'' she demanded, fighting to hold on to her self-control.

He shook his head in disgust. "You never told me," he said, quiet now. "Stay out of my path, Molly. If you come down for dinner again you'd better by God be polite or I swear I'll break your pretty little neck.''

She stood alone on the landing, unmoving, for long minutes after he'd left her to return to his guests. She glanced down at her hand as it rested on the railing, and she realized she was clutching it tightly.

He said she'd hit Ben Morse over the head and left him bleeding. Surely Mrs. Morse couldn't believe her capable of such a thing and still be as friendly to her? Not everyone believed her to be such a monster, including one of the people she'd supposedly hurt the most.

Damn Patrick and his accusations, accusations she couldn't refute. She stared after him, shaking with fury and defiance, when a stray thought entered her mind. A pretty little neck, he'd said. One he wanted to break.

Had he been the one? Had he driven her from this place, then followed her, murdered the man she was with and then bashed her over the head, hoping to have killed her?

And if he had, what was to stop him from trying it again?

Why did he want her there? Why couldn't he just let her leave, start a new life with the faint shreds of her memory? What in God's name did he want from her?

And what did she want from him?

Chapter Six

The sickness started the next morning. She woke up at the crack of dawn, a sudden churning in her stomach. She barely made it to the bathroom in time before she was thoroughly and violently sick. And as soon as the first spasm passed a second one came on, and then a third.

When it finally passed she was weak and shaken, and it took every last remaining ounce of energy to crawl back into bed and lie there, shivering. She had never felt so horribly, desperately ill in her entire life, and she wondered whether it could have been food poisoning. With her current run of luck it could have descended on her and left the others, including Lisa Canning, in perfect health.

She was just being paranoid—Mrs. Morse seemed like a careful and excellent cook. No, it must be some virus, brought on by her recent hospitalization. Maybe just an accumulation of stress. It would pass soon enough.

It was almost an hour before she felt able to climb out of bed, and she took a long, slow time to get dressed and washed and make her shaky way downstairs. Mrs. Morse took one look at her and clucked sympathetically.

"You don't look at all well, Molly, my dear," she said as she hustled her over to the seat by the blazing fire and wrapped an afghan around her. "It's not a fit day out for man nor beast, so it's just as well. Patrick said you wanted to go shopping but I think we'd better put it off for the time being. I'll make you some mint tea with honey and see how that makes you feel.'' She clucked over her like a mother hen, and Molly slowly began to relax. It was a rare, comfortable feeling, being cared for and fussed over, especially after Patrick's accusations of the night before.

"It's just some sort of stomach virus," she said nonchalantly. "I'm already feeling better—I'd like to go shopping, really!" She felt like a child begging for a treat. The thought of spending another day cooped up in that house with its atmosphere of brooding guilt was enough to make her desperate.

"We'll see," Mrs. Morse said, bustling around. "I'm going to make you some nice, nourishing oatmeal and then we'll see how you feel. Nothing like oatmeal for an upset stomach!"

THREE HOURS LATER they were on the road, and whether it was from oatmeal, natural causes or sheer willpower, Molly was feeling fine.

"All right, all right," Mrs. Morse had finally acquiesced. "Patrick and Ben won't be in to lunch today— they're busy down at the lower barn. So we might as well take off right now. You'll have to give me a hand with dinner, mind you, if I'm to spend the afternoon gallivanting around."

At the sound of Ben's name she paused, suddenly stricken. "Mrs. Morse?" she said in a hesitant voice.

"What is it, lovey?"

"Do you believe I did what they say I did? Do you think I hit your husband over the head and left him bleeding on the ground?" She held her breath, half afraid of the answer.

Mrs. Morse shook her head. "You've been accused of a lot of things this past year. Some of them you told me about yourself, bragging. But I can't believe you would have changed so much you would have hurt my Ben. Neither does he. He doesn't know who sneaked up behind him and hit him over the head, but he knows it wasn't you."

"Thank God," Molly breathed. "But who could it have been? Were there any strangers around here?"

"Just the man you ran away with."

The words hung in the air between them. "So I am responsible," she said in a low voice.

"No, dearie. You got in with a bad crowd. You were unhappy, and you didn't use your best judgment. But that's in the past. Ben doesn't hold a grudge, and neither do I."

Molly looked at her, stricken. "I'll find out what really happened," she said. "Sooner or later I'll remember."

"Of course you will, dearie. In the meantime, we have some shopping to do. Nothing like a little shopping to cheer a body up."

Molly rose, some of her earlier enthusiasm vanished. "I forgot. How am I going to get money?"

"What do you need money for, with all those credit cards?" Mrs. Morse demanded. "Besides, I wouldn't be surprised if you had money in your wallet. You always forget that you have any."

"I don't know where my wallet is," she admitted.

Mrs. Morse had the grace to look abashed. "That's right—Patrick has it in the office. Since he told me it was all right to take you shopping I'm sure he'd expect me to give it to you. You just wait a moment and I'll go fetch it."

Molly had grave doubts where Patrick had any such expectations, but she accepted the calfskin wallet with carefully concealed gratitude. Mrs. Morse was right about the credit cards and the money. If she wanted to escape from there she wouldn't have to worry about finances. She had it all in her hand, along with her driver's license.

Putting the wallet in the hip pocket of her jeans, she strode out of the room. Right then she had no intention of leaving. Not with so many questions left unanswered. Why didn't anyone know who George Andrews was? Why didn't they know for sure who hit Ben? Who killed the man in the car with her? And why in God's name was all this happening?

She was going to find out the truth if it killed her. And she had another motive as well. Lisa Canning wasn't going to have her way without a fight. Molly had every intention of staying long enough to put a stop to that relationship, finalize the divorce, and then be on her merry little way.

Somehow the idea didn't warm her in the slightest.

THE DAY IN NEW HOPE was a complete success. They had lunch in an elegant little French restaurant just opened for the season, dining sumptuously on the rich French food despite Mrs. Morse's warning glance. And then they went on a buying spree, jeans and khakis, cotton sweaters and denim shirts, leather boots, a tweed jacket, flannel nightgowns and running shoes. Mrs. Morse looked scandalized at her extravagance in an amused sort of way, and when Molly finally finished she contented herself with the comment that she didn't do things by half measures.

"Though I must say, Molly, that these clothes are much better suited to you than the ones that Mrs. Canning had you buy. I just hope you don't go through these as fast."

"I don't plan to," she said from over the tower of packages that surrounded them in the front seat and completely filled the back of the van. "I expect these will last me for a long, long time."

"Well, that's nice. And Patrick will just love the sweater you bought for him, I know he will."

Once more Molly was filled with misgivings. "Do you really think so?" she asked anxiously, her cheerfulness fading. The thick blue cotton sweater would match his cold eyes perfectly, and yet Molly doubted he had any desire to accept presents from her. Maybe she'd just put it away in a drawer until he had a birthday or something. Assuming she was going to be around for his birthday. Otherwise she could just give it to him as a divorce present. For some reason she doubted the thought would amuse him.

She was putting her new clothes away in the ugly dresser when a shadow fell across the doorway. She looked up, into the scowling face of her handsome husband.

"I thought you should have these while you're here," he said abruptly, tossing a small box onto the bed. "Despite your insistence that you'd never wear them, they *are* yours."

She knew what she'd find in that small, ivory box. Her wedding and engagement rings lay nestled against gray velvet. Neither of them struck any chord in her memory, the plain gold band nor the large sapphire in the old-fashioned setting. She slipped them on her ring finger, noting helplessly the perfect fit. Circumstances seemed determined to make her accept what her mind still found unacceptable. She was, it seemed, the selfish and spoiled wife of a brooding and very angry man. It was useless to waste any more time denying it.

She looked up at him, but there was no reading the expression on his face. "Why did I decide to take them off?" she asked. "Did I leave them behind when I left?"

"You never wore them."

He'd managed to shock her. "Why not?"

"You can cut the innocent surprise, Molly. You know perfectly well you threw them back at me the morning after we were married."

"You were that bad in bed?" she asked lightly.

He stared at her, an odd expression in his eyes. "You must have thought so," was all he said, turning on his heel to leave her.

She watched him go, wishing there was some way she could interpret that odd expression on his face. Another mystery, among too many mysteries.

She changed into a pair of khakis and a navy cotton sweater before making her way down to the kitchen. She was in the midst of peeling potatoes, temporarily alone in the vast, comfortable room, when Patrick reappeared. He looked at her, seemed about to beat a hasty retreat, and then obviously thought better of it. It appeared her husband was no more a coward than she was.

He moved into the room with that undeniable grace and leaned against the counter, a few feet away from her. "I see you decided to wear your rings," he said in that husky voice which she found so inexplicably attractive. Unfortunately she found everything about the man inexplicably attractive, from his lean, austere face to his long, muscular legs. Everything, that is, except his attitude toward his wife.

She nodded, concentrating fiercely on the potato in her hand. She felt suddenly nervous and tongue-tied with him so close, and she wondered whether that reticence was a normal part of her behavior.

Apparently not, she thought. "You've changed," he said suddenly, and she could feel those bright blue eyes on her, sense their puzzlement.

"Have I?" Her voice was carefully light. "I wouldn't

know." She looked up at him with all the courage she could muster. "You know, I really don't remember what I was like before. I can't remember a thing."

"Maybe you can't," he said enigmatically, moving closer to the table. "Or else you're a damned good actress." He leaned across her, his body brushing against hers just slightly as he turned on the lamp. "But then, you always were good at covering things up."

The faint touch of his body against hers had almost sent the knife slicing through her hand, and it took all her self-control to hide her sudden agitation. *Why in God's name does he have such an effect on me?*

He leaned back, watching her out of solemn eyes. "It's good of you to help Mrs. Morse with dinner."

She nodded, tossing one potato into the bowl of water and picking up another. After a moment she felt him move away, and she breathed a tiny, imperceptible sigh of relief.

"Come in for drinks when you're finished," he said suddenly. "We may as well try to behave like reasonable adults as long as you're here."

As a graceful invitation it still lacked a lot, but Molly found herself suddenly hopeful.

"What are you looking so happy about all of a sudden, missy?" Mrs. Morse demanded of her as she bustled back into the kitchen. "You win the lottery or something?"

Molly shrugged, hiding her face. She knew perfectly well that her reaction to his slight mellowing was all out of proportion, but it didn't matter. She had learned one thing about her loss of memory that she didn't find very comforting.

She might have forgotten names and faces and people and events, but she hadn't forgotten emotions. She cared about her husband, quite desperately, and his feelings toward her were at best decidedly lukewarm, at times bordering on hatred. But his partial civility tonight was a start. She began humming a tuneless little hum.

"You'd better let me finish those," Mrs. Morse offered after a few minutes, "and go in and get yourself a drink. I can take care of the rest. Thanks for the help."

She wanted to go find Patrick. To test out this new, inexplicable feeling. She wanted to stay in the kitchen, hidden away like a latter-day Cinderella. She squared her shoulders. "Any time."

Patrick was sitting in front of the fire, a glass in his hand, staring thoughtfully into space. He frowned when he saw her, and she firmly controlled a strong desire to run back upstairs, away from his obvious disapproval. Instead she smiled shyly.

No reaction. Since he didn't seem about to move, she poured herself a glass of the cranberry juice that seemed reserved for her and went to a seat near the fire. Near him. His eyes were fastened on her now, and she wondered what he was thinking. Probably comparing her to Lisa, she thought, and she knew who would come out ahead in that little competition.

"Why did you marry me?" she asked quietly, tucking her feet up under her. "Was it only for the money?"

He jumped, and his drink splashed onto his jeans. "Why do you ask?" he countered gruffly.

"We weren't in love, were we?"

"No, not at all," he answered after a moment. Whether he thought she was lying about her memory or not, he'd obviously decided to give her the benefit of the doubt. For now. "It seemed like the logical thing to do at the time. It was what my father wanted, and you were always eager to please my father."

"Were you? Eager to please your father, that is?"

"No," he said flatly. "I spent most of my life going

out of my way to drive him crazy. We were both too strong willed. He only had to decide something for me to take the opposite view.''

''Then if your father thought we should get married, why did you give in?''

His smile was wintry cold in the dim light. ''My father was more adept than most at getting his own way, even beyond the grave. He left his place to me, of course. I was his only child, his heir. But he left the majority of the money to you. Hadn't you wondered where it came from? Part of my father's twisted sense of humor. He knew I needed the money to keep this place going, and you needed a home. It seemed an obvious solution, and I decided to be practical for once. He was dead—there was no need to rebel against him anymore.''

Molly stared at him, appalled. ''Didn't I expect to fall in love at some point?'' she asked a bit breathlessly. ''Why in heaven's name would I agree to marry you?''

He shrugged. ''You didn't share your thoughts on the subject with me at the time. You always used to love this place—you said it was the only real home you'd ever known. And you loved my father. You wanted what he wanted.''

He leaned back, staring into the fire. ''He left the estate that way on purpose, you know. From the moment you came here he was determined that sooner or later we'd get married. Perfect blood lines, he'd decided, and once Father decided something there was no talking him out of it. He wanted to breed thoroughbred grandchildren the way he bred thoroughbred horses.''

''But we didn't.''

''Didn't what?'' he said in a rough voice.

''Breed perfect grandchildren.''

His laugh was short and mirthless. ''Neither of us were

in the mood. Don't worry, Molly, we won't have to suffer much longer from our mistake, I can promise you that. As soon as the divorce comes through you can take all your money and leave.''

''And how will you support Winter's Edge?'' she asked. ''Or is your future wife rich enough to provide you with the capital you need? It must be convenient, finding wealthy women willing to marry and support you in the style to which you seem accustomed.'' Her voice was bitter with an old, forgotten hurt.

He turned on her savagely. ''She is not my future wife, damn you. And it's none of your business how I support this place. I can manage without your help, without your money. If my father hadn't been so damned good at playing games it never would have been your money.'' He took a long pull on his drink.

''That was the only reason I married you?'' she asked, unable to leave it alone. There was something more there, something he wasn't telling her.

He looked up, a faint, cynical expression in his eyes. ''Well, there was the fact that you'd had a crush on me since you were sixteen. That may have had something to do with it.''

''I was in love with you?'' she said in a hushed voice.

''No!'' It was a sharp protest. ''You were a lonely adolescent who thought I was the perfect romantic hero. You used to follow me around like a lost puppy dog.''

She could feel color flood her cheeks, and she bit her lip. This was her fault, she'd pushed him. But she wished he'd shown just a trace more compassion. ''How very embarrassing for you,'' she said faintly. ''I must have put quite a damper on your love life.''

''Not particularly,'' he said, and she couldn't be sure what he was referring to.

"And when did I get over this embarrassing infatuation?" she asked lightly.

He stared at her, cool and removed. "On our wedding day," he said flatly. "I'm getting sick of nostalgia, Molly. Either be quiet or go away."

She stared at him out of shadowed eyes, wondering whether throwing her drink at him might help. She retreated into silence, settling back against the cushions with every appearance of unconcern as she concentrated on the dancing flames in the fireplace. Even Beastie's presence by her side was more torment than comfort, reminding her how alone she was in this place.

She glanced across the room at Patrick, unable to help herself. He was as cold as ice, and she wondered whether spring would ever touch the inhabitants of the old stone house, or whether they'd remain forever trapped in the icy winter.

CONVERSATION AT DINNER that night was stilted. Uncle Willy was his usual slightly drunken self, and decided to make up for his previous rudeness by showering Molly with effusive compliments, constantly refilling her cranberry juice until she felt bloated, trying to force vodka on her, generally being attentive and obnoxious. She would have hated it but for one interesting fact. All Willy's overbearing attentions seemed to have a most satisfying effect on Patrick, just as Toby's had the night before.

Her husband might not want her, but he sure as hell didn't want anyone else to touch her, even as elderly a lecher as Uncle Willy. He stared at them with a sour expression, and she knew he wanted to send her up to bed as he had the previous nights.

But she had no intention of behaving like a naughty little girl. Her behavior was exemplary, annoying him even further, and it was well past eleven when she finally left them. She had learned a lot that day, and had a lot more to learn. She knew where her money came from, and she had a fairly good idea of why Patrick had married her. Not because of the money, but out of pity for the poor infatuated teenager. The notion was intensely painful.

She fell into bed feeling waterlogged and exhausted, and dreamed of Patrick, staring at her out of brooding eyes.

IT SHOULDN'T HAVE bothered him, Patrick thought. That lost expression in her eyes, when he'd thrown her infatuation back in her face. If she really couldn't remember it, why should it have embarrassed her?

But suddenly he remembered what it was like. He'd just come back home after two years away, his most recent exodus the result of his worst parental battle to date. He'd gone places, seen things, done things he still hated to think about, and he felt dirty, cruel and worthless. Until he'd looked down into the sixteen-year-old eyes of his father's latest stray and seen a shining adoration he'd never deserved.

He couldn't resist it, as much as he tried. She worshiped the ground he walked on, even taking his part in battles with his formidable father.

And instead of further inciting Jared Winters's wrath, she'd merely made his father retreat with a crafty smile.

She was pretty, she was smart, she was brave, and she was unbearably loyal. If he'd been ten years younger. If she'd been someone other than his father's handpicked consort...

As it was, he'd ignored his zipper, treated her like the younger sister he'd never had, and kept his hands to himself. Each year it grew harder, and each year he was more determined to keep her at a distance. And each year his father's goading and Molly's innocent adoration eroded his determination.

He gave in, at last. After his father's sudden death from a heart attack, after the will was read and she was crying, desperate to make him take all that money that she'd never wanted. He'd come up with the obvious, logical answer, one that would salve her pride, support the expense of Winter's Edge farm, and please the ghost of his father.

Not to mention the fact that he wanted it, wanted her so badly that it was eating him alive.

He thought he'd gotten over that during their ten months of married life. She'd done her best to cure him, but he should have known better. All he had to do was look down into those innocent, green-blue eyes, and it all came rushing back.

But this time he wouldn't give in. He could keep the place going without the substantial amount his father had left her. A little economy, a lot of hard work, and things would be fine.

That was just what he needed. To work so hard he wouldn't have time to think. To remember. To want what he couldn't have.

To work so hard he'd be free of her. At last.

Chapter Seven

At six-thirty the next morning, Molly leaned over the side of her bed and threw up all over the fluffy white carpet. She rolled onto her back with bemused satisfaction. At least now something would have to be done about this awful room, she thought, and was sick again. She was too weak and dizzy to even try to make it to the bathroom, and she leaned back with a throbbing head against the immense pillows that adorned her bed.

There was no longer any way she could ignore the inevitable. She ate all the time, slept too much, and threw up every morning. Put that on top of a memory loss and the personal history of a slut, and there was only one logical explanation.

She was pregnant.

The notion both horrified and enchanted her. She looked down at her flat stomach and imagined it, round and full with a baby. She ran a tentative hand across it and found she could smile. It was a perfect image, but only with the right father to complete the picture.

It was only logical to assume that Patrick was the father. After all, he was her husband, albeit a not very enthusiastic one.

A baby might mend the brokenness between them. But

she didn't want a baby for marriage therapy, she wanted Patrick's baby because she…well, she just wanted Patrick's baby.

But what if the baby was someone else's? The man she'd run away with? Or any of the scores of lovers she'd supposedly enjoyed?

She still wanted that baby. And nothing and no one would take it away from her.

She also wasn't going to exist in a state of limbo any longer, now that she'd faced the shocking probability. She wanted answers, she wanted proof. She wanted to buy baby clothes.

She climbed out of bed, slowly and carefully, but all traces of illness seemed to have passed except for a slight weakness in her knees. She moved to the window and flung it open, letting in the fresh cool air to cleanse the room.

The sun was shining for once, proving that Pennsylvania wasn't always covered with rain or dark, brooding clouds. There was the softest hint of spring in the air, a mere suggestion of warmth and growing things, but it was enough to give Molly one of her first feelings of optimism. She showered and dressed in record time, cleaned up the mess beside the bed, and prepared to deal with the hand fate had dealt her.

"Who's my doctor?" she asked as she walked into the kitchen. Mrs. Morse already had a cup of coffee ready for her, but she paused in the act of handing it to her, clearly startled.

"What's wrong? Are you having aftereffects from your accident? We can get in touch with the hospital in New Jersey…"

"No, I just need a regular doctor. Whoever I usually

see." She took a tentative sip of the coffee, wondering how it would sit on her troubled stomach.

"You want to tell me why?"

Molly looked at her. Mrs. Morse was her only ally in this house full of angry strangers, and yet, for some reason she was loath to say anything. Perhaps she was afraid saying it aloud would make it go away. Maybe she was equally frightened that saying it aloud would make it more real.

"I just thought I needed a checkup," she said casually. "It's nothing to worry about, Mrs. Morse. I thought I ought to do something about birth control." True enough, in a way, she thought to herself.

"I'll give Dr. Turner a call for you," she offered.

"I'll take care of it myself. If you could just find me her number I'll call her when I get back from my walk. I need to get away from here for a little while, out in the fresh air."

Mrs. Morse paused, a startled expression on her face. "That's something," she said.

"What?"

"You knew Dr. Turner was a woman."

It never failed to unnerve her, these lightning flashes of knowledge that came without warning. "Maybe my memory's coming back," she said lightly.

"Maybe," Mrs. Morse said in a worried voice. "Let me just make you some bacon and eggs before you go out…"

"No, thanks!" Molly replied hastily, not feeling quite as recovered as she'd thought. The very idea of food was enough for her stomach to cramp up, and she set her coffee mug down, barely touched. "I'll have something later."

She rushed out into the early April sunshine, taking deep gulps of the clean wet air, and suddenly had the mad, determined desire to run. She took off at a comfortable lope, her body falling into the rhythm of it with effortless grace. She moved past the farm buildings, past the startled ducks, past Ben, her long hair streaming behind her, her heart pumping with a mindless joy.

She wanted to run forever, but she knew instinctively that she hadn't paced herself. After a bit she slowed, reluctantly, her heart pounding against her ribs, her breath rasping in her lungs. Her body wasn't as responsive as it had once been—she knew that without being sure how. She'd grown soft, her stamina had shattered. Perhaps it was the new life that might be growing inside her. She could only hope so.

The trees overhead were in bud, the winter brown-gray had a blush of green upon it, and all around her was the smell of wet spring earth. She inhaled it like a strong drug, wondering whether anyone could feel hopeless on a perfect day like this one, with the rich puffs of fleecy white clouds rolling around in the bluest of blue skies, and the soft spring breeze blowing in her face. As she continued down the narrow dirt track at a more moderate pace she was filled with a new hope, a new resolution that nothing could quite shake.

She hadn't gone less than a quarter of a mile when a sudden noise from the underbrush that lined the dirt road startled her into stopping. There was an eerie prickling at the back of her neck. Someone was watching her. Someone, or something, that wanted to hurt her.

She almost laughed out loud when she recognized Beastie's lumbering form charging down the road, knocking her flat on her back as he greeted her. She hugged him exuberantly, receiving a thorough face cleaning in return, then challenged him to a race down to the pile of rubble some ways in the distance.

He beat her, of course, and was waiting with ill-concealed canine smugness when she finally reached him, panting and gasping. And then she recognized where she was.

It was the charred remains of the barn she had supposedly burned down. Even after five long weeks the smell of wet, charred wood hung in the air. A part of one wall was standing, and she could imagine the flames crackling around the old structure, could even hear the screams of the poor tortured horses, could smell the sickening smell of burning flesh. She sank to the ground, dizzy, faint, and put her head between her knees.

"Are you all right?" She heard a soft voice nearby, and she looked up, blinking in the bright sunlight, to see Toby staring at her through the wire-rimmed glasses, his eyes dark and intense, his voice full of a soft concern that should have warmed her. She told herself it did, and yet she thought of Patrick.

She nodded, pulling herself together with a concerted effort and smiling up at him. "I just felt a little dizzy for a moment," she said. "I'd forgotten that I'm supposed to take it easy for a while." She looked at the incriminating ruins with sick eyes. "This…this must be the barn that burned."

He moved closer, sunlight glinting off the glasses and making his expression unreadable. "Don't you remember anything? Anything at all?"

"Not a thing," she said, resting her chin on her knees, trying to keep the guilt and misery out of her voice. Toby might have missed it, but Beastie was more attuned to her, and he whined softly, pushing his huge muzzle against her face.

Toby dropped down beside her, lying in the damp spring grass. "I've never heard of such a thing happening. Such a total absence of memory. Usually there are threads, pieces of the past.''

''And what would you know about it?'' She kept the edge out of her voice. ''Are you a doctor?''

''No. I was in premed, until illness forced me to drop out. But I remember enough to know that this is a highly unlikely scenario.''

''Whether amnesia happens this way or not, Toby, in my case it has,'' she said firmly. ''I assume it will all come back eventually, but I'm not going to waste my time worrying about it. You shouldn't either.'' She smiled reassuringly. For some reason Toby seemed to bring out her maternal instincts, which was odd, since he appeared to be several years older than she was, perhaps more than that, if he was Patrick's contemporary. But added to those strong, maternal feelings was an obscure, cynical part of her that didn't quite trust his ingenuous charm—something about him didn't seem quite right. Something in the intensity of his gaze, in the faint edge to his voice.

Her imagination had to be working overtime, she thought in disgust. She didn't have enough memories to fill her brain, so she was making things up to keep herself busy. Toby Pentick was harmless. Sweet, friendly, and far nicer than her soon to be ex-husband. So why was she looking for trouble where none existed?

''And you're sure you really remember nothing?'' Toby murmured with an intensity that seemed unnatural, and she stared at him in surprise.

''Nothing,'' she said smoothly. ''Do you?''

He paled suddenly, and she realized she had struck a nerve. ''What do you mean by that?''

''I mean do you remember anything about that night? Were you here? Did you see anything?''

He shook his head. ''I was on the West Coast, visiting

some friends. I had no idea anything had happened when I arrived back.''

There was no missing the sorrow or concern in his voice. Her memory might be gone, but her instincts were still strong. Toby cared about her. Perhaps too much.

The next thought was sudden, inevitable, and devastating. Here was another man, a close friend. He might be the father of her child, and not her husband at all. ''Toby?'' she asked in an urgent voice. ''Were we lovers?''

He blushed. It astonished her, the deep, red color mottling his skin as he stared at her. ''No,'' he said stiffly. ''Pat's my friend. I wouldn't do that to him.''

Before she had the chance to probe further, he rose. ''I'd better get back,'' he said in a strained voice. ''I promised Pat I'd take a look at one of the mares. See you.''

''All right,'' she said in a gentle voice, taking pity on his obvious mortification. She wouldn't have thought a grown man would be quite so sensitive. ''I think I'll stay here for a while. Could you take Beastie back with you?'' she asked. ''He's a little overwhelming for a playmate—I don't think I'm quite up to managing him yet.''

''Sure.'' He relaxed slightly. ''Uh...don't stay out here alone too long, okay?''

She caught the faintest trace of worry in his voice, and she stared at him sharply. ''Why not?''

He shook his head. ''I just have the feeling that it's not particularly safe around here.''

Molly stiffened her back, trying to ignore the chill of foreboding she felt at his words. ''For me or for everyone?''

''For you,'' he said, and calling Beastie, he started down the road.

She rose up on her knees, determined to call after him,

demand an explanation, but he was moving so fast there was no way she could catch him, short of sprinting, and she'd used up her energy for the morning. And she wasn't quite sure if Toby would answer her questions no matter how persistent she was.

Molly sank back in the damp brown grass and shut her eyes, trying to shut out the words of warning and bring back the feelings of peace and hope of a short while ago. But Toby's warning had done its job, and she sat up and looked around her nervously, wishing she hadn't banished Beastie. There were too many scorched and blackened trees around the ruins of the old barn, too much dark underbrush that could shield too many dangerous creatures. Dangerous creatures like Patrick, she wondered? She rose and moved closer to the barn, drawn to the blackened foundations and charred timbers, staring down at them. She had the eerie feeling that there were eyes on her, and she whirled suddenly, staring determinedly into the surrounding woods.

Of course there was no one there. She felt like an idiot as she turned back and leaned over the precipice of the barn, trying to peer into the old stone cellar of the building. She thought she saw something bright down there, something metal and flashing. Moving closer still, she suddenly felt herself hurtling face forward into the fire-blackened pit.

She must have bounced off one of the fallen beams, for she felt a sharp pain in her side, and something tore at her arm as she plummeted downward into the murky cellar. She hit bottom after what seemed like an endless fall, and she lay there in the mud, her body aching from the various obstructions she had hit on her way down, the feel of someone's hands as they pushed her still strong on her back. Without moving she could see her arm, see the long, narrow gash that was welling with dark blood. Blood that was rapidly pooling beneath her.

Her first thought was for the child that might or might not exist. Her entire body ached, but there was no worrisome cramping. The cut in her arm seemed by far the worst of her injuries, and she viewed it with sick fascination.

I'm going to bleed to death, she thought numbly. *It won't matter whether I'm pregnant or not—I'll be dead and no one will find me for years and years, and in the meantime Patrick will have all my money to spend on that woman.*

She squeezed her eyes shut, allowing her a few brief moments of misery and panic. And then she shot them open again. Life would be far too convenient if she just disappeared. She wasn't going to give them what they wanted again.

She rolled onto her back, groaning. The sides of the old cellar were oozing springtime mud, the sun filtered through the remaining beams above her and the gash in her arm no longer seemed quite so desperate. She still felt sick and weak, but from somewhere in the back of her brain came the memory that blood usually had that effect on her. Especially her own.

And then she heard the sound again, the low whine. "Beastie," she croaked weakly, but the sound was barely audible. "Beastie," she tried again, but it was useless.

There was a great crashing of wood, and an old beam thundered down, missing her head by inches. "What the hell are you doing down there?" Patrick's angry voice demanded. Molly had never heard anything so annoyingly welcome in her entire life.

"Taking a nap," she snapped. "What did you think?"

But he was gone again, and she almost called after him.

He couldn't have left her there, could he? But then, what did she really know about him? Maybe he wanted to finish what he started.

And then she heard a crashing about at the far end of the structure, and she closed her eyes in relief. He hadn't left her. If he'd been the one to push her he would hardly have come to rescue her. In a moment he was beside her, his eyes dark with a fear and an anger that were both oddly comforting. "Are you all right?" he asked unnecessarily, poking at her arm.

"I...I guess so," she stammered weakly. "I hurt my arm, but that's about it. I think."

"You did, indeed," he said grimly, his hands gentle as he probed for possible damage. She didn't like it, the impersonal feel of his hands on her body, touching her with the same care and interest he might show a wounded horse. Perhaps less. "And it serves you right," he added. "What the hell do you mean, wandering around here? It's dangerous; any fool would know that! Did you have some incredible urge to return to the scene of the crime, to see how much damage you did? If it weren't for Beastie I might never have found you."

During this tirade he managed to lift her up in his arms with a tenderness at amazing variance with the harshness in his voice, and he carried her out into the brilliant sunlight by the remaining flight of stone steps.

"Are you always so angry?" she asked wearily, leaning her head against his shoulder, too weak and tired to fight.

"With you, yes," he answered grimly, stalking down the road and jarring her poor, bruised body with every step.

"How did you happen to fall? Didn't you have enough sense to keep your distance from the edge? Or were you too fascinated by the ruins...?"

"I didn't fall. I was pushed."

The silence that followed was overwhelming, and she half expected him to drop her in the middle of the road. He didn't, but his expression grew even more grim.

"Still dramatizing, Molly?" he drawled in an unpleasant voice. "I would have thought you'd get tired of being the center of attention all the time."

"You don't believe me?" she demanded, fury wiping out the last of her shock and fear.

"Not for a moment. No one else would either, so you might as well save your breath. Why would anyone want to shove you down in the cellar? If they were trying to kill you there are a lot more effective ways."

She shoved at him, desperate to break his hold on her, but she'd forgotten how strong he was. He simply tightened his grip, almost painfully, as he stalked toward the house, and she gave up her fruitless struggle as a belated, comforting thought hit her. His anger at her story, his disbelief, was honest. If he refused to believe she'd been pushed, then he couldn't be the one who'd pushed her. The true culprit would have lied to cover for himself, or tried to throw suspicion on someone else. Her enemy, her nemesis, had to be someone else.

She was almost smiling by the time they reached the house. She sat in the kitchen, watching her husband glower at her, while Mrs. Morse clucked and moaned in distress and Uncle Willy, who was already slightly the worse for alcohol at such an early hour, kept his pale, watery eyes averted from the steadily oozing blood as he tried to make encouraging noises.

Dr. Turner arrived, a grumpy, middle-age woman who seemed annoyed at being bothered. She poked at Molly, with even less care than Patrick had evinced, bandaged her up, and pronounced her none the worse for a little shock, all with an audience of interested bystanders. "But you should be more careful, Mrs. Winters,'' she said gravely, snapping her battered case shut. ''All you'll feel is a little stiffness. It could have been a lot worse. You could have hit your head again, and then we'd have to put you in the hospital for observation. I imagine you've had enough of hospitals for the time being.''

''Yes, Dr. Turner,'' she murmured in a docile voice, thoughts racing through her head. She could have been killed. And someone *had* pushed her, she knew it as well as she... Well, she didn't know anything about herself too well, but she knew that she'd been pushed. Patrick had already made it clear that no one would believe her, and she didn't bother trying to explain. If no one would listen, why should she waste her breath?

Except that Patrick was watching her with an odd expression behind the annoyance in those blue, blue eyes. Maybe he believed her after all. Maybe he knew she'd been pushed because he was the one who'd pushed her, and he'd been afraid to finish her off for fear Toby would return and see him.

Dr. Turner was already heading for the door. Molly racked her brain, trying to think of a discreet way to call her back. Finally, Mrs. Morse spoke up.

''Wasn't there something you wanted to ask Dr. Turner about, Molly?''

Four pairs of eyes turned to stare at her, with Patrick's being the most suspicious.

''Well, young lady?'' Dr. Turner demanded when Molly didn't say anything. ''Is this an emergency?''

''Er...no.''

''Then call my office and make an appointment like everyone else. I've already been here too long as it is. Next time, Patrick, you take her to the emergency room.''

''There isn't going to be a next time,'' Patrick said in a

quiet voice. And Molly wasn't sure whether to be pleased or terrified.

"I think you'd better spend the rest of the day in bed," Patrick announced after Dr. Turner had left. "And from now on you aren't allowed out unless someone goes with you."

"But why?" she demanded, then winced in pain. She lowered her voice. "This was just an accident—it won't happen again."

"You go out with someone or you don't go out at all," he said in the kind of voice that brooked no arguments. "And if you disobey me I'll lock you in."

"Disobey you?" she echoed in a tight little voice. "Who the hell do you think you are, my father? You can't tell me what to do."

"I doubt even your father told you what to do," he said sourly, and without another word he stormed out of the house, leaving Molly in a state of stomach-churning rage.

"Well," said Mrs. Morse after a moment, "who would have thought he'd get so worked up?" She shook her head, but there was an oddly hopeful expression in her eyes. "Don't you worry, Molly. I'll fix you some nice hot soup and ham sandwiches, and some of my chocolate cake. How would you like that?"

She was hungry again. If she had been pregnant in the morning, she obviously still was. "I'd love it. Will you join me, Uncle Willy?" she asked politely of the silent figure in the corner.

He shook his head in faint disgust, the neat orange strands carefully combed over that pink and shining skull. "No, thank you, my dear. I always partake of only the lightest meal when I first wake up." He rose and wandered out of the kitchen, looking oddly disturbed about something. He hardly seemed sensitive enough to be worried

about her well-being, and Molly watched his retreating figure with vague, shapeless suspicions.

"All right, Molly," Mrs. Morse said, coming to stand
in front of her with arms planted on her ample hips.
"What's going on?"

"What do you mean? I must have tripped…"

"I'm not talking about your fall. Assuming it really was
a fall, though it seems to me Patrick's right about your
being more careful. No, I want to know why you wanted
to see Dr. Turner in private. And don't tell me some story
about you needing birth control, because I don't believe
it."

She looked up at her. When it came right down to it,
she had to trust someone. "I think I'm pregnant."

"Sweet heavens!" Mrs. Morse said. "Have you told
Patrick yet?"

"Not until I'm certain. What if it's not his?"

Mrs. Morse's face fell. "I hadn't thought of that. You
couldn't be very far along—they would have caught it in
the hospital after your accident."

"And since I haven't been home in five weeks that
would mean that Patrick…"

"Wasn't the father," Mrs. Morse finished for her.
"Why don't you ask him?"

"Not until I have to. Not until I see Dr. Turner and get
the proof. She should know how far along I am."

"Molly, dearest," she said in a gentler voice, "there's
no need to be scared of Pat. I don't know what's gone on
between the two of you, but for all his bluster he's a caring, decent man."

"Sure," Molly said with just a trace of bitterness. "He
cares about Lisa Canning."

"He cares about you, missy."

Molly shook her head, unwilling to accept the notion.

"You're not to say anything until I find out. In the meantime I suppose I need to get an appointment."

"I'll call for you," Mrs. Morse said firmly. "No one needs to know anything about it—we'll just tell anyone who asks that you were feeling dizzy after your fall."

"You don't suppose that I...did anything to it?"

She shook her head, an ancient sorrow shadowing the eyes behind the steel-rimmed glasses. "You'd feel it if you did bring on a miscarriage, believe me. I had six of them myself, before the doctor told me to stop trying, and there's no ignoring the symptoms, no matter how early along you are. No, if you're pregnant then nothing's happened to it yet." She rose. "Should I call her office?"

Molly nodded numbly.

She was lost in thought when Mrs. Morse returned a few minutes later. "Damned receptionist. You'd think Dr. Turner was the Queen of England and not some small-town family practitioner. She can't see you till the day after tomorrow, unless it's an emergency. In the meantime the best thing for you to do is go upstairs and lie down and try not to think about it. Find yourself a good book or something."

"I've read them all," she said morosely, rising slowly from the hard chair. "Maybe I'll explore the house."

"Whatever for?"

"Because I don't remember it," she said simply. "And I'm not at all tired."

"Well, you be careful if you go in the attics. There's a lot of junk stored up there," she warned. "I'd come with you but your Aunt Ermy is coming in on the 5:47 train tonight and the Lord knows I'd better have an elegant enough supper to suit her palate. You go on ahead and come down here for some brownies and tea later on if you feel like it."

"I will," she promised, setting off.

ANOTHER MISTAKE. Another botched attempt. All she'd ended up with was a gashed arm. Things were not going according to plan, not in the slightest, and it was getting more than frustrating.

Sooner or later someone was going to start getting suspicious at all her mishaps. It wouldn't matter if Molly suspected something—her credibility was in the toilet already. No one would listen to her.

The local police didn't give a damn. Stroup wanted to get into her pants and nothing more, and Ryker was so far off base there was nothing to worry about. Not yet.

But there couldn't be any more mistakes. Sooner or later it was going to come back to her. She didn't remember—there was no longer any doubt of that. Her green-blue eyes were totally guileless; she hadn't the faintest idea whom she could trust.

But that happy state of affairs wouldn't last forever. Next time they were going to do it right. Get it right.

Get her dead. And silent.

Chapter Eight

Molly couldn't rid herself of the feeling that she was Alice in Wonderland, or Dorothy in Oz. The house had grown increasingly familiar over the last two days—the beautifully comfortable living room, the formal dining room, the kitchen, the neat and uninspiring little office under the stairs where Patrick did his accounts and hid from his wife.

But upstairs was a different matter. Patrick's closed door was an enticing Pandora's box, but even Molly's courage had limits. She could explore it later, when she was sure he was nowhere around. Perhaps even tonight, while he was out picking up the mysterious Aunt Ermy from the train station.

She needed to see if she could find something to jog her memory. A hint, a clue, some tiny something to jar her stubborn mind. The longer it remained blank the more frustrated she grew.

She wasn't sure she really was in any kind of danger. Even though she'd been involved in a murder, no one had seemed interested in harming her now. So far, no one had seemed particularly interested in getting within touching distance of her.

But Patrick had touched. Unwillingly, almost as if he couldn't help himself. And she knew he wanted to touch her again. Almost as much as she wanted him to touch her.

Aunt Ermy's room was a jumble of clutter. Little ornaments jostled each other for space on her mantelpiece, her cherry wood dressers, her Queen Anne secretary. Every spare inch in the room was filled with an artifact of some sort, from exquisite pieces to the merely shoddy. Dresden ballerinas danced with plastic penguins, there were plump, overstuffed pillows everywhere, and the room felt claustrophobic. She shut the door behind her, unable to rid herself of the notion that she didn't have very much in common with Aunt Ermy.

Uncle Willy's room was exactly the opposite—practically devoid of personal clutter. That was an empty vodka bottle in his wastepaper basket, and the clothes he wore yesterday were neatly folded and placed on a Windsor chair. The atmosphere of the room was stale and tired, rather like Uncle Willy himself, and she left just as quickly.

The attics lay beyond the little turn in the hallway, down two steps and past the linen closet and the guest bathroom. She turned the doorknob, not without a small shiver of apprehension. Since this morning she distrusted being alone. It seemed to her as if there were eyes everywhere, watching her, threatening her.

"This is ridiculous," she muttered out loud, stepping into the room and switching on the light.

Mrs. Morse hadn't exaggerated when she said the attics were filled with junk. Trunks upon trunks upon trunks, ancient newspapers and magazines tied in neat little bundles, old pieces of riding tack, skis, tennis rackets needing restringing, boxes and boxes and boxes. And her furniture.

She recognized it with a swift feeling of relief and love, rather like seeing an old friend, and she moved toward it in a daze, running her hand over the warm glow of the cherry bedstead, the delicate dressing table, the blanket chest that somehow seemed to fit with the various periods of the other pieces. She was going to have it back, she promised herself. As soon as she could have that hideous modern stuff removed and carted off to the dump, she'd have her own beloved pieces back in there.

She went over to the most readily available boxes, hoping that something else might jog her memory. But nothing else tripped that frustrating, mysterious little mechanism in her brain. The prom dress that hung forlornly must have been hers, yet she remembered no magic, breathless moments, no starry-eyed excitement connected with it. It was simply a pretty dress, worn by a girl she didn't know, and she wondered vaguely where her wedding dress was. And whether it would bring her any greater recognition.

She lost track of time, poking and prying and trying to force some shred of memory. Hours might have passed. She made a mental note of all the furniture she knew belonged in her room, and lost herself in schemes on how best to arrange it. When she finally left the room and switched the light off behind her, the hallway was dark. She could hear a car driving away from the house, and she hurried to look out her bedroom window.

It was the fairly new Mercedes that she knew belonged to Patrick, and she breathed a sigh of relief. She would have time now to snoop through his room. There was no other word for it—she needed to discover the secrets he kept from his unwanted wife. Any clue to the impasse they were currently in was worth prying for, even if her methods were less than honorable. She had to find out more about him if she was ever going to remember all she had lost. And why she had married him in the first place.

And whether she had any reason to fear him.

She still wasn't quite sure why she was afraid of him. He certainly didn't seem the sort of man to be abusive. There was anger, deep inside him, and a lot of that anger was directed at her. But she still couldn't believe he'd deliberately want to injure her.

Or could she believe it? Was she a fool to trust her instincts when she had no memory to back them up? Why couldn't Patrick have bashed old Ben on the head and set the barn fire? Insurance money could be a very strong motive.

Maybe he'd paid George Andrews to lure her away and kill her. Maybe he'd tried to kill her himself.

Maybe, maybe, maybe. There were times when she thought she'd go crazy if she didn't start to find some answers to the questions that plagued her.

Including the most basic. Was her husband a dangerous enemy or a disinterested bystander? Or someone who cared more than he wanted to?

She pulled the thick cotton sweater she'd bought him out of her drawer and tucked it under her arm before attempting her final excursion. If she happened to run into Mrs. Morse or Uncle Willy at least she would have an excuse. Though why she should need an excuse to enter her husband's bedroom was beyond her comprehension. She simply knew it to be the truth.

She moved silently down the hall and opened Patrick's door with all the stealth of a master criminal. Not a sound emanated from the upstairs hall. For all anyone would know she was sound asleep in the elegant nightmare called her room. She slipped inside and shut the door.

She hadn't looked very carefully when she had explored the first day, simply noticing the air of unfrilly masculinity before she'd shut the door again. But now it had taken on an entirely new dimension. It belonged to Patrick, the enigma, and as such was endlessly fascinating.

His bed was high and wide, at least three and a half feet off the floor, the kind of bed where babies are born and old people die. The kind of bed to found a dynasty in, if one was so inclined. She ran a hand over the beautiful quilt, and wondered whether she had shared any unforgettable moments in this enticing bed. If so, she had obviously forgotten them.

She could imagine Patrick's long, lean body, tossing and turning in so large a bed, and she felt a queer little twinge in her stomach. Of longing? Or nervousness? Or both? She couldn't truthfully answer.

She placed the sweater on the bed with great care, then moved to the dresser, noting the silver-backed combs with his initials engraved on them, the loose change lying around. The photograph of a young girl standing in a field, her head thrown back, laughing from sheer joy.

Molly's hand was trembling as she reached out and took the picture. She knew that face, that moment. It was a picture of her, not that old, and she could almost remember, almost grasp…

"What the hell are you doing in here?" His voice was rough, shocking, sending whatever she was about to remember flying into a million pieces. She stared at him numbly.

He shut the door behind him and moved closer. He'd unbuttoned his shirt and pulled it free from his jeans, obviously on the way to a shower, and it was all she could do to keep her eyes away from his chest.

She had to have seen men's chests before. She had to have seen this particular one before, and she was being an utter fool to stand there, speechless. So he was tanned, even at the end of winter. So he was lean, and strong, with a triangle of hair that arrowed down toward his jeans. So it was a very nice chest indeed. There was still no need for her to suddenly find herself unable to breathe.

He moved closer, and there was just the hint of a threat in his movements, and a sinuous grace that made her look around helplessly for means to escape.

"What are you doing with a picture of me on your dresser?" she countered, trying to divert him from whatever he had in mind.

"It's not you," he said flatly. "It's a girl I once knew, but she's been gone for years. Leaving you in her place." His voice was contemptuous as he surveyed her, and then he shrugged, never slowing his determined progress toward her as she stood guiltily in the corner of his bedroom. "Call it an old weakness," he added slowly. He stopped, directly in front of her, so close she could feel his body heat, so close she could see the tiny fan of lines around his stormy blue eyes.

Her reaction made no sense to her. She wanted to run away, and she wanted to touch him. She wanted to reach out and run her hand down that lean, muscled chest, but something, some innate wisdom, stopped her. Despite the fact that she must have done that, and much more, in the past, she knew she shouldn't do it now. No matter how much she wanted to feel the warmth of his skin beneath her hand.

"You know, Molly," he said in a low, sinuous voice, "you should have told me you wanted to visit my bedroom. I would have invited you long ago."

Quite casually he reached out and took her by the shoulders, drawing her unresisting body towards him. "It's amazing that you still have some effect on me." His voice was rough, and his mouth covered hers with a sudden force that left her shocked, stunned, paralyzed. He held her in an unbreakable grip as he caught her chin in his hand and continued to kiss her, with slow, contemptuous deliberation, refusing to allow her to escape, until she was a shaking, trembling mass of confused reactions, reactions she was powerless to control. And then his mouth softened, and it was no longer punishment but a reward, and she kissed him back, sliding her arms around his waist, pressing up against him with helpless longing she hadn't quite understood.

She needed to be here. Locked tight against him, his mouth on hers, demanding nothing but complete surrender. She made a quiet little sound in the back of her throat, and surrender it was.

He pulled away, suddenly, moving back from her as if she'd suddenly become contagious. "Damn you," he said in a low, furious voice. "Get out of here."

She stared at him through the twilight room for a moment, shaken, shocked to the very core of her being. And then she ran from the room without a backward glance. Ran from him as she had run before, five weeks earlier, in the same blind panic.

When she reached her room she slammed the door shut behind her and locked it with a loud, satisfying click. Leaning against the door, she trembled in the aftermath of his touch. She had surely never been kissed like that before. She couldn't have forgotten such a torrent of emotions. As a matter of fact, she could have sworn that she'd never been kissed at all—the feel of a hot, wet mouth against hers had been a startling revelation.

But that was absurd. She was twenty-three years old, and married. Her mind must be playing even more sadistic tricks on her.

She moved through her darkened room and threw herself onto the bed. She wouldn't go down to dinner, she promised herself. She couldn't face him after...that...that.

She would lie there and starve.

"MOLLY? Molly, dear, open up. Open up right now!" An imperative voice broke through Molly's sleep-numbed mind, and she sat up dazedly. It took her a moment to remember where she was, and what had happened. Patrick's mouth on hers, the too-brief moment that had burned into her brain.

Unfortunately nothing else had disrupted her blank memory. She probed, looking for answers, ignoring the incessant pounding at her door. Still nothing.

"Who is it?" she finally called out groggily, switching on the light.

"Your Aunt Ermintrude, of course. Now open the door immediately."

What a tyrant, she thought. "What can I do for you?" she called out with deliberate calm.

"What do you mean, what can you do for me? Do as I say immediately, Molly, or I shan't answer for the consequences." Her deep contralto voice rose to a tiny squeak of rage.

"Then don't," Molly answered mildly enough, glad to have an instinct confirmed. She couldn't stand dear Aunt Ermy. "I'll open the door when I'm ready to, and not before. Go away and leave me alone."

There was an outraged silence beyond the oak door, and she could picture a rather Wagnerian lady bristling with indignation. After a moment or two she heard angry, stomping footsteps walk away and she chuckled, inordinately pleased that she had managed to rout some member of her hostile family at last.

"Molly." Mrs. Morse's soft voice broke through her

pleased reverie, and she sprang up. The woman darted into the room as soon as Molly unlocked it, with a furtive glance over her shoulder to make sure she was unobserved.

"My, my, you have put your aunt in a taking," she said with satisfaction. "Sent me up here to find out what in hell was going on with you."

Molly threw herself back down on the bed, wondering absently whether she looked any different. Could Mrs. Morse see that Patrick had kissed her? Probably not—people were kissed all the time. Everyone had made it clear she'd done a lot more than kissing, and with a number of men besides her husband. It was hardly the soul-shattering event it seemed to her overwrought imagination. "I don't care much for Aunt Ermy," Molly said in a meditative voice.

"Well, now that's a new thing, I must say. You and the old battle-ax used to be inseparable buddies, always tearing poor Patrick apart each chance you got." She sniffed. "I'm glad you've seen the error of your ways."

"We don't seem to have much in common," Molly said. "Are you sure?"

"I'm sure," she said flatly. "I'm just glad that's over and done with. I came to find out if you'd be coming down to dinner. There'll only be the three of you—Willy, Ermy, and you. Patrick took off about an hour ago in a towering rage. Said he wouldn't be in for dinner. I wondered if you would know anything about that?" Her curiosity was unabashed, but Molly wasn't in the mood to satisfy it.

"Can't imagine." She scrambled off the bed. "And of course I'll be down to dinner. Can I give you a hand?"

"It's all done. Everything to her highness's liking, you can be sure." She pursed her thin lips in disgust. "You can come down and keep her off my back, though. She and Willy are having a high old time in the living room, drinking Patrick's liquor and heaping insults on him in his absence.''

"I'll see what I can do," Molly promised, running a brush thought her hair and following Mrs. Morse's upright figure through the halls.

She paused at the entrance of the living room, just long enough to take stock of its inhabitants. Aunt Ermy was Wagnerian, all right, with a high-swept pompadour of silver hair and three determined chins, each one more determined than the last. Tiny, piglike eyes, a retroussé snout with a fierce mustache bristling beneath completed the picture, and of her massive body the less said the better: a mountainous bulk on tiny trotters. She looked as unpleasant as Molly had imagined her to be, and she was mortally glad the relationship was, at best, a distant one.

"Good evening, everyone," she greeted them airily as she sailed into the room. Aunt Ermy's tiny eyes took in the jeans, the T-shirt, the lack of makeup, and her face screwed up into a look of pouting disapproval.

"Well," she said at length, "I'm pleased to see you finally decided to come down and greet your poor aunt after your long and mysterious absence. Going off like that without a word!''

Molly smiled at her, not a bit disturbed. "Sorry," she said briefly, helping herself to a large glass of cranberry juice and slipping into the hard-backed chair left—the two relatives having commandeered the most comfortable ones in the room. "Did you enjoy your visit?"

"I might well ask the same of you," Aunt Ermy said frostily. Molly eyed her with cold-blooded calm, and she immediately changed her domineering attitude. "Molly, dear, couldn't you have told us where you were going? We were *worried* about you!"

Molly shrugged, and Aunt Ermy leaned closer, the air

heavy with the expensive but unsuitably girlish scent she had splashed all over her. ''And Willy here tells me you've lost your memory. Surely you can't have forgotten your Aunt Ermy? And all the fun things we used to do together?''

''I'm afraid I have,'' she said in a brisk voice. ''I'm starving. Mrs. Morse should have dinner ready by now—shall we go in?'' Molly rose gracefully, and Aunt Ermy stared up at her with increasing annoyance.

''Well, really, Molly, we've hardly started on our second drink,'' she began, but Molly interrupted her.

''Oh, that's perfectly all right, you can bring it in with you,'' she said, nipping her protests in the bud. Uncle Willy looked up from his chair, a gleam of amusement and something else fighting through the sodden expression on his face. He wandered after them into the dining room, bringing not only his glass but the crystal decanter of whiskey with him.

Molly watched Aunt Ermy bear down on the seat at the head of the table like a steamship. As soon as she pulled out the heavy chair Molly darted into the seat, smiling at her with all the charm she had at her beck and call. ''Thank you, Aunt Ermy,'' she said sweetly, pulling out the heavy linen napkin and placing it on her lap.

Ermintrude stood there for a moment in a floundering rage, immovable and furious. She seated herself with awful majesty at Molly's right, her mountainous form quivering with indignation.

''You used to dress for dinner, my dear,'' was all she said in an aggrieved tone, and Molly considered she'd gotten off lightly.

''I prefer to be comfortable, Aunt Ermy,'' she replied calmly.

"And where has *he* gone tonight?" she questioned half-way through the meal.

"Do you mean my husband?" Molly asked her politely. Whatever her differences were with the man, she wasn't about to let this awful old woman insult him. "He had some business to attend to, I believe."

"Business like *la belle dame* Canning, if I'm not mistaken," Willy snorted from the foot of the table.

"Perhaps," Molly said, undisturbed. "But I don't think that's any of your concern." Her calm statement put a damper on the dinner conversation, but by the time they were back in the living room and well fortified with additional alcohol Uncle Willy and Aunt Ermy grew quite loquacious once more.

"I'm glad to see you're drinking your cranberry juice," Aunt Ermy observed heavily as she accepted another tall glass from Willy's drink-fumbled hands. "At least you're following my precepts in that matter."

Molly immediately tried to refuse the drink, but Willy took no notice, trying to add a shot of vodka to the glass she held firmly out of reach.

"Come on, my girl," he pouted. "Don't go all prudish on us. You used to put away quite a bit of this stuff before your transformation into Rebecca of Sunnybrook Farm. Patrick's not here to see you—live a bit," he bantered clumsily.

Molly shook her head, frowning in annoyance. "This doesn't have anything to do with Patrick," she snapped irritably, remembering the feel of his hot mouth on hers. She shivered and sipped at the cranberry juice. She didn't want to drink. She didn't like the idea of alcohol, and if she really was pregnant it gave her an even stronger reason to abstain.

She wondered how her two so-called relatives would

react to the notion of a pregnancy. With screams of horror, no doubt. She imagined Aunt Ermy would try to drag her off to the nearest abortion clinic if she could.

"Of course it doesn't have anything to do with Pat," Aunt Ermy chimed in. "Do you suppose my poor little girl would let herself be browbeaten by that towering bully? I warned him when I saw him tonight—I wouldn't stand by and let him order you about."

"And what did he say to that?" Molly asked curiously.

Uncle Willy snorted. "Told her what she could do with her advice, and that he'd order you about as much as he pleased. Ermy didn't care for that much, did you, dearie?" He laughed again, and the sound was a high-pitched giggle.

Molly rose suddenly, disgusted by the two of them. "I think I'll go up to bed," she said. "It's been a long day and I still don't feel recovered from this morning."

"Oh, yes, Willy was telling me about your accident." Was there a slight emphasis on the word accident? Aunt Ermy seemed all solicitude. "You really should be very careful, Molly dear. Certain people could find your death very convenient. Very convenient indeed. If I were you I wouldn't go out alone." She nodded her head meaningfully, and Molly calmly considered hitting her.

"Thank you for your concern, Aunt Ermy," she said in a deceptively even voice. "Patrick has already suggested the same thing. I'll be sure to take very good care of myself." She started out of the room, Beastie at her side. He obviously cared no more for those two than she herself did, Molly thought gratefully.

"Don't forget your cranberry juice, Molly." Willy placed the cool glass in her hand.

She took it with her, managing a tight-lipped smile of thanks.

Chapter Nine

He shouldn't have kissed her. He'd done a lot of stupid things in his life, so many he'd lost count, but kissing her yesterday had to be one of the worst.

He could make all sorts of excuses. She was standing in his darkened bedroom, looking up at him as if he were a cross between Jack the Ripper and Tom Cruise, acting as if she'd never seen a man's naked chest before. When he knew she'd seen a lot more.

He wasn't sure what made him put his hands on her. His mouth on hers. The anger that consumed him whenever he saw her, thought of her. Curiosity, to see just what she'd learned from all the men she'd been with.

He'd been tempting fate as well. Checking to see whether he could remain immune to her. He should have known he couldn't. The touch, the taste of her, had burned itself into his brain.

Why couldn't life be simple? Why couldn't he have fallen in love with someone like Lisa Canning? Lisa, who'd offer him everything and expect not much more than energetic sex and a certain tolerant discretion.

Why did he have to want someone like Molly?

It had been a mistake, but not a fatal one. So he'd kissed her. So he'd felt her arms, tight around him, and the tremor that rippled through her body. He'd heard that soft, plaintive sound she'd made in the back of her throat, and he'd frozen. He'd had the sense to push her away, send her away.

And he had the sense to keep away himself.

It wouldn't happen again. If worse came to worst he'd take what Lisa Canning had been offering so blatantly, just to get it out of his system.

Sooner or later Molly would grow tired of this charade, tell the police what they needed to know, and then he could get rid of her. And in doing so, he'd spike his father's final, biggest wish.

It had to be a charade. There was no way she could possibly be the wide-eyed innocent she appeared to be.

And it was his own stupid fault for wanting to believe her. Thinking with his hormones instead of his head.

She'd have to admit the truth. Whatever the hell the truth might be. And then the two of them could go their separate ways. Forever.

So why didn't the prospect seem more like a victory, instead of petty revenge?

SHE WAS SICK AGAIN the next morning. This time she didn't wreck the carpet—she had thoughtfully provided herself with an empty wastebasket on the chance that this morning would parallel the others. She was vaguely hoping against hope that she'd be well this morning: no little babies to complicate her life. But fate didn't want to cooperate. She lay back in bed, shivering with the aftermath.

This time she didn't fall back asleep. It was stormy again, and the steady beat of the rain seemed to pound even louder in her throbbing head. There was no point in delaying—she climbed wearily out of her oversoft bed and prepared to face the day.

There was no one stirring in the darkened kitchen. And no wonder—5:30 was a bit early even for a farm. She made a full pot of coffee, lit the fire that had already been laid in the hearth, and huddled close to it. Eventually, somewhere in the middle of her second cup of coffee, the rain slackened off a bit, and she listened to the noise of an approaching car with interest. It was her dear husband in the old van, presumably back from a night in the arms of the grieving widow. The surge of anger and jealousy that swept through Molly frightened her, and she put down the cup with trembling fingers.

She saw him long before he saw her. There was a cold, discontented look on his lean face, which pleased her enormously. It certainly wasn't the proper expression for a man returning from a satisfying night of love.

He ran in the door, shaking off the clinging raindrops from his long black hair. Then his eyes met hers, and he stopped dead.

"Good morning," she greeted him evenly, willing herself sternly to forget the last moment she had seen him, the overwhelming reaction she'd had to his kiss.

He moved closer into the room, relaxing slightly. "You're up early," he observed. "Is there any more coffee?"

"In the carafe." She picked up her cup and took another sip, the trembling in her hand down to a bare minimum. "How's Lisa?" She could have kicked herself for saying that.

"Fine," he said brusquely. "She sends you her love." And, taking his cup with him, he left the room.

Cursing herself for a fool, Molly rose from her seat and began puttering around the kitchen. She discovered a cache of day-old muffins and proceeded to heat them in the oven. Placing them daintily on one of the old Spode plates and adding butter and homemade jam, she carried them into Patrick's office.

He looked up from the paper he was staring at, and frowned. "A peace offering," she stated, before he could open his mouth to order her from the room. "I'm sorry for what I said in the kitchen. It was uncalled for." She didn't honestly believe that, but she expected Patrick wouldn't agree. "Would you like some more coffee?"

"I'll get it," he said, but she took the cup from him in a peremptory fashion.

"You eat your muffins," she said grandly, sailing from the room. In a moment she was back, with two cups. She sat down opposite him and watched him out of demurely lowered eyelids, letting her gaze trail along the lean, smooth lines of his body, the tired planes of his tanned face.

"All right," he said abruptly. "You want togetherness, we'll have togetherness. Why don't you answer a few questions, dear wife? Think you can do that?"

"I doubt it. I don't have any memories."

"The convenient amnesia. I guess it must be catching—I keep forgetting that you lost your memory."

He was in a foul mood, she thought. Obviously the wrong moment for improving their relationship. She rose, but his hand shot out, clamping around her wrist, and she slopped her mug of coffee. He didn't release her, and she refused to sit. She stood there, staring down at him, wishing it gave her even the slightest advantage. It didn't.

"So tell me, Molly dear. Are you still insisting someone pushed you down the cellar hole?" he asked in a silken voice. Despite the firmness of his grip, his thumb was absently stroking the tender inside of her wrist.

"It was the truth."

"And you're such a great expert on the truth, aren't you? What happened the night you left here?"

Damn him, she thought, wishing she could break free. She knew if she tugged again it would just end up in an undignified struggle. "I don't remember," she said stubbornly.

"And you expect me to believe this miraculous case of amnesia? This incredibly convenient memory loss that lets you off the hook, as usual."

"Actually, I expect nothing from you," she said in a cool voice.

"That's wise. Because that's what you're likely to get."

"How nice that we've got that settled. Would you like to let me go?" She asked in her most matter-of-fact tone. It still took on the subtext of a cosmic question. Would he let her go? When?

"Don't you have any questions you want to ask me?" he said lazily. "Since you've been so extraordinarily frank this morning, why don't I return the favor?"

"What would you do if I was pregnant?"

It worked. He dropped her wrist as if burned, and the winter blue of his eyes turned to ice.

"I wouldn't give a damn," he said after a moment. "Unless you tried to pass it off as mine. You wouldn't get very far with that, so I suggest you don't even try. Are you?"

"Am I what? Pregnant? Or trying to pass the child off as yours?"

"Either one."

"Neither one," she said pertly. Not a complete lie. She didn't *know* that she was pregnant—she was just guessing. "I was just daydreaming."

"More like a nightmare if you ask me," he snapped. "You don't like children?"

"I like children. I don't like you."

To her horror she could feel tears start in her eyes. And it seemed to horrify him just as much, for he rose, suddenly contrite. "Molly, I..."

Before he could finish she had run from the room, anywhere to keep him from seeing her appalling weakness. She couldn't even curse him for a thoughtless bastard; his final softening had precluded that.

Perhaps it was all a lost cause, she told herself tearfully when she reached the haven of her room. She would be much better off if she did keep out of his way. He had told her to, time and time again, and she hadn't listened, stubbornly seeking him out. Looking for something. A faint sign of approval, or even affection?

She knew perfectly well she wanted more than that. And she would never get it—she'd learned that in another lifetime, and that knowledge stayed with her, even as her memory eluded her.

If she had any sense at all she would just stay in her room, passing the time as best she could until this period of waiting was over.

Unless she was pregnant. The thought came unbidden, and resolutely she pushed it away. That was one problem she would not worry about until she had to. But the period of time before her doctor's appointment stretched before her as a yawning abyss.

MUFFINS. She'd brought him muffins and coffee, a peace offering, and he'd thrown them back in her face. He didn't want peace offerings from her. He didn't want her sweet and shy, looking up at him as if she were sixteen again and he was everything she'd ever wanted.

He didn't want to believe in her again. Didn't want to be seduced by her green-blue eyes and her hurt innocence.

She wasn't innocent, and she wasn't hurt. And whatever it was she wanted from him, it couldn't be something he was willing to give.

Pregnant. What a twisted, horrible idea. Fortunately he knew she couldn't be. They'd run every test known to man on her while she was unconscious in the hospital, including a pregnancy test. There was no way she could be carrying somebody's bastard. She deserved his contempt for even thinking she could pull off a stunt like that.

But still, she never used to cry. When she'd looked at him, tears filling her eyes, he'd known a shaft of pain, sharp and deep, and he'd wanted to touch her, pull her into his arms, soothe and kiss her.

Damn her. And damn him.

He shoved himself away from the desk and headed outside. He needed to get away from here, and from her. Just until he could get his crazy, irrational yearning under control.

He wanted to believe her. That was the craziest part of it all. He wanted to trust her one more time.

He was a fool.

There was no future for them. She'd leave, and he'd get on with his life. Why couldn't he get that through his stubborn brain?

Of course, what if he was dead wrong? What if she was telling the truth, about her amnesia, about everything? She might really be in danger.

No. That was too much to contemplate. She was a tramp, a scheming little liar, and if he started believing in her again he deserved everything he got.

He'd made that mistake once before. He wouldn't make it again.

SOME PROJECT, Molly decided, was necessary if she was to survive the next twenty-four hours. There was no way she could manage to get a home pregnancy test kit without a lot of explanations, explanations she wasn't willing to make. If she was going to confine herself to her room, then she needed to do something about making it livable again.

She began clearing the dresser drawers of their meager contents. The mountain of purchases she had made a few days before had been swallowed up in the massive piece of furniture, and she was finished in next to no time. She piled the clothing on the shelves in the similarly bare closet, then began clearing off the tops of dressers, tables and night stands. Half of the junk she threw out, the rest went into the closet with the clothing. She stripped the bed and carried the dirty linen down to the kitchen and Mrs. Morse.

"What in the world is all that?" Mrs. Morse cried, brandishing a spatula.

"Laundry," she said briefly. "Could you get Ben and someone else to help me move furniture today? I've decided something has to be done about my room."

"And what furniture were you planning to put in its place?" she demanded. "I can't take another day off right now to go shopping."

"I want all my furniture from the attic," she answered her, helping herself to another cup of coffee. "I don't care what happens to the junk in my room—we can throw it out for all I care. I just want the room to look as it used to."

Her stern face softened. "Well, I've got no quarrel with that. It just about broke my heart when you did that to your pretty little room. All those fancy drapes and everything—they don't belong in a house like this. I'm just glad Patrick put his foot down when you wanted to tear up the old oak flooring."

"So am I," she said in a subdued voice.

"Go on ahead, then, dearie. I'll get you some breakfast. Coffee and muffins aren't enough to keep a body going. And next time you get up early, remember to turn off the oven when you've finished using it."

"Did I forget?" She blushed faintly, as if caught doing something naughty. "I'll try to remember next time."

"See that you do. Now sit down and I'll be with you in a minute."

Ben arrived a few minutes later, accompanied by Toby. "Just the people we want to see!" Mrs. Morse greeted them as they entered. "Molly needs some furniture moved—do you think two big strong men like you could take care of it?"

"I'd be glad to." Ben smiled, and Molly thought to herself that he surely didn't hold her responsible for hitting him on the head the night of the fire. "How about it, Toby?"

"Certainly." He smiled at her engagingly, his clear eyes warm and intense. "I was just looking for someone to go riding with me, but Patrick seems to have taken off. If Molly will take his place when we're done then I'm your man."

She looked out at the dark and drizzly sky. "It's hardly the weather for it, is it?" She couldn't imagine why she'd feel the slightest hesitation, but she did.

"Oh, the weather will clear up, my word as a gentleman," he said solemnly.

She was being ridiculously paranoid, and she knew it. "Of course I'll go riding with you," she said suddenly, ashamed of her doubts. "I've just been waiting for someone to ask." And if she waited for her husband, she thought, she'd wait until hell froze over. She rose and brought her dishes over to the sink, suddenly aware of Mrs.

Morse's subtle air of disapproval. "Follow me and I'll show you the furniture."

Within twenty minutes the room was stripped of every piece of furniture, and only the rug and drapes remained. She sent Ben and Toby off with their firm promises to return a couple of hours later for the second installment, and, armed with some tools she had purloined from Patrick's tool shed, she set to work ripping up the carpet.

It had been glued down around the corners, and the residue was a nasty, sticky mess, requiring repeated scrapings, rubbings, and washings. But by lunchtime she had the soft, downy stuff dumped in the middle of the floor with the satin curtains and valances piled on top, and her room was beginning to look more like it should.

She dragged the stuff out into the hall and down the two little steps to the attic door. Dumping it in one corner, she stood back to take a closer look at her old furniture. And then she noticed what she hadn't seen before. One of the drawers in the mahogany chest was partly open, and inside was a dried bouquet, the yellow roses faded and dead. And somewhere inside a warning bell rang. She stared at it for a full five minutes, trying desperately to force her memory to work, closing her eyes and summoning up the past. But it remained out of reach, mocking, teasing.

By two o'clock that afternoon the bedroom was once again as beautiful as it must have been before she married Patrick Winters. The oak flooring shone with the glow only old and lovingly tended wood has, the small kilim rugs setting it off perfectly. The furniture belonged in the room, as that other stuff never had, each old and sturdy piece complementing the others. She climbed up on the huge old bed, a mate to the one in Patrick's room, and stared around her with a sense of accomplishment and satisfaction. If she could put this part of her life back together with just a little hard work, surely the rest of her problems could be dealt with as successfully. Perhaps there was hope after all.

As Toby had predicted, the day had cleared off nicely, and the early spring sun was poking through the clouds with increasing frequency. Toby had provided her with one of his own horses, a sweet-tempered lady named Bess with seemingly not a bad habit in her gentle body. The moment Molly was on her back she felt at home, and she realized that at one time she must have been a decent rider.

Toby confirmed this. "It's good to see you riding again. There was a time, a few years back, when you were scarcely out of the saddle from one day to the next."

"Really?" She wasn't as surprised as she sounded.

"You and Patrick used to go to all the horse shows around, winning half the prizes at the very least." There was a touch of envy in Toby's voice, and she thought she could understand why. He sat his horse a bit like a sack of potatoes, his body stiff and unyielding. He was in perfect control of his spirited roan, but there was an unnaturalness about it, an awkwardness that struck the eye immediately. Clearly Toby had never won any prizes in the show ring.

Despite Molly's proficiency, it took a while to realize that she wasn't completely at ease on Bess's back. There seemed a tension about the horse that she hadn't noticed at first, just a small trace of nerves that communicated itself in the subtlest way. They followed the old road that encircled the farm at a leisurely pace, and Molly tried unsuccessfully to attune herself to the horse's odd mood.

"Let's go into the woods," Toby suggested as they neared the farm again. "There's a spot near the old well that should have some daffodils this time of year."

"We've been out rather long time," Molly said uneasily, her hindquarters beginning to feel a little sore from the unaccustomed exercise. "Perhaps we should save it for another day."

His face fell absurdly, and she felt a touch of guilt. "But daffodils were always your favorite flower, Molly," he said plaintively. "Please. It would mean a lot to me if I could give you your first daffodil of the year."

She didn't want to encourage his odd crush. He always seemed to be watching her, covertly, his pale eyes strangely intense, and there was a peculiar undercurrent to his behavior that she hadn't been able to define. The thought filled her with such a gnawing discomfort that she failed to notice where they were heading as the trees closed around them.

Suddenly, with no warning whatsoever, Bess gave a shrill, frightened shriek, rearing up wildly, and Molly felt herself sliding. She clawed for the reins, but it was hopeless, and she began to fall, through the air, as the ground rushed up toward her. *The baby,* she thought in sudden desperation, determined to protect something she wasn't sure she believed in.

But it was too late. She was falling, falling, and there was nothing but the winter-hard earth to catch her.

Chapter Ten

She lay on the hard ground, the breath knocked out of her, stunned. She closed her eyes, struggling to breathe, waiting for the pain, the cramping to hit her. Her breath came back in a whoosh, and she held very still, listening to her body, listening to the sound of hooves as Bess took off into the forest. Just a few expected aches and twinges. If she was pregnant, it didn't seem as if she'd done anything to hurt it.

Toby slid from his horse and knelt beside her. "Are you all right?"

Molly shook herself, sitting up slowly. "Fine," she responded after a moment, feeling only slightly dazed. It hadn't been the worst fall, she knew that instinctively, but it had still been oddly unsettling. She struggled to her feet and brushed off the twigs and dirt from her jeans. "And there's Patrick," she said, seeing his tall, lean frame at the far edge of the clearing, unable to keep the relief out of her voice. He was accompanied by Ben, and she waved to show she was all right before turning back to her companion.

Toby was standing there with a large rock in his hand, a troubled expression on his gentle face. "You could have hit your head on this and been killed,'' he said, dropping the rock back to the wet ground.

She stared at him for a moment, unnerved, still shaken by the fall. ''I wouldn't worry, Toby,'' she said finally in a determinedly light voice. ''I seem to have an awfully hard head.''

His eyes met hers with a look of sorrow. ''I have to tell you this before Patrick gets here, whether you like it or not.''

''What is it?'' she asked with a trace of annoyance. Patrick was advancing swiftly, his long legs making short work of the distance between them. There was a look of thunderous rage on his face.

''Molly, someone or something spooked that horse.''

''What?'' she exclaimed, giving him her entire attention now.

''I said that Bess was frightened deliberately. Someone tried to hurt you.'' He looked frightened, really frightened.

''How could they?'' she demanded. ''You saddled her, didn't you?''

He nodded. ''But I left her in the stables alone when I came to fetch you. Anyone could have tampered with her during that time. A small burr under her blanket that would work its way into her skin after a while, a needle. Anyone who's familiar with horses could have done it.''

She didn't want to ask the question, but there was no avoiding it. ''Who was in the stable when you left?''

''Patrick,'' he said in a hushed voice.

Panic swept over her, blind and unreasoning. She trusted Patrick—reasonable or not, she was certain he wasn't trying to kill her. But why would Toby lie?

''I don't believe it,'' she said in a horrified voice. ''He wouldn't do anything to hurt me. You must be mistaken.''

''It's no mistake, Molly,'' he said. ''I've warned you

before. You can't trust anyone, not even your own husband. Let me do the talking when Patrick gets here, all right? He's going to be mad enough that we were even out together without this happening.''

''Why should he be mad we went riding?'' she asked, startled. ''Surely there's no harm in that?''

''You really don't remember him at all, do you?'' He shook his head in amazement. ''Patrick's always had a dog in the manger attitude about you. He didn't want you for himself, but he was always damned if he would let you go off alone with anyone. And that started years before you were married.''

She looked over at Patrick's advancing figure and found a curious lightness inside her, banishing her fear. ''How very encouraging,'' she murmured, half to herself.

''What the hell is going on here?'' Patrick demanded when he reached them. ''Are you trying to get yourself killed?''

Are you trying to kill me? she almost retorted, but some long-submerged sense of tact kept her silent as Toby tried to explain the situation.

''I thought you knew more about horses, Toby.'' Patrick's contempt was withering. ''After all, you've been around them all your life. Molly hasn't ridden in over a year. You should have put her on one of our horses, not that nerve-racked Bess. And why the hell wasn't she wearing a hard hat?''

''Bess isn't nerve-racked,'' Toby protested, stung. ''She's a fine animal, and Molly always used to beg me to let her ride her.''

''That was years ago, when she was in better shape,'' he said coldly. ''And back then I told you no.''

''Oh, for God's sake, she's not a child,'' Toby said in a tense voice, and Molly noticed a faint tremor in his hands. There was something else going on here, something besides the anger over a minor riding accident. Something between them, and it involved her.

"No, but *you're* acting like one, doing a foolish and dangerous thing like that." Patrick's very calm made his stinging words all the more biting, and Toby's face took on a mottled hue.

"Well, I'll leave you to escort your *wife* home." His accent on the word was bitter. "I'll talk to you later, Molly."

"Not for a while, I'm afraid," Patrick told him firmly. "She's going to keep to the house for a few days—I don't like all these accidents that have been happening recently."

"I don't either," Toby said angrily, and rode off.

Patrick looked down at her from his six feet three inches of male irritation. "Are you satisfied now?" he demanded. "You've managed to come between me and one of my oldest friends." He started walking, and it was with difficulty that she managed to keep up with his long strides.

"*I* came between you?" she echoed angrily. "There was absolutely no call for you to speak that way to him. I think that whatever differences you two have are your own problem and none of my doing. And why aren't I allowed out riding with one of your oldest friends? Do you think he's going to throw me down and have his wicked way with me?"

He stopped and gave her a look of withering contempt. "I would say, judging from your behavior over the past ten months, that he'd be in more danger from you than vice versa." And he walked on.

Once more she had to run to keep up with him. "Then if you hate me so much why don't you let me go?" she demanded. "As long as I give the police my address I can

go anywhere I please. I haven't been accused of any
crime—I'm just a witness. If I happened to remember anything I saw, that is. So why don't you let me go somewhere
and get a quickie divorce and finish this thing once and
for all?''

"No." He kept on walking. "You put me through hell
for over ten months. I think I owe you six months of hell
in return, and I mean to see that you get it."

"WHERE'S TOBY?" Mrs. Morse asked cheerily as Molly
entered the kitchen alone.

"Gone home," she said morosely, sitting down by the
fireplace. "Mrs. Morse, why does Patrick hate me?"

"Oh, now, dearie, he doesn't hate you," she said ear-
nestly, coming to sit beside her with one of her ever-
present cups of coffee. "He just doesn't know his own
mind, that's all."

"He *does* hate me," she insisted. "And I can't remember what it is I've done to him to deserve it."

"Well, I've always said what's past is over and done
with and should be forgiven and forgotten. Unfortunately
Patrick's always had a hard time with the forgiving and
the forgetting."

"But what makes him so full of hate all the time?" she
demanded. "Isn't he ever happy?"

"Well, now, of course he is. But life's never been easy
for him. His mother ran off when he was just a kid—died
in a car accident a few years later without ever writing or
calling. It's not good for a child to feel abandoned, and
his father, bless his heart, wasn't the most nurturing soul.
He was just as strong-minded as his son, and the two of
them fought like cats and dogs, Jared trying to make Patrick do what he wanted, Patrick refusing. It was a real

battleground. Finally Patrick just took off in his early twenties, and no one heard from him for years.''

''What happened? What brought him back?''

''He never did say, and I doubt he ever will. He went through some bad times, and when he came back he was a changed man. He and his father worked out a kind of truce, and then a couple of years later you showed up. It wasn't until then that he began to be more like his old self, and I thought...well, never mind.'' She sighed, taking a deep drink of her coffee.

''Why did he marry me?'' she asked, unable to keep the forlorn note out of her voice.

''I don't know, sweetie. He treated you like a little sister—took you with him, teased you, talked with you. As for you, it was as clear as day that you were crazy in love with him. Had been since you first came here, sixteen years old and pretty as a picture.''

''He told me it was his father's idea.''

''It was. He left the estate all tied up to try to get his own way, but then, Jared was that kind of man. But there would have been ways around it. Patrick didn't have to marry you. And I never did figure out why he did.''

''It's pretty easy to guess why I did. I was willing to take him on any terms, wasn't I?'' she said bitterly, and Mrs. Morse nodded.

''I guess that was so. But it seemed like you changed your mind once the knot was tied. You weren't even friends with Patrick anymore. You became wild and spiteful and selfish, and it was just too much for Patrick to deal with. That, and all the other men.''

''Other men?'' she repeated, numb.

She shook her head sadly. ''Just like his mother. You used to go out and stay all night long with anyone you could find.''

It didn't feel right. Perhaps it was just wishful thinking on her part, but Molly couldn't rid herself of the notion that someone, somehow, was lying. "How do you know that?" she demanded.

"Honey, *you* told us! It was no secret—you made darn sure everybody knew exactly what you were doing. And Patrick just shut himself up in that office of his or went off and met Lisa Canning somewhere. I tried to tell you that wasn't the way to win him but you wouldn't listen."

Molly stared into the fireplace, trying to reconcile this image with what she had come to know about herself in the few short days since her...her rebirth. But it wouldn't come into focus, and she wondered what was the truth about her past. Her own instincts? Or other people's sharp memories?

Or neither of them.

MOLLY DIDN'T HAVE much appetite that night. She toyed with the fried chicken and creamed spinach Mrs. Morse brought up to her and barely touched the cheesecake. Uncle Willy brought up a small pitcherful of cranberry juice when he heard she was ill, and it took her most determined efforts to evict him and an oversolicitous Aunt Ermy.

She looked about her in lonely gloom. Even her new surroundings seemed to have palled, and part of her longed to be downstairs, sparring with Patrick over the dinner table, while the rest of her was happy to hide out, away from everyone.

There was something wrong, something very wrong, with this place, and the people, and the stories they were telling her. Something with their image of the past, but there was no way she could refute it.

She could only hold on, one day at a time, and hope

she'd have the answer to at least one of her questions by tomorrow.

If she was pregnant there was no way she could leave. Not unless Patrick threw her out.

But if she wasn't, then she'd stayed long enough. She had money, she wasn't charged with any crime. If she got a clean bill of health the next day she was out of here. The answers weren't coming, and whether anyone believed her or not, she was in danger. She was getting out. And she had no intention of looking back.

STUPID BUNGLER! Of course it had been miserable bad luck, Patrick showing up like that. Just a few minutes would have made all the difference. Ah, but that was too often the difference between triumph and disaster. A moment, a whim of fate, and life shifted, defeat beckoned.

But a true visionary never accepted defeat. Not when so much had been accomplished. There was too much at stake, and a whey-faced little thing like Molly Winters wasn't going to get in the way.

The subtle efforts weren't working; neither were the more flagrant attempts. It was time for more drastic measures. There was only a limited amount of time before she remembered.

And when she did, it might be too late for all of them.

Chapter Eleven

It took her over an hour to drag herself out of bed. She was so horribly sick the next morning her entire body felt numb with it, and she alternated between chills and fever, shivering and sweating, until she almost called out for help.

But any cry for help would more likely bring her husband from next door than any one else. She shut her eyes, gritted her teeth, and suffered until the sickness decided to pass.

When she finally got up it was with immense relief that she remembered the doctor's appointment. At least she could diagnose and stop this awful thing. Molly was almost afraid to go to sleep at night, thinking of the pain that awaited her upon waking. She'd have an answer today, even if it might not be the most convenient one.

It all seemed so distant and unlikely. And worst of all, Patrick made it clear there was no way he'd take responsibility for the child. She should have guessed their relationship wouldn't have included sex for a long time. And yet, she could practically feel the heat when he looked at her.

Maybe it was wishful thinking on her part. Maybe she was the tramp everyone said she was. If she was, then there'd be no way of telling what sort of person had fathered her baby. It didn't matter—she still wouldn't want to give it up, she thought stubbornly as she stepped into the shower.

She stood there in the steaming blast of water until she could stand it no longer, then toweled herself off, staring at her body in the mirror. Still the same long legs and flat stomach. Her waist hadn't thickened, her smallish breasts hadn't become tender and swollen. As for missing her period, the surest way of knowing something's wrong, her memory had only been alive for five days. Her body was as mute to her questions as her mind.

She dressed warmly and femininely, in one of the long rayon skirts she had bought and a thick knit sweater. She supposed it was some hidden maternal instinct that made her change from pants to dresses as she contemplated motherhood. She looked at the clock, and noticed with surprise that it was almost noon. She must have needed the extra sleep.

"Well, well, aren't you charming-looking this morning," Lisa Canning's voice greeted Molly as she walked into the kitchen. Molly turned around without a word and headed out, but Patrick appeared out of nowhere, halting her escape.

"Where do you think you're going?" he demanded.

She deliberately misunderstood him. "To the doctor's," she said defiantly.

He raised an eyebrow, and much as she didn't want to, she couldn't avoid noticing the beauty of the man, a beauty that had the power to move her just as his usual contempt pushed her away.

"Well, you aren't going immediately, are you? Come in and have some lunch."

She looked up at him with suspicion of this new affability. "I'm not hungry," she said mutinously.

"Too bad." One strong hand went under her arm and she was brought back into the kitchen feeling like a fish caught on a hook.

Lisa smiled at them both with that cool assurance she had in abundance. "There you are, Patrick. I wondered how long it would take you to tear yourself away from your books. And your little wife too. Did I tell you, Molly dear, how charmingly girlish that little outfit is? So country." She smiled sweetly, and Molly glowered at her in return, yanking her arm away from Patrick's viselike grip.

"You're only young once," she answered her pointedly, flopping down into the rocking chair by the cold fireplace. "How nice of you to come for lunch, Lisa," she said suddenly. "Where are Aunt Ermy and Uncle Willy? I'm sure they'd be desolated to miss you. Especially since we haven't seen that much of you recently."

Lisa flushed, and it was with surprise that Molly realized that she'd inadvertently scored a hit. So Patrick hadn't been going to see her as often as it appeared. Perhaps that situation wasn't as much of a sure thing as she had supposed.

"They've gone off on a visit," Patrick said glumly, and Molly's eyes met his dark blue ones with a tiny shock. He didn't want Lisa here either. He had forced her in here to protect him. She controlled her wry amusement.

"Really? For how long?"

"Tonight and part of tomorrow." He shrugged. "I'm not really sure."

"But then you and Patrick will be all alone here tonight!" Lisa's violet eyes were round as she put into words the thought that had been preying on Molly's mind for the last few moments. "And it's Mrs. Morse's evening off."

She seemed to know more about the domestic arrangements at Winter's Edge than Molly did. But Molly could afford to be generous. She smiled sweetly. "Oh, that's all right, Lisa. We *are* married, you know."

"I know," she shot back in a low voice, quietly declaring her enmity. She meant to have him, Molly knew, and Patrick just as definitely wanted to avoid her. Molly discovered her mood had improved substantially.

"Patrick, dear." Lisa rose gracefully and put one slim, beringed hand on Patrick's arm. "Do you think we could perhaps go for a ride this afternoon? I have so much I've been longing to talk with you about." Her violet eyes shone in her lovely face, and Molly wondered how any man could withstand her.

"Sorry, Lisa," Patrick said. "I'm taking Molly to the doctor's this afternoon."

"You're what?" Molly said in horror.

"I told Mrs. Morse I'd take you. It's her afternoon off and I might as well take on some of my marital responsibilities."

If Lisa had looked sullen before it was nothing compared to her current expression. Molly would have almost found it entertaining if she weren't so appalled at the thought of Patrick driving her to her pregnancy test.

"I'd rather have Mrs. Morse with me," she said faintly. "It's a female problem."

If she hoped to embarrass him she failed. "That's all right, Molly," he said with callous cheer. "I'm a sensitive New Age kind of guy. I want to be there for you."

And all she could do was swallow her snarl of disbelief.

THE RIDE TO Dr. Turner's neat little clapboard house was short and uncomfortable. Neither of them said a word, and Molly tried to concentrate on the countryside. It was all just vaguely familiar. Things were coming back in tiny little bits and pieces and the feeling was oddly unsettling. Most of the faint traces of memory were brief and unhappy. She could begin to recall a tiny part of her wedding night, though it all came to her from a great distance. She could remember taking off the white dress and crying, crying. But she couldn't remember Patrick by her side, taking her into his arms, drying her tears, comforting her. And when she tried to force remembrance it would vanish completely, like a wicked, willful child playing hide-and-seek.

"Do you want me to come in with you?" Patrick sounded impatient, and she realized it wasn't the first time he'd asked the question. They had pulled up in front of the doctor's office while Molly had been daydreaming.

"No!" she said with a shriek. "I mean, I'm going for a…a female exam and…"

"I believe they're called a pelvic exam," he drawled, and she could feel herself flush with embarrassment. Surely a dedicated wanton couldn't flush? "You need your birth control updated?"

She lifted her head, fighting past her mortification. "What do I use for birth control?" she asked curiously.

"I haven't the faintest idea."

That should have given her a clue. But she was too nervous, doubly so with Patrick watching her, to think about it. "It shouldn't take long," she said, sliding out of the passenger seat. "You could come back in about half an hour."

"I'll be waiting," he said. And for some reason she didn't find that the slightest bit comforting.

Comfort didn't have much to do with her exam either. After she was finally maneuvered into that embarrassing and inelegant position on the examining table she met the doctor's annoyed face with innocent trepidation.

"You're here to see me about a possible pregnancy, Mrs. Winters?" she demanded with the awfulness of a member of the Spanish Inquisition.

Molly nodded mutely. In a moment Dr. Turner drew back.

"That's all," she said brusquely. "You can get dressed. See that she gets a complete series of blood tests run on her, then bring her to my office." She started for the door, and Molly sat up, yanking the sheet up over her.

"Am I pregnant?" she demanded nervously.

Dr. Turner stared at her for one long, incredulous moment. "In my office," she repeated abruptly.

Molly was to remember that look of incredulity as she underwent the nastiness of blood tests and three painful finger-pricks. The nurse was a bloodthirsty butcher who took fiendish delight in probing for her recalcitrant veins. It was a full two and a half hours after she first entered the building, and she was practically in a state of nervous collapse by the time they brought her back to Dr. Turner's office. Molly sat there in the small, paneled room, trying to force an interest in the framed licenses and degrees, the walls of medical texts, bracing herself for the news that could change her life forever.

At least no one had brought Patrick in to hear the news. There was something to be said for good old-fashioned sexist GPs, Molly thought with a trace of gratitude.

Dr. Turner entered the room quickly, and sat down opposite Molly, her head lowered. She was the very image of the old-fashioned country doctor, lined face, tired eyes, and Molly wondered what she had done to earn her displeasure, or to cause this sudden…was it embarrassment?

"I hear you've lost your memory?" the doctor said abruptly, staring out at her from faded blue eyes.

"That's true," she answered slowly.

"I guess that accounts for it," Dr. Turner said, half to herself. "You're perfectly recovered from that fall except for a few bruises."

"I know that." Molly brushed the information aside. "What I want to know is whether I'm pregnant or not."

The doctor leaned back, a look of sudden amusement crossing her weary face. "Well, now, Mrs. Winters, virgin birth is not a medical impossibility, but in your case I think we needn't worry."

Molly stared at her in unblinking shock. "'Virgin birth'?" she repeated, astonished. "You're telling me I'm a virgin?"

She nodded. "First one I've seen on a girl over seventeen in I don't know how long." She chuckled, then sobered suddenly. "Is there something I should be treating your husband for?"

"You should know that better than I," she said bitterly. "Aren't you his doctor?"

"Well, he's never complained, but then, men are funny about that sort of thing," Dr. Turner reflected. "They're ashamed of it."

"I doubt that he has any problem in that area," Molly answered, thinking of Lisa Canning's smug self-assurance. "He just doesn't care much for me, I suppose."

"Could be, could be. I think maybe I better see him anyway." She peered at Molly across the desk. "You tell him to come in next week some time."

"I don't think so," she answered, the idea horrifying her. "We're not on very good terms."

"So I noticed," Dr. Turner said, then wheezed with laughter at her own joke. "Nevertheless, I want to see him anyway. In the meantime we'll see what those blood tests turn up—you look a bit peaked to me. We'll find out what's causing you to toss your cookies, young lady, don't you worry. Though I imagine it's nothing more than stress. We'll call you when we get the results.'' She dismissed her with a wave of her hand, and there was nothing Molly could do but leave, with one question answered and a million more started.

Patrick was sitting in the waiting room, surrounded by sneezing parents and wailing children. He was large and out of place in that feminine setting, and yet he looked curiously at ease amid the chaos. He rose when she came out, raised an eyebrow inquiringly, and then followed her out into the parking lot.

A light rain had begun to fall. She waited for him to unlock the car, climbing in as she prayed he wouldn't ask her what she'd gone to see Dr. Turner for.

She should have known it would be a waste of time. ''So,'' he said, as he pulled out into the highway, ''are you pregnant?''

She glared at him. So much for her illusion that she'd manage to fool him. ''No,'' she said in a little more than a snarl.

''Just as well. Trying to foist another man's child off on me wouldn't do wonders for our relationship.''

''I didn't know we had a relationship,'' she said in acid tones.

''We don't. Let's keep it that way, shall we? Look on the bright side—we don't have to put up with each other for much longer.''

''It's a small comfort,'' she said bitterly.

She saw him glance over at her. He didn't know where her fury was coming from, and she'd be damned if she'd enlighten him.

They completed the drive back to the farmhouse in brooding silence, and Patrick didn't bother to switch off the engine when he pulled up outside the kitchen door. ''I don't need to ask whether you can look out for yourself tonight," he said. "You're good at that. I may not be back for dinner. If you get nervous you can always give Mrs. Morse a call. Just don't bring any of your little playmates over. I'll be back sooner or later and I really wouldn't like to find you trying out whatever Dr. Turner gave you."

"She gave me vitamins," Molly snapped. She wanted to hit him. "And you needn't worry about me. I'm used to being alone."

"I'm not worried about you," he said in a rough voice. And he drove away without another word.

MOLLY SLAMMED THINGS around the kitchen in a fine bad temper. The house was cold and empty, and for the first time she wished that her so-called aunt and uncle hadn't chosen *this* Friday for their visit. Unless they left her here alone on purpose, Molly thought, suddenly frightened. She sipped at the ginger ale she had poured herself, heartily sick of cranberry juice, and stared out the window at the darkening countryside. She had had two near-fatal accidents in the last two days. Rather an uncomfortable coincidence, she thought.

With an athletic grace she hadn't known she possessed, she swung herself up onto the scrubbed counter and sat, lost in reflection as the sun sank lower and lower behind the farm buildings. Perhaps Patrick wouldn't be back at all tonight. Perhaps some hobo would come and finish the job on her and they would find her body in a tangle on the floor. There was something going on here, something she didn't like, and the vague snatches of memory that were coming back to her had taken on an ominous tinge. The night of the fire was slowly coming back. She could remember her absolute fear and horror at the sight of the flames licking their way around the stable, could remember

Patrick, his face lit up by the orange-red fire, fighting desperately to get in and free the poor, tortured horses. And there was someone beside her, someone laughing quietly, deep in their throat, at the horror in front of them. And she remembered when she was alone, she ran.

But this wasn't enough to go to Patrick with. For one thing, he wouldn't believe her; for another, she had absolutely no idea of the identity of her companion. It could even have been a woman, for all she knew.

No, there was nothing she could do until more of the past decided to reveal itself. In the meantime she could only wait, and watch out, as Toby had warned her.

She thought back to his gentle concern, knowing she should feel some sort of reassurance that someone cared. But all she could think of was the sharp, strange look in Toby's eyes as he'd warned her about Patrick. His urgency somehow struck her as odd and eerie.

It could have been wishful thinking on her part. She didn't want to think Patrick was capable of hurting her. But what did she really know about him, apart from the fact that half the time he seemed to despise her? He couldn't be the one out to hurt her, could he?

Mrs. Morse thought the sun rose and set with him, but then, she was admittedly prejudiced. And everyone else Molly had met, from Toby to Aunt Ermy to old friend Willy, even to subtle remarks from Lisa Canning, had warned her to beware of her husband.

She'd stupidly refused to listen. She was certainly not being very wise. But as she stared out the window at the coming night she knew she would continue to shut her ears. To trust her heart, even if it made no sense at all.

She finished her drink and jumped down from the high counter. It was past six, and no sign of Patrick. Perhaps he wouldn't return tonight, she told herself, irritation simmering within her at the thought. Perhaps Lisa's arms were too strong a temptation even for such a saint as Patrick Winters. She set the stew on the back burner and started it at a low flame. Such a noble man her husband was. She slammed the oven door. Such a considerate gentleman. She threw a handful of silverware onto the table. Such an excellent, restrained fellow. She kicked savagely at the trash can in her way.

She finally ate a furious and solitary meal at half-past eight. At that point she was beyond rage. She knew that if he came in she would hurl her plate with its scorched meat and vegetables at him without a second thought. It was probably just as well that he was nowhere to be seen.

And then she began to brood. Steadily, as she sat in front of the sputtering logs she had tried to coax into a fire. Beastie appeared at the door and elected to keep her company, and for this small, or actually quite mammoth piece of companionship, she had to be grateful.

Her nerves were on edge. She sat huddled in that great chair, her feet tucked under her, staring over her shoulder every few minutes. The hours passed slowly, so slowly, and she knew her nervousness was pure foolishness. All the doors were locked and bolted; no one could enter without her knowing it. She had no intention of letting her errant husband return to his bed without a few choice words.

She must have dozed off, for the next thing she knew the grandfather clock in the hallway was chiming midnight. She stretched, and rose, some of her pique abated from the uncomfortable little nap.

"I suppose we might as well go to bed, Beastie," she said to her companion, and he seemed to nod his massive head sagely, following her up the stairs. She gave no thought to her husband's possible return. He could find his own way in, she thought savagely. If he bothered to return before daybreak.

She washed, brushed her teeth and changed into one of those flimsy nightgowns before climbing up into the firm confines of her ancient cherry wood bed. She was tired, angry, and troubled, and what she needed more than anything was a good night's sleep.

She fully intended to get it.

PATRICK KNEW just what kind of trouble he'd be in if he went home that night. The house was deserted—no one would be there but Molly. Asleep in her room, her blond hair flowing over the pillow, her mesmerizing eyes closed. As long as he waited until she was thoroughly asleep he'd be safe.

He found he was smiling in grim amusement. It was a strange situation indeed, when a man over thirty was afraid of his child bride. He hadn't thought he was afraid of anything, but Molly scared the hell out of him.

No, it wasn't Molly who scared him. It was the way she made him feel. Like there was a chance for them after all, when he knew only too well that love was a delusion and women were hopelessly fickle. Hadn't his mother taught him that? Hadn't Molly made certain he'd learned the lesson all over again?

There was no sign of Toby at the small apartment he rented over a nearby stables, a fact which under normal circumstances would have bothered Patrick. Toby was an odd one. He'd known him since they were kids, but Toby had always been a little off center, a little shy, just the slightest bit obsessive.

He had no other friends as far as Patrick knew. No love life whatsoever. So where the hell was he at twelve o'clock at night?

His apartment was locked, or Patrick would have let himself in and made himself at home.

There was nowhere else for him to go.

Well, that wasn't strictly true. He could go to Lisa Canning's, and be sure of a welcome. He'd succumbed a few times, when he was mad, when he was lonely, when he'd had too much to drink to be able to refuse what she so blatantly offered.

But Lisa wasn't what he wanted. He knew what he wanted. She lay sound asleep in her bedroom back at Winter's Edge, and he couldn't have her. Wouldn't have her.

Not if he had any sense of self-preservation. He was going to leave her strictly alone.

If he could.

Chapter Twelve

The door slammed open, ripping Molly from a sound sleep, and the light in the hall streamed in her room, silhouetting the tall, furious figure who stood there.

"What the hell do you mean by locking me out of my own house?" Patrick's voice was dark with anger.

She turned to the little clock beside the bed, trying to squash down her initial panic. Three-thirty. "I assumed you weren't coming home tonight," she answered haughtily, pulling the sheets around her thinly-clad shoulders. "I'm nervous when I'm left alone at night." She switched on the light and met his angry gaze with a cool assurance that matched Lisa Canning's most intimidating stare.

"Oh, but you weren't alone, were you?" he demanded with mock sweetness, coming to stand by the bed. He was even more handsome than usual, the anger and frustration making his deep blue eyes glitter in the dim light. He'd been drinking, not enough to make him drunk, just enough to give him an edge. It should have frightened her, but instead she wanted to reach out and soothe away the angry lines in his forehead. She didn't dare. Besides, she was equally furious.

"What do you mean by that?" she said stonily. "Of

course I've been alone. Which is more than I can say for you."

"Then why did I see Toby Pentick's blue car driving away from here as I came in?" he demanded in a voice as cold as ice. "At three o'clock in the morning!"

"You're crazy," she snapped. "There was no one here, and even if there was, it's none of your concern, now is it? It's not as if you have any use for me." She stared at him defiantly, trying to hide the pounding of her senses, the heavy, frightened beating of her heart.

"I suppose he's been with you all afternoon and evening, ever since I left you. No wonder I couldn't find him. I should have known if I left you alone you'd be up to your old tricks. Lisa warned me."

"She certainly did, didn't she?" she said tartly. She felt her mouth curve up in a taunting smile, almost of its own accord. "Why shouldn't Toby spend the night?" she asked him slowly, mockingly. "After all, if my husband spends his night with a lover, why shouldn't I?" So this was how rumors got started, she thought almost absently. By her own destructive mouth.

"I told you I wouldn't have you whoring around any more." His voice was calmer now, almost frightening in its quiet fury. "I meant what I said."

"This dog in the manger attitude is absurd. You don't want me, but no one else can have me, is that it? Well, how are you planning to stop me?" She goaded him, goaded him purposefully. Perhaps she knew what would happen, what she was pushing him toward, perhaps she didn't. Tension and violence were strong in the air, and she rose to meet them, mocking him.

There was something else in the air, something familiar yet foreign, in the sudden stillness of his angry blue eyes, the silky menace of his body that had nothing to do with violence.

"That's the second time in the last minute you've accused me of not wanting you," he said in a slow, mesmerizing voice. "Are you trying to tell me something, Molly?"

Now her fear had suddenly become real. "Listen to me, Patrick," she said urgently, clutching vainly for the covers.

He'd reached down and yanked them away from her. "It's a little too late for modesty, isn't it?" he said with deceptive gentleness, undoing his shirt. "I assume you don't mind if I take up where Toby left off." He pulled the shirt from his jeans. "You've made it clear to me that every man in town has had you. I think it's about time that your husband tried out your talents."

Molly watched him in a daze as he went over and kicked the door shut. He yanked off his shirt, coming closer, and she looked up at him with a fierce panic mixed with an undeniable desire. He was strong, lean, muscled, with just a faint matting of hair on his chest. No wonder she hadn't remembered making love with him. She never had. Never touched him. Never lay in his arms. And she'd wanted to. Quite desperately.

She wanted him now. But not with rage and contempt, not by pushing him so far into anger that he couldn't pull back. "No, Patrick," she whispered helplessly, trying to move back out of his reach. "Not this way."

"'No, Patrick,'" he mocked. "Why ever not, Molly?" He reached out and caught her arm, pulling her upright toward him. "You've always maintained you liked it rough."

Curse my big mouth, she thought numbly, trying to jerk away, but he reached out and caught her, pulling her against the heat and hardness of him. The feel of his bare skin against her set off new sparks of longing and panic, and she pushed against him, not certain what she wanted. He was too strong, too determined, too furious. He pushed her down on the bed, and a moment later his body covered hers.

She almost gave up fighting then. He put his mouth over hers, and there was no denying the harsh, demanding sensuality of his lips, his tongue, thrusting against her.

He was aroused, angry, and she should have known better than to let her humiliation and anger get the better of her. She should have known better.

If she had any sense she'd tell him no. He might be furious, he might have been drinking, but she knew, instinctively, that all she had to say was no, one more time, and he'd walk away from the bed, from her.

And she didn't want him to do that.

She slid her arms around his neck and kissed him back.

It seemed to startle him. She didn't know whether it was her lack of expertise, or the very fact that she was responding. If he was bent on hurting her, punishing her, he would have pulled away.

But he didn't. His kiss gentled, teased at her lips, teaching her, kissing her with slow, deliberate delight that sent waves of pleasure through her body. There was no longer any question as to what was going to happen, and she wondered if she should tell him the truth. Tell him to be gentle, to go slow, to seduce her, love her.

She said nothing. If he left her now he would never come back, and she had no doubt whatsoever that he would leave. Abandon her to her unwanted purity.

She could feel him, hard against her belly. She could taste the desire and reluctant passion in his kiss, and all she could think was, at least he wants this much from me. And there was no way she was going to keep him from it.

He reached down and fumbled with his belt, one strong hand more than enough to keep her captive in a prison she didn't want to escape. He moved her unresisting legs apart, and then paused, staring down at her from his dark, stormy eyes.

"Tell me to go away," he said, and it was a plea, a dare, a taunt. "Tell me you don't want me. Tell me no."

He was resting against the center of her, and she'd never felt such heat, such longing, such emptiness in her life. "Yes," she said, clutching at his shoulders, pulling him to her, over her, into her.

He filled her, sinking in deep, and she cried out with the sharp pain of it and then was silent. She thought she could feel the start of surprise in his body, and for a moment he was still. She could hear his breath rasping above her in the darkness, and she was terrified that now he'd pull away. Leave her.

But he didn't. His hands loosed their bruising hold on her wrists and reached up to frame her face, and his mouth gently, lovingly kissed away the tears from her cheeks, her eyes, her mouth. Tears she hadn't even known she'd shed.

Those kisses were a blessing, an apology, a promise, and she could feel the initial panic begin to fade. Heat returned, as he began to move, slowly at first, coaxing her along, bringing her with him, until she was clinging to him, desperately, as he thrust faster, deeper, carrying her to a place of darkness and delight. Everything became lost in a swirl of dizziness, a dizziness that was bringing her closer and closer to something she couldn't quite comprehend. She moved with him, instinctively, and she held him fiercely, wrapping her arms and legs around him as they climbed higher and higher. Until the world and Patrick exploded within her.

When he finally moved she made a soft sound of protest.

He left the bed and walked out of the room, and she closed her eyes to let the tears pour down her face, no longer fighting them back.

And then he was back, drawing her trembling, unresisting body into his suddenly tender arms and holding her close against the warmth and strength of him. It felt safe, it felt indelibly right. This was where she'd always wanted to be. This was where she belonged.

When her crying finally halted, he pulled back slightly, just far enough to see her face. "What the hell is going on, Molly?" he asked quietly.

She concentrated with deep interest at his muscled shoulder, too shy to meet his fierce blue gaze. He put one hand under her chin and drew her head up. "I said, what's going on?"

She tried to shrug, but his body was wrapped so tightly, securely around hers that she couldn't. "It seems obvious enough," she answered in a low voice. "I was a virgin."

His other hand moved the curtain of tangled hair from her face. "And all those men, all those stories—they were lies?"

"I suppose they would have to be. I don't remember." She shut her eyes in exhaustion and moved closer still, pressing her body against his, instinctively, as if searching for warmth and comfort.

"Don't do that," he said sharply, making no effort to move away. She laid her head against his chest, aware of the sudden response in him, exulting in it. She moved her face, pressing her mouth against his shoulder, and the pulse seemed to jump beneath his smooth flesh.

As if against his will his hands moved over her body, caressing her, healing her, soothing away the battered and bruised feelings and replacing them with rapidly escalating need. He ducked his head down, and almost involuntarily, his mouth found hers, and she came alive under his skillful touch. She lay beneath him, trembling with delight as his hungry mouth covered her breasts, his hands inciting feelings she had never imagined she could possess.

And when he entered her this time she couldn't restrain a sigh of pleasure, holding him fiercely, arching against him. And this time it was so beautiful she wept. And this time, when he exploded within her, she was ready too, and through a daze she heard their voices cry out together.

WHEN MOLLY AWOKE he was gone, and she was alone among the tumbled and stained sheets. Sunlight was pouring in the windows, and she could hear Aunt Ermy's magnificent bellow through the thick stone walls. She must have returned early, Molly thought, reaching out for the discarded blankets and covering her pleasured body lazily. And not a minute too soon.

"Why are you still in bed?" Aunt Ermy demanded from the doorway. She was a symphony in peach crepe. It wasn't her color.

"Don't you knock?" Molly countered mildly, snuggling down into the bed, in the meantime taking a surreptitious glance around the room to see if there was any telltale evidence of Patrick's presence last night. Except for the condition of the sheets there was none, and she almost wondered if she had dreamed it. Dreamed the feel of his warm, smooth skin beneath her hands. His mouth on her breast, his body, thrusting, pulsing....

She turned back to Aunt Ermy's suspicious gaze. "I was tired," she said vaguely.

Aunt Ermy edged into the room, her steely eyes raking over the disordered condition of the covers. Molly was obsessed with the atmosphere of passionate lovemaking that permeated the room, and she wondered that Aunt

Ermy could be impervious to it. She obviously could tell something was different but she couldn't quite tell what. She watched Molly out of uncertain little eyes, moving closer, and it took all Molly's strength of will not to scramble away from her.

"Are you all right, my dear?" she inquired in an oozing tone. "You look overwrought. Are you sure you had enough sleep? You might even be a bit feverish. Your eyes are bright and your cheeks are flushed."

No wonder, Molly thought, feeling the color deepen on her exposed skin. She kept her expression determinedly vague. "I'm fine, Aunt Ermy. If anything, I've had too much sleep."

"Well, you needn't be afraid your husband's going to bother you." She sniffed in distaste at the mention of Patrick. "He went off early this morning, leaving absolutely no word with either Willy or me. According to his beloved Mrs. Morse he won't be back for a day or two."

Molly grew cold inside. "How nice," she said woodenly. She felt as if she'd been slapped in the face. Aunt Ermy's next malicious words made it even worse.

"I thought you should know. And apparently Lisa Canning's gone visiting." She moved a little further into the room, her massive front heaving with spurious indignation, her nose wrinkled in rage. "I think it's a shame and a scandal, the way that man treats you. After all, he should leave you with some pride." A sly smile cracked her powdered and rouged face. "But then," she cast a speaking glance around the room, "you at least have been able to find your own sources of entertainment, haven't you, my dear?"

So the atmosphere of the room hadn't escaped her spiteful eye. But naturally, she assumed Molly had brought a lover up here.

"By the way, Molly, Toby's coming over for lunch," she added meaningfully as she started out the door. "I thought you might want to dress." The door shut behind her majestic figure and Molly was left alone with her hurt and humiliation.

She leaned back against the pillows, pulling the sheet up to her neck as she contemplated her future. Last night had changed her world.

Yet last night had meant nothing to him. He'd simply taken pity on the love-starved teenager who'd always worshiped him.

Except that last night he'd known perfectly well that she was no longer a teenager, and he presumed that she was far from love-starved.

Except when it came to Patrick, she always would be. Love-starved, adolescent, and bereft.

She climbed slowly out of bed. While she filled the tub she stripped the bed, hiding the stained sheets in her mammoth, empty closet. She didn't feel like sharing last night with anyone, even Mrs. Morse or whoever did the laundry. Obviously, as far as Patrick was concerned, it hadn't happened, and that would be her attitude as well. Things would go on as before, they would get their divorce, and then he could marry whomever he chose. After all, hadn't she heard that men feel differently about these things? What seemed like an act of love for a woman could be merely scratching an itch for a man. His itch was thoroughly scratched after last night. And she thought that now she finally, truly hated him.

She lay in the tub and soaked for fully three quarters of an hour, trying to wash away some of the stain from last night. She should have known it would be useless. Perhaps it was better that he left. Or perhaps she was imagining all sorts of problems where none existed. But couldn't he at least have said goodbye to her?

When she arrived in the kitchen Toby was waiting. He was silhouetted against the window, and for one, brief, joyous moment she'd thought he was Patrick. And then he turned, his light, intense eyes watching her with an odd stillness, and it was all she could do to hide her disappointment.

She greeted him with lukewarm pleasure. "How are you this morning, Toby?" At that moment she was heartily sick of the whole male half of the species.

"Afternoon," he corrected, smiling. "I'm fine. You're looking absolutely beautiful, Molly."

She heard a snort from the corner, and Mrs. Morse hovered into view. "Patrick said he'd be back sometime tomorrow," she said loudly, determined to bring the specter of Molly's husband into the conversation before Toby could get any ideas. "He had some business to attend to, some things to check up on. He said you were to stay close to home, Molly." The look she cast Toby was one of pure dislike, and Molly glanced at her in surprise. Toby was one of the most innocuous human beings she'd met since she'd returned to Winter's Edge.

"Did he?" she said coolly, angry at the arrogant manner of her absent husband's orders. "We'll see." She wandered over and poured herself some coffee, noting with sort of an anguished longing the unaccustomed stiffness in her hips.

"And Dr. Turner's office called." Mrs. Morse was determined. "The results of your tests are in. She said it wasn't what you thought."

"So soon?" She picked up a still warm muffin and bit into it.

"She said she wanted you to come in and see her right

away.'' Molly couldn't miss the note of worry in her voice. ''I told her Patrick took the Mercedes and wouldn't be back until tomorrow. The van's out of commission.''

''I can take you,'' Toby offered eagerly, and Mrs. Morse glared at him, slamming a pan down on the wooden counter.

''She said you should call her as soon as you wake up.''

''All right,'' Molly agreed, strolling out of the room into Patrick's office, trying to still the sudden spurt of fear that filled her. She had cancer, she thought dismally, or some fatally crippling disease. And for some odd reason, this was the first morning she hadn't been sick in days. Perhaps sex agrees with me, she thought bitterly, dialing the doctor's number. Perhaps it was a case of terminal lust.

''Mrs. Winters?'' She recognized the gruff voice at the other end of the line. ''I need you to come in and talk with me today. We've got the results of your blood tests and it's serious. Very serious indeed.''

''Really?'' Molly replied in a wooden voice. ''I'm afraid I can't make it in. My husband's taken the only working car. You'll have to tell me over the phone. Have I got cancer?''

''Certainly not. Perhaps Mrs. Morse could drive you in.''

''I told you I couldn't make it,'' she said, anxiety making her angry. ''What's going on? If I'm dying of some strange disease you might as well tell me. At this point I really don't give a damn.''

Dr. Turner took a deep breath at the other end. ''Mrs. Winters, has anyone else in the house been troubled with nausea recently?''

''Not that I know of. Why, is it communicable?''

''I'm afraid, Mrs. Winters, that you are suffering from arsenic poisoning.''

"What?" Molly let out a shriek, then lowered her voice to a conspirator's whisper. "Arsenic?"

"That's right. There can be no doubt of it. Clear traces were found in your bloodstream. Not enough to kill you, just enough to make you quite ill. And of course, over a long period of time it could prove quite dangerous."

"I'm sure it could," she replied numbly, sinking down in the well-worn leather chair in shock.

"I've notified the police, as I'm required to do in cases of this sort. In the meantime, I suggest you only eat what everyone else is eating, and preferably fix your own meals."

She managed to stir herself long enough to protest. "Mrs. Morse wouldn't hurt me!"

"I'm not saying she would," Dr. Turner said patiently. "I'm just saying you should watch out. I expect the police should be out sometime in the afternoon—in the meantime, sit tight and don't worry."

"Don't worry," she echoed, leaning back in shock and the first stirrings of justifiable outrage. "Hell and damnation!"

Chapter Thirteen

He had considered going out and getting thoroughly drunk. However, Patrick had never made a habit of blotting out his memories with alcohol, and six o'clock in the morning wasn't the time to start. While part of him wanted to forget everything that happened the night before, from the moment he'd let his fury give him just enough excuse to enter her bedroom in the middle of the night, until the moment he left her, lying there, sound asleep, the saltwater tracks of dried tears on her pale face, her lips swollen from his mouth, her face flushed and absurdly happy in sleep.

Why the hell had he touched her?

And even more important, why had she lied to him?

If he'd known, he would have been even more determined to keep away from her, though right now he was so angry and twisted up inside that he wasn't quite sure why. After all, he'd married her. They'd entered into a sensible, business arrangement, based on mutual affection and good judgment, and it had turned drastically wrong even before their wedding day.

They'd never discussed just how much of a marriage it was going to be, and he'd assumed that sooner or later they'd get around to sex. To make those grandchildren his father had wanted so damned much.

But as things had gone from bad to worse, and she'd flung her lovers and her hatred in his face, his own mixed longing had chilled. He'd always wanted her. But he'd been just as determined not to have her.

And now it was too late. He'd spent a night in her bed, doing at least some of the things he'd dreamed about when he'd had no control of his fantasies. And he wanted to do more.

He wasn't going to. He was getting the hell out of there, long enough to cool down. To come to his senses. To figure out what the hell was going on here.

Because it was finally getting through his thick skull that something was happening around here. Nothing was as it seemed. In the last few hours his life had turned upside down.

If he'd been wrong about Molly he could be wrong about a great many other things. Like whether or not she'd been pushed into the cellar. Like whether someone was really out to hurt her, as she'd insisted.

Something had been nagging at the back of his mind, some hidden scrap of memory. He wasn't going to sit around on his butt and wait to see what happened. He was going out to find a few answers himself. Just to assure himself that she wasn't in any kind of danger.

When he got back maybe he and Molly could come to some sort of amicable agreement. She could go where she wanted, do what she wanted.

Anything to get his peace of mind back.

And by the time spring rolled around he probably wouldn't even think about her more than once a day.

All day long.

WHEN MOLLY RETURNED to the kitchen she looked at the inhabitants with new eyes. Mrs. Morse was cleaning with a violence, her stern and spare body radiating disapproval. Toby was staring out the window, an odd, abstracted expression on his face, the sunlight reflecting off his wire-rimmed glasses, and Uncle Willy had just come down, hung over as usual, the orange hair combed with its usual finicky neatness, his eyes pale and bloodshot and weary.

"Well, well, Molly," he murmured as he poured a cup of Mrs. Morse's excellent coffee. "You're looking absolutely stunning this morning."

"Afternoon," she said absently, staring at all of them in turn.

"I've already told her so," Toby announced in a playful voice that still held a slightly possessive edge.

Uncle Willy thumped Toby on the back. "Sly young dog," he said approvingly. "Don't miss a trick, do you? Ah, well, when I was your age..."

"Where's Aunt Ermy?" Molly broke in suddenly.

"Ermy?" Willy repeated, befuddled. "I don't know, my dear. She should be around somewhere."

Molly drew herself together with a monumental effort. "I believe the police might be coming by later. They'll probably want to have a word with all of you."

The silence was absolute, as the three other inhabitants of the kitchen stared at her in horror that might have been mixed with guilt.

Mrs. Morse spoke first. "You'll not be saying something's happened to Patrick?"

Uncle Willy snorted bravely. "Not him. He's got nine lives, that one has." His face remained a ghastly white, despite the determined smile. "What are you talking about, Molly? Why should the police be coming here?" he demanded. "Have they...have they discovered something new about your accident?"

"I doubt it," Molly said, sipping casually on her cold

and bitter-tasting coffee. "I think they want to find out who's been poisoning me."

Uncle Willy's cup slipped out of nerveless fingers and crashed back onto its saucer. He opened his mouth to speak, then closed it again. "Well," he said finally, his normally affected voice high-pitched and squeaky. "Well."

Toby had already moved to her side, laying his soft, gentle hands on hers in tender concern. Hands so different from Patrick's strong, demanding ones. She pulled away firmly. "This isn't true, is it, Molly?" His voice was low and impassioned. "If it is, I swear to God I'll kill him!"

"Now who do you think you're talking about?" Mrs. Morse demanded in a blaze of fury, slamming down another pot and marching across the room, hands on her hips. "You have one hell of a lot of nerve, my boy, if you think you can come around here, playing up to your so-called best friend's wife, and slander him behind his back. Patrick wouldn't harm a hair on that girl's head, and well she knows it!"

Apart from breaking her heart, she thought wryly. "Mrs. Morse is right, Toby," she said aloud. "What's between Patrick and me is no one else's concern."

Mrs. Morse nodded with grim approval. "You listen to her, young man. If I didn't know better I'd get awfully suspicious of the way you're trying to throw the blame on Patrick."

"This is all nonsense." Aunt Ermy spoke sternly from the kitchen door, her tiny, piglike eyes glistening avidly. "What's all this about Molly being poisoned?" She looked at Molly with an expression of heavy solicitude that was almost believable. "That was a nasty blow you took on your head, and I think you must be suffering delusions of persecution along with your amnesia. Heavens, no one would want to poison you! Now, you just put that idea out of your head and we'll call the police and tell them it was all a mistake.''

"I'd love to do just that, Aunt Ermy, if it weren't for one simple thing," Molly said in her calmest voice. "It's Dr. Turner's idea that I'm being poisoned, and it's more than a stray fancy. There was arsenic in my bloodstream."

"Then you took it yourself, for the attention it would bring you," Ermy said flatly, the look in those tiny eyes hostile. "No one in this house would try to kill you. We all love you."

Molly's deadly calm turned into a slicing rage. "Of course you do," she said bitterly. "You're just dripping all over with concern, aren't you? There's something going on here, and if my memory wasn't such a total blank I could figure it out. But I'll remember. Sooner or later it'll come back to me, and I'll have the answers."

Her words hung in the air like a palpable threat. And she found herself wondering if her angry words had just sealed her fate.

THE POLICE ARRIVED a half an hour later. Molly had taken refuge in her bedroom, and when she heard a car pull up she ran to her window, hoping against all possible hope that it was Patrick. She felt more than a twinge of dismay as she recognized her old friend, Lieutenant Ryker, as he climbed out of the gray sedan.

She was downstairs in time to open the door for him. "You're looking a lot better, Mrs. Winters," he greeted her, stepping into the hall and looking around him with calm, professional detachment. That detachment made her uneasy.

"I'm feeling much better," she said with deceptive politeness. "Why are you here? I would have thought the local police could have handled this."

"I'm sure they could have," he answered in his clipped, emotionless voice, "but they decided it was more my concern than theirs. And rightly so. Sergeant Stroup came along to represent their interests."

Molly's eyes flickered over the man standing behind him, recognizing the leering animosity with faint despair. It only needed this, she thought wearily.

"Is your husband here, Mrs. Winters?" Ryker continued smoothly. "I'd like to have a few words with him."

"I'm afraid not. He doesn't even know about this…this poison business. He left here before I woke and I don't think he's expected back until tomorrow."

"And could you tell me where we could get in touch with him?" There was absolutely no reason for her to be bothered by the simple questions. But she was.

"I'm afraid I have no idea," she finally answered, her voice stiff. "Perhaps Mrs. Morse might know. I assume you'll want to talk with her?"

"All in good time, Mrs. Winters, all in good time," he said in that chilling tone. "Suppose you take me to a nice quiet place where we can talk, and we'll get this business over with as quickly and painlessly as possible."

He didn't appear to be the kind of man who wished to avoid causing pain, but there weren't really any options. She led him to Patrick's office to begin one of the most harrowing half hours in her life.

Every answer she gave to his sharply barked out questions, every statement she made, was pulled apart and delved into as if she were on the witness stand. He patently believed not one word she said, yet Dr. Turner's evidence was impossible to refute. Through it all she was conscious of Stroup's smirking, leering presence, his damp, slightly bloodshot eyes lingering over the leather chair she sat in and the antique desk with the same covetous intensity that he directed at her.

She answered Ryker's tersely worded questions calmly and rationally, keeping her voice level, and in the end he was forced to concede defeat. He hadn't been able to make her cry, as he'd all too obviously wanted, and blurt out the truths of all her so-called crimes. She stared across the desk stonily.

"All right, that will be all for now, Mrs. Winters." He leaned back in Patrick's chair affably. "But I suggest you stay close to home for the time being."

"It seems to me that home is about the most dangerous place for me right now," she said in a cool voice. "But I suppose I really have no choice in the matter."

"No, I suppose you don't," he answered. "Could you ask William Winters to come next please, Stroup? I don't think we'll be bothering Mrs. Winters any more today."

Thank God for that, she thought as she left the room, brushing unshed tears of anger and humiliation from her eyes. The only consolation in the miserable affair was that Willy and Ermy would have to go through the same thing. Though there was always the chance Ryker would behave toward them with at least a trace of charm.

She saw him before he left, his arms full of little bottles and packages, Stroup's beefy arms similarly encumbered. "We'll be leaving now, Mrs. Winters," he said coolly, his colorless eyes distant and unfathomable.

"What are all those?"

"Samples, samples. We want to see how the poison is being administered, if, indeed, it is. According to your information and that of your relatives, these are things only you could have eaten and drunk in the past four days. We should come up with some answers pretty soon."

"And in the meantime...?"

"In the meantime, I'd be careful, if I were you, Mrs. Winters. Very careful."

MOLLY WANDERED into the living room and poured herself a glass of ginger ale. If ever she needed a stiff drink now was the time, and she wondered wistfully when her ban on alcohol would be lifted. There was no one in sight—she thought she could hear a heated discussion in the kitchen, and she had no desire to join in. One of these people was trying to kill her, had tried three times. Once with the poison, twice with her socalled accidental falls. She wondered if Ryker found those accidents suspicious. He'd been far too quick to dismiss them—doubtless he thought she imagined them as well.

Dinner that night was an uncomfortable affair. Toby stayed and stayed, far longer than anyone wanted him to, watching out of pale, brooding eyes, and helped polish off the roast chicken and tomato casserole Mrs. Morse had fixed. Molly had helped with the dinner preparations.

She didn't for one moment suspect Mrs. Morse. She simply wasn't taking chances on letting any of the food out of her sight for even one moment.

Apparently Lieutenant Ryker hadn't been any more tactful with Aunt Ermy's dignity, for she spent the entire evening in a state of towering indignation. Of all the possible suspects, Molly would have preferred Aunt Ermy to be the guilty one.

Except that the poisoning had begun before Ermy returned home. So had the fall down the cellar hole in the burned-out stable. No, it didn't seem as if Ermintrude was the villain, even if she was patently unlikable.

It seemed forever before Toby was ready to leave. In desperation Molly walked him to the front door. One of her many mistakes. Before she knew what was happening his arms were tight around her and his hot, whiskey-laden breath was in her ear, urging her to do all sorts of things, including leave the house and spend the night with him. The very thought disgusted her, not from an actual dislike of Toby, but more because of her helpless longing for last night and for Patrick. Who'd made love to her, finally, and then left her.

She pushed Toby away with an unnecessary vehemence. "Please, Toby," she said angrily, straightening her clothes.

"Please, Toby," he mimicked bitterly. "You used to care about me. You used to say I was your only real friend. Remember when we'd talk about going away together? Leaving here, leaving Patrick and all those others. I don't know what's happened to you. I'm only trying to help you. I just don't think you should be alone here tonight with them."

"I thought you decided that Patrick was the guilty party," she said. "In that case I'm perfectly safe with Aunt Ermy and Willy."

"There's no way of knowing who's to blame," he said darkly, making a grab at her. She dodged him neatly.

"Listen, Toby, of course you're my friend. I like you very much," she said wearily, backing away from him. "But I'm too tired to play post office in the hall of my husband's house. I think you should go home and go to bed and try to get over this...infatuation or whatever it is."

"It isn't an infatuation. I love you!" he whispered urgently, obviously affronted. "You promised me..."

"Toby, I don't remember," she said, desperation creeping into her voice. "Whatever I said, whatever I did, whatever I promised. I simply don't remember it."

He stared at her, his face shrouded with hurt. Without another word he turned and left, slamming the heavy door shut behind him.

Molly leaned against the door in exhaustion, and if it wasn't for an odd impulse she would have left it at that. But, for some reason she drew back the little curtain beside the door. Toby was standing by his car, staring up at the house, and there was the oddest expression on his face. A look of strange intensity that was illogically frightening.

And then it was gone, and he climbed into his car. It must have been a trick of the light, or a figment of her imagination, Molly told herself, moving back from the window.

But she was unable to shake the eerie feeling that danced over her shoulder blades, as she pictured Toby's face.

THE BITCH WOULD DIE. Not tonight, much as she deserved it. Tomorrow, when there was time to plan.

She'd die in pain, struggling, calling for help. The life would be choked out of her, and no one would come to her rescue. They would find her body the next morning, eyes open and staring. She would be punished.

And she would accept that punishment, that sentence of death, gratefully.

Chapter Fourteen

Molly woke up early the next morning, her stomach calm. Whoever had sprinkled arsenic in her food had obviously thought better of it now that the cat was out of the bag. Unless, of course, her poisoner was simply gone from the house on unexplained business.

The old stone house was silent and still as she tiptoed through the halls, bundled in a warm blue wrapper, her bare feet moving noiselessly on the wooden floors. It was Mrs. Morse's day off, and it was up to Molly to make the coffee and muffins this morning if she expected to have any. As a matter of fact, it was just as well—at least she was safe from an accidental seasoning of rat poison.

The muffins were just out of the oven, the sun was rising higher in the early morning sky, and she was sitting cross-legged on the counter, wiggling her toes in the sunshine when he walked in the door.

He clearly hadn't been expecting to see her so early. He stopped dead, and they stared at each other across the shadowy kitchen with only the dawning light in it. She set down her coffee cup with great care.

"Good morning, Patrick." Her voice was astoundingly even. "When did you get home?"

"Just now." His husky voice sent chills down her spine.

He came over to the counter and poured himself a cup of coffee, and his nearness seemed to set off all sorts of reactions inside her, reactions that she wasn't sure if he was quite immune to. And then he spoke.

"I've come to a decision," he said in a flat, unemotional voice. "I'm letting you leave here. You can go anywhere you want while we wait for the divorce to be final. Nevada and Mexico are known for fast divorces—why don't you take a little vacation and speed things up?"

She stared at him in numb surprise. Then, without thinking, she picked up the cast iron muffin tin and hurled it at his head. He dodged it easily, and it fell with a terrible clanging noise, muffins scattering over the slate floor.

Before she had time to move he had caught her wrist in a tight grasp, the long, strong fingers biting into her flesh. There was a fury about him, held strongly in check, that matched and overwhelmed her own anger, and she was suddenly afraid. He looked like a man who had reached the end of his endurance.

"There's been enough of your tantrums around here, Molly," he said in a low, angry voice. He yanked her down from the counter and she stumbled against him. "Now go pick that up and put it back where it belongs."

There was no way she could resist, no way she could defy him. Without a word she did as she was told. When he finally released her she backed away from him towards the door, ready for a quick escape if need be. "You enjoy forcing your will on helpless women, don't you?"

He didn't even have the grace to look ashamed. "The day you're a poor, helpless female will be the day hell freezes over," he said shortly. "I'll get your good friend Toby to drive you to the airport this afternoon."

"I'm not going."

"What the hell do you mean by that?"

"Simply that I'm not going," she answered with deceptive calm, holding the trump card. "I doubt I'd be allowed to, anyway. Interesting things have been happening while you were off with Lisa Canning this time."

He didn't bother to deny it. "What interesting things?"

"Oh, not much," she said with mock calm. "Someone's been poisoning me, but apart from that life has been going on as usual."

"What the hell are you talking about?" There was no play-acting in the shock that paled his tanned face. Before she could answer him the telephone rang harshly through the quiet house.

"It's probably for you," she added offhandedly. "The police have been trying to reach you since yesterday morning. I think they suspect you." Actually she didn't think any such thing; she just wanted to annoy him.

He didn't give her the satisfaction of a response. Without a backward glance he went into his office, shutting the door quietly behind him. She would have felt better if he'd slammed it. She stared after him as she contemplated listening in on the extension, then dismissed the idea. For one thing, it was terribly dishonorable, for another, more important reason, she was afraid she'd get caught. She trudged back to her bedroom and did her own door slamming.

When she returned downstairs she felt a bit braver. She was showered, dressed, armored against the world, against Patrick, against her own vulnerabilities. Ermy and Willy were still asleep—the twin snores coming from their rooms assured her. Patrick's office door was still shut tightly, and she went on into the kitchen for another cup of coffee and to work on the Sunday crossword puzzle, determinedly oblivious to the man just out of sight. Forever out of reach.

A half hour passed, then an hour, before Patrick finally

removed himself from his inner sanctum and came to stand before her. His belt came to about eye-level as she looked up from the table, and it was with great concentration that she kept her eyes above rather than below it.

"Molly," he said, and his voice was gentler, "I want to talk with you."

She wasn't going to like this, she thought suddenly. And once more she felt like running, from Patrick, who'd never loved her, from Winter's Edge. From her own, helpless longing.

But running was no longer an option.

"All right," she said, bracing herself.

He pulled out a chair, apparently at a loss for words. He's going to say something about that night, she thought in relief. It's going to be all right.

But she was wrong. "That was Lieutenant Ryker on the phone a while ago. You're right, there's no question of your leaving right now."

She nodded, saying nothing, determined to hide the hurt in her eyes.

"They've found out something else, Molly. They found out who the man was. The one in the car with you."

She stared at him blankly. "I thought they knew who he was. A small-time crook named George Andrews."

He winced. "That was one of his names. I can't believe it took them so damned long to come up with a real one, but then, he was always good at covering his tracks. He was born Gregory Anderson." He waited for a response, one she was unable to give.

"Should this mean something to me?" she asked. "If you want it to then I'm afraid you'll have to explain the connection."

"Gregory Anderson was your father."

She took a deep, shaky breath, shocked. "Really? I thought you told me he was dead."

"He is now," Patrick said sharply. "Don't you care at all?"

She stared at him openly. "I don't remember him. How many times must I tell you before you get it through your head—I don't remember. I must have known he was my father. Otherwise why would I have been with him? But I don't remember anything about it." Her voice rose uncontrollably. "How many times must I say it? I don't remember, I don't remember, I don't remember!" She bit down on her lip to stop the hysteria that threatened to overwhelm her, and she turned away, unable to look at him any longer.

"All right," he said after a long moment. "I suppose I have to believe you." His face was unreadable. "The question of the money was also explained. It was yours, withdrawn from your various accounts, all legal and proper." He gave her a cool look. "It's been redeposited, by the way."

"But why?" she echoed, puzzled. "What did I want with that much money?"

"You're the only one who can answer that, if you choose to."

"Damn you, Patrick, I..."

"All right, if you *could*," he amended.

"You know what it sounds like to me?" she said after a long moment. "It sounds like blackmail money."

"What could you have done to warrant blackmail that we didn't already know about?" His voice was cynical.

She opened her mouth to protest, then shut it again. It would be useless to argue further. He'd believe what he wanted to believe.

He rose, his tall body towering over her, and she shivered slightly, longing for all sorts of things, longing to simply lean her head against his hip. "Lieutenant Ryker said he'd keep in touch. He also found out how you were being poisoned."

"So he believes me?" she said in a defeated voice. "Finally. How was it done?"

"It was in the cranberry juice. No one but you touches the stuff, so whoever put it there knew you'd be the only one likely to drink it." His face was impassive. "I'll go get rid of it."

"Why don't you have some yourself?" she muttered sweetly, low enough so he couldn't hear as he started out the door. He stopped and turned for a moment, and she thought perhaps he had heard her after all.

But he hadn't. "About Friday night," he began, his voice huskier than usual.

She froze, and she could feel her face draining of color. "Yes?" she said without looking at him, very busy with the newspaper.

"I should have never come in your room. I shouldn't have lost my temper, and I certainly shouldn't have touched you, considering our situation. It won't happen again."

He left the room before she could answer, and she stared unseeing at the crossword puzzle in front of her. The pencil point broke.

"Oh, won't it?" she said to herself softly, determinedly. "We'll see about that."

WHEN ERMY and old friend Willy arrived downstairs, somewhere between noon and one, Molly was in the midst of luncheon preparation, and she turned a deaf ear on their requests for eggs and sausage.

"It's lunch time," she said flatly. "And I'm not used to cooking. You'll have to make do with coffee and muf-

fins until I'm finished, which should be in about an hour."
She pushed a stray strand of hair off her sweating brow.

"Now, Molly, dear, you don't know how to cook,"
Aunt Ermy said heavily. "If you'll simply let me take over
I'm sure I'd do a much more competent job. And then
Willy and I could have our breakfast. Surely you must
realize that you're being unreasonable?"

"Am I?" She looked at them coolly. "Well, this time
you're going to have to humor me. I intend to cook all the
meals that Mrs. Morse isn't here for." She smiled sweetly,
turning back to her labors. There was a moment of annoyed silence, and then Aunt Ermy stomped into the dining room.

What with clearing off their messy dishes, resetting the
crumb-strewn table, and dashing back and forth between
recipe book and stove, the lunch was more than an hour
in coming, a fact which bothered her not one bit. When it
was almost ready she started out the back door to look for
Patrick, who'd disappeared somewhere in the vicinity of
the barns.

Molly saw her before she came up to him. Lisa Canning
was dressed all in pale lilac, the pants fitting her perfect
legs with nary a bulge or wrinkle, a scarf tied carelessly
around her throat. Molly ducked behind some hay bales,
then edged closer, eavesdropping shamelessly on their conversation. It was wrong. It was an invasion of privacy. It
was irresistible.

"Where were you yesterday?" she was asking in her
low, attractive voice. "I waited and waited. I thought we
had decided we were going to meet."

Patrick's withdrawal was clear even before he spoke. "I
had things to think about, Lisa," he answered shortly, with
less sympathy than he usually seemed to direct toward her.

"What things?" she demanded, pressing her lithe body

closer to him until Molly wanted to scream. "I thought we'd made all the decisions that had to be made."

"You made the decisions, Lisa," he answered. "I neither agreed nor disagreed."

Lisa moved away then, and from Molly's vantage point she could see the anger in her beautiful eyes. "I never thought you'd be like this." Her voice was petulant. "I'm not used to being jilted, Pat. If that's what you're doing. Ever since that baby-faced little bitch of a wife came back you've been making excuses for not seeing me. It wasn't like that before she went away." She moved back to him, her slender body swaying seductively. "Come on, Pat. You don't love her. You're just piqued that she'd have nothing to do with you, and you know it. She's a child, darling, and a spoiled one at that. Why don't you send her off to get a divorce and put an end to this charade? And then we'd have time to learn whether there might be something for us? Don't you think we deserve it?"

He pulled away from her. "I suppose it would be too much to ask if you'd leave me alone?" he asked coolly.

"Yes, it is! You can't do this to me, playing the devoted lover one minute, the model husband the next. I want to know where I stand in your life! Are you going to divorce her?"

Molly held her breath, an impossible hope building inside her, but it was useless. "Yes, I'm going to divorce her," he said. "But it doesn't have a damned thing to do with you. Look, Lisa, it's been over a long time, and it wasn't much to begin with. We were both lonely, you and I, but we both know it was a mistake."

She stared up at him. "That brings me to the second question, though it sounds like you already answered it. Are you going to ask me to marry you?"

There was a long pause, and Molly almost felt sorry for

her. "Lisa, I couldn't afford you, and well you know it." His voice was suddenly gentle.

She laughed unhappily. "How very flattering of you, Pat. The truth of the matter is that you don't want to marry me. And I think, if you were really honest with yourself, you'd admit that you don't want to divorce that unfaithful wife of yours either. There's nothing you'd like better than to play love's young dream with her, regardless of the fact that she's ten years younger than you and she's cheated on you with every man she could lay her greedy little hands on."

"She doesn't have anything to do with you and me, and I'm not about to discuss her with you."

"But there is no you and me. There hasn't been really, since before you married her. And there never will be."

"No," he said with great finality. "There never will be."

She stared at him for a moment longer, then she reached up and ran her hand along Patrick's face with a longing gesture. "It's a shame, darling," she murmured. "It could have been marvelous." She sauntered out the door with more self-assurance than Molly knew she possessed, and she felt a moment's compassion for the woman.

Without another word Patrick turned and started toward the door. Molly ducked back among the bales of hay, but she needn't have bothered. His mind was on other things, and, as she watched his closed face, she wondered what she had done to him, why things had gone so terribly wrong in that shadowy past, and she could have wept with frustration and nameless guilt.

It took her a moment to compose herself. She couldn't very well spend the rest of the day out in the stable, and the conversation she had just overheard was having a belated effect on her. If he didn't want Lisa Canning, then there might, just possibly, be a chance. For the future. For them.

She entered the kitchen close on Patrick's heels, unable to keep a little bounce out of her steps.

"Oh, there you are," she said blandly. "Lunch should be ready. We're eating in the dining room for the time being." She gestured to the table littered with dirty bowls, cutting boards, and cookbooks.

A brief smile lit his forbidding face. "You cooked it?"

"I did, indeed. And very tasty it will be, if I haven't burned it looking for you." She pulled the cast iron skillet out of the oven and noted with satisfaction the golden crust.

"I was in the barn," he said, looking at her curiously and not without suspicion.

"Really?" she said ingenuously. "Well, that's where I should have looked, I suppose. Would you call the others?"

Chapter Fifteen

"What the hell made you decide to wear that dress?" Patrick demanded explosively after a moment of dead silence.

Molly stared down at the white eyelet dress, one of the few pieces of clothing left from her original wardrobe. "You told me I usually dress for dinner. I thought I would tonight. What's wrong with it?" she asked, touching the delicate material. "It's pretty."

Uncle Willy snorted into his drink, and Patrick continued to glower, so it was up to Aunt Ermy to explain the situation.

"That, my dear, was your wedding dress."

It struck no chord of memory. She stared down at it, trying to force some faint glimmer of recognition, but it meant nothing to her. Just a pretty dress.

"I would appreciate it if you'd change, Molly," Patrick said heavily after a moment, and there was pain in his dark blue eyes, a pain she recognized with an unholy pleasure. He couldn't be indifferent to her.

"Yes, my dear. Something in black would be more suitable on today of all days," Aunt Ermy said.

"Why today of all days?" she inquired innocently.

"Because your poor father's death has just been made known to us," she snapped back. "Granted, no one had seen or heard from him for a decade—Patrick's father, rest his saintly soul, assumed poor little Molly was an orphan when he fetched her home here. You'd been staying with some distant cousins, but they no longer had any room for you, so Jared took you in. Such a kindly man, always taking in waifs.''

''Yes, wasn't he?'' Molly said with a pointed look at Ermy's smug direction.

Ermy, however, was oblivious. ''I'm certain Jared would want proper attention paid to your father's death. After all, he was Jared's third cousin. Or something like that. A little more decorum and proper feeling wouldn't hurt you one bit, my girl. Go and change.''

Molly smiled sweetly. She knew what she looked like in the dress, and nothing was going to make her take it off. Nothing short of Patrick's strong, clever hands. ''I don't think my father would mind,'' she said coolly. ''Now, if you're all finished your drinks you might go into the dining room and I'll bring dinner in.''

''Don't you want a drink first, dear?'' Uncle Willy spoke up suddenly from his seat in the corner, his voice surprisingly clear for someone in his usual state of inebriation. ''Some of your cranberry juice? You've been working hard all day, I should think you'd deserve a break.''

Patrick's eyes met Molly's for a pregnant moment, then he let out a deep breath. ''Molly's only drinking Diet Coke nowadays, Uncle Willy,'' he answered smoothly. ''She's been putting on weight.''

She considered hitting him, then thought better of it. She glared at him, only to find the expression in his dark blue gaze to be curiously tender. And suddenly she felt sixteen again, in love with the man who always teased her unmercifully. The unbidden memory was like a sharp pain, one that vanished almost as swiftly as it came.

She was in the midst of the tedious job of cleaning up after dinner when Patrick appeared in the doorway. Aunt Ermy and old friend Willy had retired with full stomachs to the living room without offering to help, and she'd somehow managed to use just about every pot and pan in the well-equipped kitchen. The place was a disaster area, and it took her a moment to realize she was no longer alone. She looked at him questioningly, up to her elbows in grease and soap.

He put his strong, beautifully shaped hands on her waist and pulled her gently away from the sink. At his touch she stiffened, then willed herself to relax. She wondered idly whether he was going to kiss her, but after a moment he released her, and she had no choice but to step back.

"You put the dishes in the dishwasher," he said quietly, "and I'll finish these."

She stood motionless for a moment, watching him as he started to work. Then she began clearing the table, slowly, so as to savor every moment of this odd harmony between them. She would brush her body against his as she bent to load the dishwasher, and each time she did so she could feel the little quiver that ran through his body. At least, she thought with satisfaction, she was having the same effect on him that he was having on her.

It was an odd, ritualistic sort of dance they did, their hands touching as they both reached for things at the same time, his body glancing against hers as he moved around the kitchen. The tension in the room built, slowly at first, and the air grew warmer, tighter, darker, until her hands were trembling with pain and love and desire and hurt all rolled into one mass of emotions, the foremost of which was desire. She didn't want to think about what she felt for him. She wasn't ready to admit that she loved him completely and forever, the way a woman should love a man. She didn't know him well enough in this new life to make any such rash statement. But the more she edged away from such a commitment, the more she knew deep down that it was true. Had always been true, since the first moment she'd seen him, back in the forgotten past.

Together they cleaned everything in that kitchen: the toaster, the stove top, the counters, the cupboard doors, the sink, the floor, anything to put off the moment when they had to face each other. And then it was spotless, and there was nothing left to do, no way they could postpone acknowledging each other's presence.

They were standing close together, too close, and Molly finally looked up into his eyes, and what she saw there, beneath all the hostility and hurt she had dealt him over the past, was the man she had fallen in love with seven years ago when she was sixteen and he had just come back from his self-imposed exile. The look in his eyes was as hungry and yearning as the feeling in the pit of her stomach, and she wanted, needed him to touch her. To take her. The moment stretched and held.

And then he broke it. "I'm going to work on accounts," he said abruptly, turning from her.

She felt a slap of total despair and rejection. How could he ignore what was between them? "You do that," she said tonelessly. "I think I'll just go up to bed and read a bit. I'm very tired."

"That sounds like a good idea," he said absently. "The weather report said we might have thunder-showers tonight. You'd better be prepared—maybe you should take one of Ermy's sleeping pills."

"Why?"

"You're terrified of thunder and lightning," he answered shortly. "I want you to promise me you'll take a sleeping pill. You need a good night's sleep."

She stared at him, wondering about his insistence. Perhaps if she was knocked out then she wouldn't be a temptation to him. That was the last thing she had in mind.

"No, I don't like to take pills," she answered calmly. "Especially not someone else's. I'll be all right. It seems like such a silly thing to be frightened of."

He hesitated a moment, and she wanted to throw herself into his arms, wantonly, shamelessly. She waited for a sign, a weakening. There was none.

"Well, good night, then," he said after a moment.

"Good night," she answered, not moving. He stood there for a second longer, torn between conflicting emotions. She knew, she just *knew*, he wanted her. But apparently his control over his desires and emotions was much better than hers. He turned and resolutely walked out of the kitchen.

MOLLY COULDN'T get to sleep. For a moment she contemplated taking one of Ermy's proffered sleeping pills, then shut the thought out of her mind. She had to be awake tonight, she thought grimly. He would come to her tonight, she was sure of it. She lay in the wide bed, the light off, listening for footsteps.

Aunt Ermy came up first, her heavy, determined tread unmistakable on the old oak flooring. She paused for a moment beside the door, and Molly could hear her heavy breathing.

"Molly?" Her voice called out softly.

"Yes?"

There was a surprised pause. "Are you sure you wouldn't like a pill? I don't like the sound of that wind."

"I'm sure."

Her footsteps moved on, and a short while later Uncle Willy's tired, slightly unsteady feet followed hers down the hallway. He didn't bother to stop along the way—he made his way to his bed with single-minded enthusiasm. She lay there in the dark, listening to the ominous sound of the strong April wind rushing through the trees.

And then came the sound she had waited so long for. Patrick's footsteps, firm and resolute, climbing the twisty stairway slowly, reluctantly, perhaps. She lay perfectly still, breathless, waiting, as she fingered the soft white nightgown she wore, its bridal lace. She could hear his footsteps coming closer, closer. And then he too stopped outside her door, and her heart stopped beating for a second, then slammed into action again, faster now. Before she could call out he left, continuing down the hall back to his own bedroom. Molly turned and wept silently into the pillow.

She must have dozed off. There was a flash of lightning in the room, an enormous crack of thunder, and she was sitting bolt upright, trembling with an instinctive fear. She had to stay calm, she told herself shakily. *There's no place to run to this time.*

She lay back reluctantly, shivering slightly, willing herself to go to sleep. So he didn't want her. He'd already tried to make that clear, and she'd been an adolescent fool to ignore it, hoping against hope that her heart was right and her common sense was wrong.

Well, she'd just had a salutary lesson. He was in his own room, he had no interest in her, and the night loomed ahead, long and endless.

She closed her eyes, trying to will herself back to sleep, when she thought she heard a movement by the bed. Before she could reach to turn on the light something loomed over her, something huge and dark and dangerous. Lightning split the sky, illuminating the room, but the creature

looming over her seemed huge, faceless, as his hands
latched tightly around her neck, pressing, pressing tightly.

She fought, kicking out, her hands beating at his iron
strong arms. She couldn't make a sound as the breath was
slowly squeezed out of her. She scratched at him in desperate fury, kicking.

The lamp beside the bed toppled over with a resounding
crash, and he cursed, a muffled obscenity, in a voice eerily
familiar.

And then suddenly she was free, the death-dealing hands
had left her, and she was alone in the room, in the darkness, gasping for breath.

She struggled out of bed and turned on the light. Whoever had been in the room had knocked over a chair when
he made his escape, and the door to the hallway stood
gaping open. She held herself motionless, listening for the
sound of escape, but there was nothing but the sound of
the storm outside, covering any retreat. And then the thunder crashed again, shaking the ancient stone foundations
of the old house, and she let out a shriek of terror, dropped
the blanket and ran from her room straight into Patrick's.

She headed blindly for the bed, throwing herself into his
arms, sobbing desperately. "Someone just tried to kill
me," she said in a hoarse, raw voice. "He came into my
room and tried to strangle me!"

He was already sitting up, trying to disengage himself
from her panicked, clutching arms. He switched on the
light and stared at her in disbelief. "That's impossible,"
he said flatly, doubting blue eyes narrowed against the sudden light. "You must have had a nightmare."

"I didn't, I swear I didn't!" she cried, hysteria and
something else shattering her tenuous control. "Someone
came into my room and tried to kill me. Can't you hear it
in my voice—I can barely talk. It's true, I swear it! You

can go and see for yourself—he knocked over the furniture as he escaped.''

''Why did he run? You're hardly formidable enough to fight him off. Why didn't he just finish the job?'' Patrick asked flatly.

She stared up at him, pain and fear subsiding into shock. ''I don't know,'' she said numbly.

''You must admit you don't have much of a record for truth telling,'' he said.

She started to pull away from him, but his hands suddenly tightened on her arms, as if he regretted his harshness. ''If you're afraid of the storm, Molly, you just have to say so.''

''I'm not…'' She started to deny it, but another flash of lightning sparked through the room, followed by a crash of thunder, and she jerked, clutching at him more tightly.

A tentative hand reached out and smoothed her tumbled hair. ''I think you must have dreamed it, Molly,'' he said, more gently now. ''Thunderstorms always affect you that way.''

''Why won't you believe me?'' she demanded hoarsely.

He sighed, and with surprising tenderness reached down and pulled her into the bed beside him. He leaned over and turned out the light. ''Lie down and go to sleep, Molly,'' he said patiently, slipping down under the covers, for all the world as if that was exactly what he intended to do himself.

In the meantime Molly was making some interesting discoveries. In the first place, Patrick slept naked, and the feel of his warm, smooth skin next to hers was having a predictable effect. She wanted to move closer, to press herself against him, to breathe in the feel and the scent of him.

It was also becoming apparent that she was having the same effect on him.

Lightning lit up the room for a moment, and she shivered and drew closer to the warmth of his body. The thunder followed a moment later, and she could barely resist hiding her head. Tentatively she put her face against his shoulder. His arm came around her waist, almost by its own volition, and he pulled her closer as she snuggled against him, the warm, lean hardness of his body. He put his hand under her chin, moving her head up, and his lips tasted hers, gently, almost wonderingly. With a sigh of pure abandonment she put her arms around his neck and moved closer still.

She couldn't have imagined it could be any better, but amazingly it was. His mouth was soft on hers, tasting, demanding, his hands exploring her body with a tenderness she would never have expected from a man of his temper and passions. He slid the nightgown from her, pulling it up slowly until it came free, and then it was as if he'd finally given himself free rein.

He was everywhere on her body, hands and mouth, tasting, touching, arousing her to a fever pitch she hadn't imagined possible. And when he entered her this time she clung to him, sobbing lightly, wanting more and more of him. She felt she would die if he left her; this sweet, soft dream should go on forever, when he suddenly turned rougher, exciting her in ways she hadn't even known existed, and her fingernails raked his back as she held him, straining with a passion as savage and dark as his own.

And when it was over, when she fell back, panting and warm in her dazed completeness, she still held on to him, determined not to let him leave her, not to let him shut her out.

She fell asleep in his arms, his body wrapped tightly with hers.

Chapter Sixteen

When Molly awoke the next morning he had already left the bed, and she lay calm and contented beneath the covers, watching the sun grow brighter and stronger, waiting for her husband to return. She had almost drifted back into a blissful sleep when the door opened and he came back in, dressed only in his faded blue jeans, his long black curls dripping from the shower onto his strong shoulders. His eyes slid over her lying in his bed, for all the world as if she belonged there, and the same old expression of distrust filled his dark blue gaze.

She couldn't stand it. Without thinking she slipped out of bed and ran across the room to him. Throwing her arms around his neck, she pressed her warm, naked body against his. "Don't look that way, Patrick," she pleaded, with tear-filled eyes. "Whatever I've done, whatever way I've hurt you—that's in the past. I can't change it, I can't even remember it." Reluctantly his dark blue eyes met her intense gaze. "All I can do is love you, Patrick," she said in a quieter tone of voice. "I know that I always have. And I just wish you could accept that and try to trust me. Just a little bit."

"Molly, this is hopeless," he said wearily. But his hands had reached up and caught her arms, holding her against him, his long fingers stroking her skin. "We have too many strikes against us, not the least of which is I'm of a different generation."

"You're ten years older, for heaven's sake!" she snapped, seriously annoyed. "That hardly makes you Methuselah. If you try really hard you should be able to come up with a better excuse than that."

He looked down at her, stroking, stroking. "And what if I don't want to?" he said in a husky, uncertain voice.

She held very still. "Want to what?"

"Don't want to come up with any more excuses."

The tension between them was fragile, tentative, and unbelievably delicate. She almost didn't dare breathe, for fear she'd shatter the possibility in his words. He leaned over and brushed her lips against her eyelids, first one, then the other. Feathered across her cheekbones, danced across her mouth, clung for a moment, then moved on. When he moved back she was dazed, so lost that she couldn't move, couldn't react as he grabbed a shirt and left the room.

He'd kissed her many ways, in many places during the nights she'd spent with him. He knew how to use his mouth, to arouse, to satisfy, to delight.

But he'd never kissed her with love before.

SHE PUT OFF going downstairs for as long as possible, using every speck of hot water the old house possessed, turning on her radio and humming loudly while she moved around her room. She didn't want anything, any noise, any creature, to intrude on the burgeoning hope that was burning inside her. She didn't want to face Patrick in front of Ermy and Willy's knowing eyes, and she didn't want to frighten Patrick away.

So she tried on half a dozen changes of clothing, finally ending up in a huge cotton sweater and faded jeans, put on makeup and then washed it off, tucked her hair in French braids and then ripped them out. It took all her concentration to wipe the smile off her face a mere second before she entered the kitchen.

The sight that met her eyes was enough to depress anyone. Willy was up early and sitting in the corner, looking even paler than his nightly imbibing usually made him, and the carrot-colored strands of hair were disarrayed on his balding skull. Mrs. Morse was slamming pots and pans around in a bad humor, causing Willy to wince dramatically.

"What's wrong with everybody?" she demanded brightly. "It's a beautiful day, the sun is shining. What…?" she noticed that Aunt Ermy was snorting and snuffling and dabbing away at red-rimmed eyes. "What's happened?" she continued in a lower voice.

Aunt Ermy looked up, dislike and disapproval emanating from her tiny, tear-filled eyes. "You're a fine one to ask! Why should you care, spending the night romping around with that man while all the while…all the while…" She dissolved into noisy tears.

Molly could feel the color flood her face as she struggled to remain impassive. "What are you talking about?"

Uncle Willy took over, a look of stern condemnation on his ruddy face. "Your Aunt Ermy was referring to your behavior last night. You left your door standing wide open, my dear. There was no doubt in our minds where you'd gone. Besides which, his bed creaks."

She could feel her color deepen. It had squeaked noisily, rhythmically, most of the night. There'd been other sounds as well, but at least Uncle Willy didn't seem likely to mention them. "I spent the night with my husband," she said, a little too loudly. "I don't know what's so shocking and immoral about that." She poured herself a cup of coffee with a deceptive show of nonchalance. "Surely that's not cause to make you burst into tears?"

"Sometime in the night, my dear Molly," Willy began portentously, "while you were disporting yourself with your husband, Toby Pentick was murdered. Someone cut his throat."

"What?" She sat down abruptly, feeling faint. "That's impossible."

"I'm afraid it's not only possible, it happened, Molly," Mrs. Morse broke in from her stance by the sink. "The police came by not half an hour ago and took Patrick with them. For questioning, they called it." She snorted. "Seems like they found something of his by the body. What you might call circumstantial evidence." She shook her iron-gray head. "And now God only knows what's going to happen."

For a moment Molly couldn't move. It was as if a dark cloud had hovered over them all, and with the advent of the thunderstorm, disaster had broken free. She crossed the room and put her arms around Mrs. Morse's spare figure, trying to still the sudden spurt of despair that had shot through her heart. "He'll be all right, Mrs. Morse," she said, not certain if she was trying to reassure the older woman or herself. "It's all a stupid mistake, you'll see. He was with me last night—there was no way he could have killed Toby. Why in the world should he want to do such a thing?"

"Jealousy, my dear," Willy said from his seat in the corner in a firm voice. "He was mad with jealousy over you. Everybody knew it."

"And you made sure that the police found that out too, didn't you?" Mrs. Morse turned on him wildly. "You nasty, sponging drunk, ready to stab a man in the back when he's not looking."

"Now, now, my dear Mrs. Morse, I was only doing my duty," Willy protested mildly, unmoved by her attack. He rose from his seat. "You don't seem well today. This business has upset you—why don't you take the rest of the day off?"

"I don't have to discuss it with the likes of you if I do!" she flared back, turning to Molly. "As a matter of fact, I thought I might ask Ben to take me home after lunch. This has got me all upset—I don't know whether I'm coming or going. You can manage, can't you?"

"Of course I can," she said soothingly, stilling her own doubts. "You leave whenever you feel like it, and I'll give you a call as soon as Patrick gets back home."

"You'll be waiting a long time for that," Willy said with a smirk, and Molly nearly threw a pan at him. Fortunately there was nothing close at hand, so she had to be content with glaring at him fiercely.

"Willy and I were also planning on leaving this afternoon," Ermy piped up in a watery voice. "A short round of visits with our friends the Sturbridges would get our minds off this distressing business. We should be back in a couple of days. Unless, of course, you're afraid to stay alone?" she hinted slyly.

"I won't be alone," Molly shot back grimly. "My husband will be here."

"Of course, he will," Willy said in a soothing voice. "You could come with us, if you wish. I don't think it's really your thing though—nobody under fifty and all we do is play bridge. A dull party for a lively young thing like yourself. I'm sure if Patrick doesn't get home you'll find some other way to console yourself. After all, there are plenty of young men in town. All old friends of yours, I believe."

"I'll be just fine, thank you," she answered coldly,

pouring herself a cup of coffee with an unsteady hand. "Why don't you leave as soon as you're ready? I'd welcome some time alone in my own house."

"Ungrateful bitch," Ermy murmured malevolently, lifting her overdressed bulk majestically. "I need to get away from this depressing place and all the depressing people in it." She paused and turned to Molly. "And when did you decide to take Patrick into your bed?" she demanded frostily.

Molly stared at her. Ermintrude used to frighten her, she realized. She'd lost her power over her, sometime in the last few days. "When I was sixteen," she replied calmly, turning away.

"You are an ungrateful, scheming little slut," Ermy said boldly. "When I think how I wasted some of the best years of my life guiding you, advising you, trying to teach you a bit about the ways of the world..."

"You did a good job, between you and Lisa," she answered, staring out the kitchen window. The day looked warmer, the winter-dead grass had a faint tinge of color. It was no day for a young man to lie dead. No day for her husband to be in jail. She turned back to her so-called relatives. "It's too late to change the past. When you get back from your visit I think you'd better start making plans to find some other place to live. I think you've worn out your welcome around here a long time ago. You and Willy."

"Listen to me, you conniving little brat!" Aunt Ermy started toward her, grabbing her wrist in a bone-crushing grip. As a matter of pure reflex Molly kicked her in the shins, and Ermy pulled away, shrieking curses. Some of the phrases were rather good, and Molly was sorry she couldn't remember them for later use. Willy hurriedly helped his cousin out of the kitchen, hushing her with words Molly could neither hear nor imagine. By the time they reached the stairs she had quieted down, and the sound of their whispering was barely audible.

"What mischief are they hatching up now?" Mrs. Morse demanded. "If I were you I'd keep an eye on them before they leave. You might find the best silver gone with them if you're not careful."

"Don't worry," Molly said. "I wouldn't trust Aunt Ermy farther than I could throw her, which is about half an inch. And Willy's not any better." She turned to Mrs. Morse. "Why don't you go on home now? Everyone can get their own lunch around here—there's no reason you should wait around for *their* sakes. I'm just going to call the police and then go for a ride. After a few minutes with those two I feel like I need a breath of fresh air."

Mrs. Morse nodded sagely. "I know how you feel. You sure you won't mind being all alone here?"

"Not a bit," Molly lied, smiling bravely. After all, there'd be no one left to hurt her.

SHE WAS OUT for several hours on the back of old Fountain, the mellowest horse in the stable. The police had refused to release any information, either about Toby or Patrick, and Molly had slammed down the phone on the unhelpful Sergeant Stroup in a blazing fury.

Oddly enough, they didn't seem interested in trying to search her blank memory one more time. Maybe they already had the answers, she thought, unnerved. She needed the ride to burn off some of the helpless frustration that swamped her, and she had no intention of spending another minute in the company of her hateful relatives. That last little battle with Aunt Ermy was the final straw.

It was a gorgeous day, giving lie to the storm that raged in her heart. The fresh spring air did its best to convince her that all was right with the world. The budding trees, the daffodils and crocuses, the soft spring smell of wet, warm earth were an intoxicant, and she prayed that when she returned to the old stone house Ermy and Willy would be gone and Patrick would be back.

She should have known the latter would be too much to hope for. The house was very still as she made her way slowly, reluctantly through the barns toward the kitchen door. Her sixth sense, such as it was, was working overtime, and she had the unshakable feeling that something very bad awaited her inside the flagstoned hallways of Winter's Edge.

She opened the door with deceptive boldness. "Anyone home?" she called out, thinking of the day just over a week ago when she first remembered entering this house. It seemed astonishing that so much could have happened in such a short time.

Slowly, bravely, methodically, she went through each room of the house, calling out as she went. By the time she reached the attic she should have been satisfied that the house was empty except for Beastie's slumbering form, and yet she couldn't shake her sense of panic. Of disaster lurking.

She hadn't even had time to think about Toby's death. It felt unreal—that intense light in his eyes suddenly snuffed out. She wanted to mourn, but all she could think about was Patrick.

She went back downstairs, determined to be calmly reasonable as she locked all the doors and windows, whistling tunelessly as she moved through the house. What she was locking them against, she didn't know and refused to try to imagine—she was nervous enough already. The sun was already sinking lower in the sky, and eerie shadows were growing in the spotless corners of the house.

Briskly she walked into the kitchen and made a pot of coffee. Five-thirty. She picked up the discarded newspapers, grabbed a plate of home-baked muffins and went back into the living room to be near her sleeping canine friend.

Someone had already laid a fire, and she lit it, despite the warmth of the late afternoon sun shining through the multi-paned windows. She needed every bit of cheeriness and warmth she could get. Someone had murdered Toby Pentick, and the one person she knew couldn't have done it was the only one in custody. Whoever had killed Toby was most likely the same person who'd been trying to kill her. And here she sat, alone in the house, a perfect sitting duck. The idea was not exactly heartwarming.

Something incriminating was found by Toby's body, Mrs. Morse had said. For some reason her mind went back to the handkerchief still hidden away in the bedside table. The handkerchief with Patrick's initials and the mysterious rust-colored stains. And with a sudden horrid sinking feeling she recognized the short spurt of memory that came rushing back. The handkerchief wasn't an ancient love token. She had found it clasped in her father's murdered hand. And in a last moment of consciousness she had hidden it away from the police's prying eyes. Something incriminating, her brain echoed.

On an impulse she couldn't quite understand she made her way back up to the attic, to the gloom-shrouded shapes of the abandoned furniture. The handkerchief was exactly where she had left it, tucked in the back drawer of the ugly dresser. She stared at the orange, bloodlike streaks thoughtfully, some distant memory teasingly out of reach.

She slowly returned to the living room and the fire, the scrap of incriminating cloth in her hand. Settling back in the chair, she stared straight ahead. Beastie snored beside her, snuffling noisily in his sleep, bringing her back to her senses. If she doubted Patrick, what did she have left? She picked up the newspaper again, determined not to think about it.

The crossword puzzle proved almost too easy, the coffee had none of its usual wakening effects, and the warmth from the fire made her suddenly drowsy. In between clues she fell asleep, the handkerchief clutched in her hand.

Chapter Seventeen

It was an odd sort of dream, even from the beginning. It was too logical, too familiar to be a fantasy. And yet at the beginning it was as pleasant and somehow frightening as most dreams are.

It was her wedding day. She was dressed in the lace and eyelet dress that hung straight down past her shoulders, and the antique veil sat delicately upon her head. Her slanted green-blue eyes were filled with angry tears as Aunt Ermy and Lisa Canning bustled around her, making busy, critical noises.

"You look absolutely lovely, darling," Lisa crooned, arranging the veil about her shoulders. "I'm sure Pat will be most pleasantly surprised."

The bride felt a stab of resentment, one she hid quite well. After all, she had won, hadn't she? He was marrying her, for whatever his reasons. He hadn't waited for Lisa Canning to divorce her gentle-mannered older husband.

"For goodness sake, Molly, smile!" Aunt Ermy ordered in exasperation. "One would think you were going to your funeral instead of to a wedding. It's not as if we all don't know you're in love with him, and have been ever since you were a teenager. I only wonder how you managed to hook him."

"I was wondering the same thing," Lisa murmured lazily, fingering the opulent hot-house bouquet with the yellow orchids that she and Aunt Ermy had chosen for her. They had wanted to pick the wedding dress too—a dumpy-looking satin creation that had taken their fancy, but on this point she'd had a strange moment of stubbornness. She had taken her little car and spent the day shopping, returning with the simple, old-fashioned dress she now wore, and the slight victory gave her confidence as she watched her pale, nervous face in the mirror of her pink-and-white room.

"You don't think he's in love with you, do you?" Lisa leaned closer. At the betraying expression on the bride's face, Lisa laughed. "Oh, you poor dear, you do! Did he tell you so?"

"No," she whispered, unwilling to confide in the older woman. She had believed, held the idea firmly in her heart of hearts, that underneath his friendly exterior he really cared for her. That he just hadn't realized it yet. Otherwise why would he have asked her to marry him? The money wasn't that important—she would have given it to him anyway, and well he knew it.

"Of course he didn't!" Lisa said in quiet triumph. "That's because, my dear, he loves me. But you know that—heaven knows we've tried to be discreet about our little affair, but word does get around. Just last night he begged me to run off with him, to put a stop to this atrocious masquerade. His very words, my dear—'atrocious masquerade.'" Lisa was lying, but how could the girl have known it was merely the prompting of a feverishly jealous mind? She believed every word.

"He needn't go through with it," Molly muttered sulkily, her unhappiness building. "All he has to do is come and tell me and we'll end it right now."

"With the guests arriving at the church already?" Lisa raised one beautifully molded eyebrow. "Pat doesn't like fusses made, my dear. If you want I could give you quite a few pointers on what Pat does like in a woman. After all, you are going to be his wife. A few little secrets as to what pleases him sexually should help your rather desperate situation, sweetie." Her smile was like a cat's. "No, he won't back down. It was too much wine and passion last night that made him suggest it. He needs your money too much. Winter's Edge means more to him than any woman." Lisa's voice was laced with bitterness, and the bride felt a small stirring of revenge. At least he didn't love her enough either.

Aunt Ermy was strangely silent through all this, watching the scene with satisfaction in her mean little eyes. She was magnificently overdressed as usual, in a powder blue full-length suit with matching turban and eye shadow. Attached to her noble breast was a cluster of gardenias—the scent overpowered the lighter fragrances in Molly's bouquet and made her slightly ill.

"Before your wedding night, my dear, I feel I ought to warn you," Lisa continued, her ripe, full mouth a crimson curve against her artificially tanned skin. "He has certain sexual...shall we say, aberrations...that might frighten a young girl if she isn't warned—"

"Enough!" Molly cried suddenly, angrily. "I'm leaving now." She grabbed her bouquet and headed for the door. "I'm getting married in less than an hour," she told them coolly, taking pleasure in reminding Lisa. "It wouldn't do for the bride to be late."

"But the limousine hasn't arrived yet," Aunt Ermy protested.

"I'm driving myself," she answered them with icy calm, recognizing the hatred behind their tender concern.

Wondering why she had never seen that hatred before. "*You* can ride in the limousine."

"And what will Pat think of this little outburst?" Lisa asked slyly. "You know how he hates things to be changed at the last minute."

"Pat," she said slowly, "can go to hell."

THE WIND BLEW her hair wildly as she sped toward the church, driving twenty and thirty miles above the speed limit. She had taken off the veil and stuffed it behind the seat with her bouquet. She very carefully didn't cry—it had taken her over half an hour to apply her makeup and she didn't propose to ruin it on *his* account. "Bastard," she said out loud, savoring the sound of the word. "Bastard, bastard, bastard!" she shouted to the blue, blue skies.

So he had spent the eve of their wedding with another woman, had he? And what right had she to complain? He had made her no promises, not even a word of affection when he had made his startling proposal. And she had jumped at it, because for seven long years he had been the only thing in her life that had mattered. Even if things had been strained between them since Jared had died and the terms of the will made public, she'd hoped, she'd prayed, that at least his tolerant affection for her remained. And that her love for him would be enough to support her.

"Not anymore," she said grimly, speeding over the rutted macadam roads. "Not anymore."

Her wedding passed in a daze. Lisa Canning stood beside her, her gleaming eyes carefully lowered, only the small smile that hovered around her full lips hinting at the pleasure she found in the uncomfortable situation.

Aunt Ermy cried, and kissed her cold face. "Molly, dear, you make such a lovely bride. Who would have thought you'd have the dignity to carry it off? Try to smile, dear.'' A sharp pinch accompanied the admonition, and she could barely restrain a little outcry. Aunt Ermy was fond of delivering painful little pinches for improper behavior.

And so she was very gay. The reception was one lavish feast, with the bride dancing and flirting and smiling and laughing and kissing everyone there. Except her husband. With her husband she was even shriller, even gayer, desperate to hide the mortal blow Lisa had given her. His dark blue eyes followed her, doubt turning into a slow rage that built as the hours went on, until, when it was time to leave, he snapped at his child bride.

She shouted something obscene and very nasty back to him and fled the hall. Then she drove away, back to Winter's Edge in her bright red sports car, leaving her husband fuming with rage. A perfect setup for Lisa Canning.

That night seemed endless. She sat in her huge, soft bed with the pink satin sheets and waited for him, dressed so carefully in her bridal nightgown of sheer gauze. It made her itch. And she rehearsed the things she'd say to him. How she'd apologize for making a fool of him in front of all those people. How they would lie there and talk about their marriage, and come to some sort of understanding of what they meant to each other. Things they should have talked about before the wedding, but she had been frightened of scaring him off.

The hours passed, and he didn't come. Then she planned the things she'd say to him, demanding where he'd been, why he'd left her for so long. And then they would forgive each other and make love in this soft, too elegant bed that Lisa had picked for them, and everything would be fine.

And when morning finally came, and Patrick hadn't bothered to come to his foolishly virginal bride, a core of anger grew and hardened in her, fed with the hurt of his rejection and the humiliation of having been left on her wedding night. She had saved herself for him, because no other man would ever do for her; she had waited for Patrick to want her. But he hadn't wanted her.

From that night on she locked her door against him. A locked door he had barely seemed to notice, much less mind. The warmth and friendliness that had existed between them before their marriage was gone and in its place was a hurtful, implacable hatred. That was very close to love.

Until the night when it had all become too much for her. She was a stranger in her own house—it seemed that Patrick found her presence an annoyance, and the others considered her a selfish little slut. All except one of them, who was her friend.

The dream then became fraught with danger, and Molly stirred in the armchair, trying to wake up. She didn't like this. She didn't want to remember, to relive what happened next. But the dream moved on.

That friend had been the only one she could confide in. But he was shadowy and unclear; even his voice seemed to come from far away, telling her to leave Patrick, to run away where no one could ever find her. If she went with her father, taking her money, he would see to it that Patrick would never use her again.

She tried to see him clearly through the mists, but he remained maddeningly out of reach…until that night when old Fred Canning finally succumbed to his cancer, and her friend told her that Patrick was going to divorce her.

She went out with him to the far barn, where Patrick kept his breeding stock, and watched with numb, drugged horror as he set fire to the place after striking poor old Ben and leaving him in a pool of blood.

"What are you doing?" she screamed at him. "You said you were going to help me leave here!"

"You are leaving here, Molly dear. You're leaving here for good, in that fire." He started dragging her screaming, kicking body toward that inferno, the heat scorching their faces, and whatever he had put in her drink earlier made her unable to stop him.

And then, before he could shove her struggling, helpless body down into the funeral pyre, they heard shouts from nearby, and the slow scream of the fire engine. He cursed, and loosened his hold for a moment, and she pulled away and ran, blindly, hysterically, through the woods that no one knew as well as she did, back to the deserted house. She grabbed a handful of clothes, took all the spare money Patrick kept in the petty cash box, climbed into her car, and drove all night long, her terror fighting the effects of the sleeping pill he'd given her. When she reached New York state she checked into a run-down motel and slept for eighteen hours.

HE WAS THERE in the room. If she opened her eyes the shadows would pass away and she would see the man who wanted to kill her quite clearly. But then, she thought craftily, if she kept her eyes closed he might disappear and she would be safe. All in all, it was a problem, but with her newfound courage she slowly opened her downcast blue-green eyes and stared at the crumpled handkerchief in her hand. With its streaks of orange hair dye. She raised her eyes.

"Hello, Uncle Willy."

Chapter Eighteen

"You don't seem very surprised to see me," he said, and Molly stirred in the chair, determined not to show for a minute the absolute terror he instilled in her. She remembered everything now, and she desperately wished she didn't.

"Oh, Molly." He moved forward into the room, and once again she was aware of the lingering cruelty in his soft pink face, the cruelty she'd refused to recognize in the past week of blessed forgetfulness. "I've told you before you never were much of an actress. You've remembered."

"Yes." Her voice came out in a rusty croak, and she cleared it hastily.

Beastie snored loudly beside her, and she tugged silently at his collar. "It won't do you any good, my dear," Willy said smoothly, running a slightly trembling hand over his carroty strands of hair. "He's drugged. I decided I didn't want him interfering with my plans tonight—he's too fond of you, you know."

"And what exactly are your plans for tonight?" She sounded almost unnaturally calm. She'd been through too much in the last few days, the last few weeks. All she could do was pull this false serenity around her, watching him while she thought feverishly of escape.

"Now, now, Molly, I'm sure you can imagine." He seated himself in the chair opposite her and crossed his legs, at home and urbane. "I'm going to have to kill you." He sighed. "I suppose I should tell you that it grieves me, but quite frankly, it doesn't bother me in the slightest. You've been an annoying little pain in the rear ever since Jared brought you home, and your indestructibility is absolutely infuriating."

"Why do you want to kill me?"

"For the oldest reason in the world, my dear. Money. You have lots of it, I want it. It's really quite simple." For once the man was quite sober, and the effect had a horrifying charm to it.

"My money goes to Patrick if I die." She couldn't keep a note of desperation from her voice. She was strong, but Uncle Willy, despite his alcohol-induced flabbiness, had overpowered her before, the night of the barn fire, and he could doubtless do it again.

"It does, my dear. But not if he's convicted of murder. And it looks pleasantly as if it will work out that way. I had planned to make it a triple play, as they say in baseball. You, your father and Toby. But I might have to settle on a suicide for you."

"You killed my father," she stated flatly.

He nodded benevolently. "Well, no. Actually I arranged for Toby to do it, but I was there, watching. I've learned it never pays to leave important tasks to underlings. People need supervision nowadays—they have no incentive. Toby was eager enough to please, but he wasn't very good at improvising. I see you're clutching my important piece of evidence. I was very distressed that Patrick's handkerchief wasn't found with the body, Molly. That upset a great many careful plans."

"It had your hair dye on it." She held up the square of linen.

She was pleased to see his ruddy complexion turn a sickly pale. "Good heavens, how careless of me! And how very fortunate that you thought to save your husband. Fate has been on my side after all, it seems. Things should work out very well this way, very well indeed."

"We were bringing you that money." Memories were flooding back at a terrifying, dizzying rate. "Why did you have to kill him?"

"It was necessary. Your father, petty little swindler that he was, knew what was going on the minute you turned up. He thought he could blackmail me for half of that money. You didn't know that, did you? He soon found out otherwise. That was my only mistake, Molly dear." He eyed his hands reflectively. "I thought that blow on your head killed you. Crushed your stubborn little skull. I should have known you were far too hardheaded. Imagine my displeasure when the police called and you were still alive. And no handkerchief! I thought all my plans had failed dismally." He shook his head sadly. "But you had that convenient loss of memory that no one believed, and now, everything has worked out splendidly. Just splendidly." He sighed.

"Just splendidly," she echoed in a daze.

"Ah, I can see you had some of your ginger ale tonight. It's much harder to hide drugs in soft drinks, you realize. Tonight it's just a strong sedative. You're too willful, my dear. But it's already slowed you down, I'm pleased to notice."

She hadn't touched the ginger ale. She looked up at Uncle Willy with feigned blankness.

"I don't plan to make it painful," he added. "As much as you've annoyed me, I'm basically a decent human being. I try not to hold grudges. And I can be fairly certain that no one has the faintest idea that I had a hand in either your father's death or Toby's. For one thing I have no motive—or not as strong a one as your dear husband. And for another, my dear Ermy will provide me with excellent alibis. Did you know, for example, that right now I am visiting our old friends the Sturbridges over in Devon? They had to go out on a previous engagement, but when they left I was there and when they return I will still be there. And there will be one less member of the exalted Winters family in the meantime."

There was a sneer in his voice as he rose and poured himself a stiff drink. His hands were suddenly still, unlike the usual mild tremor that afflicted him. Just another part of his elaborate charade.

"And what if they don't convict Patrick?" she asked, speaking in a deliberately thickened voice.

He shrugged his shoulders. "That's no problem, really. He won't marry again. He's in love with you, my dear. We all knew it, even if you were too heartsick and adolescent to realize it. Your untimely death by suicide will deal him a mortal blow. He'll continue to support Ermy and me because he's foolishly generous, and in a few years he'll meet with a recalcitrant horse or faulty brakes. He does drive too fast, you know. Such an angry, impetuous man. You could have been the making of him, but alas, that isn't to be. We can wait, once our goal is in sight. Infinite patience, that's what's required in a really first-class criminal mind." He drank deeply from his drink and stared into the fire. "Yes, my dear Molly, I consider myself a criminal, and I am proud of it. An ordinary man couldn't do what I've done. I can plan extraordinarily complicated schemes, I can kill when it's necessary, without compunction, and that all requires a truly high degree of dedication and skill.''

''I don't understand what Toby had to do with this,'' she said, trying to keep Willy talking while she searched for any possible avenue of escape. The keys were in the car—she could probably run faster than he could, especially if she took him by surprise. He thought she was falling into a drugged stupor; instead the adrenaline was surging through her body. ''Why would he be willing to kill? And why would you turn around and kill him?''

''Toby?'' he said blankly. ''Toby was becoming somewhat of a problem. He was the one who tried to kill you by the ruins, you know. And he was all set to crush your clever little brain in when he tripped up the horse. If Patrick hadn't made his untimely appearance it would all be over with, and you would have been spared a lot of needless fuss. But then, that's what life's all about, isn't it? Needless fuss.''

He swirled his rapidly disappearing drink with one fat, pale finger. ''That's a good lesson to learn, my dear. Never take a psycho into partnership with you. Toby was not what you'd call well-balanced. He'd always been consumed with a strange passion for you, and when you married Patrick it tipped him over the edge. He decided since he couldn't have you then nobody could. I'm afraid finding out your sexual liaison with your husband rather set the seal on his…problems. When he failed to strangle you last night he was going to come back with a gun, and that seemed far too sloppy. I suppose I could have taken the chance and let him do it. I could have hoped he wouldn't talk and just let all my work be handled by a poor deranged boy. But chances are not my style at all. Not at all. So I took care of him myself.'' He sighed heavily. ''If you hadn't gone creeping off to Patrick's bed I could have finished what Toby had so sloppily started. The coroner probably wouldn't have noticed that Toby's death preceded yours.''

''And you left something incriminating of Patrick's by his side? As you tried to do with my father?'' she questioned, watching him as he rose and made his way to the bar.

''Naturally. I had had the foresight to arm myself ahead of time with another of his handkerchiefs and his watch. There's no way he'll be released—the police are an awfully gullible lot. That ox Stroup would just love to lock Pat up and have you all alone out here. But when he comes to call he'll find Pat's poor wife dead by her own hand, and he'll…''

She was on her feet and out of the room before he could turn around. She slammed open the front door and ran out into the cool night air. A light rain was falling, and the sounds of Uncle Willy's furious pursuit were unmistakable. She raced toward the garage, dodging through doorways, as she heard him come closer and closer, his heaving, panting breath loud in the stillness.

Finally she reached the old van. The night was oddly silent—Uncle Willy must have gone in the wrong direction. She jumped in the car and reached for the ignition.

The keys were gone. She felt around on the floor, in the glove compartment, fright and desperation making her oblivious to the threat moving up behind her. When she straightened up she looked directly into Willy's pale, murderous eyes.

Like a fool she sat there, too numb with horror to lock the doors against him. He yanked her out of the driver's seat, insane fury mixing with some ghastly trace of amusement.

''I warned you I consider myself a master criminal,'' he

said in his soft voice, his pale fat hands on her arm, squeezing with surprising strength. "You just made a fool of me, Molly. Even though I had the foresight to remove the keys, you shouldn't have gotten this far. You didn't drink anything at all tonight, did you? You thought you could fool me. Most annoying of you. And it would have been a waste of time—the van isn't working properly, remember? No," he said, dragging her back through the barns and the courtyard, into the kitchen, "I'm afraid you're going to have to be punished for this. The loss of my dignity will come very dear. I was going to try to make it easy for you, for old times' sake, but now it's going to hurt. It's going to hurt quite a bit." His eyes glistened and Molly noticed he was drooling slightly.

For a moment she thought she saw a flash of light in the distance, but it was gone before she could look further, and she didn't want to alert her would-be murderer. Help was highly unlikely. If she was to stay alive it was up to her, and right now her chances didn't look too promising.

"How are you going to do it?" she asked him humbly when they reached the living room once more and he'd shoved her down into the chair.

He chuckled pleasantly, running his pale, sluglike hand across his mussed orange strands. "You'll be found hanging from one of the rafters in the attic. And it should take quite a while to find you—a typewritten note will serve to distract everyone for a few days. Until you begin to smell, my dear." He sat and reached for his drink. "I had meant to be generous and snap your little neck with a quick jerk of my wrists so that you'd only have a moment of blinding pain before it was all over." He smiled through the cheerful firelight, and Beastie snored blissfully on. "But now, my dear, I'm going to strangle you, slowly, so I can watch your eyes bulge out, watch you gasp and scream for mercy, watch you pleading as I rip your life away with my bare hands." It all sounded like a recipe: detailed, but simple and effective.

Shuddering uncontrollably, she let her hand trail nervelessly, and noticed, an aching fraction of an inch out of her reach, the lovely old brass-handled fire tools. He would notice in a second if she appeared to reach for them, and her one final chance of salvation would be gone.

Willy looked at his watch in a businesslike fashion. "I'm afraid it's getting late, my dear," he announced affably. "This is pleasant but I do have to allow enough time to get back before my hosts return." He rose, and came toward her slowly, very slowly. She watched him out of hooded eyes, concentrating desperately on the fire poker just out of reach, thinking of Patrick, and of poor, sick, dead Toby. Of her father, whom she'd barely known. She'd thought she could go to him for help, for a place to hide from Willy and the danger, a place to hide from the husband who hated her. Instead he'd been ready to betray her for money. But in the end he was the one who was betrayed.

Willy moved closer, running a quick tongue over his dry, flabby lips, his eyes moist and shining, his fat pale fingers twitching.

And then a sound, the briefest of unexpected noises broke in the room. He whirled around, his back presented for only a second. It was all Molly needed. Without an instant's hesitation she smashed him over the head with the lovely brass-handled fire poker, the fastidious orange hairs providing no padding. His squat body sank to the floor in a curious attitude of surprise. She looked up and met the astonished deep blue eyes of her husband, followed closely by Lieutenant Ryker and his posse.

After a moment Patrick broke the stillness. "How the

hell,'' he asked in a faintly disgruntled tone of voice, ''am I supposed to save you when you prove entirely capable of rescuing yourself?''

She shrugged, and smiled, took one step toward him and quite calmly passed out on the body of dear Uncle Willy.

Epilogue

She slept in his arms that night, curled up snugly against his body as if that was where she belonged. Patrick lay beside her, drifting in and out of sleep, his arms tight and possessive around her.

He'd tried to reason with her. "I'm too old for you," he'd said. "I have too foul a temper."

"I'm mature for my age," she'd said, an arrant lie, as she bit his shoulder. "And I'm fairly grumpy myself."

"I should never have married you," he tried to tell her, later, when she was licking his navel. "I took advantage of you. I knew you had a crush on me, that you'd do anything for me…"

"I would," she agreed, moving her head lower.

His voice grew tight and husky. "But it's not fair to you."

"Let me decide what's fair," she said.

"You'll find someone better suited to you."

"There isn't anyone better for me."

"You'll regret it."

Her mouth was too busy to reply to such a patently ridiculous statement, and he found he couldn't manage to come up with any more arguments for the time being. But later, when they were curled tight around each other, he slid his hands through her thick tangle of wheat-colored hair and tilted her face up to his. She looked sleepy, sated, immensely pleased with herself, and he didn't want to care that much.

"I won't hold you here," he said in a harsh, quiet voice.

She stared at him, her eyes wide. "You can't make me leave you." She reached up her own hands to cup his cheeks, and her voice was intense. "Don't you love me, Patrick?"

He'd never meant to tell her. He's always thought it would take unfair advantage of her. But there was no way he could not answer her simple, heartfelt question.

"Completely," he said.

She smiled, a bright, tear-filled smile. "I know," she said.

And he wondered if he'd just made the worst mistake of his entire life.

WHEN MOLLY WOKE UP the next morning he was gone. She hadn't felt him leave. She could hear Mrs. Morse humming to herself in the kitchen below—Patrick had left the door ajar. Mrs. Morse was in a very good mood. She was singing out of tune and quite loudly.

Molly jumped out of Patrick's bed and stretched luxuriously. Bright sunlight was pouring in the open windows, and it seemed as if winter was finally coming to a close. It was good to be alive on this April morning, though she doubted poor Willy felt so. She had only managed to daze him, and he was now unhappily incarcerated in the county jail, awaiting arraignment.

She showered and dressed quickly in cutoff jeans and the tightest T-shirt she owned. She wanted to see Patrick. To see whether the slowly burgeoning trust and friendliness survived outside the bedroom walls. To see whether he still knew that he loved her.

And yet she was almost afraid to find out. If he turned that cold, stony face on her once more she didn't think she could bear it.

"And how are you this fine morning?" Mrs. Morse greeted her with almost tasteless good cheer, considering the circumstances. Bringing coffee and muffins to the table, she pulled out a chair invitingly. "Eat, for goodness sake!" she ordered. "Patrick told me all about your fright last night—you need rest and good food after an ordeal like that!" She shook her head meaningfully. "Willy confessed all nice and neat when he saw it was useless. No, we won't have him to worry us ever again. They'll lock him away for hundreds of years, you mark my words. I'm only thinking it's a shame they don't use capital punishment more often." She paused for breath. "And as for your Aunt Ermy, why she just disappeared off the face of the earth, as far as anyone can tell. Doesn't seem like they'll ever find her, more's the pity. What's the matter, child, don't you have any appetite?"

Molly shook her head and smiled nervously. "I don't care whether they find Ermy or not," she said truthfully. "As long as she keeps away from here it doesn't matter to me what she does with herself. I don't imagine she was anything more than a pawn in Uncle Willy's game."

Mrs. Morse sniffed. "That's as may be. She was still one of the meanest women I've ever known, and don't you doubt it. Still, I suppose you're right—as long as she's gone that's all that matters. It still horrifies me to think of the years that have gone by with them living here as friendly as you please, all the time planning such wickedness." She shook her graying head with wonder. "Come on now, dearie, eat something. You need to get some meat on those bones." Her eyes reflected a mild disapproval for the scantiness of Molly's clothing.

"Where's Patrick?" she asked suddenly, the suspense unbearable. Before any more time passed she had to find out what his attitude toward her might be.

"He was out in the yard last time I looked. He said to tell you that you and he would have to go into town later on to give statements to the police..." Her voice trailed off as Molly ran out the door.

The sun was pouring down, the first really hot day of the year, and she had to squint her eyes against the glare. There was the faintest hint of a breeze, and it blew her hair in her face. She pushed it away impatiently, looking for him, half afraid of what she'd see when she looked into his eyes.

She saw him first, his lean, strong body bent over some piece of riding tack, his eyes narrowed in concentration, his black hair curling around his neck in an endearing way that made her long to reach out and touch it. So far she hadn't quite dared.

She moved closer, casting a shadow across his work, and he looked up swiftly. "Hullo," she said rather breathlessly, trying to hide her nervousness, all the while listening to the pounding of her heart, the jumping of her nerves, her flat out panic that this was all going to end in disaster.

He stood up, looking at her for a moment, his face cool and expressionless. And then his eyes warmed. He reached for her, and without thinking she ran into his arms.

His mouth came down on hers with such casual, automatic intimacy that she knew it was going to be all right. She reached out and ran her fingers through the tangle of hair at the back of his neck. He drew back slightly, and his smile was brighter than the blazing sun.

"Hullo, yourself," he said. "I love you."

And winter was over at last.

SAFE BY HIS SIDE

Debra Webb

Many thanks to an outstanding guide, Lee Lewis,
for his superior knowledge of Smoky Mountain
trails, and to a terrific friend and
expert drawer of maps, JoAnn Reynolds.

A special thanks to Natashya Wilson,
a wonderful editor, for believing in my work
and giving me this opportunity. This book is
dedicated to the man who helped make all my
dreams come true—my wonderful husband, Nonie.

Prologue

"Failure in this assignment is almost a given," Victoria Colby told the investigator sitting on the other side of the immense oak desk that had once belonged to her late husband, James. "And should you choose to accept it, your life will be in constant danger—perhaps from more than one source," she added cautiously.

"I understand," Katherine Robertson replied.

Victoria eyed the young woman with more than skepticism—uncertainty...maybe.

Did she really understand?

Victoria wasn't so sure that she understood, herself. This was the most sensitive assignment the Colby Agency had undertaken in the ten years since she had assumed the helm. She'd been reluctant to take charge at first, but the small Chicago-based private investigations firm her husband had operated for the final years of his life had been near and dear to his heart. So Victoria had worked hard to make the agency the best in the business. It was the one thing she could still hold on to and feel close to James.

She passed a thin manila folder with a red "Top Secret" cover sheet on the front to the eager investigator, who immediately opened it to review the meager contents.

"Who does Jack Raine work for?" Katherine asked, glancing up only briefly.

"He used to work solely for the CIA, but four years ago he shrugged off the brass and became a contract agent. Since that time, he's worked for them all—NSA, DEA, CIA. He'd been under deep cover for the FBI for seventeen months when things went sour. The story is that he left the son of a prominent mob leader named Ballatore dead and an extraordinary sum of money missing."

"He turned?" Katherine looked from Victoria to the folder and back in disbelief. "A guy with a record like this?"

Victoria nodded slowly. She could hardly believe it herself. Jack Raine's work history might be restricted reading—which meant no significant details were available for their perusal—but his reputation was spotless, not to mention unparalleled. The man had every commendation his government could give him. Somehow, between the known and the unknown, things just didn't add up—at least, not for Raine's longtime friend Lucas Camp. Lucas had asked Victoria to take this assignment as a personal favor. Raymond Cuddahy, Lucas's boss and the new director of Special Operations, didn't like the idea of a civilian agency's involvement. He had, however, given his consent—eventually, and off the record.

Like Raine, Lucas had worked for the government in one capacity or another for most of his adult life. He had recruited Raine into the CIA and was probably the only man alive who'd had an up-close-and-personal relationship with the elusive Jack Raine. Both men now worked, in different roles, for a highly covert special operations unit created to provide support when all else failed.

Lucas had shared a cage with Victoria's husband as a

prisoner of war during Vietnam. The two men had helped each other to survive. And Lucas had been a key factor in Victoria's own survival in this cutthroat business after her husband's death. Had it not been for Lucas, the Colby Agency might have gone under long ago rather than becoming the elite organization it was today.

Victoria owed the man.

"It's your job to find out if he's turned." Victoria leaned forward and propped her elbows on her desk. She laced her fingers and rested her chin atop them. "And to bring him in, either way."

Without responding, Katherine turned her attention back to the file in her hands and frowned.

Victoria noted again what a lovely young woman Katherine was. She had only been with the agency for one year. At twenty-five, she still lacked the life experience Victoria usually preferred in her investigators, but Katherine was an especially quick study. Her looks were definitely deceiving. She had a model-perfect build, with long dark hair and even darker eyes. But beneath that pretty exterior lay the wit and intelligence of an excellent tracker. Instinct and guts—that's what had gotten Katherine noticed in recent months.

Victoria couldn't help wondering why such a beautiful young woman didn't seem to have much of a social life. Of course, the world was different now than it had been when Victoria was twenty-five. She studied the woman seated across from her. Perhaps Miss Robertson had the right idea, she mused. *Career first and foremost—and then maybe a husband and family later.* Those had been Katherine Robertson's exact words in her interview thirteen months ago, and she'd been true to her word. She concentrated on work with a determination Victoria seldom saw in a person her age.

"How did the Colby Agency end up with an assignment like this?" Katherine asked, breaking into Victoria's thoughts. "This case has federal jurisdiction written all over it."

"For six months Raine's own people have been unsuccessful in their attempts to bring him in. It's difficult to capture a man who, for all intents and purposes, doesn't exist. That—" Victoria gestured toward the folder Katherine held "—is all there is on Jack Raine. Each time his whereabouts have been locked on to, he's managed to slip through their fingers.

"Unfortunately, Raine knows too much about too many things to simply write him off. If he's turned, the government needs to know so they can defuse the situation. If he hasn't, then he needs protection. Ballatore wants him dead."

Katherine examined the one and only photograph the file contained of her target. "Well, if he's a criminal, he's certainly a handsome one," she said without looking up.

"He is that," Victoria agreed. With sky-blue eyes and sandy blond hair, Jack Raine was a breathtaking, lean and rugged six foot two. Victoria never doubted for one minute the other reputation Lucas had warned her followed Raine—lady-killer. But, beneath those devastatingly good looks, the man was a highly trained soldier, specializing in death and deception.

"Why me?" Katherine looked up, her surprise at being handed such an important assignment evident.

Victoria sighed. This was the part that bothered her most. "Raine is an infiltrator—the best in the business. He's spent the past twelve years of his life living on the edge, getting in and out of places no one else could. He's good, maybe too good. *If* you can find him, the extrication will be extremely risky. I have reason to believe that he's playing some sort of game—dropping clues like bread crumbs. It's more than possible that the few times he has been located were intentional. We might not get so lucky this time.''

Victoria paused a beat before she continued. ''To answer your question as to why you were selected for this assignment, you're a woman, and you're young and beautiful. That will get you closer than anyone else in our agency. The fact that you don't have a great deal of field experience will probably keep you alive.''

Katherine arched a dark eyebrow. ''How do you figure that?''

''If Jack Raine suspects for one second that you're tracking him, he won't take the time to find out which side sent you.''

''Oh.'' Katherine dropped her gaze to the folder in her lap and studied it for a moment. ''I see.''

Victoria straightened and leveled a serious gaze on the Colby Agency's newest investigator. ''I'll understand completely if you choose to decline. I'd never ask one of my people to take a job they didn't feel comfortable with.'' She drew in a heavy breath and added, ''I have to admit, Katherine, this one worries me, but you're our best shot at getting close to this guy.'' And Lucas is depending on me, she didn't add.

As Victoria had anticipated, Katherine met her gaze with a determined one of her own and, without the slightest hint of misgivings, asked, ''When do I start?''

IGNORING THE DRIZZLING November rain that dampened her hair and chilled her to the bone, Katherine tossed the one duffel bag she'd allowed herself into her rented car. She checked her small shoulder bag once more to confirm that a full prescription of her heart medication was there. She shook the small bottle of pills and smiled. She was definitely ready. Her little secret would be safe as long as she took her medicine and steered clear of an in-depth physical examination until she had proven herself. Then it wouldn't matter, the agency would keep her anyway. She had worked too hard for this opportunity to lose it because she couldn't measure up to someone else's perception of acceptable physical condition.

Finding Jack Raine hadn't been as difficult as she'd imagined it would be. It had taken her only two weeks to pinpoint his location based on the latest information Lucas had given her. It seemed almost too easy. She wondered if Jack planned it that way. Did he savor the chase?

Catch me if you can?

She shook her head at the thought of the kind of man who would get his jollies that way. What purpose could it possibly serve for him to yank around the very system for which he had once worked? Something just wasn't right. Katherine had that feeling—the one her father called cop's instincts. Except she wasn't a cop. She had failed the required physical. The same type required by the Colby Agency for investigators. But Katherine had already been employed by the agency as a researcher, so she had delayed the appointment after her promotion. Now all she had to do was prove herself. Then the results of the physical wouldn't matter.

After arriving in Gatlinburg the afternoon before, Katherine had checked into a hotel. Within a few hours of her arrival she had located Raine's residence and done a little advance scouting.

His place was the typical Smoky Mountain retreat, a rustic rental cabin that probably had a fabulous view of the surrounding mountains and valleys. The place sat a good two miles off the blacktop in a particularly remote area.

The rendezvous point and estimated time of arrival had been arranged with Nick. All was go.

Katherine slid behind the wheel of the green Ford Taurus and checked her reflection in the mirror. She swiped the raindrops from her face and immediately banished the flicker of uncertainty she caught in her eyes. This was her big chance—she wasn't about to blow it by getting cold feet.

"You can do this, Robertson," she whispered sternly.

Despite her dislike of the reasons she'd been chosen for the assignment, she intended to make the best of it. She might be young and she might be new, but she was a damn good investigator and tracker. And she intended to prove that her physical limitations wouldn't hold her back.

Nick didn't approve. And her father would likely blow a fuse when he found out. But by then it would be a done deal and they would both see.

She could do this.

She would do it.

Katherine started the engine, set the transmission to Reverse and put her plan in motion.

Thirty minutes later, the drizzle and the fog making the curvy mountain road even more treacherous, Katherine neared her destination. She quickly reviewed her strategy one last time, then took three slow deep breaths to calm her racing heart. She assured herself once more that she could do this.

Katherine spotted the sudden movement on the highway in front of her too late. She slammed on the brakes and swerved hard to the right. She felt the wheels lock. Heard the squeal of tires.

And then everything went black.

Chapter One

Jack Raine jerked his front door open and stared down at the drenched woman standing on his deck. The freezing precipitation had gone from bad to worse in the last hour, and she appeared to have gotten the worst end of it. He had lived in this remote location for over a month without a visitor and he damn sure didn't want one now. This wasn't the sort of place that attracted door-to-door salespeople or that a passerby merely stumbled onto.

"If you're lucky," he said roughly, "you're lost."

The woman drew back a step at his brusque tone. "I'm...I had an accident," she stammered.

"Accident? Let's see some ID," he demanded. He would never understand why anyone would be out on a crappy morning like this. In the mountains, days like these weren't fit for man or beast. And whoever his visitor was, she certainly didn't fit either category. She didn't even have on a coat. "Where the hell's your coat?"

"What?" The woman stared up at him as if his question made no sense at all.

For the first time, Raine noted the dazed look in her dark eyes. Her arms were wrapped around her waist, and she swayed slightly before she caught herself. With one trembling hand she pushed long, dark strands of hair from her face. Rivulets of water slid down her pale cheeks. A blast of cold November wind whipped across the deck. She shivered. And damned if her teeth didn't chatter as well.

Raine swore under his breath and yanked her inside. This was the last thing he needed. He slammed the door and stared down at the trembling female with complete irritation and utter distrust. She was dripping wet from head to toe.

"I—I just need to use your phone," she said weakly. Her frail attempt to free herself from his grasp only served to send her swaying backward. When he steadied her, she almost wilted in his arms.

"Whoa," Raine said, concerned. "You need to get out of those wet clothes and warmed up before you do anything else."

"The phone…I just need to use the phone," she whispered before she closed her eyes and sagged against his chest.

Instantly he felt the wet and cold invade the warmth of his dry clothes. Raine blew out a breath of frustration and did the only thing he could—he picked her up and carried her to the bathroom. He had to get this lady warmed up fast. As cold as she was, shock and hypothermia represented definite threats. Concern overrode his usual self-preservation instincts.

He settled her on the closed lid of the toilet and watched for a moment to ensure that she wasn't going to fall over. She shivered uncontrollably. He crouched in front of her and removed her hiking boots and rolled off her socks. She sat there, seemingly unaware of his movements.

Raine opened the shower door and twisted the hot-water valve to wide open. Once the water was steaming, he adjusted it to a bearable but still plenty hot temperature.

"Okay, lady, let's see if we can't get your body temperature headed in the right direction,'' he muttered more to himself than to her. If she heard him, she didn't react.

Raine pulled the dazed woman to a standing position and then helped her into the shower. When the hot water hit her she gasped, shuddered violently and sagged against the translucent glass wall. Before Raine could catch her, she slumped to the tile floor, the water spraying directly on her face.

''Damn,'' he growled. He reached inside and tried to pull her to her feet, she only whimpered and huddled more deeply into a fetal position. Muttering expletives, Raine stepped into the cubicle and pulled her to her feet, then wished to hell he had turned off the water first. Too late now. Besides, she needed the heat a lot more than he needed comfort.

''You have to get out of these clothes,'' he told her. Liquid heat pelted his skin through his flannel shirt.

She lifted her hands to her blouse and worked on a button, her movements stiff and awkward. Raine swore under his breath. At this rate, she'd never get her clothes off. Raising her body temperature was top priority. He had hoped to allow her some privacy during the process. But if she couldn't do it, he'd just have to do it for her.

What the hell? He'd undressed plenty of women in the past. He pushed her hands away and deftly began to release the remaining buttons.

She jerked back and stared up at him. He could see that it took her a while to bring him into focus. ''What are you doing?'' she asked weakly and clutched at his hands. Her pupils were unevenly dilated.

He cursed through clenched teeth.

Concussion.

She had a damn concussion. Why hadn't he noticed that before? He knew the signs. Her left temple was bruised.

Gingerly he touched the discolored spot. She winced and drew away but not before he felt the size of the lump that had formed there.

"We need to take the rest of your clothes off. We have to get you warm and into something dry," he said as he resumed the unbuttoning process. To his relief, her hands fell away and she made no further protest.

"Thank you," she said softly, her breath whispering across his downturned face.

Raine tightened his jaw. He wouldn't say she was welcome—because she wasn't. He didn't want her here... didn't need her here. But he couldn't just let her die out in the cold any more than he could neglect an injured animal. He looked at the woman silently watching his fingers undo the final button of her blouse and wondered if he was making a big mistake.

He peeled the wet blouse down her arms and pitched it to the bathroom floor. Steam billowed around them and sweat beaded on his forehead as he reached for the hem of her undershirt. She automatically lifted her arms and closed her eyes. When he pulled the undershirt over her shoulders and then her head, he tensed. The scrap of cotton slipped from his fingers and joined her blouse on the wet tile floor.

Raine's gaze riveted to her naked breasts. Not particularly large breasts, but they were nicely rounded and the rosy tips tilted slightly upward. He had the sudden, insane urge to draw one into his mouth and taste it.

She shivered and he forced his gaze back to her face only to find her watching him from beneath half-closed lids. Her lips parted and for one instant Raine allowed himself to want her, but then she whispered, "I'm so cold."

Raine turned his back and silently cursed himself for the

bastard he was. "You can do the rest," he said harshly. Surely she could get her jeans off. Hell, she probably could have gotten the blouse off if he'd given her time. Perverted SOB, he cursed himself once more.

What the hell had gotten into him? It hadn't been that long since he'd had a woman. Ogling an injured female was about as low as a man could go. A muscle in his tense jaw jumped when he heard her small sounds of frustration and fatigue as she struggled with the wet jeans. Raine clenched his fists and ignored the urge to turn around and look at her. The spray of hot water on his chest did nothing to calm his mounting tension or the hard-on he had acquired in the last sixty seconds.

He flinched when she touched his rigid shoulder. "I can't do it," she said wearily.

Raine licked his lips and swallowed tightly. This was damn ridiculous. He'd seen more than his share of naked women, what the hell was the big deal with this one?

He turned around slowly and met her pleading gaze with an annoyed glare.

"I'm sorry," she managed to say weakly before collapsing against the shower wall.

Raine set his jaw so hard he thought his teeth would crack. He grasped the waistband on either side of her slender hips and tried without success to peel the material down as he'd done with the blouse, but the tight-fitting jeans wouldn't cooperate. He sucked in a deep breath and did what he knew he had to. Raine pushed his hands inside and worked the material, panties included, down over her icy skin.

She was lucky to be alive. The last time he'd touched skin this cold, it had belonged to a dead man.

As chilled as her body was, his was getting more heated by the moment. His groin tightened painfully when his hands moved over the swell of her hips and glided down several inches of thigh. He straightened, held her firmly by the waist, placed his bare foot between her legs and pushed the jeans and skimpy panties down to her ankles. He immediately averted his gaze from the triangle of dark curls between her thighs.

He almost groaned. He'd been in these woods longer than he'd realized.

She braced both hands against his chest while she struggled to kick her feet free of the soggy material.

"Thank you," she murmured on a frail breath when she'd finally freed herself. She squeezed her eyes shut and swayed back against the wall.

Raine kicked the jeans to one side. "No sweat," he lied.

He knew the hot water wouldn't hold out much longer, so he stripped off his own shirt, pulled her against him and turned her back to the hot spray. She sucked in a sharp breath and clung to him helplessly. He bit the inside of his jaw to stifle the groan that rose in his throat at the feel of her firm breasts pressed into his chest.

Damn, this woman was going to kill him and she didn't even have a weapon.

They stood in the steamy shower until the water began to cool and her shivers had subsided. Raine held her steady with one arm while he turned off the water. He guided her out and helped her dry. He focused intently on the job rather than the peach-colored skin flushed from the hot shower.

He used another towel to squeeze her long, thick hair dry. Neither spoke during the drying process. Raine refused to acknowledge how good her made-for-loving body looked. Curvy and firm, yet soft. Tall, but not too tall, with long, shapely legs. Chestnut-brown hair and dark chocolate eyes—eyes that would surely darken even more with passion.

When her hair was as dry as it was going to get without a blow-dryer, Raine wrapped a clean towel around her and tucked the corner beneath her arm. He quickly dried his chest and arms and tossed his towel to the floor, then swiped his wet feet.

She gazed up at him with those dark, shimmering eyes, a ghost of a smile touched her lips. "I feel much warmer now."

Before he could respond, her knees buckled and Raine barely caught her before she hit the floor. He drew her into his arms and carried her into the bedroom. After depositing her on the bed, he rummaged through the chest of drawers until he came up with a bulky sweatshirt. It would fit more like a dress on her, but it would have to do. Besides, he decided, beggars couldn't be choosers. He looked at his unwelcome visitor as he retraced his steps to the bed. At the moment she didn't look as if she cared about much one way or another.

"Hold up your arms," he ordered. She obeyed and Raine immediately regretted his command. With her arms extended above her head, the towel fell away from her upper body, giving him another good look at her perfect breasts.

Raine shoved the sweatshirt sleeves onto her arms and then pushed the neck opening over her head with a bit more force than was necessary. She winced as the material slid down her face.

"Dammit," he muttered. He'd hurt her, and all because he couldn't prevent his body's reaction to hers. Raine stepped to the side of the bed and drew back the covers. When he had readjusted the irritating bulge in his wet pants, he walked back to the foot of the bed and lifted the woman into his arms. She pressed her cheek to his chest and closed her eyes. He frowned when his heart skipped a beat or two at the feel of her soft cheek against his skin. What the hell was wrong with him? He didn't usually get so worked up over a blasted female.

Raine placed her in the middle of the bed and covered her with every blanket and quilt he could find. He stalked into the great room, fingered the thermostat to a higher setting, then placed several logs on the fire. He stoked the blaze until he was satisfied that it wouldn't go out for a while. Then he trudged back to the bedroom and adjusted the blinds to let in the warm glow from the sun that had finally broken through the thick clouds hanging in the sky. The rain had stopped.

The newscast had said that the temperature would reach a pleasant forty degrees today, if the clouds cleared. Raine blew out a disgusted breath and turned back to the bed.

There was no telling how far his mystery guest had walked before she had stumbled upon his place. Raine had picked this particular cabin because of its seclusion. With the high volume of tourists floating in and out of Gatlinburg, his was just another face in the crowd on the rare occasions that he went into town. The last thing he had expected way out here was company.

As soon as he was sure the woman was out for the count, he'd put on dry clothes and take a ride to check out her vehicle. There would likely be some form of identification in her car. He wanted to verify her accident story as well, for his own peace of mind. She certainly seemed harmless enough, but Raine hadn't survived this long by letting his guard down—even for a beautiful woman in distress.

If she had merely had an accident and showed up at his door for help, she had nothing to worry about. He'd keep an eye on her and rouse her every couple of hours just to be safe. When she awoke, he would drive her into town and drop her off at the emergency room. He had enough medical training to know she would probably be fine, but medical attention wouldn't hurt.

If *anything* at all appeared suspicious about her ID or the means by which she had arrived at his door, she wouldn't need medical attention—she'd need an undertaker.

HER EYES OPENED and she blinked to focus. She stared at the white ceiling for a long time before it occurred to her to try to move. Her head ached and felt oddly heavy. She licked her lips. Her mouth was as dry as sandpaper and she could hardly swallow.

On her left, sunlight poured into the room from a large window, spreading its golden glow across deep green carpet. The bright light hurt her eyes, but at the same time felt good against her face. She was tired and it was quiet. Maybe she should just go back to sleep, she thought, her eyes closing of their own accord.

"How's your head?"

She snapped her eyes open and jerked her attention to the right, toward the deep male voice. Every aching muscle in her body tensed, and her head screamed in protest of the sudden move.

He sat in a chair a few feet away, watching her. She blinked and then frowned. Did she know this man? He looked vaguely familiar. She inspected his features more closely. Blond hair, light blue eyes. His face was lean and angular, exceptionally handsome. He seemed tall, but it was hard to tell with him sitting down. Still, she couldn't put a name with his face. What had he asked her? Her head…yes…*how was her head?*

"It…" She cleared her rusty voice and tried again. "It hurts."

"My guess is that you have a concussion. You probably need to see a doctor. I'll take you into town to the hospital."

He didn't sound as if he relished the idea. She wondered if this man had some reason to dislike her. She pushed up into a sitting position and the room spun wildly for a sickening moment. Her stomach roiled. She groaned and rested her head in her hands.

"Where am I?" she asked in a thready whisper.

"Don't you know?"

She thought about that for a while, but no matter how hard she tried to form an answer she couldn't. She had no idea where she was. She shook her head and immediately regretted it.

"Your license says Virginia. Is that where you're from?"

Virginia? Was she from Virginia? She should know where she was from. If her license said so, then she must be. "Yes," she finally told him for lack of a better answer.

He didn't speak again for a while, but his intense gaze never left her. His close scrutiny made her uneasy. "Who are you?" she ventured hesitantly.

"What's *your* name?" he asked, ignoring her question.

"What?" That was a ridiculous question. He'd seen her license, he should know her name without asking. She scanned the room once more. Besides, why would she be in a strange man's bedroom? He must know who she was. He had to be playing a joke of some sort. Well, she didn't want to play. Her head ached.

"Tell me your name," he repeated sternly.

She opened her mouth to speak, but nothing came. She frowned and snapped it closed. Her name…what was her name? She had to know her own name. Panic slid through her veins.

Everyone knows their name.

She threw the covers back and stood too quickly, only to plop back onto the bed. As soon as the dizziness had passed, she stood again, a bit more slowly this time. "I have to go," she announced as calmly as she could. She concentrated on putting one foot in front of the other. She had to get out of here. Away from this man. Away from his questions.

"Your name is Denise."

She silently tested the name as she took another step toward the door. *Denise.* It didn't ring a bell, but if that's what her license said… "Yes, that's it."

He snagged her arm and pulled her around to face him. He shook his head and swore, an ugly four-letter word. "Then why does your driver's license say Kate?"

How had he moved up behind her so quickly, so quietly? Why was he holding her arm so tight? "I…I don't know," she stammered, her voice faltered as fear mushroomed inside her.

He pulled something from his pocket and placed it in her hand. A driver's license. "That's you." He pointed to the picture. "Kate Roberts."

She stared at the picture, concentrating. Was that her? She suddenly realized that she didn't know what she looked like. Hysteria bubbled up in her throat. How could she not know what she looked like? She jerked free of his grasp and half ran, half stumbled to the dresser. She peered at her reflection in the mirror.

Terror gripped her. She didn't recognize the face staring back at her. She moistened her lips and swallowed tightly. She looked at the reflection again, mentally inventorying the details. Dark hair and eyes, pale skin. She looked at the picture on the driver's license once more. It was the same face. Kate Roberts, she read. *Kate.* That sounded right.

"Your clothes should be dry by now. When you're dressed, I'll take you to the hospital." He started toward the door.

"Wait," she called after him. When he faced her, she asked, "Why don't I know my name? Is there something wrong with me?" The panic tightened like a steel band around her chest now. She braced her left hand against the dresser for support. The license dropped from her slack hold as her right hand fluttered to her throat where her breath had caught.

He hesitated, seeming uncertain of how to answer. "You were in a car accident. It looks as if you hit a deer. I think maybe you bumped your head pretty hard." He shrugged. "They'll be able to help you at the hospital."

She released the breath she'd been holding as she watched him disappear. She turned all the way around in the large bedroom then. Absolutely nothing looked familiar. She noticed the bathroom door open and walked slowly in that direction. At least she knew she had to relieve herself, that was something.

After she'd taken care of necessary business, she picked up a comb from the vanity and fought with the tangles in her hair. She stared at her reflection. "Kate," she whispered. She looked like a Kate—didn't she?

When she was satisfied with the state of her hair, Kate walked sluggishly back into the bedroom. She found that if she didn't move too quickly, the dizziness didn't overwhelm her. The man stood quietly waiting for her. He'd piled jeans, panties, T-shirt, socks, shoes and a wrinkled blouse on the bed.

"The sooner you're dressed the sooner you'll get the medical attention you need."

"Thank you," she murmured. Kate moved to the bed and inspected the stack of clothing. Were these the kind of things she liked to wear? She had no idea.

Kate heard the door close and she looked around to find herself alone. She pulled off the huge sweatshirt and tossed it on the bed. After donning the panties, socks and jeans, she pulled on the T-shirt. Kate reached for the wrinkled blouse, but thought better of it. She'd just keep the warm sweatshirt. She sat on the edge of the bed and tugged on the high-top boots.

Kate picked up the driver's license and tucked it into the pocket of her stiff jeans. She looked at herself again in the mirror and summoned her courage. A doctor would know why she couldn't remember who she was. Everything would be fine just as soon as she got to the hospital.

Kate firmed her resolve and went in search of the man who had promised to take her to help. She found him in the great room warming by the fire. He'd already pulled on his coat. He stepped to the sofa and picked up a parka and a small purse. "These were in your car."

Kate accepted the items and draped the long, narrow strap of the purse over her shoulder, then pulled on the tan-colored coat. The sweatshirt hit the tops of her thighs, the coat only came to her waist. What a fashion statement, Kate mused. But at the moment, she truly didn't care. Remembering the license, she stored it in the purse.

"Do you know what these are?" he asked, holding out what appeared to be an unlabeled prescription bottle for her inspection.

Kate took the bottle and twisted off the cap. She peered at the small blue pills it contained, then shrugged as she

recapped it. "Are they mine?" She met his watchful gaze.
Why did he look at her like that?

"They were in your purse, so I would assume they belong to you." He plucked the bottle from her hand and
jammed it into his coat pocket. "There was a duffel bag
in the trunk, I've already put it in my Jeep. Are you
ready?"

"I'm ready," she told him, somehow as anxious to be
away from him as he appeared to want to relieve himself
of her. Though she didn't quite feel threatened, something
about him made her uneasy.

Katherine followed the man out into the cold sunshine.
It looked to be late afternoon. The sun hovered just above
the tops of the evergreen trees surrounding the cabin and
the small clearing. A gravel driveway veered down the
slope and off into the woods. Did she know this place?
Had she been here before? With him? Her gaze darted to
the handsome stranger who appeared to be her reluctant
savior.

He reached to open the door of his Jeep, but hesitated.
He cocked his head and listened, his gaze narrowed.
"Damn," he muttered and quickly shoved her against the
closed door.

"What's wrong?" she asked, frowning at the throb in
her head generated by his sudden move. Then she heard it
too. The distinct sound of gravel crunching beneath tires.

He spouted another curse and then turned to her, his
gaze fierce. "Listen to me, Kate," he said harshly. "If
that's who I think it is, we're in deep sh—"

"I don't understand," she broke in, fear snaking around
her chest and squeezing like a boa constrictor.

"Listen," he growled, giving her a little shake. "They
won't hesitate to kill both of us, do you understand *that?*"

Kate nodded, ignoring the intense ache it caused. She

couldn't breathe…she couldn't think. Kill them both? What was he talking about? Why would anyone want to kill her?

Call in…

The phrase flitted through her mind. What did it mean? Oh, God. What was happening? Her panic was complete now, fueled by her inability to comprehend the situation. She shuddered against it. Closed her eyes to make it go away.

His hands were under her sweatshirt, probing the waistband of her jeans. Kate snapped her eyes open. "What are you doing?" she cried, tears burning behind her lids.

"Kate, you're our only chance at surviving this little party." He captured her gaze with his, and the sheer determination there forced her to pay attention. "This—" he shoved something hard and cold that she somehow recognized immediately as a gun into her waistband. She instinctively recoiled, but he caught her by the waist and held her still "—is our only chance." His cold blue gaze pierced hers. The feel of his roughened palm against her bare skin felt strangely soothing. "Just listen to me, and when the time comes, do what I tell you—don't hesitate—just do it no matter what it is. Can you do that?"

Before Kate could respond, a car skidded to a halt right beside them. Two men jumped out of the black sedan, big, ugly guns in hand.

Oh, God. They were going to die. And Kate didn't even know why. How had she gotten in the middle of all this? She lifted her gaze to the man standing beside her. What had this man done to deserve to be hunted down like this? Wary and uncertain as to how to react, she aimed her attention at the two men stalking purposely toward them.

"Well, well, Danny, looks as if we've found our man," the larger of the two men said with a sneer. He waved his gun and added tauntingly, "And it looks as if he's got the little woman with him, too."

The man beside her shifted his body closer to hers. "She's just a lay I picked up in town last night."

Instinctively, Kate started to refute his words, but before she could speak, the goon with the gun moved closer.

Vinny grabbed her purse from beneath her jacket and looked inside, fishing out her license. "She looks a little worse for wear." He winked at Kate and shoved license and purse back at her. "What'd you do, Rick, ride her all night?"

Rick... His name was Rick. Kate looked at the man standing next to her and tested the name. She frowned. He didn't really look like a Rick. But what did she know?

"Maybe she's still got a little fun left in her." The goon moved closer, snagging Kate's chin in his beefy hand.

Kate gasped. Rick pushed between them. "Don't touch her," he warned in a voice so deadly it sent shivers skipping down her spine.

"You ain't in no position to be giving orders, Ricky boy. Pat him down, Danny," he directed the other goon.

Rick stood stone-still while the man named Danny frisked him. The whole scene took on a surreal quality. It suddenly occurred to Kate that this was just like in the movies. Two big guys in black suits arrived in a black sedan carrying scary black guns and...*she was going to die*.

The urge to vomit burned at the back of her throat. Kate fought the impulse. She felt certain that such a move would not endear her to these men. If they thought she was sick they might just shoot her on the spot.

"That's it, Vinny," Danny announced as he handed the other man a gun that looked very much like the one they both carried.

Rick had been carrying that gun. Kate suddenly recalled that she, too, carried a gun. Did it look like that? She tried not to breathe too deeply now, remembering the cold steel object tucked into her jeans. Her head throbbed insistently.

"How the mighty hath fallen," Vinny sneered, the words filled with sheer hatred. He stepped closer, until he was toe to toe with Rick. Vinny stood there for a long moment and stared before he spat in Rick's face.

"You don't deserve to live another minute. If I didn't have strict orders to take you to Dillon, I'd kill you myself, right now." Vinny's mouth twisted in anger. "But the old man, he wants you to look him in the eye and tell him what you did. Otherwise I would do you right here."

Rick rubbed his hand over his face to rid himself of the man's spittle, then cocked his blond head. "What's stopping you, Vinny? I won't tell if you don't," he said in a patronizing tone.

"Shut up, you piece of crap," Vinny bellowed as he shoved the tip of his gun barrel under Rick's chin. "I might forget orders for once."

Kate's heart almost shuddered to a stop then, but Rick only laughed derisively. "Don't kid yourself, Vinny, you're a made guy all the way down to your Gucci loafers. You don't take a piss without orders."

"Get in the frigging car." Vinny shoved Rick in the direction of the sedan.

Rick pulled Kate close to his side. She didn't have time to decide if being near him was a relief or not. Gun barrels stuck in their backs, Kate and Rick were ushered forward.

"You, up front," Vinny said, and propelled Kate toward Danny.

Danny half dragged her to the passenger side of the car and pushed her inside. Kate glanced at Rick in the back seat. She wondered if he had a plan. She hoped he had a plan. Was the gun in her waistband part of that plan?

Once Danny slid behind the wheel, they headed down the sloping driveway. Kate took one last look around her in hopes of remembering something, anything, but nothing came.

She studied the driver. He appeared young and almost innocent upon first inspection, early twenties maybe, but he looked as mean as a junkyard dog on closer examination. She listened to the heated conversation between the two men in back. Rick—the name still felt strange— goaded the other man unnecessarily, in Kate's opinion. It looked as if he intended to get them both killed long before they reached a destination.

"How does it feel to know you slept with a killer?"

Kate jerked her head up and stared at the driver, Danny, who'd directed the question at her. "What?"

"Didn't he tell you?" he quizzed with a widening grin. "Rick's a cold-blooded killer. There's no telling how many men he's killed. Hundreds, I'd guess."

Kate moved her head slowly from side to side in denial of his words. Why was he telling her this? She didn't want to hear it.

"Well, it's true." He shot her a sidelong smirk. "But he's going to pay now."

Could she possibly believe anything this man told her? Who were these people? She closed her eyes. Maybe he was only taunting her, trying to scare her. He didn't need to do that, she was already scared to death. God, her head hurt.

Call in…

The words skittered across her mind again. What did they mean? *Call who?*

"Too bad you had to be in the wrong place at the wrong

time, baby," Vinny said as he kicked the back of Kate's seat.

"Kate's a lifesaver," Rick remarked wryly. "She gave me a second chance."

"A second chance at coming, maybe," Vinny scoffed. "Kate?"

Kate tensed at the sound of Rick's voice when he said her name. The tiny hairs on the back of her neck stood on end. Something was about to happen.

"Remember what I told you, Kate. You're my only chance," Rick said slowly. "*Our* only chance."

"Shut your frigging mouth," Vinny commanded. Kate heard the grunt that followed a hollow thud, knowing that Rick had just been whacked across the abdomen by the goon in the back seat.

Kate's head swam. What was she supposed to do? How could she save them? She could feel the cold steel jabbing into her pelvis. What did he want her to do?

And suddenly she knew.

Slowly, while keeping a close watch on the driver, she eased her right hand across her thigh and under her sweatshirt. With a swiftness that shocked even her, she drew the gun and expertly pointed it at the driver's head. She even held it with both hands just as she'd seen in the movies.

"Stop the car," she commanded in a voice she hardly recognized.

"What the hell?" Danny shouted, almost losing control of the speeding car.

"Give me that gun, bitch, or I'll blow your man's head off!" Vinny barked.

"Squeeze the trigger, Kate," Rick ordered coolly.

Kate looked from Rick to the man driving the car. Was he insane? She couldn't do that? How could she do that?

"Gimme the gun!" Vinny roared, pressing the barrel of his own gun hard into Rick's temple.

Kate's eyes darted back and forth between the men. What was she supposed to do? Everyone was yelling at once. Danny shot her quick, nervous glances, his knuckles white as he clutched the wheel. Vinny screamed vulgarities alternately at her and Rick. The car careened faster and faster down the winding mountain road, yet the events inside the vehicle seemed to lapse into slow motion.

"Squeeze the damn trigger, Kate! Now!"

The car suddenly swerved, Kate squeezed, the gun fired and all hell broke loose. She could hear the muffled curses and grunts of pain as Rick and Vinny wrestled for control of the gun. Danny struggled with the steering wheel, trying to pull the car out of its tailspin. A slim shaft of sunlight poured in through the small hole the bullet had made in the car's roof. Kate peered at the perfect circle in total amazement and then at the man fighting the inertia pulling the car round and round.

As if she had done this sort of thing all her life, Kate pressed the barrel of the gun to the driver's perspiring temple and said, "Stop the damn car or I'll blow your head off."

When the car skidded to a sideways stop in the middle of the road, Danny immediately stuck his hands up in the air. *Just like in the movies,* Kate thought again, a faint smile tugging at her trembling lips.

"Put your weapon on the floor and kick it under the seat, then get out of the car."

It was Rick's voice. He had Vinny's gun now.

"You heard him," Kate told Danny, her aim still level with his forehead. God, this was amazing. Had she done this before?

The two goons got out. Rick marched them to the edge

of the blacktop. Kate followed behind him, her gun hanging at her side from a hand that had long since gone limp with aftereffects.

Rick cocked his head to one side, lifted his weapon and took aim. "Now run!"

"Hey, man, we can work this out—" Vinny began nervously.

"Run!" Rick roared.

"You're not going to kill them?" Kate shrieked.

Gunfire erupted and Kate gasped. She squeezed her eyes shut and dropped to her knees on the cold, hard pavement. *Oh, God.* She clamped her hand over her mouth to prevent the scream that twisted her throat. She didn't want to see this. Didn't want to be a part of it. Had no idea how she had gotten involved in it.

"Let's go."

Kate forced her eyes open, expecting to see two dead bodies lying in the ditch.

No one…no bodies.

She looked up at Rick. "I thought you shot them," she croaked.

He grinned, a dangerous yet ridiculously sexy widening of his lips. Kate shivered at the insane turn her thoughts had suddenly taken.

"Who says I didn't?" He grabbed her arm and pulled her to her feet.

Kate stood on shaky legs and stole another glance at the thick woods beyond the ditch. She still saw no bodies. She settled her gaze back on the face of the man guiding her back to the car. Savior or crucifier, she wondered.

"What do we do now?" she asked, her voice thin.

He opened the car door. One eyebrow quirked when he swung that intense blue gaze back on hers. He lifted the weapon from her loose grip and said, "We get the hell out of Dodge."

Chapter Two

Raine mentally reviewed every move he had made in the last four weeks as he drove like a bat out of hell down the steep mountain road. How had Ballatore's hired guns found him? He hadn't made a single mistake—he never did. The two times he had been found by Lucas's men in the last six months were intentional. Allowing only a glimpse, he had wanted Lucas to know that he was alive. The man deserved that, if nothing else. Raine couldn't quite bring himself to believe that Lucas was the leak who had blown his cover and almost gotten him killed.

But it was definitely someone in Lucas's organization. Raine knew that for certain now. He had called Lucas's private voice mail only three days ago and left the number to a downtown Gatlinburg pay phone. The information had to have filtered down to Ballatore—there was no other way the old man could have known to look here for Raine. But how many were involved in working Raine's case? Cuddahy, Lucas's boss, for sure, and at least three other special ops agents. Raine would have to find a way to narrow down that tight little group. But right now he had to concentrate on not getting caught.

Raine groaned when a stab of pain knifed through his

gut. Vinny hadn't broken anything, but he had damn sure given Raine something to remember him by.

Steering the car onto Highway 321, Raine decided his best course of action would be to get out of Gatlinburg in a hurry. He would worry about dumping the car and picking up another means of transportation farther down the road. It would take Vinny and his sidekick a while to walk down to civilization. Not much traffic found its way to where he had left them. And even if someone did come along, no way would they pick up two strange men—especially a couple of guys who looked like refugees from Alcatraz.

He should have killed them, but he hadn't. *She* had distracted him. He glanced at the woman clinging to the passenger-side door. He never allowed anyone to distract him. Raine could analyze that bit of irony later.

He estimated he had about two hours before a new and much more intense search began. Maybe he'd get lucky and Vinny would get lost in the woods and freeze before finding help. "Scumbags," Raine muttered.

"You…you were going to drop me off at the emergency room."

Raine snapped his head in the direction of the small, hesitant voice. She trembled beneath his irritated glare. He forced his gaze back to the road and the ever-increasing traffic as they headed south on 441 and into Gatlinburg proper.

What was he going to do with her? If he let her go, *they* would find her and kill her. A professional never left loose ends. If he took her with him, she could easily be caught in the crossfire and wind up dead anyway. Raine set his jaw and considered his options. He didn't owe this woman a damn thing, but if she ended up wearing a toe tag it would be his fault.

He released a frustrated breath. Kate Roberts was an innocent bystander in his world of death and mayhem and Jack Raine didn't off innocents—directly or indirectly. She was his responsibility now whether he liked it or not, and he sure didn't like it. If he kept Kate with him, she had a chance of surviving, slim though it might be.

Slim? Who the hell was he kidding? *Anorexic* would be a more accurate description. Raine knew the odds of his being able to evade capture much longer without doing a permanent disappearing act. And they weren't good, especially now.

But he had to find that leak. To do that, he couldn't afford to get caught—at least not yet.

Raine no longer owed the government anything, but he did owe it to the other men, like himself, who put their lives on the line for that government. Contract agents were especially vulnerable since the very agencies that hired them denied them when an assignment went south. If a leak existed at a high enough level to have access to Raine's assignments, then no one was safe.

He snatched another glimpse of the woman in the passenger seat. Kate would just have to come along for the ride until he could tuck her away someplace safe.

"I'm afraid there's been a change of plans," he told her. He might as well get this over with. No point in keeping her in the dark.

"What do you mean?" she asked, her eyebrows knitted with concern. Her hands twisted together in her lap, her face looked pale and drawn.

She was scared to death, Raine decided after giving her another sidelong glance. "It would be a mistake for me to leave you behind. These people don't like loose ends and you're definitely a loose end."

"I don't understand." The pitch of Kate's voice rose

steadily. "You said I needed medical attention…I don't understand," she repeated.

Raine cursed under his breath when he saw tears slip down her cheeks. He had no tolerance for crying females. What the hell had he done to deserve this? Raine swallowed the hard, bitter answer that climbed into his throat. He knew what he'd done. He'd sold his soul a long time ago and now he was going to pay for it, in the form of a weepy female amnesiac.

A tiny sound, almost a sob broke loose from Kate, jerking Raine from his reverie. "There are a lot more guys like Vinny after me—a helluva lot more—if any of them get their hands on you, medical attention won't do you any good." He shot her a fierce glare. "That's just the way it is, so shut up and let me think."

Raine focused his full attention on the road before him. The next town with transportation possibilities was his destination. He had to get somewhere—anywhere—as fast he could without taking a chance on speeding and drawing attention to himself. He couldn't allow any distractions, not Kate's whining or his own uneasiness. He had to concentrate on driving. He didn't have time to waste. This sedan would soon be a heavy liability.

KATE'S MIND RACED like an out-of-control roller coaster. She had to do something. This man, Rick, wasn't going to drop her off at the hospital as he'd promised. She should have known better than to trust him. Of course, her options had been limited. He certainly seemed considerably less threatening than the other two goons she'd met today. He was definitely the lesser of the evils.

But would he drag her along with him and get her killed? Kate might not remember her life, but she instinctively knew she wouldn't have a death wish if she did. She shot the man driving an assessing glance. And this guy certainly had himself some unsavory enemies. Kate had to think of something...something that would provide her with an avenue of escape.

If she could get away from this man, she could call the police and tell them everything. The police would get her to a doctor who could help her to regain her memory.

The harshness of that reality slammed into her with such force that it sucked the air right out of Kate's lungs. She didn't just not know her name—she didn't know anything. Where she was from, what she did for a living, whether she had any family. Nothing...she knew nothing.

"Oh, God," Kate muttered. Panic clawed at her throat, making her want to scream despite the knowledge that it would do her no good. Her heart pounded in her chest and her head ached unmercifully. She had to get out of here. A definitive click of the power door lock told her that he knew exactly what she was thinking.

Kate refused to look at him, afraid she'd give away her swiftly deteriorating condition. She had to calm down and think of a plan.

Any kind of plan.

Call in.

The words shook her with their intensity. That inner voice louder now, demanding action.

Call in, she repeated silently. "555–4911," she mumbled involuntarily. The numbers spilled from her mouth as naturally as breathing.

"What?" he demanded, his eyebrows crunched in irritation.

"I have to use the phone!" Kate blurted. "I have to...call in," she added more slowly.

"What the hell are you mumbling about?" he growled, glaring at her as he stopped for a traffic light.

"Rick, I have to—"

"Don't call me that," he warned.

Kate blinked, confused. "But those other men called you that."

"And look where it got them."

Kate stifled a gasp. Was he trying to shock her?

He chuckled and turned his attention back to the busy street. "You," he said, tossing her an unreadable look, "can call me Raine."

Fear trickled through Kate. *Raine.* She swallowed tightly. *Your life will be in constant danger.* Words, images, sensations crashed through her consciousness. Kate trembled with the effort of maintaining her composure under the mental assault. This man was dangerous. She didn't know how she knew, she just knew. And every moment she spent with him put her in danger. *Constant danger.*

She had to get away from him. "Please," she began in an unsteady voice. "You have to let me find a telephone."

"I don't have to let you do anything," he told her flatly, without ever taking his eyes from the road. "Besides, who will you call? You don't even remember who you are. Remember?" he taunted irritably.

"I...I remembered a number. I think maybe it's my mother's. Maybe she lives here and I was visiting her when I had my accident. I need to let her know that I'm okay," she pleaded with all the vulnerability and femininity she could muster. Kate had no idea if she even had a living mother, but neither did he.

"No." The single word was cold and emotionless.

Anger shot through her, but Kate tamped down the emotion. She had to approach Mr. Hardass with something a little different. Like an actress given her cue, Kate burst into tears. "Oh, please. You have to let me call. Maybe if

I can hear her voice it will help bring my memory back. Please," she pleaded.

Raine ignored her completely.

Kate moved on to plan B: she sobbed relentlessly. The occasional peek she dared take in his direction reassured her that she was winning the battle. Raine literally squirmed in his seat. She kept the theatrics going at a steady pace.

Hey, she thought, maybe I'm an actress.

"All right, all right. Just shut up, for Christ's sake." He plowed his hand through his hair. "One phone call and then I don't want to hear another peep from you."

"Thank you," Kate murmured humbly. She stared out at the passing landscape and gave herself a mental pat on the back. She allowed her tears to dry slowly, swiping her eyes occasionally for added effect. Kate was certain that this man was smarter than most; it would be better not to regain her composure too quickly. No point in risking his finding out that she had pushed his buttons to get what she wanted.

Maybe she was a psychologist, she mused, biting her lower lip to prevent a tiny smile.

A large visitors' center came into view up ahead on the right. Kate felt her hopes rising. Somehow she'd find a way to ditch him there. She could easily get lost in the crowd. Raine passed the center and her hopes plummeted.

"Why didn't you stop? You said I could have one phone call."

"Too crowded," he told her, keeping his gaze fixed straight ahead. "The fewer people who see us the better."

Kate huffed an indignant sound and crossed her arms over her chest. She leaned back in the seat and forced herself to relax. She had no choice but to acquiesce to his authority—she was, after all, his hostage. Kate frowned at the thought, but it was unfortunately accurate. For all intents and purposes she was the hostage of this Raine character.

He's the best in the business. The words echoed inside her aching skull. She glanced at the man driving and considered again if somehow she did know him. The best in the business of what? she wondered.

A strong profile defined the angular features of his handsome face. His forehead and nose were prominent, but not too much so. A strong chin and chiseled jaw finished out the lean lines. He wore his thick, sandy hair a little too long. And those eyes. Kate closed her own eyes and summoned the image of those stormy blue eyes. Among his many assets, including a strong, muscular body, Raine's eyes were definitely the most appealing. His personality, unquestionably the least.

Kate opened her eyes wide. What had gotten into her? There wasn't the first thing appealing about the man! He was hell-bent on getting her killed, and besides, her interest in him was purely professional.

Kate started. Her heart rate accelerated. *Professional.* She did know this man. Then why didn't he know her? Vivid images of her naked breasts pressed against his bare chest flashed through her mind. Him removing her clothes…his strong arms wrapped firmly around her. *In the shower.* Oh, God, they'd showered together—naked.

Oh, God. Raine had told the truth. She wasn't an actress or a psychologist. She was a bought-and-paid-for whore! Oh, God. Kate closed her eyes and willed the tears to retreat. Every fiber of her being rejected the idea. But what else could those snatches of memory mean?

Raine slowed the car and took a hard right. Kate blinked rapidly to clear her blurred vision. He parked the car in a slot in a large, vacant parking lot. As had been the case when she'd stepped out of his cabin that afternoon, they were surrounded by dense woods. Nothing looked even remotely familiar.

A large painted sign read Alum Cave Bluff Hiking Trail.

Kate didn't realize Raine had gotten out of the car until he opened her door. "Get a move on," he ordered in a military tone.

Kate dropped her feet to the pavement and pushed herself up and out of the car only to be slapped in the face by a cold blast of wind. She sucked in a sharp breath of frigid air and shivered. The only thing that kept her convinced that she hadn't died and gone to hell was the arctic chill of this damn place. At least it wasn't raining. She glanced around the unfamiliar area. In fact, it looked as if it hadn't rained here at all.

Raine ushered her toward a pay phone that looked strangely out of place in the deserted parking lot surrounded by trees. He picked up the receiver and listened for a dial tone.

"Okay," he said roughly. "You've got one minute and don't say anything you'll regret." He pulled some change from his pocket and thrust it at her, then leaned against one side of the open blue canopy that served as the telephone's protection against the elements.

Kate nodded mutely. She accepted the change and receiver and tried to pretend that he wasn't so close, but no way could she completely block out his powerful masculine presence. His scent, leather and something vaguely citrus, invaded her senses, making her feel even more disoriented.

She deposited the coins, then reached a shaky hand toward the numbers on the face of the telephone. Call in, she silently repeated to herself over and over. No matter how often she said it, the numbers she'd remembered so clearly only minutes ago would not resurface. Kate licked her lips nervously and stabbed a string of meaningless numbers, stopping after the seventh one. She quickly replaced the receiver in its cradle, the change rattled into the coin return.

Now…she had to think of something now!

"It…was busy," she stammered. "May I try again?" She bit her lower lip and prayed he wouldn't realize what she'd done.

Raine straightened and she almost gasped. He glared at her impatiently. "So try again. I don't want to be here all night." His gaze darted from her to the entrance of the parking lot and back several times while she dropped the coins in and redialed.

It was during one of those split seconds when he looked away that Kate propelled herself into action. She brought her right knee up into Raine's crotch as hard as she could. She nailed him square between the legs with all her might.

A wounded, animal-like grunt sounded from deep in his throat. Surprise flashed through his blue eyes and then he was on his knees on the ground. Instinct absorbed all thought, Kate dropped the receiver and ran as fast as she could toward the trail disappearing into the woods.

Kate pushed forward trying to stay off the main trail. Branches and undergrowth slapped at her arms and legs.

Faster! She had to run faster or he would catch her. Thick old growth and trees forced her to return to the main trail. She ran as rapidly as she could, despite the fact that her legs felt like rubber and her head throbbed as though it might explode any minute.

Tripping and clutching at anything in her path for support, she didn't look back. She couldn't stop. Run! She had to run!

Kate's lungs felt ready to burst. Her chest hurt. She

gasped for air, but she couldn't stop. She had to keep going.

What was that sound?

Louder…it got louder with every step she took. Her heart hammered in her chest, her blood roared in her ears.

Water. It was only the river running alongside the trail.

Run, Kate, run. She pushed forward a little faster. Her entire body stung now from a lack of oxygen, but the desire for survival spurred her on.

What was that?

Kate shifted to look back, lost her balance and tumbled to the ground. It took a few moments for her mind to catch up with her sprawling body. Kate jerked herself up and turned around, fully expecting to find Raine towering over her.

There was no one or nothing there.

Kate shook herself, trying to shrug off the prickling feelings. She had to keep moving.

She moved swiftly but cautiously across a footbridge that was nothing more than a fallen tree with the top side hewn down flat. A primitive handrail provided support. After crossing the footbridge, she walked up the massive stone steps of a natural-rock formation. Under different circumstances, the formation might have captured her attention, but not now.

Right now she had to move as quickly as she could.

The steps took Kate through the huge rock and back to the trail. There was still no sound behind her. She smiled to herself. Undoubtedly Raine was still on the ground curled into a fetal position holding his pride and joy. She'd really nailed him good. He'd be in serious pain for a while yet.

Or maybe, she considered hopefully, he had decided going after her would be too much trouble and had already taken off in the car. Could she be that lucky?

Just to be sure the coast was still clear, Kate glanced over her shoulder once more as she started to run again. At first the sight of Raine moving swiftly toward her didn't register in her brain—then suddenly it did.

He was only a few yards behind her. Kate lunged up the trail's steadily climbing grade as fast as her weak body could take her. She couldn't let him catch her.

Faster! She had to move faster!

The trail made a sudden left. Kate veered a bit too sharply and lost her balance. Raine's powerful arms closed around her and they both tumbled to the ground.

They skidded to a grinding halt in the rocks and dirt. Kate struggled to free herself, but Raine pinned her to the ground with his full body weight.

"Let me go!" she yelled vehemently as she managed to grab a handful of his sandy hair.

A string of curses exploded from his mouth when he jerked her hand out of his hair. His eyes blazed like fire. He clenched his jaw so hard a muscle jumped furiously in his cheek as he immobilized her completely beneath his strong body.

Kate could do nothing now. The run and subsequent struggle had drained her already weak body.

For several seconds, neither moved or spoke. The only sound was the wind shifting through the trees and their ragged breathing. He felt hard and heavy on top of her. She watched his nostrils flare and that same muscle tic in his jaw. His mouth looked hard and grim. When their gazes collided, he tightened his hold on her wrists to a bruising intensity. For one fleeting instant sexual awareness sparked between them, strong and hot. Then it was gone, replaced by fury.

"Let me go," Kate demanded once she'd caught her breath. Fear zipped through her at the possibility of what lay in store for her. He was really angry. A number of unpleasant scenarios flitted across her mind.

"I ought to do just that," he growled as his blue gaze burned into hers. Kate could see the depth of the barely checked rage there. "You're nothing but a pain in the ass—more trouble than you're worth. I should just leave you for the cleanup team. That would put us both out of our misery."

"I don't know what you're talking about," Kate managed to say with the last bit of strength she could muster. "I want you to let me go." Her entire body trembled as much from weakness as from fear of the man crushing her into the ground.

"You just don't get it, do you?" His tone was cold and impatient, his piercing gaze ruthless. "They've seen you with me. You're marked…history…dead meat." With a frustrated exhale and a pained groan, Raine pushed himself up, pulling Kate up in the process.

Kate watched in confused disbelief as he dusted himself off and shoved the hair from his face. It pleased her immensely when Raine's face paled slightly and his hand went to his stomach as a wave of nausea obviously hit him.

"Why should I believe you?" Kate crossed her arms defiantly over her chest. She was covered with dirt and her hair was a mess, but she didn't care. She only wanted to get away from this man…this killer. Danny's words replayed in her head. *There's no telling how many men he's killed.* Kate backed up a step. "I…I don't believe anything you say," she stammered.

"You know, I really don't give a damn whether you believe me or not. If you think those guys we left back there weren't for real, then maybe you've lost more than your memory.''

Kate tried to decide what to think. How could she know what was real and what was not—who she could trust and who she couldn't? She didn't even know who she was! Completely overwhelmed and scared out of her mind, she broke down and cried, real, soul-shattering sobs. She couldn't take any more, she was truly at the end of her emotional rope.

''Don't start that again.'' Raine ran both hands through his hair and shifted uneasily.

''What am I supposed to do?'' Kate gasped out between sobs. ''You got me into this mess.''

Raine blew out a long breath, his eyes softened just a little as he took the step she'd retreated. ''I know I got you into this mess.'' He looked away for a moment before continuing. ''You have to understand that as long as you're with me and I'm breathing, I'll keep you safe. But if you pull another stupid stunt—'' Anger flared in his eyes again. ''You could get us both killed.''

Kate's knees went weak. He was right. She had no idea what was going on. She didn't stand a chance without him. ''Are you still going to take me with you?''

With a resigned sigh, he replied, ''Yes.'' His eyes locked with hers. ''I just hope I don't die regretting it.''

Relief flooded Kate at his response. She didn't understand the situation, but she felt certain he did. She would just have to trust him to straighten things out.

''Thank you.'' She swiped at her tears. ''I promise I'll do whatever you say from now on. You won't regret it.''

''I already do.'' Raine turned and headed back in the direction of the parking lot.

Kate combed her fingers through her mussed hair and let out a weary breath. Relief rushed through her, calming her frazzled nerves. She dusted the dirt from her clothes and started out after her less than saintly savior.

Raine stopped abruptly and turned around. He grabbed Kate by the shoulders and squeezed hard. His expression was stone cold as he stared into her eyes for a seemingly endless moment before he spoke. "But, I swear, if you do anything else that pisses me off, I'll kill you myself." With that said, he released her, turned and stalked away.

Judging by the look in his eyes, Kate had no doubt that he meant exactly what he'd said. She hugged herself tightly for a moment and watched his angry retreat.

He was crazy. He had to be. But, she was hopelessly at his mercy. Those other men were killers. It would take a killer to protect her from them, if everything he said was true. Kate had no alternative but to follow him and do whatever he told her.

And she did, still feeling dazed and brushing the dirt from her rumpled attire.

The last of the sun's warmth showered down on them through the opening canopy of tree branches as they neared the parking area. Kate noticed that her breath fogged the cold air. She wondered, as she marched behind Raine like a prisoner being led to her execution, where in the world they were. She had no idea even what state they were in.

Without warning, Raine stopped and Kate smacked into his wide back. He motioned for her to keep quiet as he stepped closer to the edge of the woods and surveyed the parking lot.

Kate peeked around him. A uniformed man was inspecting their car—the car they'd left in the parking lot, she amended. It wasn't really theirs, it belonged to the two goons. After the man in uniform circled the vehicle, he returned to his truck and spoke into his radio mike. He wasn't a policeman. Kate strained to make out the markings on the truck.

A park ranger.

So they must be…she suddenly made out the rest of the words: Great Smoky Mountains, Gatlinburg, Tennessee. A ranger! He could help them. If only… She looked at Raine.

"Damn." Raine pulled back from his viewing position. He glanced at Kate and then frowned. "Don't even think about it."

"What's he doing?" she asked innocently, as if she had no idea what he'd insinuated. How could he know that she'd had the overwhelming urge to scream her head off?

"He's running the plates." He swore. "They're strict about abandoned vehicles around here. Let's get moving." Raine turned and headed back up the trail.

"Where are you going? We can't go that way," Kate exclaimed in a stage whisper. She flung her arms heavenward in mute frustration and then muttered heatedly, "There's nothing back there but trees and mountains." Kate stood her ground. She wasn't about to go back into those woods, not when a perfectly good car waited in the parking lot. If Raine didn't want to talk to the ranger, all they had to do was wait. He would leave eventually.

Raine glared at her impatiently. "The guys who are after us will be monitoring reports made by the local authorities, especially the report of an abandoned car with a bullet hole in the roof. Not to mention a couple of loaded nine millimeters under the seat. When that ranger ran those plates he gave them our exact location. They'll be here soon, you can bet on it."

"Don't you mean the guys who are after *you?*" Kate set her hands on her hips and glared back at him, all memory of the promise she'd made gone.

"Same difference. You're either going or you're staying. I'm going." Raine stalked off, leaving her to decide for herself.

"But the ranger could help us!" Kate called after him, still clinging to the hope that she might separate herself from this whole nasty mess.

"Dream on," he called back without stopping.

Kate rolled her eyes and sighed in exasperation. What was she supposed to do? Run to that park ranger and risk being turned over to the *other* bad guys, or follow a man who could very well be a deranged killer himself?

One thing was certain, Raine could have killed her already if that had been his intent, but he hadn't. He had, in fact, done everything he could to protect her. She hadn't forgotten how he'd stepped between her and Vinny.

Maybe Raine was a good guy. Instinct told her to go with the known rather than the unknown. But could she trust her instincts? She didn't even know who she was, how could she know whether to trust her judgment?

Still less than convinced, Kate headed in the direction into which Raine had already disappeared.

Chapter Three

Crossing the primitive footbridge again, Kate reminded herself that following Raine was her only logical option. Besides, even if she had decided to make a mad dash for the park ranger, Raine could easily have stopped her. She watched his strong, confident strides. He moved with more fluid grace than a man his height and size had any right to. And quietly as well. Hardly any sound at all accompanied his steps.

Raine.

Kate concentrated with all her might to grasp that fleeting hint of recognition that flitted through her consciousness each time she looked into those piercing blue eyes or considered his name. She just couldn't quite latch on to it. She knew him, yet he was a total stranger.

Maybe in another life? *Right, Kate, you can't even remember this life.*

Kate shook off the mental frustration and climbed the steps that would take her back through the large, unique rock formation. She paused to admire the natural beauty of the awesome rocks. She smoothed her hand over the cold, rough surface, tracing the imprints time and the elements had left forever embedded.

Maybe, Kate thought with a smile, she was a geologist.

"You're wasting daylight."

Startled by the sharpness of his voice cutting through the silence, Kate snatched her hand back like a child caught reaching into the cookie jar.

He stood some ten yards away, as still as the stone she'd been admiring, hands on hips, glaring at her. Damned if he didn't make a hell of a picture when he was angry, she suddenly thought. Tight jeans encased muscular thighs and a worn leather bomber jacket filled to capacity covered his broad shoulders.

He glanced up at the sky and then directed his scowl back at Kate. "The sky's clear, it's going to get really cold tonight. Unless you plan to sleep under the stars, you'd better get a move on. I won't stop to remind you again," he added before he turned and continued.

Kate had the sudden, almost overwhelming urge to click her heels and salute. God, he would make a great drill sergeant. She quickly scanned the vast, blue sky. It looked much bigger somehow from here. There wasn't a cloud to be seen. He could be right, Kate supposed. Obviously she wasn't a meteorologist. She didn't know one cloud from another, or what their absence meant in regards to their current circumstances. She shrugged and forced her weak, wobbly legs into gear. She'd have to hurry to catch up or risk being left behind.

The trail climbed steadily upward. Kate was a little winded by the time she got within conversational distance of Raine. Not that he would be interested in conversation—he'd made that point quite clear. Her chest still ached, but she attributed the discomfort to fear. This man, she glowered at her leader, scared her. His friends—no, make that his enemies—scared her.

The trail took a hard right, which brought them into an area of total and unexpected devastation—a raw, open gash in the side of the mountain. Kate was taken aback by the stark contrast to only moments before.

There was absolutely nothing growing—no trees, no bushes, no nothing. The large expanse looked like the aftermath of a savage hurricane. Massive boulders lay scattered like marbles. Huge trees had been tossed about like toothpicks. In the distance, trees, logs, mud and rocks lay piled at least fifty feet high, a decaying monument to whatever had taken place to wreak such destruction.

Raine trudged on relentlessly, taking little note of their surroundings. Kate had been so engrossed in the unnatural phenomenon that she'd fallen way behind again. True to his word, Raine didn't appear concerned about whether she kept up or not. Pushing herself to move faster, Kate soon caught up with him.

"What caused all that? It looks like an artillery battle was fought here." She took one final look back over her shoulder at the naked area. In some stretches the earth had been scraped down to the bedrock. How could that spot look as if it had been hit by a holocaust and everything around it still appear so lovely and tranquil?

"A flash flood." Raine stopped and looked back as if he'd only just noticed his surroundings. He stared at the devastation for a long moment.

Just when Kate was sure he didn't intend to say anything else, he continued. "They say a monster storm hit, dumping massive amounts of water in a matter of minutes. Cresting at—" he shrugged "—more than twenty feet, it was like a highland tidal wave surging through and taking with it everything in its path."

Kate looked around warily. "That doesn't happen on a regular basis around here, does it?"

One corner of his mouth lifted in a half smile. "You don't have anything to worry about as long as you don't stand in one place too long,'' he said, and then pushed off, heading ever upward toward wherever the hell they were going.

Kate didn't find his little jab amusing. She heaved a frustrated breath and obediently trudged after him. In her efforts to keep up with his long legs, she tripped over every exposed root and loose rock in the trail. She glared at his broad back. Raine seemed to know exactly where to place each step. His self-assuredness frustrated her all the more. Just once she'd like to see him lose his footing or trip over one of nature's obstacles, she mused as she kicked another rock out of her path.

Kate shivered in her parka. The sun was dropping slowly but surely behind the mountains in the distance, taking its waning warmth with it. Orange and purple streaks slanted across the sky behind the slope of majestic trees that gave way to the valley below. The view was breathtaking. Though Kate felt sure she had heard of the Smoky Mountains, somehow she knew she'd never before seen a view like this one.

An occasional squirrel scampered into the open, gave Kate a curious look and then disappeared back into the forest. Birds went about their business, flying overhead or squawking from their perch on a nearby tree limb. Kate didn't readily recognize any of the varieties. She obviously wasn't a bird-watcher.

Raine, on the other hand, seemed to know his way around this place. How did he know so much about the mountains? she wondered. Had he always lived around here? For that matter, what did she really know about him at this point?

Nothing.

Except that he was dangerous, she reminded herself. She had no idea where they were headed, either. She was cold and achy. Dusk had descended upon them. And she was starving.

She had a right to know where he was leading her, didn't she?

Damn straight, she did.

Kate stamped off after him. "Excuse me!" she shouted to his back.

As she had anticipated, he ignored her.

Her anger brought with it a burst of energy, Kate broke into a dead run. "I said, excuse me," she repeated when she skidded to a halt right beside him.

He paused, turned to her and lifted one eyebrow, a look of bored amusement on his too-handsome face. "I'd be more careful where I stand if I were you," he warned. He inclined his head toward her side of the trail.

Kate glared at him for half a beat before looking in the direction he'd indicated. Her eyes widened in fear when she realized she stood on the edge of a precipice. Instinctively, Kate flung herself at Raine. His arms went instantly around her as her feet shifted in the loose dirt and rocks that scattered over the edge.

"Holy cow," she muttered as she clung to his jacket. His arms felt strong and reassuring around her. "I didn't even see it."

Raine set her away from him and on solid ground. "You should be more careful," he said smugly, giving her an amused look.

"Thanks for the warning," she retorted, her heart still thundering painfully in her chest. She called him every vile name she could think of under her breath.

Raine reached out and grasped a heavy wire cable that had been strung alongside the trail for some sixty or seventy feet. "Hold on tight and watch your step," he called back to her.

Kate uttered a nasty four-letter word, one she didn't even realize she knew until it rolled off her tongue.

Raine didn't have to tell her twice to be careful. She held on to the cable with both hands as she cautiously edged forward. She took one hesitant look at the drop-off and cringed. It plunged a good hundred feet down. If a person survived the rolling, tumbling fall, climbing back up would be a real problem. Kate felt fairly certain that Raine wouldn't be interested in helping her climb back up.

To her surprise, he waited for her on the other side of the drop-off. When Kate made it to his position, she wrinkled her nose and asked, "What's that smell?" The deep woodsy scent was gone, replaced by some sort of chemical odor. She couldn't quite identify it, almost a metal smell.

"Alum Cave Bluff. The rain and subsequent slides bring out the metallic odor," he told her flatly. He offered no further explanation, just turned and continued forward.

Kate stuck our her tongue at his broad back, but followed obediently. A regular Mr. Personality, she fumed.

The trail grew steadily steeper as the ground beneath her feet became more powdery and less rocky. Her close encounter with the precipice had caused her to forget the demand for information she had intended to make. She still didn't know where they were headed.

The trail led them underneath the overhang of a bluff. The interesting terrain momentarily distracted Kate as she squinted to make out the formations. The natural beauty of the rocks and landscape grew more and more difficult to see as darkness closed in around them.

"Watch out for the icicles."

Kate shifted her gaze from the rock wall to him. He pointed skyward and then moved swiftly beyond the craggy overhang.

"Icicles?" Kate frowned. What icicles? She looked up

just in time to see a rather large one drop like a heavy dagger. The ice crashed to the ground a mere three or four feet in front of her. No further explanation required, she thought as she hurried past the overhang.

Raine had already resumed his trek upward. Kate plodded after him. They passed two more drop-off areas. She held her breath past both—each time seemed worse than the last with nothing more than moonlight to guide them.

Kate was freezing now. As she peered into the dense black forest, she wondered how long it would take to find a person's body in this environment. A body out in the middle of nowhere like this probably wouldn't be found until spring and by then it would have been something's lunch. She shivered at the thought.

Bears. She suddenly wondered if there were bears in these woods. She opened her mouth to ask, but then snapped it shut. She wouldn't give him the pleasure of knowing her concerns.

Lost in thought, Kate looked up to find that she'd almost run into Raine again. He stood waiting near a particularly steep area. The trail inclined so sharply that log steps had been embedded in the mountainside to assist with the climb. Raine took the steps two at a time. Kate swallowed tightly. If he could do it, she could do it. By the time she reached the top her heart fluttered wildly, but she had done it.

Before long the trail leveled out somewhat and Kate's breathing finally returned to normal. She hoped they would get to their destination soon, her feet and ankles were aching. Her head joined in the symphony of pain and her chest felt oddly tight.

The trees grew dense, almost blocking out the moonlight and making their trek even more precarious. Fraser firs soared high into the sky like giant Christmas trees. The crisp evergreen scent teased Kate's senses. She smiled and wondered if there were evergreens where she came from.

Virginia. Raine had said she was from Virginia. Virginia had evergreens, didn't it?

Her next step sent her feet in opposite directions. *Ice,* she realized too late. A shriek escaped her lips at the same time that her feet skated out from under her.

Raine's arms encircled her waist, catching her a split second before her bottom slammed against the hard dirt. He steadied her on her feet, but kept his arms wrapped tightly around her.

"I guess I'm not an ice skater," Kate whispered hoarsely.

"Guess not," he said, his warm breath feathered across her mouth. His ice-blue gaze seemed to capture the sparse moonlight and do strange things with it. Kate found herself mesmerized by his eyes, his nearness. She couldn't move or take a breath, she could only hold on to that worn-soft bomber jacket and absorb the heat emanating from his powerful body. Her mouth traitorously yearned for the taste of his, her fingers tightened on fistsful of leather.

"We're almost there," he said finally, breaking the charged silence. Raine dropped his arms, turned and strode off into the darkness.

Kate's legs moved of their own volition. She was too stunned to do anything but operate on autopilot. She blew out a long, slow puff of air that fogged against the cold night.

Get a grip, Kate. It was nothing. Just exhaustion, hunger and the play of moonlight.

A sign welcoming hikers to LeConte Lodge came into view. Kate silently thanked God for some form of civilization. She hoped this was their intended destination. Rustic though it might be, she added when they entered the clearing and the unobstructed light of the moon gave her a better look.

Several cabins, maybe a dozen or so of varying sizes, dotted the clearing. Not a single light pierced the night. It wasn't that late, someone should still be up.

The trail wound to the right of the lodge compound and disappeared into the blackness. A welcome center of sorts stood at the entrance. To Kate's distress, rather than enter the compound, Raine stayed with the trail.

"We're not staying here?" Kate hastened her pace to catch up with him again.

"The lodge is closed for the winter. There's no one here except maybe a caretaker, and we can't chance him seeing us."

"So, what are we going to do?" she asked, almost afraid of the answer.

Without bothering to respond, Raine took a sudden left through the knee-deep weeds and headed in the direction of a small cabin at the very back of the compound.

Kate followed, relieved to be heading toward shelter. She waded through the thick dead-for-the-winter grass. Sharp, prickling pain brought the sudden awareness that the grass was accompanied by saw briars, which pulled at her jeans and the skin underneath.

Raine made it to the cabin well before Kate. She watched him survey the door and windows—deciding on the best method of breaking and entering, she realized. By the time she made her way to the cabin, Raine was already inside.

The single room held one narrow bed, a kerosene lamp sitting on a table, two chairs and a small kerosene heater. The floor and walls were rough, unpainted wood, as best Kate could tell.

Rustic had been an understatement. Primitive was a

much more apt description. But at least it would provide shelter from the cold wind and damp ground. She appraised the narrow bed once more. Anything was better than sleeping on the ice-cold ground.

But where would Raine sleep? she wondered absently.

Kate shivered. Shelter or no, it was still cold. She took the few steps that separated her from the bed and sat down with a satisfied sigh.

Dear God, it felt wonderful just to sit. Kate closed her eyes and succumbed to the exhaustion she'd been holding at bay. She pulled a scratchy wool blanket up around her and relaxed more deeply into the thin mattress. She licked her lips and imagined strawberry lip balm and almond oil hand lotion. That would feel so good about now, she thought with another sigh.

"Stay put," Raine ordered.

Kate opened her heavy lids to look up at him. He stood in front of the door, blocking the dim light the moon provided.

"If I have to run you down, you'll be the one doing the regretting."

"Where are you going?" Kate asked. He didn't have to worry, she didn't plan to move, much less run.

"If we're lucky, there'll be some canned food left in the dining cabin."

"Okay," Kate muttered, but Raine had already vanished from view. He left the door open, for the light, she supposed. The constant sound of the wind rustling through the treetops lulled her toward sleep as the cloak of moonlight and nocturnal silence folded around her.

WHEN RAINE RETURNED to the cabin with his booty, Kate was fast asleep. He set the cans of beans and franks and the bottled water he had found on the table, along with a couple of spoons.

He thought about just letting her sleep. She'd been nothing but a pain in the ass the entire trek up the mountain. But he knew she hadn't eaten anything, at least not since early morning, and he wasn't comfortable with her sleeping too much in the first twenty-four hours since her accident. Eating was a necessity. She'd need her strength to make the rest of this hellacious trip.

With a frustrated sound that was more groan than sigh, Raine walked over to the bed and shook Kate. "Kate, you need to eat." He shook her again. "Wake up."

Kate's eyes popped open, she sat bolt upright, quickly scanned the room and then assessed him. "What?" she eventually asked.

Raine frowned. Most people didn't wake and immediately take stock of their surroundings. She peered up at him with those dark, chocolate eyes. Maybe he'd startled her.

"I found some food. You need to eat," he told her firmly.

Kate seemed to consider his words then said, "Okay." Still shrouded in the blanket she had found on the cot, she struggled to her feet and followed him to the table. After claiming one of the two chairs, she watched as he popped the tops from two cans and passed one to her.

"What is it?" she asked, trying to read the label in the almost complete darkness.

"Beans and franks."

"Ugh. I hate beans and franks," she complained.

Raine paused, spoon halfway to his mouth. "How do you know if you like them or not?"

Kate paused, frowning at the stuff inside the can she held. "I don't know. I just know."

"Eat it anyway," he ordered, then nudged the water in her direction. "And drink. You'll need lots of energy tomorrow."

She met his gaze across the table. "What happens tomorrow?"

"More of today," he said flatly.

"Oh, God," she groaned.

Reluctantly she drank from the water bottle then poked a spoonful of the beans and franks into her mouth and chewed. She shivered when she swallowed. Raine didn't know if it was from the cold or the cuisine. He bit back a grin and opened a second can. Food equaled survival, and the sooner Ms. Roberts learned that, the better off they'd both be.

"Have another," Raine teased when she'd at last finished her can.

"No, thank you," she said with another shiver.

"I'll just save the rest for tomorrow," he taunted.

"Great," Kate muttered as she stumbled back to the bed. She plunked down on one end, leaned against the iron railing and hugged the blanket around herself. "I'm not moving until the sun comes up and sheds some warmth on this cold, godforsaken mountain," she mumbled from beneath the blanket.

Raine didn't say anything. No point in bursting her bubble, he decided. She'd find out soon enough that his day started well before dawn, and on this trip they followed his schedule.

He sat down on the other end of the bed and leaned against the iron headboard. He watched her for a long while, wondering about this woman of mystery. Raine had particularly good night vision and his eyes had long since adjusted to the lack of light.

He ran through his mental notes regarding his inadvertent hostage. She didn't wear any rings, so he assumed that meant she didn't have a husband somewhere searching frantically for her. Her hands were soft and her nails well manicured, indicating a white-collar job of some sort. Her clothing sported designer labels, as did her pricey hiking boots. Whatever she did, she got paid well.

Judging by her vocabulary, she appeared well educated. As her strength returned so did her confidence. She seemed in good physical condition considering her injuries. If the transformation thus far was any indication, she tended toward bossiness.

Raine didn't know a lot about amnesia except that it could be temporary and usually returned sporadically.

"What?" she snapped from behind the blanket. All that remained visible were her eyes and that cloud of dark, silky hair.

Raine realized then that he had been staring at her for some time. She'd caught him. "I was just thinking that it's going to get a hell of a lot colder before this night is over and we'll need to do whatever we have to in order to survive."

She jerked the cover down from her face, her eyebrows veed in confusion. "What do you mean?" she asked warily.

"I mean, we'll need to share that one blanket." He lifted one shoulder in a careless shrug. "Or we could use it in shifts," he suggested.

She stared at him, aghast. "You must be kidding. I'm freezing!" She shook her head. "If you were a gentleman you wouldn't even have made such a suggestion."

"I'm glad that's settled," he said dryly. Raine cocked his head and eyed her with blatant amusement. "Just to prove I'm not completely uncouth, I will be happy to share my body heat with you if you're willing to share the blanket.''

''*Pleeease,*'' she cried in disgust.

''All you have to do is come over here and cuddle up with me. Nothing more.'' He pulled his jacket open wide and smiled invitingly. ''It's a known fact that sharing body heat has saved many a poor soul from freezing to death. Between our jackets, that blanket, and whatever body heat we can work up, I'm sure we'll stay nice and toasty.''

''I'd rather freeze.''

''Suit yourself.'' Raine grinned and pulled his coat back around him. He crossed his arms over his chest, exaggerated a shiver and watched her struggle with her conscience.

''Can't you light that kerosene heater or the lamp?''

How refreshing, he thought. He hadn't spent time with anyone who had a real conscience in ages.

''Sorry, I don't smoke, so I don't carry a lighter.''

''Well, don't...don't you know how to rub two sticks together or something?''

''I hate to lower your perception of me any further,'' Raine said, his smile widening into another grin. ''But I was never a Boy Scout.''

Kate sat up and sighed loudly. ''All right.''

''All right what?'' he baited.

She glared at him. ''We'll share the blanket.'' She made room for him beside her. ''But don't get any ideas, because I'm fully trained in self-defense,'' she added sullenly.

Raine stood, moved to the other end of the bed and then lowered himself next to her. ''How do you know you're fully trained?'' he whispered near her ear.

''I don't, but you should,'' she said pointedly. Kate relinquished part of the blanket and turned her back to him.

Raine winced at the memory of her knee in his groin.

She'd definitely knocked him on his can. Maybe...hell, all women knew where a man's weakest points were.

He'd gotten what he wanted anyway. He grinned as he snuggled in behind her, spoon fashion. She inched her body as far away from his as possible without falling off the edge.

Raine breathed deeply of her womanly scent. A hint of whatever shampoo she'd last used still lingered in her hair. "Mmm, you smell nice," he murmured.

She jabbed him in the gut with her elbow. Raine grunted from the unexpected blow to the already sore spot. "Hold your breath," she said icily.

Not a masochist at heart, Raine lay perfectly still until he heard the gentle, rhythmic breathing that indicated she had fallen into a deep sleep. Keeping warm on a night like this wasn't going to be easy. He slid his arm around her waist and pulled her body against his. Some concessions were necessary.

Despite the stomach-churning blow she'd delivered to his groin earlier that day, and then the sucker punch he'd gotten only minutes ago, he hardened like a rock in record time. Damn, he would never get any sleep like this. Between her neediness and soft body, he was completely and painfully aroused. Raine had worked with women plenty of times in the past and never had he lost his perspective like this.

His professional ethics had gone out the window practically from the moment he'd opened his door and found her standing there in the falling rain. Kate Roberts threatened even his most deeply entrenched habits of self-preservation.

Raine had always been a loner, taking care of no one but himself. What was so different about this woman? He had thought of little else but her all day. Never before had he felt such a need to take care of another person. Never before had he wanted a woman so much.

Nevers weren't supposed to happen to him.

It couldn't be just the circumstances. He'd been in a race for his life hundreds of times before. The odds had certainly been stacked against him numerous times in the past. Even the fact that he didn't know all the players in the game wasn't so unusual for his line of work.

But something was definitely different this time.

Kate was the difference.

Or maybe he was just getting old and soft...

...or stupid.

Chapter Four

Raine woke as the first faint glimmer of light streaked the sky with color. His backside felt half-frozen, but his front was warm and fully aroused. The ache he still felt from Kate's knee had not prevented his almost constant state of arousal since climbing into bed with her.

He was sprawled half across her body, his arms wrapped tightly around her waist, hers draped around his neck. Their legs were tangled, with his thigh resting snugly between hers. His arousal pressed into her soft belly. There was no way he could move that wouldn't cause unbearable friction between them, and possibly send him out of control. He didn't trust himself even to breathe. He felt damn close to embarrassing himself at the moment.

There had to be a way out of this. Raine had built his reputation on his ability to get in and out of death-dealing situations. Disentangling himself from one female should be a piece of cake.

Finally, he had to breathe. His chest expanded from the depth of the breath. Kate stirred beneath him and Raine gritted his teeth.

Each time he'd woken her during the night, she had burrowed closer to him. Now, she stretched languidly and tightened her hold around his neck, then arched against his thigh. Sweat popped out on his forehead. When she kissed his throat, he closed his eyes and bit his tongue to stifle the groan. Kate practically purred beneath him, planting soft, sweet kisses from the base of his throat all the way to his chin.

He couldn't take it any longer. The groan escaped, loud and gut-wrenching. He felt ready to explode. If she arched against him once more, his self-control would be history.

Kate tensed. Raine didn't have to look to know her eyes had opened, the earsplitting shriek that escaped her lips clued him in well before her hands pressed against his chest in an effort to shove him off.

''Give me a minute to—''

Kate cut him off as she arched her entire body like a bow and propelled him over the edge of the bed, her in tow. His back thudded against the wooden floor. A loud *ummph* escaped him as the wind whooshed out of his lungs from the weight of her body slamming into his.

''You sleazy bastard,'' she shouted angrily as she scrambled to free herself from the twisted blanket and his arms and legs. ''How could you take advantage of me while I was sleeping?''

''Hold on just a damn minute!'' he rasped. Raine grabbed her shoulders and held her still. ''I didn't do anything. You were the one kissing me.''

She huffed. ''You must be insane! I did no such thing.'' She struggled against his hold, her every move grinding the heat between her thighs into his arousal. Suddenly she stopped fighting him. Kate's eyes widened in horror when she realized she was sitting astride his hips.

Kicking and tripping and cursing, she freed herself and stumbled to her feet.

If Raine hadn't been so painfully aroused he would have

laughed at the whole situation. As it was, there wasn't a single thing funny about it.

Raine got to his feet and stormed out the door into the cold. He felt immensely thankful for the bitter wind whipping around him. He needed a long walk and some relief.

KATE SHOVED her hair back from her face and hugged her parka around her. "Jerk," she muttered as Raine disappeared from sight. She grimaced at the pain shooting through her body. Yesterday's adventures had left their mark in the memory of every muscle. Her head felt foggy and achy.

Why had he gotten up before the sun? It couldn't be more than thirty degrees outside. Kate picked up the tangled wool blanket and cocooned herself in it, then plunked back down on the bed. Raine could do whatever he wanted, but she wasn't going anywhere until the sun rose above the treetops. She snuggled into the scratchy cover and closed her eyes. Just five minutes more of sleep and she would be good to go. Five little minutes…

"Wake up. It's time to go."

Kate's eyes shot open and she came instantly to attention. She tamped down her automatic reaction of fight or flight as she recognized Raine towering over her in the dim predawn light, a scowl on his face. "What?" she grumbled.

"It's time to go," he repeated impatiently.

"But it's not even daylight yet, why do we have to go now? It's still freezing outside." Literally, Kate didn't add as she hugged the blanket closer.

That annoying tic began in his angular jaw. Even in the shadowy light she could see his scowl deepen. "Because," he said slowly, drawing out the word, "it's over twenty miles to Cherokee, and if we don't make it today, we'll be spending tonight under the stars. There may not have been any heat in this cabin last night, but it was a hell of a lot better than spending the night out in the open.''

"Twenty miles?" Kate echoed. Nothing he'd said after that mattered at the moment. ''You expect me to walk twenty miles—*today?*'' He was insane. The man couldn't possibly mean *twenty miles.* Her muscles told her in no uncertain terms that walking twenty miles was not something she wanted to do anytime soon. Twenty miles, right.

"Give or take a couple," he said flippantly.

Kate stared at him in disbelief. "You're serious." It was a statement, not a question. Instinct told Kate that this man wasn't a kidder.

He crossed his arms over his chest and angled his head toward his right shoulder. The same way he'd done when he had taken aim at those two men yesterday. A shiver skated over Kate's skin.

"Dead serious," he told her.

Kate swallowed. "What would be the harm in waiting until daylight?"

"In case you've forgotten," he said, emphasizing the last word, "there are people after us who want us dead."

"You mean who want *you* dead," Kate clarified sarcastically.

Raine exhaled loudly. "We had this discussion yesterday." He cocked one sandy eyebrow. "Or have you *forgotten* that, too?"

"You're not funny." Kate shot him a reproachful glare. Her efforts only sent one corner of his mouth upward in a half smile.

"I wasn't trying to be. Now let's go."

Reluctantly, Kate stood. "I still don't see the need to hurry. We're in the middle of nowhere. What fool would look for us here?"

Raine slowly paced the room, scanning each square foot. "If we're lucky, no one. Hopefully, they'll assume that we picked up some other means of transportation. I don't think they would expect us to take this route, but I don't plan to stick around and find out."

Kate unzipped her parka and pulled the small purse she had forgotten she was wearing back around to her side. Small though it might be, it probably accounted for at least one tender spot on her back. She had been so tired last night that she hadn't thought to take it off. Raine's strong arms and muscular body accounted for numerous other discomforts. Some Kate didn't want to consider, like the hot ache deep inside her. She shivered and rezipped her parka, then tightened the blanket around her shoulders. She needed all the help she could get staying warm and shielding herself from *him*.

When Raine completed his survey of the room, he bent over and began to put the bed back in order.

"What are you doing?" Kate asked, puzzled by his actions. She wouldn't have taken him for a neat-freak.

"I'm making sure things are left the way we found them. So we don't leave a trail."

Kate frowned. He certainly seemed to think of everything. She wasn't complaining on that score though, the view from her position was pretty good. Faded jeans strained against his tight butt as he bent over the bed. His bomber jacket covered his back and shoulders, but she already knew exactly what that broad torso looked like. Kate concentrated hard on his long, muscled physique and tried to recall exactly how he had looked naked. A ripple of awareness made her shiver again as she closed her eyes and allowed the images to flood her mind. Tanned skin stretched taut over ridges and planes of hard muscle. Heat rushed through Kate as her breathing grew shallow and rapid.

If she had to be stranded in the wilderness, this was definitely the man to be stuck with. He was rugged, handsome, strong...*he was a killer*. What the hell was she thinking? Kate forced her eyes open to face the reality of her predicament. Raine stood right in front of her, studying her closely. Those piercing sky-blue eyes made her heart skip a beat.

"Are you all right?" he asked, a hint of concern tinging his low, husky baritone.

"Fine. I'm fine." Kate retreated a step and stumbled on the blanket hanging around her feet.

Raine advanced the step she had retreated and tugged the blanket from around her. "I don't think you'll need this." He folded the blanket and draped it across the foot of the bed just as she had found it.

Kate pushed her hands through her hair, careful of the tender spot on her scalp, and tried to smile, but her efforts fell far short of her goal.

"Let's go." He flicked one last glance at her before striding out the door.

Drawing in a fortifying breath, Kate followed him into the biting cold. She hesitated at the corner of the cabin. "Wait," she said suddenly. Already a half-dozen yards ahead of her, Raine stopped and turned around. "I need to...do something," she stammered, heat rising in her cheeks.

He adjusted the collar of his jacket higher around his neck. "So do it."

"I...I can't do it here." Kate shifted with growing discomfort. Obviously she hadn't been awake enough until just this moment to realize she had to go—bad. Or maybe it was the cold. Whatever it was, she had to go now.

He nodded toward the cabin. "Go around to the other side and make it fast. We're wasting time." All signs of concern had vanished. The cold, emotionless man who had mocked death when it came in the form of two armed goons was back.

Not wanting to be left behind, Kate hurried through the knee-deep grass and briars. The dead blades crunched beneath her hiking boots.

After finding a spot that represented the least possible threat to her bare bottom, Kate took care of business. She checked her purse for anything useful, like lip balm. Nothing but a hairbrush, her driver's license, and a wallet that contained a few small bills. Knowing his lack of patience, she quickly rejoined Raine. He might be cold and emotionless, but he was all she had. She met his impatient gaze and produced a smile.

"You're ready now?" he asked archly.

"Do I have a choice?"

"I knew I would regret this." His tone matched the implacable expression on his face. Raine turned and strode toward the trail they had abandoned the night before.

Kate followed quietly. She focused on trying to remember how she had ended up in this man's company. He had said something about a car accident. Her head ached from the concussion she had received, according to Raine, in that accident. But Kate didn't really remember anything before waking up in his bed. Fleeting snatches of memory about his naked body and their being in the shower together were about all she could recall. Except those sensations of knowledge that plagued her from time to time. She frowned. She would experience a sudden feeling or sense of knowing, but not quite a memory.

Kate sighed. Surely it was only a matter of time before her full memory returned, with or without medical attention. Wasn't that the way it happened in the movies? How would she know? she mused bitterly. Who was to say that the flashes of insight she experienced weren't scenes from movies? They could be fragments of her life just as easily. Maybe she was some sort of spy or cop or something, she thought, laughing bitterly at herself. Whatever she was, Kate decided reluctantly, she had definitely been hanging around with the wrong crowd.

The trail climbed steadily for a short distance before they reached the crest and began the descent. Kate felt immensely grateful for the downward trek. She took care to watch for icy patches this time. Before long she even got the hang of stepping over the many hazards of the rocky trail. She felt immensely more coordinated today, and not as weak.

Raine waited for Kate at each of the slide areas. He warned her to stay away from the edge and to move slowly since there were no cables to hold on to this time. He stuck to her like glue as she braved the more precarious areas. Kate didn't bother to thank him since he didn't seem in the conversational mood. A hundred questions flitted through her mind, but she didn't vocalize them, either. She had a bad feeling she wouldn't like the answers. What were the old sayings? *Ignorance is bliss. What you don't know won't hurt you.* Kate hoped like hell that at least one would prove true.

Each time Raine took her hand and helped her across a particularly hazardous spot, a tingle zipped through her. Kate didn't really understand her physical reaction to the man. Did they know each other intimately as she feared? Did they have a history? If they did, he wasn't telling. Raine was the kind of man who probably had women falling at his feet all the time. For a man like him, she was most likely nothing more than another roll in the hay. Too bad she didn't remember the roll. She shook herself mentally.

Kate clenched and unclenched her fists against the numbing cold. She glanced down at her coat and for the first time realized she had pockets. Stuffing her hands inside the protective material, Kate also discovered gloves. An appreciative smile spread across her cold, stiff lips. She tugged the gloves out to slip them on and something fluttered to the ground. Kate frowned as she reached for the small object. *Matches.* A small book of matches. The kind people in bars always wrote their telephone numbers on and then gave to a prospective date. The cover was plain white, no advertisement. Kate opened it. No telephone number was scrawled inside. Why would she have matches? Did she smoke? If she had known she had matches in her pocket, Raine could have lit that kerosene heater in the cabin.

"What's the holdup?"

Raine's steely voice jerked Kate from her reverie. She stuffed the matchbook back into her pocket and hurried to catch up with him. She could mull over the mysterious matches later. Right now she had to follow her fearless leader.

Like a big orange ball of fire, the sun finally rose above the treetops in the east and bathed the beautiful mountains in a golden glow. Its warmth melted away the thick blue mist that had enveloped the majestic trees that covered the landscape around them. Kate stopped and held her face to the sun, allowing its kiss to warm her. When she opened her eyes once more, she viewed the solitude and serenity of her surroundings with renewed interest. This was surely the most beautiful place she had ever seen. She sensed it in the deepest recesses of her soul.

A distant *whop-whop-whop* sound suddenly cut through

the serene fabric of the morning, the cacophony wholly out of place in the beautifully untamed environment.

Raine had already turned toward the sound, his searching gaze roaming the treetops.

"What's that?" she asked. Dread filled her midsection, followed swiftly by fear. Kate knew instantly that whatever it was, it wasn't good.

"Trouble," he told her, his voice low.

Kate tried to rally her intellect. To determine exactly the source of the sound or what he meant by that one word, but she couldn't. She could only stand there, frozen with the fear of the unknown.

The bad guys. It had to be the bad guys. She could feel her forehead wrinkle with worry. Was it the bad guys? Or was *he*, she turned her attention to Raine, the real bad guy? *He's good, maybe too good.* The words sifted through the empty sieve of her mind. Kate's frown deepened. How could she know that? Good at what?

"It's a copter, they're looking for us at the lodge," he said mechanically. "We have to move faster, Kate."

He was beside her now. She hadn't even realized he had moved. Kate blinked rapidly, trying simultaneously to focus on him and the whirlwind of emotions churning inside her. Raine took her hand, wrapping his long fingers around hers and urging her forward.

"We have to hurry," he repeated grimly.

She didn't ask any other questions and he offered no further explanations. Kate simply allowed him to pull her along behind him. Raine moved with lightning speed and absolute silence. Kate stumbled frequently, but he always caught her. Soon the sound of the helicopter's blades cutting through the air faded entirely. Kate focused intently on the task of keeping up once Raine had released her hand.

Faster and faster they moved down the trail as it followed the contour of the mountain. Kate didn't know exactly how long they had been running, but surely the danger had passed. Raine continued to push forward anyway. She needed to slow down, but forced herself to keep his pace. If he could do it, she reminded herself, she could do it.

Just when Kate thought she might collapse, the unmistakable sound came again, blades beating through the frigid air. Kate turned to look out over the valley. Fear slithered up her spine. Without warning, Raine pulled her into the thick underbrush.

"Don't move," he whispered against the shell of her ear.

Kate nodded, too breathless to speak. She forced herself to ignore the feel of his hard body beneath her backside. He held her in his lap, his arms firm around her as if he feared she might suddenly make a run for it.

Her eyes widened and the breath vaporized in her lungs when the helicopter rose above the cliff and hovered over the trail on which they had been running only moments before. Kate turned into the protection of Raine's embrace. His powerful arms tightened around her, and for reasons she could not comprehend, she felt safe, no matter that the helicopter veered ever closer.

The wind whipped around them. Branches slapped at their bodies. The thunderous sound of the propeller echoed through Kate's body, making her heart pound harder. She closed her eyes and pressed her face into the curve of Raine's neck. She inhaled the scent of leather and man and took comfort in the promise he had made to protect her.

What felt like a lifetime later, the sound once more faded into the distance. Kate lifted her gaze to find Raine watching her. Something about the way he looked at her unsettled her, yet drew her. She couldn't look away. His gaze dropped to her lips, and her breath stalled in her chest. Just when she felt sure he intended to kiss her, he reached up and tucked a tendril of hair behind her ear. Slowly, gently, he traced the bruise on her temple. Desire, unbidden yet hot and insistent, raced through her veins.

"Raine," she murmured.

That steady blue gaze returned to hers. Kate moistened her lips, suddenly as afraid he might just kiss her after all as she was that he wouldn't, and asked, "Do you think they're gone for good this time?"

"Maybe...probably." The low, raspy sound of his voice sent goose bumps skittering across her skin.

"What do we do now?" Kate wasn't sure how much longer she could bear the unmistakable sexual tension sizzling between them. She wanted to fight it, to push him away as she had earlier. But she simply could not bring herself to move. She felt safe by his side. Safe from the men chasing them. Safe from the bitter cold. *Safe.*

His warm breath whispered across her lips as he exhaled. "We stay put until we're sure they're gone."

She hadn't noticed just how full and well shaped his lips were until now. Their movement as he spoke mesmerized her. The heat of his body tempted her to burrow more deeply into him.

"Kate."

She forced her gaze upward, away from those lips. "Yes." He was closer now, she felt sure of it.

Long fingers curled around her neck and pulled her closer—so close that their lips almost touched. Almost.

The faint sound of propeller blades jerked Raine's attention skyward. Kate followed his gaze. "Are they coming back?"

Raine listened intently a moment longer. "No, they're

headed back toward the lodge.'' He got to his feet, pulling Kate up as he went. "Let's get moving.''

Still unsettled by the intensity of that near kiss, Kate followed the man who had promised to keep her safe from the bad guys.

But who would keep her safe from Raine?

FOR HOURS they continued the downward trek that took them through several shallow streams. Using rocks and fallen tree limbs, Raine helped Kate keep her shoes and feet dry and to avoid icy patches. It was definitely too cold to get wet. From time to time, he offered her a drink from the water bottle he carried.

Kate had accused him last night of not being a gentleman. This morning she'd had to eat her words. He was proving more of a gentleman than she would ever have imagined.

And Raine had been wrong this morning, as well, when he'd said that there hadn't been any heat in the cabin last night. Not to mention the nuclear meltdown that occurred while they hid from the helicopter. Kate's skin still burned from the feel of his strong body against hers. Even through the layers of clothing, she'd felt the strength of him and the power he emanated. She shivered at the recollection.

Focus, Kate. This wasn't the time to fantasize about a man who might be more killer than hero. Thankfully they hadn't heard the helicopter anymore. With the thick canopy of trees overhead she doubted they could be seen from the air at this point even if their pursuers decided to come back. Kate didn't know if she had ever been chased by killers before or not, but it wasn't an experience she wanted to repeat anytime soon.

Kate shuddered when she imagined the sound of barking dogs behind them. How could she remember all these scenarios from movies—if that's what they were—when she couldn't remember anything about her own life? Maybe she was a writer or director or film critic?

That's rich, Kate. If that were the case, what the hell would you be doing in the middle of nowhere following James Bond? Kate had to laugh at herself then; she was pathetic.

She wondered briefly what god she had antagonized to deserve this fate. Whatever she had done in life to bring this penance, Kate prayed she would eventually remember it so she could be sure never to do it again.

Your life will be in constant danger—perhaps from more than one source. Kate jerked to a stop as the words slammed into her mind. She swallowed the fear rising in her throat. Why couldn't she remember what those words meant? Or who'd said them?

Kate pushed aside the haunting questions and forced herself forward. She had to keep up. It would all come back, eventually. It had to.

They reached an intersection of sorts and Raine took the left fork, announcing that it was the Appalachian Trail. Kate wasn't sure if she had known anything about the Appalachian Trail before today, but she'd had her fill now. The trail seemed more like a ditch at times. Heavily eroded, it was even rockier than the previous terrain they had plodded over. Fir, spruce and birch trees surrounded them on both sides as they continued their downward descent. The only views were of trees and sparse patches of sky.

She scanned the now-familiar landscape and sighed. They had walked for hours with no sign of anything in the distance but trees. For the first time since they had started their journey, Kate wondered if Raine really knew where he was going.

A large, treeless outcropping came into sight. A huge rock jutted up the side of the mountain. It looked oddly out of place, as if someone had lifted it from some faraway spot and deposited it here as a conversation piece. Kate surveyed the strange sight. The trail wound right in front of the large, naturally misplaced rock. Raine again warned Kate not to veer off the trail. His concern was needless—she had no intention of getting more than a few feet from him. The possibility of getting lost or running into Raine's "friends" again tormented her thoughts. Not to mention the possibility of being attacked by a bear.

Lions and tigers and bears. The Wizard of Oz. This time she knew the memory was a movie. She even remembered the name of it. Bears? Kate wondered again if there were bears in these woods. She opened her mouth to ask, but thought better of it. If there were no bears here, Raine would laugh at her stupidity, and if there were bears, he would think her afraid. Besides, any self-respecting bear would be hibernating this time of year, she reminded herself. Kate dismissed the worry as one she could definitely do without.

Raine took a hard right, leaving the Appalachian Trail behind. If this man did not know where he was going, they were in serious trouble. Kate could not have found her way back to the lodge if her life depended on it—at this point she truly hoped it didn't. According to Raine, this part of the trail was rarely used. It continued downward, becoming weedy and even rockier. It soon opened up into a wider, somewhat grassy area. Kate was so exhausted by then that she hardly noticed the lovely mountain views around them. She stored away the glimpses of nature's beauty in its purest form for later consideration. Much later, when she had her life back and wasn't running for it.

The mountains jutted toward the sky on either side of

them now as they moved steadily downward. Kate trudged on, numb and beyond exhausted. Snags of old chestnut trees stood on either side of the trail, haunting remnants of times past.

Raine moved forward, seemingly oblivious to anything and everything except advancing toward their destination. Wherever the hell that was. He hadn't uttered more than a sentence or two in hours.

Kate didn't have a watch, so she had no idea how long they had been walking. But her body was telling her that it had been a very long time and that she needed to rest.

No way would she even ask him to slow down. If the bad guys caught up with them, it was not going to be her fault.

RAINE STOPPED at the creek and waited for Kate to catch up with him. She dragged at this point. He had known this journey would be tough on her and he felt bad that it was even worse than he had anticipated. She was young and certainly fit, but the head injury and overall battering she had taken in the accident had left her in a weakened condition. But they had to keep moving.

When she came alongside him, Raine gave her a moment to catch her breath before he spoke. "We'll take a breather now."

Kate dropped on the old bench next to the No Camping sign, the first indication of civilization they had seen since leaving the lodge. They hadn't covered as much ground as he would have preferred, but they could still make up for lost time. Raine scanned the valley around them. They had the worst of the journey behind them, but there was still a ways to go.

He pulled a can of beans and a spoon out of each pocket and handed one of each to Kate.

"Gee, thanks," she said wryly. "You certainly know how to treat a girl right."

Raine allowed her a near smile as he pulled the top from his can. She'd been a real trouper most of the time, the rest of the time she had been a pain in the ass. Though he couldn't help respecting her adaptability, he couldn't make himself trust her. Too many years of not trusting anyone but himself, he supposed. He wasn't about to change now. But that didn't change the fact that he wanted her. And that was an unacceptable complication.

He shifted his gaze to Kate. Even with the dark crescents of fatigue beneath her eyes and the unnaturally pale quality of her face, she was still a hell of a looker. The memory of the shapely body that lay beneath that thick parka had permanently etched itself on the backs of his lids. Every time Raine closed his eyes, he could see her naked, the water from the shower sluicing over her toned body and the steam rising around them as he held her close against his own bare skin. Remembering the feel of her firm breasts against his chest made his groin tighten.

Raine shook off the images and forced himself to swallow the rest of his food. His only intention toward Kate Roberts was to keep her alive until he could get her someplace safe. She was an innocent bystander in all this, and he intended to make sure that she survived this close encounter with the game of life and death. But even Kate's safety remained secondary to his mission. He had to stay focused on his goal: to find Dillon and the mole in Lucas's organization. Even if that turned out to be Lucas himself. Every fiber of Raine's being resisted that possibility.

Raine clenched his jaw against the rage that boiled inside him at the mere thought of Dillon. Dillon would die, and the mole would be tried for treason if he didn't die first. Raine hadn't decided if he would let the bastard live or not. This game would be just like any other, he would play the hand dealt him. He glanced at Kate. She represented a wild card. Raine hadn't decided yet if she would make his hand or break it. Time would tell, and time was his enemy. He retrieved the half-empty water bottle and passed it to Kate, then drank the rest when she finished. They'd have to make it to a source of food and water tonight.

After they had eaten and Raine had buried their cans and spoons, they resumed their journey. Darkness descended as rapidly as the temperature. Raine felt a rush of relief once they emerged into Smokemont campground. The place amounted to nothing more than vacant open spaces for campsites, cold fire rings and a scattering of trees of varying sizes. A paved road circled the grounds. The last tourist had left more than a month ago. Raine had grown up in a nearby community, and there wasn't much about this area that he didn't know.

"What now?" Kate asked, exhaustion evident in her tone.

"Seven miles to Cherokee." Raine didn't look at her, but he heard her little gasp of disbelief.

"But it's dark already."

"Don't think about it, just keep walking. It looks like rain." With growing dread, he scanned the thickening cloud cover. The temperature hadn't dropped low enough for sleet or snow, but precipitation appeared inevitable. And as long as they were moving, Raine could keep his mind off the woman. He needed to be physically exhausted before he spent another night in her company.

An hour later they reached the highway. Raine headed in the direction of Cherokee. The long, black road lay before them like a dark, endless river. The wind had gotten stronger, determined to blow up a storm.

"How far now?" Kate asked wearily.

She hadn't complained at all during the past hour, but Raine knew she had struggled to keep up. He had pushed hard, he knew, and now she was paying the price. Damn, he'd done nothing but screw up since meeting her.

"Not far," he assured her. He would flag down the first vehicle that passed if he had to use his Beretta to get the driver's attention. It was obvious now that Kate couldn't make it much farther, and carrying her would only slow them down. "We'll be there soon."

"Thank God," Kate muttered. "I hope I never get another assignment like this one."

Chapter Five

"What did you say?"

Kate didn't know whether it was the stone-cold blue eyes that glittered at her through the darkness or his bruising grip on her left forearm, but uneasiness stole over her. She'd said something wrong—something Raine didn't like.

"Wh-what are you talking about?" A fist of fear squeezed in her chest.

"You said," he replied tightly, "you hoped you never got another assignment like this." He stepped closer, his size and strength bearing down on her now. "What did you mean by that?"

Kate held her ground—she couldn't have moved if she had wanted to. Her weak and exhausted body had gone limp with absolute fear. She stared into the icy depths of his arctic gaze and said the only thing she knew to say, "I don't know what I meant." Straining with the effort, she swallowed. "I didn't realize I had said it until you repeated it to me." That same gaze that had singed her with heat only a few hours ago now chilled her to the bone.

Kate knew one thing for certain, she would never forget the hard, unflinching expression on his chiseled features. If he felt anything—anger, disbelief, sympathy—neither his face nor his eyes showed any hint whatsoever of what might be going on inside his head. His piercing blue gaze bored into hers, searching, analyzing.

The noose of uncertainty tightened around her neck.

Call in filtered through her haze of fear.

Headlights seemed to come out of nowhere, the flash of light flickering across Kate's face, breaking the charged moment. Raine glanced over his right shoulder at the approaching vehicle before settling his gaze back on hers.

"I'm telling the truth, Raine," she said quickly, in a last-ditch effort to convince him. "I don't know why I said that. Maybe I'm a reporter or something. I just don't know." She released the breath she'd been holding and then added, "You'll...you'll have to trust me on this."

"There's only one person I trust, Kate, and that's me." He turned toward the twin beams of light steadily growing larger, extended his arm and stuck out his thumb in the universal gesture indicating that he wanted a ride. He cut Kate a sidelong look. "But, if it makes you feel any better, I do believe you."

Kate closed her eyes and uttered a silent thanks. He believed her. That's all that mattered at the moment. *If Jack Raine suspects for one second...* Kate's eyes snapped open at the sound of the voice echoing inside her head. *Suspects what?* And how the hell did she know his first name was Jack? Had one of the goons from yesterday called him Jack? She replayed the words over and over, but the answers would not come. What did that warning mean? Who did the voice belong to?

"Is it safe to be hitching a ride?" she suddenly heard herself ask. Kate didn't know if she was cautious by nature, but the thought that their pursuers might be driving down this same road made her uneasy. Not to mention the voices inside her head, and the man standing next to her.

Come to think of it, Kate decided, she had a number of things to be uneasy about.

''Not driving something that sounds like that,'' Raine said impatiently.

An old pickup truck that was surely built before the invention of mufflers lurched to a stop in front of them. Raine opened the passenger-side door and leaned into the vehicle. Kate listened as he asked the driver about a ride to Cherokee. The old truck didn't look as if it would make it another mile much less all the way to Cherokee, but anything was better than walking in the frigid darkness with a storm threatening.

The man mercifully agreed to give them a lift. Raine stepped aside for Kate to climb in first. She eased onto the worn bench seat, the sensation of warmth inside the cab almost making her light-headed. Even the musty odor of stale tobacco and something resembling oil couldn't detract from Kate's appreciation of a ride. The heat blasting from the heater far outweighed all other unpleasantness.

Kate glanced at the driver as he struggled to grind into first gear. The old man eyed her with more interest than curiosity, his mostly toothless grin and scraggly beard doing nothing for his weathered face. Kate moved closer to Raine, putting as much distance between her and the leering old man as possible.

As if sensing her discomfort, Raine slid his arm around her shoulders and pulled her possessively against him. She was thankful for his strong presence as the truck jerked into forward motion. Kate had watched Raine in action. There was no doubt in her mind that he could handle whatever this strange man attempted.

Despite her misgivings about the driver, Kate leaned her weary head against Raine's solid shoulder. At the moment she didn't care if the man turned out to be Jack the Ripper, as long as she could rest for just a little while. Raine had promised to keep her safe and she had to trust him, even if he didn't trust her.

She still couldn't figure out why she would have used the word *assignment,* or why he had reacted so fiercely to it. Why would she hope never to get another *assignment* like this one? Wait a minute, did prostitutes consider their johns assignments? Kate shuddered at the thought. It had to be something else, she wouldn't allow herself to believe that distasteful possibility. Maybe she was a reporter and somehow she had latched on to Raine's story. Or, maybe she knew Ballatore's story. Kate tensed.

Ballatore. Who the hell was Ballatore? Had Raine used that name? Or had one of the goons who'd tried to kill them mentioned it? Kate closed her eyes and forced the questions away. She didn't know how she knew that name. She didn't know why she called this an assignment. She didn't know what her relationship with Raine amounted to. She didn't know why she didn't know.

God, she was so tired. Kate snuggled closer to Raine, and his arm tightened around her. He would keep her safe and that's all that mattered right now.

FIFTEEN MINUTES LATER, they were in the middle of Cherokee. The town was one long strip nestled between the soaring mountains. Neon signs flashed, advertising typical tourist-trap junk. Casinos, restaurants, motels, and other tacky, run-down buildings dotted the main street through the small town.

"That service station on the right will be fine," Raine told the driver. His voice sounded harsh after the long silence during the ride.

Without question, the old man pulled into the parking lot. Raine thanked him, opened the door and got out. Kate scooted across the seat and hurried out behind him. When her feet hit the ground, her legs felt rubbery beneath her. The cold night air seemed more brutal after the warmth of the truck.

"What now?" Kate asked, watching Raine as he surveyed the street in both directions. "A motel, I hope," she added when he didn't answer right away. "Or a restaurant, I'm starved."

"Not yet," he told her, his attention still focused on the mixture of gaudy and dilapidated businesses lining the long street.

"What then?" Kate hated the slight whine she heard in her voice. Every muscle in her body screamed in protest of taking another step; a dull ache had settled inside her head, or maybe it had been there all along but the task of keeping up with Raine had distracted her from the pain. Her chest still felt tight. She needed to eat—anything but beans and franks. And she was thirsty again, she suddenly realized.

"We need transportation out of here," he said as he started down the dimly lit street toward the busier end of town.

Kate flung argument after argument against her mental sounding board, but she trudged after Raine without protest. She had followed him this far, no point in changing her strategy now, no matter how much she wanted to check into a hotel and sleep for days. If he wanted to keep moving, she certainly didn't have a better plan. He obviously had some sort of plan, and any kind of plan was better than none.

Raine wandered through the casino parking lot, looking over each vehicle as if he was about to purchase one. Kate shivered. The cold night air had consumed the last of the warmth her body had managed to build up during their ride to Cherokee. Kate wrapped her arms around herself. She would walk until she dropped. Raine had to be tired, too. If he could keep moving, so could she.

Finally Raine opened the driver's-side door of an old Chevy sedan. After surveying the interior, he looked across the top of the car at Kate and said, "Get in."

"What?" She frowned at his curt demand.

"Get in, dammit."

Kate felt her eyes go round in genuine horror. "You're going to steal this car!" she hissed, glancing around to see if anyone was watching them. A thief! The man was a thief as well as a killer. She shook her head slowly from side to side in disbelief. He was crazy. *She* was crazy for tagging along with him.

"Get your butt in the car!" Raine commanded. He shot her a look that would have spurred a dead man into action.

Kate jerked the door open and plunked down onto the seat. Maybe his plan wasn't so great after all, she decided. Stealing! And she was an accessory. Grand theft auto, wasn't that a felony? Kate yanked at the obviously never-before-used seat belt. It wouldn't budge. She pulled harder. By God, she might be forced to ride in a stolen vehicle, but at least she would ride safely. The engine suddenly roared to life.

Kate's startled gaze bumped into Raine's. "How'd you do that so fast?"

One of those rare, breath-stealing smiles spread across his lips. "Trade secret." He winked, then leaned across Kate to reach the seat belt.

A tiny curl of awareness coiled inside her as she watched Raine pull the belt over her lap and snap the buckle into place. Kate had certainly been this close to him before, but there was something different this time. His protective gesture, that was it. Just like when he'd stepped between her and Vinny, and when the helicopter had come back he had pulled her to safety. She hadn't asked for his help with the seat belt, he had simply taken the initiative, as if her safety was important to him. As if she mattered in all this madness.

"Thank you," she murmured, sounding too breathless.

Still leaning across her, Raine paused. His gaze lingered on her mouth for a moment. Neon lights flashed and flickered, filling the car with a mixture of garish light and eerie shadow. When his gaze lifted to hers, the lean, hungry look in his eyes twisted that little curl of desire until heat funneled just beneath Kate's belly button.

Raine abruptly banished the hunger in his eyes and straightened. He put the car in Reverse and muttered, "You're welcome." Without another look in her direction, he backed the car out of its slot and pulled out of the parking lot.

Kate rubbed her hands up and down her arms as if she could warm herself by sheer determination. She relaxed against the cloth seat and tried to forget the needy look she had seen in Raine's eyes. She knew it wasn't right, but she couldn't help thinking of the way she had felt when she woke that morning in his arms, tingly and warm all over. Although she had been fighting mad with him for having responded sexually to her, she was more angry at herself for her own body's traitorous reaction. And then in the woods. She had wanted him to kiss her, and he would have if they hadn't been interrupted. On some level it pleased Kate to know that he felt the pull of desire too.

Maybe he was a bad guy, but he had some good points all the same. Especially, she thought with a little smile, those amazing blue eyes. She could imagine how really touching him and losing complete control would feel.

Stop it, Kate! She bit her lip. She couldn't think that

way. *There's no telling how many men he's killed,* Danny's words rang out inside her head. Jack Raine was a killer.

...*this one worries me.* That other voice echoed right behind Danny's. Kate squeezed her eyes shut and tried to place the voice that haunted her. It was a woman. Someone she trusted. That's all she knew. But who? Her mother? A sister? *Who?*

Kate sighed and stared into the darkness beyond the headlights. Was her past so awful that she couldn't bear to remember it? Or was it her that was so unmemorable?

The beam of the headlights moved over a road sign up ahead that read Bryson City 10 Miles.

"Bryson City, is that where we're going?" Kate turned to Raine, hoping he would choose to gift her with a straight answer. "What's in Bryson City?"

"That's where we're headed. Bryson City has public transportation." Raine didn't look at her, and, if his tone gave any indication, he wasn't interested in conversing. As usual.

Too tired to care, Kate leaned against the door and watched the first fat drops of rain splat against the windshield. The heater had finally kicked in, filling the car with its warmth. Soon the pelting against the glass grew steadier, turning the highway in front of them into a long line of black ink. The desolate road stretched out before them, taking Kate away from a past she didn't recall and into a future she understood nothing about. Her mind felt as empty and desolate as the highway. She shivered again, but this time it had nothing to do with the cold.

The hypnotic swish of the wipers lulled Kate toward sleep. Her lids felt so heavy...she needed to sleep...to rest her aching muscles and ease the tightness in her chest. She finally closed her eyes and welcomed the heavy blanket of inner darkness.

KATE SAT UP with a start as she felt the tires leave the pavement and bump over uneven ground. She glanced at Raine to see if he had fallen asleep at the wheel. He was wide awake and braking the car to a stop.

"Where are we?" Kate peered through the dark and drizzle in an effort to get her bearings. She saw trees but couldn't make out anything else.

"We walk from here." Raine opened his door and got out of the car.

It took a few moments for his words to register, then Kate realized he intended that they walk in the rain. "But it's raining," she protested when he opened her door.

He reached inside and unbuckled her seat belt, then glared at her. "No kidding."

Kate sat there, stunned. She wasn't about to leave another perfectly good automobile. Especially a nice warm one. He was definitely crazy—worse than crazy. He was…he was… Kate couldn't think of a fitting description at the moment, but whatever it was, he was it.

"Get out of the car," he ordered, giving her one final threatening stare. His breath fanned across her face. A muscle twitched in his tense jaw. The dim interior light cast his stony features in shadows and angles that enhanced the impatient scowl on his handsome face. She couldn't possibly win in this battle of wills. Raine had no intention of giving one centimeter.

Kate exhaled in frustration. One corner of his mouth lifted the tiniest fraction—he'd won and he knew it. Raine straightened and waited for her to get out. Kate silently recited every swearword she could remember, twice. With equal measures reluctance and anger, she forced herself out of the nice warm car, then slammed the door. Raine had the grace not to allow that smile to completely form as he adjusted the collar of his leather jacket. Without another word, he strode toward what Kate recognized as the highway they had left behind. Raine had pulled the car onto a dead-end side road just far enough that it would be hidden from view.

Cursing under her breath, Kate struggled to unzip the thick collar of her parka and pull out the hood. By the time she had the hood pulled over her head, her hair was already damp. She shivered as the icy liquid slid down the collar of her sweatshirt and absorbed into the T-shirt beneath. Seething inside, she flung a few expletives at Raine's broad back. As usual, he ignored her.

Once they were on the pavement, Kate could see that Bryson City lay only half a mile or so away. At least they wouldn't be walking for long. It dawned on Kate then that Raine had abandoned the vehicle because it was stolen. Tucked in the cluster of trees, it would be days or weeks before the car would be found. The man left as few clues as possible. By the time the car was found and traced back to them, they would be long gone. He seemed to think of everything to cover his tracks. Maybe he was crazy. Yeah, right—crazy like a fox. Kate supposed that he had done the right thing, even if she was getting all wet. They hadn't come this far just to get caught because he made a stupid mistake.

He's managed to slip through their fingers. Kate frowned. That voice. She knew that voice. But what did the words mean? She looked at the man she struggled to keep pace with. *Him?* Whose fingers had he slipped through? The police? The other bad guys? Kate shoved her gloved hands deeper into her pockets and sighed. She had to remember. Every instinct told her that her life depended on remembering.

But she was too tired now to think about it anymore. She shuddered as the wind whipped the icy droplets against her face. God, how she hated to be cold. As if on cue, her stomach rumbled. She hated to be hungry, too.

When they reached civilization, Raine used a pay phone at a service station. Kate had no idea who or where he called. She was too wet and too cold even to wonder. She shivered almost uncontrollably now. The only thing on her mind at this point was getting somewhere warm and dry. She didn't care if she ate, only that she got warm.

After the brief call, she followed Raine to a seedy-looking motel on the edge of town. She wondered vaguely how he managed to keep from shivering as she did.

Because he's a machine, that's how. He doesn't have any feelings, she added decidedly. Jack Raine, if that was his full name, was a cold, heartless *killing* machine. Kate shuddered at the thought. Then she remembered the way he could make her feel with just the right look. Maybe he wasn't *all* machine.

Kate could only guess what her financial standing might be, but somehow she knew that this place—she scanned the shabby room once more—was beneath the usual for her. The term "motel" had been used very loosely, in her opinion.

"There's only one bed," she said, suddenly noticing among the decrepit furnishings the one bed, slightly wider than the last one they had shared, but singular nonetheless.

"This was the only room available. You heard the manager say so yourself. So put a lid on it and get in the shower. We have to get out of these wet clothes." Raine cut her a look that dared her to argue with him. He dropped his coat onto a chair behind him and quickly moved his hands down his shirtfront, releasing button after button with stiff, clumsy fingers.

"What are you doing?" Kate retreated a step only to bump into the lone bed.

"The same thing you're going to do, if I have to help you do it." His hard-edged tone and the implacable expression on his face reinforced his words.

When Kate hesitated, he added, "Don't worry, I'm too tired to be dangerous."

At that same instant he peeled his shirt off his shoulders, revealing more than Kate needed to see right now. Her mouth went incredibly dry. He walked into what was obviously the bathroom and came out wiping his awesome chest with a towel, wordlessly offering her the first shower. He might be tired, but somehow she doubted the other. She decided right then and there that it would be safe to assume that Raine was definitely dangerous, even in his sleep.

Kate hurriedly unzipped her parka, shouldered out of it and dropped it to the floor next to the bed. Without sparing Raine a glance, she walked past him and locked herself in the minuscule bathroom. She stared at the still-unfamiliar reflection in the mirror. Her dark hair was wet and disheveled. The smudges under her eyes looked black against her pale skin. She was a mess. Shivering to the point that her teeth chattered, Kate quickly stripped off her wet clothes and stepped into the shower with the water as hot as she could tolerate it.

After unwrapping a new bar of soap, she closed her eyes and allowed the heat to relax her sore, stiff muscles. The wonderful sensation of liquid warmth was almost enough to make her forget about food. *Almost,* Kate thought as she rubbed the soap into a lather. She hoped they wouldn't have to wait for their clothes to dry to get something to eat. She was starved.

Since their pathetic excuse for lodgings didn't offer amenities such as shampoo, Kate had no choice but to wash her hair with the bar soap. She worked the lather into her hair, then she moved to her shoulders and arms, and on to her breasts. The steam rose around her, filling the tiny room with moist heat. Kate's breathing became slow and shallow as vivid memories of her shower with Raine reeled through her tired mind like images from a hot, steamy movie.

His broad, muscular chest and strong arms. Hands that were both gentle and comforting as he'd held her in his arms, warming her with his own body heat. Kate vaguely remembered him drying her skin and then carrying her to his bed. She braced her hands against the dingy, tiled wall when the terrifying events of yesterday and today replayed before her eyes. Raine stepping between her and Vinny, the out-of-control car ride, the loud, echoing sound of gunfire, the helicopter, and then the long trek across the mountain.

Just when she had decided once and for all what a bad guy Raine was, he did something like putting his arm around her in the truck, protecting her when she felt uneasy. Buckling her seat belt when she couldn't. And now, letting her shower first. Nothing about him fit one particular mold. And absolutely nothing about him could ever possibly be considered less than dangerous.

Then there was the intense desire she had seen in his eyes this morning and the lean, hungry look she'd noticed there tonight. Maybe he wanted to be nice to her in return for sex. Her eyes popped open and she pushed the water and hair back from her face. After all, they were pretty much joined at the hip for the duration of this little adventure. And he hadn't exactly said that they hadn't done it already. Surely if she had slept with a hunk like Raine, she would remember. Kate shivered involuntarily despite the hot water warming her skin.

Maybe the intense awareness between them was simply

hormones. Or, maybe the man was flat out horny. Kate shivered at the thought of Raine's naked body moving over hers. Banishing the images, she turned off the water, pushed the curtain aside and stepped out of the tub. She pulled a clean, rough terry-cloth towel from the stack on the back on the commode. Kate hugged the towel to her breasts as she leaned forward and swiped the fog from the mirror. Would a man like Raine consider her attractive? she wondered.

She bit her lower lip and studied the reflection staring back at her. She was attractive, she supposed. Kate turned her head slightly and inspected the ugly bruise on her left temple. It had turned an unflattering shade of reddish purple. She lowered the towel from her breasts and scrutinized them as well. They weren't large, but, she decided as she surveyed her nude body, they did seem properly proportioned to the rest of her. Her waist was slim, her hips flared a bit, and her legs were long and toned.

All in all, Kate felt reasonably satisfied with what she saw. Now, if only she could remember the past and the personality that went with the body.

Raine pounded on the closed door, startling Kate. Her heart thudded out her panic at the possibility that they had been found already. Were the bad guys here? Raine pounded on the door again. Instantly Kate covered herself with the towel as if he might see her through the door.

"What's the holdup?" he demanded impatiently.

Kate pressed a hand to her throat. Thank God. He only wanted his turn. She blew a breath out slowly and licked her lips nervously. "Just a minute," she yelled back.

Quickly, she dried and wrapped a clean towel around herself. She retrieved the brush from her purse and hastily tugged it through her hair. Kate gathered her wet clothes and took another deep breath before she opened the door.

He waited, blocking her exit, irritation etched in his features.

"Hang your clothes over by the heating unit. I've turned it on high so they'll dry faster." Raine had already undressed, leaving nothing but the towel draped precariously around his narrow hips.

Kate kept her gaze above his waist as she waited for him to step out of her way. The scattering of hair on his chest was blond too, she noticed, and it looked gold against his skin. Several thin, jagged lines drew her attention. Scars, she realized. Before she could ask about them, he stepped aside.

Kate hurried past him. She couldn't look him in the eye, not after the thoughts she'd had in the shower. God, she must be insane, fantasizing about a man who was a thief as well as a killer. And a kidnapper if she added the fact that he had dragged her, unwilling, into this nightmare. She draped her clothes over the heating unit next to his and valiantly fought the impulse to turn around. Kate knew he was watching her, she could feel his gaze on her body.

She straightened, swallowed hard, then turned to face him. He stood at the closet with the door open. "I'll need you to wait in here while I shower."

Anger unfurled inside Kate. "You're kidding," she suggested, giving him an opportunity to retain his current status as a gentleman in her opinion.

"I never kid," he deadpanned. "I can't trust you not to make a run for it." He opened the door wider and motioned for her to step inside. "I won't be long."

Raine slipped down Kate's opinion poll several notches, all the way back to jerk, in fact. She recognized the futility in arguing with him, so she squared her shoulders and stamped across the room. Kate paused at his side and shrugged. "Why not? I've been subjected to numerous other indignities since making your acquaintance.'' She stepped into the tiny, dark closet and kept her back turned until he closed the door.

Kate huffed a disgusted breath. Of all the amenities for a dump like this to have—a real closet. She stood stone still in the middle of the unadvertised and unusual feature and mused over the irony of it all.

RAINE EXHALED in disgust as he closed the door and jammed a straight chair securely under the knob. He didn't exactly feel good about locking Kate in the closet, but he couldn't risk her running. And, though she appeared harmless enough, there was something about her that ate at him. He knew better than to get involved with Kate. She was an unknown factor...a risk. Swallowing back that ridiculous guilt he felt every time he so much as raised his voice to the woman, he entered the bathroom, leaving the door open so he could keep an eye on the closet door.

Raine stepped into the hot spray of water and closed his eyes. He pressed his forehead against the tiled wall and allowed the hot water to sluice over his tired muscles. He relaxed a moment longer before making short work of washing and rinsing. He didn't want to leave Kate stuck in the closet for too long. She might beat on the door or scream at the top of her lungs. Raine had quickly learned that Kate was almost as unpredictable as he was. And that was a helluva scary thought. Especially since he still didn't know much about her.

Except that he wanted her—wanted her bad. Raine swore. He was a fool. A damn fool. He'd had the hots for the woman practically since the moment he'd laid eyes on her. She was just so bloody vulnerable. And beautiful, with an innocence that tugged at something deep inside him. Raine had spent so much time in the company of scum,

he had forgotten that there were still truly innocent people
in the world. Kate struck him as one of those. There was
something undeniably attractive about that part of her.
Something that drew him like a moth to flame.

And he would probably get burned…or worse.

He was a fool all right.

After drying off, Raine secured a towel around his waist
and hurried to remove the chair and open the closet door.
Kate didn't look at him as she stepped out of her two-foot-
by-four-foot prison. The towel effectively covered her
slender body, but fully displayed those long, shapely legs.
Need punched him in the gut again as he watched her walk
straight to the bed and burrow between the sheets. Raine
shook his head in self-disgust at how easily she could
make him feel like a heel.

And want her even more. This woman was going to get
him killed. Raine scrubbed his hand over his face and then
through his hair. He had spent more than a dozen years
facing death and dealing it out as well. For the first time
in his life, he felt unprepared for the situation. He could
look a target in the eye when that target took his last breath
and feel little remorse, but every time Raine looked Kate
in the eye something moved, twisted inside him.

This was bad, real bad.

Get a grip, Jack old boy, before you get yourself killed.
He swallowed. Kate Roberts was just a woman. He only
felt protective because she couldn't remember who she
was or where she came from. That was all.

Yeah, right. Raine jammed his hands at his waist. Kate's
memory loss was the least of their problems at the moment. Being with him was likely going to cost this pretty
lady her life, that's what bothered him. But he couldn't
chance leaving her behind at this point. Even if she turned
out to be the enemy.

Shrugging off the thought, Raine walked to the bedside table and pulled the telephone book from the drawer. He was tired. He would be able to deal with all this better tomorrow.

"What kind of pizza do you like?" he asked as he thumbed through the Yellow Pages for a restaurant that delivered.

"I don't care," she said, her voice muffled by the cover. "I'm not going to eat with you and I'm not going to talk to you." Kate kept her back turned, refusing to look at him.

"I'm devastated," he muttered, then reached for the telephone and called in an order. How in the hell had he gotten himself into this situation? It wasn't bad enough that Ballatore's men were after him, even his own people had jumped on the bandwagon. The mole's doing, no doubt. And, as if that weren't trouble aplenty, he had to be saddled with—he glared at Kate's back—a helpless and annoying female who pushed all his buttons.

He was definitely screwed.

Raine had always known that he was going to hell for his multitude of sins, he just thought he'd die first. Not once had anyone ever warned him that when he got his it would come in the form of a high-priority assignment gone sour and a woman who turned him inside out.

Kate continued her silent treatment even after the pizza and drinks arrived. The smell alone was enough to make Raine salivate. He sat down in one of the two chairs flanking the small table and propped his feet on the end of the bed. Kate continued to face the wall while Raine ate his fill. He commented frequently on the delicious ingredients and the thick crust, but she ignored him completely. He knew she needed to eat, but he couldn't make her if she didn't want to. Damn, the woman irritated the hell out of him.

Finished, Raine stood, scratched his chest and stretched his arms over his head. He was tired. He made himself comfortable on the side of the bed next to Kate's back. She immediately wiggled to the edge, as far away from him as possible. Then, as soon as he had gotten situated just right and turned on the news, she edged off the bed on the other side and went to the table. He frowned. What the hell was she doing now?

Kate plopped into one of the chairs, picked up a large slice of pizza, and closed her eyes as she savored the taste.

"I thought you were on a hunger strike."

She took a gulp of soda, then flashed him a look. "I didn't say I wasn't going to eat, I said I wasn't going to eat with you."

Raine suppressed the grin that tugged at his lips. Kate had no intention of allowing him to get the better of her. He was beginning to wonder if maybe she was going to get the better of him. Kate Roberts had gotten deeper under his skin in the last thirty-six hours than anyone had in his adult life. It wasn't just the physical attraction either, and that was stronger than any he had experienced. It was the way she could turn his resolve to mush or make his insides twist just by looking at him. The sound of her voice made him want her.

Raine didn't want to want her. Somehow he had to get this crazy need back under control. He forced his gaze from her towel-clad body. Looking at all the silky skin revealed by her lack of clothing wasn't going to help.

Raine scanned the television channels for a while. As usual, nothing caught his interest. Eventually Kate got back into bed. Perched on the far edge, she kept her back to him. Still bored and restless, he allowed his gaze to linger on Kate's bare shoulders. His groin tightened. Damn, he had to get this woman out of his system. Disgusted with himself, Raine ran through the channels once more.

But how could he not think about her when he was stuck with her at least for a few more days?

Fear. She was definitely afraid of him on some level. That was the ticket. If he could keep her afraid of him, then she would never let him too close. That was the answer. Raine pushed the power button on the remote, turning the television off. He settled farther down into the bed without getting under the covers. No way was he going to chance coming in contact with her bare skin. That would be a big mistake.

And tomorrow he would concentrate on fear and intimidation, his specialties. Sweet little Kate would never know what hit her. She would keep her distance then. Raine felt a smile pull at his lips as he drifted into much-needed sleep.

RAINE WOKE at 6:00 a.m. His left arm was draped over Kate's breasts, his face buried in the curve of her neck. His left hand had tangled in her soft hair. Even the smell of cheap soap couldn't mask her womanly scent. He could feel the heat of her body all along the front of his. It would be so easy to tug the sheet down, ease his body over hers and take what he wanted. Would she resist after he used his lips and hands to persuade her? He didn't think so. Raine had seen desire in her eyes more than once. She wanted him, too. Maybe not as much as he wanted her, but the need was there.

Raine rubbed a strand of dark, silky hair between his thumb and forefinger. So soft, so sweet. He doubted that Kate had had much experience with men—especially men like him. His whole body tightened at the thought of how hot and snug she would be. He wanted to taste her, to bury himself inside her. To forget for just a little while.

Raine set his jaw hard. He allowed himself one last deep draw of her scent before he moved away from her enticing body. That line of thinking would get them both killed. He had to keep his mind on business. Disgusted with his intense state of arousal, Raine picked up his jeans and shirt and headed for the bathroom. He'd give Kate a few more minutes to sleep. She had tossed and turned a lot during the night. He wondered what demons chased her. She seemed entirely too young and innocent to have any significant demons, but looks could be deceiving, as he well knew.

Maybe she wasn't what she seemed at all. Maybe, she was bait—sexy, beautiful bait. Raine tensed. He hadn't considered that particular possibility until now. He stared at his reflection in the bathroom mirror. It wouldn't be the first time a woman had been used that way to trap him.

''You're a fool,'' he told his doubting reflection. He had already lost his perspective entirely when it came to Kate Roberts.

That was a mistake, a big mistake.

After he had dressed, Raine picked up Kate's clothes and sat down on the side of the bed. He turned on the lamp and looked at her closely. The sheet and towel had slipped down, revealing one firm breast, but that wasn't what caught his eye. She was even paler than she had been the day before. The bruise on her temple looked a nasty shade of red. Her rose-colored lips weren't quite as rosy as before and the dark circles under her eyes were much darker.

Something was wrong, but they had to put more miles behind them before they stopped for any length of time.

Still, Raine had an uneasy feeling about the way she looked. He glanced at his watch. Six-fifteen. They had to get moving.

"Kate, wake up." Raine shook her gently. "Kate, you need to get up and get dressed."

She sat bolt upright, pulling the sheet over her as she went. She surveyed the room, her searching gaze instantly alert. Raine frowned. This was the second time he had noticed that waking reaction. He eyed her suspiciously. This kind of response definitely warred with his instincts about her. Whatever Kate had to hide was lost to her as well, and that provided Raine with a safety net of sorts. But what about when she remembered? He would deal with that when and if the situation presented itself.

"What now?" she asked, shoving long silky strands of hair behind her ears.

"Get dressed. We have to get moving." Raine pushed up off the bed and crossed the room. He stared out the window while he waited for Kate to get ready. One way or another he would refocus his perspective, especially where she was concerned.

After a full ten minutes in the bathroom, she finally pulled on her coat and announced that she was good to go.

Though the sun was shining, the early-morning air cut straight to the bone. It was a damn good thing they didn't have to do any mountain climbing today. Raine glanced back at Kate, who had fallen behind. He frowned again. She didn't look as if she'd make it the few blocks they had to go. He waited for her to catch up before continuing.

Kate didn't ask any questions or make any comments when he led her into the bus station and used a clean credit card to purchase two tickets for New York City. She sat quietly and obediently. Another indication that something wasn't quite right.

When they boarded the bus, Raine ushered Kate to an empty seat in the back. Still, she didn't protest.

She sat next to the window, staring into the distance. Raine relaxed into the seat and closed his eyes. He hadn't ridden a bus in a long time; now he remembered why. Noisy, uncomfortable and smelly, just to name a few of the less pleasant points. But, it was a means to an end. His pursuers wouldn't expect him to take a bus.

"Why are we going to New York?"

Raine cracked one eye open and looked at his traveling companion. "I thought you were giving me the silent treatment?"

"Never mind," she muttered, then turned back to the window.

That damn guilt again. Raine cursed himself for feeling it. "I have a command performance in New York," he said quietly, irritated that he felt compelled to give her an explanation. "An old friend wants the pleasure of my company so badly that he's willing to kill for it."

Friend? Raine almost laughed out loud at his misnomer. He didn't have any friends in the true sense of the word, least of all the man he had most recently betrayed. Raine forced the image of Sal Ballatore from his mind. They were enemies, nothing more.

Kate turned back to him, her eyes wide with uncertainty and the slightest hint of fear. Raine knew that he had to pursue that avenue if he was ever going to keep his sanity. He'd been in this business too long to screw up because he couldn't control his lust for a woman.

"Have you really killed hundreds of men?" she asked in a tentative voice.

Raine smiled at the question. Where in the hell had she heard something like that? Danny, maybe. He leaned a bit closer and pulled his most intimidating face. "Do you really want me to answer that question?"

She swallowed tightly. Her voice trembled a little when she answered, but she kept her gaze locked with his. "Yes."

Raine lifted one shoulder in a careless shrug. "I don't know. I never really kept count. It's probably a fairly accurate estimate. But there is one inaccuracy." Raine leaned even closer, crowding her. "They weren't all men, some were women."

Kate drew back as far as possible against the window. She tried without success to mask the stark fear that stole across her features. "Are you...do you kill people for money? Is that what you do?"

Raine laughed softly. His answer had evoked just the response he had hoped for, but he really hadn't expected the second question. "No. I don't kill people for the money, *exactly*."

She sucked in a sharp breath, licked her lips and then hit him with another one. "Then why do you...kill people, exactly?"

Raine forced the smile to fade from his lips and turned up the intimidation a notch. "If I told you the answer to that, then I'd have to kill you, too."

Chapter Six

He was only joking, Kate told herself for the one hundredth time that day. She had asked a stupid question and she'd gotten a stupid answer. Kate twisted in her seat and stared out the window into the blackness.

The day had stretched into a lifetime. Kate's head still ached, but not as much as the day before. The pain and weakness in her muscles had grown undeniably worse. Maybe she wasn't accustomed to such a rigorous physical workout. Mountain climbing obviously wasn't her forte. Whatever the case, Kate felt exhausted and limp, as if her bones had melted, leaving her incapable of the slightest exertion. Even after a night's rest and the endless morning sitting on a bus, she still didn't feel refreshed. If she had ever been this tired before, she didn't care to remember that particular event.

She had hoped that with the dawning and passing of a new day, more memories would surface as well, but they hadn't. Raine had remained distant, in his own little world. He had spoken to her only once the entire day and that was to inquire whether she wanted to eat during one of the extended layovers. They had eaten in silence at a fast-food restaurant next to the bus station.

Kate passed the afternoon away watching the landscape

go by and mulling over the few snatches of memory she could recall. The words and warnings didn't make any sense. The voice—the woman's voice—seemed familiar, yet no name or face emerged from the gray haze that hid her past. The phrase "call in" stirred the most emotion for her. The words seemed deeply entrenched, like a lesson gone over many times. On an elemental level Kate knew that she needed to follow that instinct the moment she remembered the number again.

Eventually the day had turned once more to night, and darkness enshrouded them. Kate relaxed back into her seat and, with the gentle rocking of the large silver bus, drifted toward sleep. Just before sleep took her, the thought occurred to Kate that she had yet to catch Raine in even a nap. Vaguely she wondered if he slept at all. Of course not, she decided as she gave in to her body's need to shut down, machines don't need to sleep.

THE GENTLE, rhythmic rocking had stopped.

Abruptly, Kate jerked awake. Raine was telling her to get moving. The other passengers had lined up single file down the long center aisle to wait their turn to exit the bus. Ignoring her body's protest, Kate pushed out of the seat and followed Raine off the bus and into the all but empty station. A handful of travel-weary people waited for their connections or for a loved one to pick them up. Kate scanned the sleep-deprived faces and wished she was like them—on her way home.

Home. Where was home? she wondered.

Virginia. Her driver's license had been issued in Virginia. Maybe that was home.

"What time is it?" Kate asked, then shoved her hands into her pockets and huddled into her parka as they exited the building. The night air seemed colder than it had been in Bryson City. They were traveling north, so that would make sense. "What time is it?" she repeated, increasing her pace to keep up with Raine's long strides on the uphill trek. The landscape seemed hilly, as if the city was carved into the side of a mountain, but nothing Kate saw clicked any recognition. In fact, she had seen about all the mountainous territory she cared to see in this lifetime.

"One thirty-five," he said without slowing down.

The bus had stopped so many times, with a couple lengthy layovers, there was no way Kate could gauge the distance they had traveled in time. She surveyed the sleeping town Raine seemed determined to cross on foot and came to one conclusion very quickly—they definitely weren't in New York City. She had been to New York. She didn't remember when or how, but she had been there. Kate remembered the skyscrapers, the traffic at all hours of the night. This wasn't the Big Apple.

Raine walked up the dark, quiet sidewalk as if he had a specific destination in mind. The long bus ride had made Kate's overworked muscles stiff and lethargic. She grimaced with each step she took. She hoped like hell that Raine didn't intend to walk from wherever they were to New York. If so, she was out.

"Where are we?" Kate forced herself to maintain his pace so he couldn't ignore her question.

"You don't recognize it?" He stopped, and leveled his penetrating blue gaze on her.

Kate's feet stopped before the rest of her did. When she had steadied herself, she hesitated before answering. Was this a trick question? Should she know this city? She looked around again, taking in the one- and two-story buildings and an array of storefronts. Nothing at all looked familiar. "No," she finally admitted.

"Charlottesville, Virginia," he told her.

Raine watched her reaction carefully. Kate struggled to keep her face clear of emotion. Virginia. That was supposed to be home, but nothing about this place felt like home. Panic swept through her, a cold, harsh reminder that she had lost her past. Lost herself.

Suck it up, girl. Don't let him get to you. Just because you lived in Virginia doesn't mean you've ever been to this particular town. "I thought we were going to New York," she reminded. Good move. Turn the tables on him. Make him squirm for a change.

He looked away then. "There's something I have to do first."

Without further explanation, Raine resumed his journey to God only knows where. Kate had little choice but to follow. After all, she had practically no money, no memory, no nothing. She could only stick to him and hope it was the right thing to do.

After crossing two more streets, they entered the dimly lit cobblestone entrance of a large hotel. Now this, she acknowledged thankfully, was a hotel. The well-kept exterior beckoned to the weary traveler. The lobby looked warm and welcoming.

Fortunately there were plenty of rooms, so Kate was able to have a separate bed. The moment they entered the room, she dropped her coat to the floor, kicked off her shoes and sprawled out on her big soft bed—the one farthest from the door, per Raine's insistence. Kate closed her eyes and sighed. She had died and gone to heaven. Now, if only she never had to move again. Well, just one last move, she told herself as she tugged the spread over her body. Kate burrowed into the thick cover and relaxed completely. She didn't care what other amenities the room might have.

She didn't open her eyes again, but she could hear Raine

moving around the room. Kate didn't care what he did as long as he left her alone. She was so very tired, even breathing seemed an effort. The aroma of coffee brewing couldn't even rouse her. Tomorrow she would worry about trying to find home. If Virginia was home, surely she could find her way from here. All she had to do was give Raine the slip and hide from the bad guys who were after him. Simple enough.

Kate sleepily moaned her disbelief. Giving Raine the slip wouldn't be quite so easy. He didn't miss a single detail. Sometimes she wondered if he could read her mind. What a strange man. A paradox.

A cold-blooded killer. Kate shuddered and hugged the spread more closely. Danny had said that Raine had killed hundreds of men, and Raine hadn't bothered to deny it. In fact, he seemed rather proud of it, unremorseful. But something inside her—intuition maybe—kept telling her to trust him. She had no idea if she could really trust him or not, but one thing remained certain—Raine could have killed her long ago had that been his intent. He had taken care of her so far. She would just have to go with the flow. What else could she do?

FOUR A.M. The lighted display shone brightly in the darkness. What had awakened her? Kate strained to listen. Thunder exploded and lightning flashed across the darkness. It was storming outside, she realized with relief. She squinted at Raine's empty bed. Where was he? The next flash of lightning answered her question. Raine stood at the window staring out at the storm.

Kate disentangled herself from the covers and slid out of bed. She padded across the room to stand next to him. "What's wrong?" she asked as she rubbed her eyes to clear them. The brooding silhouette he made against the dim glow of neon and violent displays of nature's fury made her shiver.

"Nothing. Go back to sleep." He didn't spare her a glance, but continued his relentless gaze into the stormy night.

Lightning streaked across the sky again, followed closely by two more brilliant flashes, giving Kate a heart-stumbling view of Raine's bare chest and unsnapped jeans. Her eyes followed the golden trail of wispy chest hair until it disappeared into the half-zipped fly of his jeans. Desire coiled, sending a spear of heat through her middle. She blinked when the darkness returned as suddenly as it had vanished. Had she been openly gaping at the man's body? Yes, she had. Kate couldn't bring herself to meet the gaze she felt analyzing her. No doubt he had also noted her preoccupation with his bare torso.

Kate pushed a handful of hair away from her face and wet her lips. She had to say something—she couldn't just stand there like an idiot. The next flash of light brightened the entire room and the clap of thunder boomed so loud that Kate jerked, then staggered in its wake.

Raine grabbed her by the shoulders and steadied her. There was nothing tender about his grasp. He held her too tightly and too close, willing her to look at him.

"I'm okay," she managed to say, though her body denied her words by trembling uncontrollably. She couldn't look at him. Part of her wanted desperately to touch him, but another part—a much wiser part—wanted to pull away, to run. "I'm okay," she told him again when he didn't immediately release her.

"Somehow I doubt that," he said, his words blunt, his voice low and husky. The sound shivered over her nerve endings, both terrifying and tantalizing.

"Look at me," he ordered, cupping her face and forcing her gaze upward.

Kate looked at his mouth first, that full tempting mouth that was almost too beautiful to belong to a man. Two days' worth of golden-brown stubble covered his jaw, lending a definite roguish quality. Finally, reluctantly, Kate met that piercing gaze. Ice blue, with an underlying fierceness that drew her and pushed her away at the same time.

He caressed her cheek with the pad of his thumb, all the while his eyes weaved a sensual spell of their own. "Are you afraid, Kate?"

"Yes." The one word came out breathless, a mere whisper. A thought spoken.

"Tell me what you're afraid of," he commanded.

Kate swallowed. It was difficult to think clearly with him so close and his eyes so...so intent on her. "I'm afraid those men will find us."

His thumb slid over her lower lip, Kate shivered. "You're not afraid of me?"

Wariness had stolen into his intent gaze. Kate nodded, once. "A little," she admitted. "But you said you would keep me safe, and I believe you." She bit her lower lip to erase the sensation of his touch.

He made a small sound of satisfaction in his throat. "What is it about me that puts fear in you, Kate?" She stiffened when he lowered his head and pressed his lips to her cheek in a lingering kiss. "Is it my infamous reputation?" His fingers curled around her nape, tangled in her hair and pulled her head back while he planted a line of slow, steamy kisses down her throat. Kate shuddered when need erupted inside her.

"Or maybe—" Raine traced a path back to her ear with the tip of his tongue, leaving a trail of gooseflesh "—you're afraid of how I make you feel."

Kate's breath stilled in her lungs. Even the storm seemed to quiet for one long, electrifying moment.

He hummed a knowing sound against the shell of her ear. "So that's it." He nipped her earlobe with his teeth. Kate gasped. Her heart thundered in her ears, drowning out the renewed sounds of the storm raging outside. "Sweet little Kate doesn't want to admit that she lusts after a killer."

Instinctively she flattened her palms against his chest and pushed. "Stop," she said in a shaky voice. "I want you to stop."

Raine's grasp on the handful of hair at her nape tightened, keeping her from turning away when he drew back to look into her eyes. His arm snaked around her waist and pulled her closer, until their bodies touched intimately. Kate's pulse reacted to the intense desire she saw in his eyes and the feel of him against her. He was aroused. She sucked in a sharp breath. He smiled. An insanely sexy, irritatingly confident gesture that affected only one side of his mouth.

"You're sure you want me to stop?" He pressed his hand into the small of her back, forcing her to mold to his unmistakably male contours.

Kate squirmed, but suppressed the urge to arch against the hard ridge straining into her belly. "Yes," she murmured, though yes was far from her thoughts. She wanted him to take her. She wanted to feel him inside her. God, how could she want him?

Instantly, Raine's hold relaxed, but he didn't release her completely. "All right," he rasped. "I just have to do one thing first."

Kate's gaze collided with Raine's a heartbeat before his mouth captured hers. Unlike his gruff words, his lips were soft, his siege tender. He tasted like coffee and something else, something dark and mysterious. A staggering swell of desire surged through her, making her dizzy with want. Without thought, Kate's hands slid over his muscled chest and her arms twined around his neck.

No, she didn't want him to stop. Kate tiptoed, pressing her body more intimately against his. She didn't ever want him to stop. Raine's answering groan set off a series of shock waves deep inside her, the pulsating aftershocks weakening her knees. His tongue pushed inside her mouth, hot and demanding. Kate moaned her acceptance as he explored, retreated, and thrust again.

His hand was under her sweatshirt, beneath her T-shirt, seeking, caressing. Each brush of his callused palm over her bare skin sent spasms of desire to her core. And then he had her breast in his hand; his thumb grazed her nipple, and it puckered and her feminine muscles clenched. Raine kissed her harder, commanding her body with complete mastery.

You're a woman…you're young and beautiful. That will get you closer than anyone else… The words exploded inside Kate's head. This was a mistake. She had to make him stop. Kate struggled to push Raine away. To stop his sensual assault. He broke the kiss and stared down at her, his breath ragged, his eyes glazed.

"I can't do this," she gasped, fighting for her next breath. She needed to get away from him. Kate pushed harder, trying to put some space between their heated bodies.

"It's all right," he assured her. "I'll stop." He took his time removing his hand from beneath her shirt, allowing his palm to glide slowly down her rib cage. Kate stood stock-still, afraid to move at all for fear of throwing herself back into his arms.

He lifted that hand, still warm from clutching her breast,

and traced the outline of her cheek. "But next time I won't." He leaned closer, filling the tiny distance she had managed to put between them. "Next time I'll be so deep inside you that you won't know where you end and I begin." He dropped one final kiss on her cheek, his lips lingering there as he said, "Be careful what you let yourself lust after, Kate, you might just get it." Then he straightened and resumed his distant stare into the night.

Anger shot through Kate's veins, pushing strength into her boneless limbs. "You bastard! I didn't want that!" Her hands tightened into fists at her sides.

Raine leaned against the window frame and shot her a look over one broad shoulder. "Oh, you wanted it all right. Maybe you didn't *want* to want it, but you wanted it just the same."

Kate had no idea if she tended to be short-tempered under normal circumstances, but these circumstances were anything but normal. And her hold on her temper wasn't just short, it was nonexistent. Her breath came in ragged spurts. "You started it! You kissed me!"

Raine faced her then, and crossed his arms over his mile-wide chest. "You don't have to justify what happened, Kate. Many women have fantasized at one time or another about having wild, hot sex with a bad boy, especially one on the run. Why should you be any different?"

Raine manacled her wrist before her palm connected with his jaw. He shook his head slowly from side to side. "You don't want to do that," he said in a low, warning tone.

Kate jerked her arm from his hold and took a step back, out of his reach. "Don't touch me again."

Lightning flashed, giving Kate a good look at his face. He didn't smile, but she didn't miss the gleam of triumph in his eyes. Somehow he considered himself the winner in

what had just taken place. The winner in what respect she
didn't know. If she was smart, she wouldn't want to know.

Kate whirled away from him and strode back to her bed.
She didn't want to look at him. She didn't want to talk to
him. And she sure as hell didn't want to want him. Sliding
beneath the covers, she squeezed her eyes shut and willed
herself to sleep.

THE SOUND OF WATER spraying woke Kate from a drug-
ging sleep. She forced her eyes to obey her brain's command to open, but it proved a difficult task. A thin ray of
sunlight sliced through the dark room from the crack where
the drapes met. On the bedside table, the clock's display
read 10:00 a.m. Sitting up, Kate stretched and groaned
with satisfaction at finally feeling rested.

Raine. Images from their early-morning kiss flooded her
mind. She shivered and pulled the covers up around her.
She scanned the semidark room. Where was he? The sound
of water invaded her consciousness again and Kate realized he was in the shower.

In the shower—and she wasn't locked in the closet. Obviously he had given up on her waking anytime soon and
decided to shower on the assumption that she would sleep
through it.

Call in… The words raced through her mind, sending a
rush of adrenaline through her veins. Call in. She had to
call in. Numbers spilled into her head: 312–555–4911.

"Call 312–555–4911," she repeated aloud. Kate threw
back the covers and dropped her feet to the floor. She
stared at the telephone for all of three seconds before she
turned the base to face her. Kate listened for Raine; he was
still in the shower. She quickly read the instructions for
making a collect call. She didn't want any charges to be
added to the room.

Kate swallowed the lump of fear rising in her throat and dialed the appropriate numbers. When the operator asked for her name, she had to whisper Kate Roberts twice before the woman understood her. Finally the call was connected. One ring sounded across the line, then another.

"Hello."

Kate frowned at the strangely familiar male voice. She listened as the operator asked if he would accept a collect call from Kate Roberts. The man agreed without hesitation.

"Kate? It's Nick, honey. Are you all right?"

She couldn't put a face with the voice, but no warning bells went off inside her head, so Kate took that as a good sign. "I'm all right," she replied tightly.

"We've been worried sick about you. Why haven't you called in before now?"

Kate shivered. How could this man know her and she not know him?

"Kate, are you there?" Concern colored his voice.

Kate blinked. "I'm here," she said softly.

"Aunt Vicky needs to speak to you. She's been beside herself for *two days.*"

Two days. Did that mean something? The man emphasized those words. Should they mean something to her? Kate creased her forehead in concentration. And who was *Aunt Vicky?*

"Kate, if you're safe that's our main concern. But…" He paused. Then, "Did you reach your destination? Was it everything you had anticipated?"

The water shut off in the bathroom. "I have to go," Kate muttered distractedly.

"Wait, please wait. I need you to stay on the line a *little* longer. Vicky needs to speak with you about your missed appointment. Don't hang up."

Kate glanced from the bathroom door to the telephone.

If he caught her on the phone, what would he do? Should she tell him she had remembered this number?

"Kate? Are you still there?"

Kate stared at the handset. The voice…it was her. The woman's voice she always heard in her head.

"Kate, it's Aunt Vicky, are you all right, dear?"

The toilet flushed. Fear gripped Kate's heart. "I have to go." She quietly replaced the receiver in the cradle before the woman on the other end could respond, then pushed the phone back to its original position on the table.

Kate stood just as Raine stepped out of the bathroom. Quickly, she stretched and then brushed the hair back from her eyes. "Thanks for letting me sleep late," she said, trying her level best to keep the fear from manifesting itself in her voice. Those same old warnings kept echoing inside her head. *If he suspects for one second…*

Raine didn't say a word. He simply stood there, showered and dressed, and scrutinized her from head to toe. The thickening beard on his chiseled features made his presence even more fear-inspiring. When he at last seemed to be satisfied with the results of his visual inspection, he spoke, "You needed the rest. As soon as you're ready, we have things to do today."

Kate only nodded and hurried past him to the bathroom. Once inside, she closed the door and sagged against it. *Aunt Vicky. We've been worried sick. Two days. Was it everything you anticipated? Missed appointment?* Kate closed her eyes and willed the voices away. She couldn't think about that right now. None of it made sense anyway. And she could never let Raine suspect that she had made that call. *He won't take the time to find out which side sent you.* Which side of what? she demanded. No answer came.

Kate opened her eyes. She could do this. She had to do this.

RAINE UNLOCKED the door to their hotel room and entered first. The room faced the rear parking lot—not the usually requested view, but he preferred direct access to the outside. He set the packages containing their purchases on the table. A late-afternoon storm had kicked up, rivaling last night's. Raine didn't allow himself to waste any time dwelling on the kiss he had stolen from Kate. To say it had moved him would be a vast understatement. He didn't like the way she made him feel, but his actions were a means to an end. Kate had kept her distance all day. She didn't let him get close and that was what Raine had wanted.

Want really didn't have anything to do with it, he amended. He *needed* the distance. He had to keep his head on straight or they would both wind up on ice. Raine swallowed hard as he checked inside the closet. He didn't want to die himself, but the thought of Kate lying lifeless on the ground with a bullet through her head appealed to him even less. He wouldn't let anything happen to her. *And if she proves to be your enemy, what then?* Raine ignored his own warning.

When he was sure the room was clear, he motioned for Kate to come inside. She sighed and pushed from the door frame she had leaned against. The day had taken its toll on her. She dropped her coat onto the bed and curled around one fluffy pillow, then closed her eyes.

Raine frowned. The impression that something was wrong with her still niggled at his conscience. He pulled off his coat and tossed it across the bed. Maybe she needed some sort of special diet or vitamins. But he didn't have time to worry about that at the moment. Right now he had to consider the information Lucas had given him. Such as it was.

He shoved his hand through his hair and paced the

length of the room. He hadn't wanted to make that call, but being saddled with Kate had left him little choice. Raine hoped like hell he hadn't made a mistake. He desperately needed Lucas to keep the various government agencies off his back for just a little while. Of course, putting the feds on Raine's trail wouldn't have been Lucas's idea anyway. That order had to have come from Cuddahy, the director of Special Ops. He was relatively new to the organization and intent on making a big name for himself. Raine didn't know much about the man, but he had the reputation of being a ''by-the-book bastard.''

Raine slowly turned and retraced his steps. He hadn't given Lucas their location and he'd made sure that he hadn't stayed on the line long enough for a trace. That's why he had made several different calls, and always from a different location. Kate hadn't complained about all the walking, but she had later protested the shopping.

He had bought new clothes and necessities for her as well as himself. Raine expelled a weary breath. He had to admit that Kate was the first woman he'd ever had to coerce into shopping. She hadn't wanted to do anything but come back to the room.

New clothes, dining at a nice restaurant, none of it appealed to her, as it would have to most women. She was tired, she'd said. Raine scrutinized her pale features. Maybe she had some sort of health problem. The bruise on her temple looked much better. But overall she seemed weaker now than when she'd first staggered into his cabin from the cold.

Raine suddenly remembered the unmarked bottle of pills he'd found in her purse that first day. The medication she hadn't recognized. He retrieved the bottle from his coat pocket and peered through the colored plastic at the small blue pills. Maybe this was the key to what was going on with Kate. He glanced at her still form and made a decision. If he had remembered the pills earlier, he could have done this today, but he hadn't given them a thought since the day he'd shoved them into his pocket.

Now he would just have to go out again and locate a pharmacist still open at 6:00 p.m. to find out what the bottle contained. Raine clenched his jaw and strode over to her bed.

"Kate." He shook her gently. His frown deepened when he noticed the sheen of perspiration on her face. He brushed the back of his hand across her forehead. Her skin was cool and clammy. "Damn," he muttered. She was definitely sick. Raine shook her again. "Kate, wake up."

Kate opened her eyes and stared vacantly at him. "What?" she murmured.

"We have to go out again. There's something I need to check."

She shrugged off his hand and turned back into her pillow. "No way. I'm exhausted. You go without me."

Raine blew out a puff of air. "No can do, Kate. Where I go, you go."

She rolled to her back and glared at him. "You don't have to worry, I won't run away. I don't have the energy to do anything but lie here. Just go and leave me alone."

Raine considered that possibility for about two seconds. As easy as it would be to do, he knew better. Kate might not take off on him, but he couldn't take the chance.

"Sorry, but I can't do that. Now get up."

Raine straightened as Kate struggled to her feet. When she had steadied herself, she planted her hands firmly on her hips and glared at him. "It's pouring down out there, I'm not going with you." She lifted her chin defiantly. "And you can't make me."

Raine bit back a grin. At least she still had some fight

left in her. "I think you know better than that, but if you'll promise to behave yourself I'll let you stay."

"I swear," Kate said quickly. "I'll be an absolute angel."

"And you won't make a sound?"

She nodded adamantly. "Not a peep."

Raine shrugged. "Okay, suit yourself." He took the eight steps necessary to reach the closet and opened the bifold doors. "I'll let you out the moment I get back."

Kate's mouth gaped in disbelief. She glared at him, crossed her arms over her chest and said, "No."

"That's not an option. You either come with me—" he gestured toward the closet "—or you stay in here until I get back."

Kate marched across the room, muttering things he couldn't and didn't want to understand. She stepped into the close quarters and whirled around to give Raine what could only be called the evil eye.

That grin he'd been holding back broke loose. "If looks could kill," he suggested.

"Don't give me any ideas," she retorted.

Raine reached out and took her chin in his hand. "Now that's not very sporting of you, Kate. Where's your gratitude for the man who saved your life more than once?"

Kate turned away from his touch, refusing to look him in the eye. That intense, protective feeling overwhelmed him again. Along with it came desire so strong that it shook him like nothing else ever had.

Every instinct told Raine to walk away from this lady and never look back, but he couldn't. He just couldn't. He brushed his knuckles down her soft cheek. "I won't let anything happen to you, Kate." Again she drew away. "I'll be back as soon as I can," he told her, then closed the door. Since he couldn't prop a chair under the knob as he'd done before, Raine slid his belt off and looped it around the side-by-side identical knobs. He tightened the cinch he'd made and checked its hold. That would do, he decided. This way he didn't have to worry about her making any unauthorized calls or slipping out.

Raine jerked on his coat and cursed himself all the way out. He locked the door and double-checked it. What a fool he was. Letting a damn female get to him like this. He'd thought if he scared her off, he'd be safe from the relentless physical attraction. All he had managed to do was strengthen this insane need to protect her.

He was a fool. If he kept going at this rate, he'd be a dead fool very soon.

KATE STAMPED her foot and blew out an indignant breath when she heard Raine shut and lock the door. She called him every bad name she could think of and a few she made up as she went. If he hadn't locked her up like an ugly stepchild, she could have called that number again. She still hadn't remembered anything else and she felt like death warmed over, but she'd been hoping to get the chance to call again.

Damn Jack Raine. Maybe she would be better off trying to get away from him. All she had to do was make herself scarce until all this whatever was over. She frowned. But how would she know when it was over? And what if something happened to Raine?

Kate gave herself a mental kick. She didn't care what happened to him. She shifted and took a deep breath. Well, maybe she cared a little—but not a lot.

The door to the room opened. Kate stilled. Was he back already? He fumbled around in the room for several minutes. Had he forgotten something?

Yeah, by God. He had forgotten she was locked in the

damn closet. Kate balled her fists at her sides and glared at the slits of light angling upward through the louvered door in front of her. "Raine, what are you doing? Let me out of this closet this instant!" She muttered a couple more of those inventive expletives as she waited for him to obey her demand.

She heard him at the closet door then. Three seconds later the doors folded open. "It's about—" Kate's outrage died a swift and total death as she stared into the eyes of a stranger.

Chapter Seven

Raine cursed himself a dozen times over as he walked across the hotel parking lot. He had known this would be a mistake, and he'd been right. He should have left Kate Roberts at the hospital emergency room back in Gatlinburg as he'd originally planned. But he hadn't. He'd foolishly thought he could protect her. His need to play protector may very well have put her in even more danger. Raine blew out a breath and slowed a moment to stare at the bottle of pills clutched in his hand.

Inderal. Most common usage: heart conditions.

The pharmacist had said that the medication in the bottle could be prescribed for a number of ailments ranging from migraines to serious heart problems. And, if the patient was taking it for a heart condition and suddenly stopped, the result could prove life-threatening.

Raine swore again as he double-timed around the corner and down the stretch of sidewalk that led to their room. The pharmacist had also given Raine the name of a doctor who ran a clinic in his home just outside town. The doctor had gone into semiretirement some years ago and didn't carry much of a patient load these days, so he should be available. Of course, at 7:00 p.m. it was well past office hours, but Raine didn't intend to let that stop him. He needed to know if there was something wrong with Kate's heart. And there was only one way to confirm or rule out the possibility. He needed a doctor to examine her.

Raine swallowed hard when he considered the trip they had made on foot. Kate had held up pretty well, but he knew that the journey had been tough on her. He cursed himself again for being a stupid bastard. He should have taken her waxy complexion and complaints about being tired a little more seriously. But this was all new to him. He'd never really had to take care of anyone but himself. The flip side to what he had just learned was that he now had little reason to suspect Kate of having an ulterior motive for showing up at his door. No one in this business would send in an unreliable player—not in a game this serious. And a medical condition, especially one involving the heart, would definitely be a risk.

Raine paused at the door to their room. He took a long, deep breath and, key in hand, reached for the knob, then frowned when the door swung inward at his touch. He'd locked the door, no question about it. Raine reached beneath his jacket, drew his Beretta and automatically released the safety.

Cautiously he entered the room, his gaze swept from left to right and then shot back to the open closet doors.

Kate was gone.

He didn't have to step over to the closet and look inside. He didn't have to check the bathroom or look under the bed. He felt the answer in his gut. Emptiness echoed deafeningly in the room.

She was gone.

Adrenaline surged, sending his senses into a higher state of alert. Tension vibrated through every muscle as he crossed to the closet and checked the belt he had used to secure the doors. The belt had been loosened and removed, then tossed aside.

Someone had let Kate out. There were no obvious signs of a struggle, he noted as he slid his belt back into the loops of his jeans. Raine inhaled deeply and considered the possibilities. If Kate had decided to scream her head off and a passerby heard the cries for help, it was feasible that the hotel manager had been alerted. Raine glanced again at the open door to the room. If that were the case then the police would have been notified by now. But the parking lot remained dark and quiet. Maybe he had jumped to the conclusion that she was innocent too soon. Maybe she was involved. She had shown up rather conveniently at his cabin. Raine shook his head. Her injuries were real, her amnesia was real. The medication, he touched the pocket containing the prescription bottle, was real. She couldn't be involved. Could she?

A cold chill skated down Raine's spine as he contemplated the only other alternative.

Dillon.

The shrill ring of the telephone sliced through the silence. Raine jerked around to glare at the infernal instrument. It rang again. He didn't take the time to wonder who would be calling, because he already knew.

Raine retraced his path, kicked the door to the room shut and strode to the table between the two beds. He waited two more rings, then snatched up the receiver. "Yeah." Raine kept his voice low and steady. There would be no hint of the degree of tension he felt for Dillon to enjoy.

No one else would play it out this way.

"Hello, Raine. Long time no see."

The hair on the back of Raine's neck bristled at the sardonic sound of Dillon's voice. The Puerto Rican roots he'd inherited from his mother still surfaced in the lingering accent Dillon had worked hard to lose. The image of the face that went with the voice filled Raine's head, taking his senses to another level of tension.

"Not long enough," Raine replied as he dropped onto the bed and leaned against the headboard. He planted his left foot on the floor and pulled his right knee up to brace his firing arm. He kept the closed door sighted, just in case Dillon's henchmen showed up for seconds. "Can't say that I've missed you," Raine added when the silence on the other end stretched too long for comfort.

"Have you missed Kate?"

A trickle of fear managed to slip past Raine's brutal hold on his emotions, his heart rate increased to accommodate the uncharacteristic sensation. Raine swallowed the scathing response that formed in his mouth. Dillon already knew too much, no point giving away just how badly Raine wanted to keep Kate safe.

"She's quite a pretty lady," Dillon continued, his tone slick and coolly menacing. "Such beautiful dark eyes. I can't imagine why anyone, even you, Raine, would let such a lovely creature out of your sight. Whatever possessed you to lock her in the closet? Have you finally happened upon one you can't handle?"

Anger flooded Raine, drowning that tiny glimmer of fear. "What do you want, Dillon?"

"Why, I thought you knew." He chuckled, a harsh, emotionless sound. "I want you, Raine. Are you willing to trade yourself for this sweet young thing?" A frightened shriek from Kate punctuated Dillon's question.

It took Raine two full seconds, but he cleared his mind, banished all emotions. "Don't yank my chain, Dillon, just give me the details." Raine wished he could reach through the telephone and strangle the ruthless son of a bitch on the other end, but that would have to wait. Right now he had to focus on playing out this sick little game.

"There's a quaint place on Route 29 called Chances. Meet me there at midnight. I've reserved the proverbial room in the back."

A resounding click ended the conversation. Raine dropped the receiver back into the cradle. He should have killed Dillon months ago. The world would certainly be a better place without him. Raine couldn't bear the thought of Dillon touching Kate, but it was Dillon's specialty that worried him the most.

Juan Roberto Dillon specialized in killing. He was one of Sal Ballatore's right-hand men and he had no qualms about taking human life. Race, sex, age or circumstances never entered the picture. Dillon enjoyed killing. The only thing he liked more was the hunt. And that's what tonight was all about.

Raine replayed every move he had made in the last seventy-two hours and could find no mistake. He didn't know how Dillon had found him. No way Lucas could have traced Raine's call. But somehow he'd been found. Dillon could just as easily have stormed the room and taken them both, but he hadn't. He had waited until Raine was out and taken Kate.

Dillon wanted to play. He liked the thrill of the chase, the sudden twists of fate. Everything was a game to him. Raine gritted his teeth against the rage that rose in his throat. This whole business was just one big walk around the Monopoly board to Dillon. Toss the dice and see where the game takes you. In the end, the player with the most money, and still breathing, wins.

The man was a real opportunist too. Rather than going to Ballatore after discovering Raine's true identity, Dillon had seized the opportunity for another, more self-serving purpose.

Raine allowed the vivid images to reel through his mind, his heart pounding harder with each passing frame of memory. Raine, Dillon and Michael, Sal's son, had picked up two million dollars in cash from a major cocaine distributor working for Ballatore. They had done it together numerous times before, but this time was different.

After the exchange went down, the three of them were alone in the warehouse. Vinny and Danny had waited in the car like always. Dillon was slapping Michael on the back one minute and praising his ability to close a deal, then putting a bullet through the kid's head the next.

Dillon had then turned to a stunned Raine and said, "I know who you are and why you're here." He'd pressed the barrel of his Ruger against Raine's forehead. "The only thing I don't understand," he continued with a sadistic smile, "is why *you* killed Mr. Ballatore's son."

The momentary distraction of Danny entering the warehouse was all that had kept Raine from winding up on the cold, hard concrete floor next to Michael with blood pooling around his shattered skull. Raine had barely escaped with his life, but he had managed to snag the briefcase containing the money on his way. It was his only security, and he'd hidden it safely away.

When a mob-ordered hit went down or a play for power took place, it rarely happened without warning. The one thing that could be counted on in this business was murmurings in the ranks or, at the very least, a gut instinct that something was about to go down. Raine had not once anticipated Dillon's move.

He had gone over and over every minute of the seventeen months he had worked with Dillon and found nothing to indicate that such a hit was in the plan. Raine had come to the conclusion that it hadn't been planned. Dillon had somehow learned who Raine was and used the information for an opportunity to kill his boss's only son and make himself two million dollars richer in the process. And, by simultaneously eliminating Michael and placing the blame on Raine, Dillon had put himself in the position of second in command to the grieving father. The perfect move—swift and efficient. Too bad for Dillon that Raine had escaped with the money.

Every perfect plan had its flaw. Raine hadn't played along and died for Dillon. Of course, when Dillon told his version of the story, Ballatore had ordered Raine found and brought to him personally for punishment. Then the feds had joined the party and decided Raine had turned. All in all, Raine had been left between a rock and a hard place.

But he'd been in tight spots before.

His plan was simple—he'd use the money as bait to entice Dillon. Dillon was a greedy bastard, he would want the money back. If Raine's plan worked, the mole who had blown his cover would eventually make a move to tie up his loose ends—including Dillon. So Raine had had to act fast. Luring Dillon would be easy, staying alive when the good guys as well as the bad guys were after him was a little more complicated. If Raine was lucky, Lucas would keep the feds distracted. Then Raine could concentrate on the old man. Ballatore wanted him brought in alive, but Dillon would try everything in his power to prevent that from happening. Dillon wanted Raine dead.

Dead men tell no tales.

And Kate…

Well, Raine scrubbed a hand over his bearded chin, Kate was still a wild card at this point. But he would soon know whose side she stood on.

KATE COMMANDED her trembling body to still as she watched the man named Dillon end the conversation with Raine. Her chest ached with fear and her heart fluttered like a butterfly trapped in her rib cage.

"Well, Kate, it looks as though everything is going to work out perfectly," Dillon announced to her, his voice dark and evil, his thin lips sliding into a sinister smile.

Kate swallowed the fear and blinked furiously at the moisture burning behind her lids. She lifted her chin and glared at the man who had forced her from the hotel at gunpoint. "He won't come. Raine won't trade himself for me. He hardly knows me," she said, surprised at the strength and challenge left in her voice. "He'll be long gone before midnight."

The idea that Raine would walk purposely into his own death trap to rescue her was absurd. What did Dillon take him for? A fool? Kate didn't know much about Raine, or fully trust him for that matter, but the one thing she felt certain of was that he was nobody's fool.

At least Dillon's proposition had given her a few more hours to live. Kate wasn't kidding herself. This was bad. Very bad. Raine had been right, at least about this much. These guys were killers and they intended to kill both of them. She should never have made that call. Kate had no proof of her suspicions, but instinct told her that it had been a mistake. A mistake that had brought the devil himself sweeping down on her like a hawk after a frightened field mouse.

Kate surveyed the private room Dillon had bribed the bartender into renting him for the night. It was small, maybe twelve by fourteen. Kate supposed the Thursday-night guys used the place for poker games or small private parties. The decorating enhanced the doom and gloom of her circumstances—circa early seventies with dark paneling, shag carpet and a wagon-wheel chandelier. A round table with eight chairs sat in the middle of the room, and a smaller one sat against the far wall. The only color to break the monotony was a large, rather garish, framed print of huge blue and gold flowers.

Country music blared from the jukebox on the other side of the paper-thin wall that separated her from the crowd of patrons drinking beer and having a grand old time. No one out there would pay any attention to the events taking place in the back room tonight.

Kate swallowed the fear and panic bubbling in her throat. Tonight there would be no poker or party. Tonight people were going to die and, unfortunately, she appeared to be one of the unlucky candidates.

Kate's gaze flitted back to Dillon's. His sick smile widened into a grin at the fear she knew he saw in her eyes. He wore his long black hair in a ponytail, giving a clean, unobscured view of his sharp hawklike features. High cheekbones dipped into hollows on either side of his thin lips. A straight blade of a nose, and a dark ledge of eyebrows that hovered over beady eyes. Excitement sparkled in those black depths as he watched Kate's chest rise and fall too rapidly.

The bastard got his kicks from watching his prey squirm. A jolt of anger shot through Kate and she suddenly wished for a weapon. A Glock nine millimeter, her weapon of choice. That would put a nice, clean little hole smack in the middle of his forehead, while taking off a large portion of the back of his skull.

Kate started. Her attention instantly focused inward. How did she know all that? Why would she have a favorite gun? She had never killed anyone, had she? She shuddered at the thought.

"Oh, he'll come," Dillon said, drawing her attention

back to him. "You see, Kate—" He leaned back in his chair and rubbed his Ruger against his jaw. Kate flinched. Why would she recognize the brand of gun he carried? "Unfortunately for him, Raine fancies himself a good guy. It goes against his nature for the innocent to suffer." Dillon licked his thin lips as he screwed a silencer onto his weapon. With blatant challenge, he placed it on the table in front of him and crossed his arms over his chest. "It's his way of justifying what he does the rest of the time. My stealing you away and forcing him to come to me is an insult he'll have to answer."

Kate's gaze moved from Dillon's to the table, then back. She balled her fists in her lap and gauged the distance between her and the gun, between Dillon and the gun. Behind her, Danny and Vinny paced like caged lions. Even if she could get her hands on the gun before Dillon, which was highly unlikely, she would never be able to shoot all three of them before one of them shot her. Kate relaxed her rigid muscles and eased out a ragged breath. A bead of sweat trickled between her breasts.

Dillon smiled knowingly. He leaned forward, grabbed Kate's wrist and jerked her close. "You know," he whispered harshly, his lips brushing her temple, making her shiver uncontrollably, "I love this stuff." He pressed her trembling hand to his crotch, his arousal proving his statement.

Kate choked out a shriek and jerked free of his grasp. Dillon laughed at her, his eyes twinkling with the insanity that no doubt drove him. Vinny and Danny teetered like bullies in the schoolyard, backing up their leader with sound effects.

Kate closed her eyes against the sound, and against the image of Dillon, the personification of evil. Ice slid through her veins, immobilizing her body with cold, solid fear. If Raine showed up to rescue her, he would die. If he didn't, she would die. Kate opened her eyes and stared at the man in front of her. Who was she kidding? She was dead either way.

RAINE HAD KNOWN that Chances would be a dive in every sense of the word—cheap and disreputable. The place was definitely in keeping with Dillon's taste for the underbelly of life. Raine slid from behind the wheel of the Thunderbird he had "borrowed" and smiled at the one thing that didn't quite fit: country music. The sound wafted into the dimly lit, quiet parking lot. Neon lights flashed from the front of the building, advertising Budweiser and Miller beer.

Dillon hated country music. In fact, he hated most anything that had its roots below the Mason-Dixon Line. Raine had seen him kill a man simply because his Southern drawl grated on Dillon's nerves. Sick bastard.

Raine adjusted his jacket and then the all-but-worthless handgun he'd tucked up his right sleeve. He despised .22's, but finding the weapon—loaded and ready—stashed in the glovebox of the stolen car had been a stroke of luck. Satisfied with his unexpected contingency, he checked his watch: 12:05. Dillon would be pissed. He hated to wait. The move would throw him off balance, make him more likely to make mistakes. Raine needed whatever edge he could find to save Kate and get them both away alive. He checked the position of the .22 automatic once more and headed for the door.

He stepped into the crowded, smoky bar and took a moment to survey his surroundings. The bar extended the length of the room on one side. Only one bartender appeared to be on duty. Two waitresses skirted the tables filling the rest of the place. The crowd consisted of mostly men and no one seemed to pay Raine any mind, with the exception of one table. The one nearest the door. A group of wannabe cowboys looked Raine over with the slow, easy confidence of being on their home turf, then went back to the business of beer and bullshit.

Raine took his time, checking out the place as he crossed to the bar. He ordered a beer and asked about the room in the back. The solemn-faced bartender plopped a cold, long-neck bottle in front of Raine and angled his head toward a door at the far end of the room. Raine paid the man and took a long pull from the bottle as he settled onto a stool. The cold liquid slid down his throat and pooled in his stomach, doing nothing to quench the fire burning inside him. He forced himself to drink the rest despite the tension urging him to act. He had wanted to rush over here and wait for Dillon's arrival the minute he'd hung up the phone. But he had forced himself to wait. To fill the time, Raine had showered and shaved, then changed into the new clothes he had bought that day. He knew Dillon too well, he would have considered the possibility of an early arrival. Most likely, he had already been at this joint when he'd called.

Raine glanced at the Red Dog clock above the mirror behind the bar. Twelve-ten. Dillon had waited long enough, any longer and he might take his anger out on Kate. Raine slid off the stool and strode to the door, opened it and stepped inside. His gut clenched at the sight of Kate sitting at a table with Dillon standing behind her, caressing her hair. Raine's jaw tightened. Dillon looked mad as hell, his tall, thin features taut, his eyes as dark as smoke off burning rubber. Raine's gaze flicked from the pompous twisted bastard back to Kate. She was scared to death. His thoughts went immediately to the bottle of little blue pills in his pocket, but that would have to wait.

The door slammed shut behind Raine. Danny and Vinny stepped up to stand on either side of him.

"You're late," Dillon hissed.

Raine lifted one eyebrow in the beginnings of a shrug that didn't quite make it to his shoulders. "I know."

"I *hate* to be kept waiting," Dillon added, his knuckles going white as he grasped the back of Kate's chair.

"I know," Raine intoned.

Vinny jabbed him hard in the gut, but Raine absorbed the blow with nothing more than a soft grunt. He stood statue-still while Danny patted him down and removed the weapon at the small of his back, then held up the Beretta like a trophy.

Vinny sneered at Raine. "You shoulda killed me while you had the chance, Ricky boy. Now I'm gonna watch you die."

Raine smiled mockingly down at the shorter man. Vinny knew his real name wasn't Rick, but he kept up the pretense. "I'm saving you for later, Vinny, when it's just you and me." Raine instinctively tightened his stomach muscles a split second before the next blow was delivered.

Muttering expletives, Vinny moved back to stand guard at the door. Danny followed suit.

"Kate leaves now." Raine leveled his gaze on Dillon's. "That was the deal. I'm here, she goes." He shifted his gaze to Kate. "The car's outside, the engine's running," he added so she'd know which car he meant. The surprise and momentary disapproval that flitted across her face told him that she understood that he'd stolen another vehicle.

Kate stood. Raine saw the violent tremble that rocked her body. Her brown eyes were huge and liquid. A single, crystalline tear slid down one cheek. Something inside Raine twisted and he felt weak with regret that any of this had happened to her. If he had learned nothing else, he now knew that Kate was in no way connected to Dillon.

"Let's not be in such a hurry, Raine." Dillon snaked an arm around Kate's waist and pulled her against him, knocking over the chair she'd vacated. She gasped, her fingers automatically working to pry loose his restraining arm. "I was rather enjoying Kate's company."

Raine tamped down the rage that jolted him. "I'm not in the mood to debate the point. I'm here, so let her go."

Dillon rubbed his cheek against her hair. Kate whimpered and closed her eyes. Before he could prevent it, Raine's fists clenched at his sides. Dillon smiled at the reaction and Raine cursed himself for allowing it.

"So this one means something to you?" Dillon scrutinized Kate for a time, then righted the chair and pushed her into it. His gaze moved back to Raine. "Don't worry, I'll take good care of her for you."

Raine moved in Dillon's direction, ignoring the snap of weapons engaging behind him. "*I said,* let her go," he repeated, the sound coming from some foreign, guttural place deep inside him.

Dillon rounded Kate's chair, waved a hand at his two henchmen then took the final three steps to bring himself face-to-face with Raine. He drew his weapon and aimed it at Raine's heart, the tip of the silencer creasing his shirt. Kate's sharp intake of breath broke the quiet that followed.

Raine briefly considered announcing that Dillon was the one who had killed Ballatore's son, but why bother? Kate wouldn't know what he was talking about, and the other two in the room would never believe him. Besides, Raine still needed Dillon—at least until he could draw out the mole. He had no choice but to play the hand he'd been dealt. As bad as it sucked, this was it.

"The old man wanted me to bring you in alive." Dillon

shook his head and sighed. "But I think I'll save him the trouble of dealing with you personally. I wouldn't want to further tax his failing health." Dillon smirked and pressed the barrel more firmly into Raine's chest. "Are you prepared to die, Raine?"

Raine flashed an answering smile. "I'm always prepared, *amigo*."

Dillon flinched. He hated to be reminded of his heritage. Raine leaned into the weapon. "Why don't you cut the small talk and just do me? No need to complicate things. I'm here, the weapon's engaged with the target, why waste time yapping? *Just do it*," Raine challenged.

Dillon's face contorted with rage. "I say when. I set the pace." His face relaxed into a feigned smile. "And I say, *now*." Dillon's grip tightened on the weapon in anticipation of the recoil.

"There's just one thing," Raine began, his words stopping Dillon a heartbeat before his trigger finger applied the slight pressure required to fire the weapon.

"What the hell would that be?" Dillon snapped. Sweat beaded on his forehead, anger blazed in his eyes.

"The money," Raine offered with a nonchalant shrug. "If you kill me, you'll never know where I hid the money."

Irritation flared in Dillon's angry gaze. "To hell with the money! There will be more where that came from."

It was during that fleeting moment of transition between anger and irritation, just before the final decision was made, that Raine acted. His left arm darted under Dillon's right and shoved it upward. A shot hissed through the silencer and lodged in the ceiling. Before either of the other two could assimilate what had happened, Raine had the .22 automatic pressed to Dillon's temple.

"Hold it right there," Raine ordered when Vinny would

have moved closer. "Everybody just take a breath." Two beads held steady on Raine. "Kate, move over here behind me." She quickly obeyed.

"Now." Raine tightened his choke hold on Dillon's scrawny neck. "Place your weapons on the table." Nobody moved. Raine nudged the .22 a little deeper into the thin skin protecting Dillon's temple. "*Now,* gentlemen." Dillon tossed his Ruger on the table. The two men on the other side of the room remained motionless.

"Do it!" Dillon screeched when Raine's finger snugged around the trigger.

First Vinny, then Danny relented, placing their weapons on the table and backing away.

"And mine," Raine reminded Vinny.

His insolent gaze fixed on Raine, Vinny slid the Beretta across the table. "Good." Raine smiled his appreciation, which only earned him a heated glare from both men. "You two, back over here—" he angled his head toward the far side of the room "—on the floor, facedown."

When the two were prone on the floor, Raine shoved Dillon in their direction with one hand and snatched up his Beretta with the other. He watched Dillon reluctantly slide into place next to his cohorts. "Kate, grab those weapons."

He didn't have to tell her twice, Raine noticed when he shot a glance in her direction. To his surprise she snatched up the Ruger, deftly unscrewed the silencer and slid it into her back pocket, then put the weapon on safety and set it aside. Despite the rampant trembling he had observed in her only moments ago, her hands were steady and efficient now. She put each of the other two weapons on safety as well before stowing them in the waistband of her jeans beneath her sweatshirt.

Watching her warily, Raine took the Ruger from her and

shoved it into his waistband. Now wasn't the time to ask how she knew her way around a handgun. Getting the hell out of here was top priority.

"It's only a matter of time before I catch up to you again," Dillon said from his position on the floor. "You're a dead man walking, my friend."

Raine ushered Kate across the room, keeping his gaze trained on the three men on the floor. "Well," Raine said as he reached behind him to snag the doorknob, "at least I'm walking." He turned and propelled Kate into the crowded barroom. He pulled the door closed behind him, leaned toward her and ordered, "Get in the black T-Bird. The engine's running. I'm right behind you."

She spared him a panicked glance, but took off without question. Raine knew Dillon would burst through the door any moment. He waded quickly through the crowd, but paused when he got to the door. He moved back to the last table he'd passed and leaned down to speak to the nearest wannabe cowboy.

He had to shout to be heard over the jukebox, which had just boomed back to life. "Hey, buddy, that fag with the ponytail—" Raine glanced up just in time to see Dillon's anger-twisted mug glaring at him from across the room "—called you and your friends here a bunch of redneck yahoos."

Raine straightened and backed up the four steps between him and the door. A quick glance over his shoulder before he slipped out revealed Bubba and his five buddies forming an intimidating line across Dillon's path. Raine smiled. Satisfied that he had a few minutes to put some distance between them, he headed for the T-Bird.

"Are they right behind you?" Kate's frightened voice met him when he opened the driver's-side door.

"They'll be busy for a few minutes." Raine shoved the car into gear and spun out of the parking lot.

"What are we going to do now?" she demanded, twisting around to peer out the rear window.

"Slide those weapons under my seat." Raine suppressed the other demand he wanted to make. Now wasn't the time.

"What?" She shifted her wide-eyed gaze to him.

"Put the Smith & Wesson and the Beretta under my seat," he said slowly, watching her reaction in his peripheral vision.

"You have the Beretta and the Ruger, the two I have are both Smith & Wessons," she clarified as she pulled the weapons one at a time from beneath her sweatshirt and slid them under his seat just as he had instructed. The silencer followed.

Raine clenched his jaw and drew in his first deep breath since walking into the hotel room and finding Kate missing. She was safe now and that gave him some sense of relief. But he had seen more than enough to resurrect his suspicions about her identity. And that made him madder than hell—mostly at himself. He took a right onto the unpaved side road that led to the doc's house. A couple miles down the rutted, muddy passage he took another right. Water and mud from the day's storm splashed from the deeper ruts. The driveway to the house-cum-clinic was more than a mile long and dark as pitch save for the unearthly glow of the moon bearing down on them through the barren treetops.

Raine parked a good distance from the house, cut the engine and got out. He skirted the hood, anger and questions pounding in his head, then jerked Kate's door open and demanded, "Get out."

"Where are we?" she asked hesitantly, glancing from

side to side with mounting uncertainty. Despite the reluctance in her voice, she scrambled out of the car.

Raine slammed the door and glared at her. She shivered and rubbed her hands up and down her arms. Dillon had dragged her off without her coat. The coat was in the car, but Raine was too pissed off right now to offer it to her.

"What's wrong? Why are you staring at me that way?" Her eyes were wide with fear, her lips trembled, and Raine hated himself, which only pissed him off all the more. He reached behind him and drew his weapon. Kate gasped and edged back against the T-Bird.

Brutally squashing the guilt that immediately rose, Raine forced her chin up with the cold, steel barrel. The weapon wasn't aimed at her, but the effect was the same, she trembled and tears welled in those big dark eyes. "Tell me about the weapon I'm holding," he rasped.

"I don't know what you mean," she shuddered the words. A tear slid down her cheek, then another and another. She blinked furiously, but they came anyway. "Why are you doing this?"

Raine clenched his teeth until he had ruthlessly steadied his control. "How did you know that the two nine millimeters you carried out of there were Smith & Wessons?" His tone was fierce and Kate all but crumpled under his glare.

She shook her head. "I don't know. I just knew."

"You removed that silencer without thought, Kate." Raine leaned in closer, keeping the weapon between them, his fisted knuckles hard against the slim column of her throat. "As if you'd done it many times before."

"I...saw Dillon attach it." She pressed a shaky hand against his chest, a frail attempt at protecting herself. "It was simple. And maybe they mentioned the names of their guns. I just don't know!'' A sob shook her body with such force that it pained him to watch.

With a disgusted exhale, Raine shoved his weapon back into his waistband. He braced his hands against the car on either side of Kate and held her fearful gaze a long moment before he spoke. ''Here's what I know.'' He paused for effect. She trembled. ''I know that I didn't make any mistakes, and still Dillon walked right up to my door. How do you suppose he knew where we were, Kate?''

She shook her head and pushed a handful of dark hair behind her ear. ''I don't know,'' she insisted. ''I didn't tell him. I'd never seen the man before in my life until he dragged me out of the closet.'' She shuddered in a harsh breath. The pulse at the base of her throat fluttered too fast, way too fast.

Raine wrenched himself away from her. He muttered a colorful phrase about his birthright. Here the woman might have a heart condition and he was doing his level best to send her into cardiac arrest. Damn him all to hell.

''All right.'' He reached out to brush the fresh tears from her cheek and she flinched at his touch. His gut twisted with regret when she trembled beneath that simple caress. Her skin was unbelievably soft. Raine willed away the desire that immediately rose inside him. How could he want her so much? He couldn't let his guard down around her, that was becoming all too clear, but he wanted her anyway. She drew in another shaky breath and he longed to press his lips to hers. To soothe away the fear. But something about Kate Roberts didn't add up.

''Let's go,'' he said tiredly, and took a step back, out of her personal space.

''Where are we going?'' she murmured, her voice weak with relief.

Raine turned from her. "We need a doctor," he said, then started toward the house he couldn't yet see.

Kate grabbed his arm and pulled him back around to face her. Concern had replaced the fear. Her gaze moved frantically over him and then landed back on his. "Are you hurt?"

Guilt stabbed like a knife deep into the center of his chest. "Don't ask questions, Kate," he said tightly.

She glanced around, and frowned. "But where are we going to find a doctor at this time of night around here?"

"Trust me, I have a plan."

Chapter Eight

"Just stay calm, Doc, and there won't be a problem."

Kate glared, agog, first at Raine and then at the elderly man staring into the business end of Raine's Beretta.

This was his plan?

"What are you doing?" she demanded. "*This* is your idea of a plan?"

Raine looked at her for a long, charged moment, then smiled. It wasn't pleasant. Turning his attention back to the doctor, he shoved the unmarked prescription bottle Kate had completely forgotten about into the man's hand. "I'm told this is Inderal. I need you to tell me if my friend here has a bum ticker."

Kate drew in an audible breath. Was he talking about her? On cue, her chest ached and her heart fluttered. Oh, God! Was it possible that she could have some sort of heart problem and not remember? What other horrible things had she forgotten? Panic surged through her veins, urging her possibly faulty heart into an erratic rhythm.

His eyes huge behind the bifocal lenses, the doctor nodded his understanding of the question. "I'll…" He cleared his throat. "I'll need some background information on the patient."

Raine shook his head slowly from side to side. "No questions, Doc, just answers."

Still somewhat reluctant, the doctor opened the door wider and allowed them entrance into his home. "This way," he said as he started down the long, dimly lit hall.

Pressing his hand to the small of her back, Raine urged Kate forward. "This is insane," she hissed, and shot him an irritated glare. She was young. How could she have a heart condition? The poor old doctor, on the other hand, could very well drop dead of fright, considering his age and the weapon Raine was waving around.

Raine ignored her. "You live here alone, Doc?" he asked as if he'd just commented on the lovely country decorating of the man's home.

Kate gaped at Raine's audacity. "Why don't you just ask him where he keeps his life's savings buried while you're at it?" she huffed in a stage whisper.

"I stopped burying my money years ago, missy," the doctor called over one stooped shoulder.

Heat flooded Kate's face as humiliation dropped around her like a black cloud. Raine coughed in an obvious attempt to cover a chuckle, which earned him the nastiest look Kate could marshal. How did she get mixed up in all this? Though she still couldn't remember anything, she knew in the farthest reaches of her soul that she was not a criminal. Except, she grimaced, for the fact that she had participated in using two stolen vehicles and now, in holding a poor, innocent old man at gunpoint.

The doctor opened a door at the end of the hall and flipped on a light. "To answer your question, young fella—" he stood aside so Kate could pass "—yes, I live alone. Does that make a difference in the services you require of me?"

"No." Raine shrugged, a faint smile playing on his lips. "I just don't like surprises."

"You won't find any surprises here. I'm fresh out." The doctor eyed him speculatively. "You won't need that fire-arm either. The only one I own is upstairs behind the bed-room door. Hasn't been fired in more than twenty years, so I doubt that it would even work."

"That's good to know." Raine angled his head toward the open door. "After you, Doc."

The doctor appraised Raine a moment longer before he relented. Kate released the breath she had been holding when the two men seemed to reach some sort of unspoken understanding. The doctor shuffled over to an examination table. Raine, perpetually wary, settled into a chair near the door. At least clean shaven he didn't look quite so dangerous. Her eyes had feasted on the sight of him when he'd walked through that door to rescue her. Freshly showered and wearing the new clothes he had bought earlier that day, he took her breath away.

"On the table, missy. But first you'll need to shed some of those clothes."

Kate shrugged out of her coat and purse, then pulled the sweatshirt over her head, leaving just the T-shirt. She tossed them aside, then braced her hands on the examination table and hoisted herself onto it. Thankfully, Raine had put his gun away, or at least it was no longer in sight. The doctor placed his stethoscope around his neck.

Kate took her first good look at the old man. He had on flannel pajamas and well-worn house slippers. She had to clamp down on her lower lip to prevent a smile at his bedtime attire.

"It *is* the middle of the night," he offered, one shaggy gray eyebrow arched as if he'd just read her mind and taken good-hearted offense. "Besides—" he scrutinized her face, then angled her head to get a better look at her bruised temple "—you look a fright yourself."

Kate smiled then, warming to the old man's fatherly nature. "I've been through a lot lately."

"This," he said quietly as he touched the fading bruise on her temple, "doesn't have anything to do with your companion, does it?"

Kate shook her head. Her gaze flitted to Raine, who didn't seem to be paying any attention to their conversation. "I was in an automobile accident."

He nodded. "I see. Are you in trouble?" he asked quietly, his gaze searching hers.

"No." Kate hoped he couldn't read the truth in her eyes.

"Are you afraid of him?" He inclined his head in Raine's direction. This time Raine's jaw tightened and he shot the doctor's back an impatient look.

Kate moistened her wind-chapped lips. She summoned the small amount of strength she had left to keep her voice steady. "He saved my life."

"Who prescribed the heart medication for you?"

Before Kate could answer, Raine broke in. "No questions, Doc. That was our agreement." His tone left no room for bartering.

The doctor released a breath, then nodded. "Let's see what we can find then," he suggested. He settled the stethoscope into place, then warmed the contact piece in the palm of his hand before reaching beneath Kate's T-shirt to press it to her chest.

Kate tried to smile kindly for the old doctor, but Raine's words kept replaying in her ears. *I need you to tell me if my friend here has a bum ticker.*

"WHAT'S THE BOTTOM LINE, Doc?" Raine asked over his second cup of coffee.

Kate couldn't finish her first cup. She'd managed to swallow the little blue pill, but nothing else wanted to go down. She didn't want to hear any of this. This whole heart thing made her want to run away and hide her head in the sand. The feeling wasn't new. Kate recognized the familiarity of the old pain, but the recognition gave her no comfort. This was something she didn't want to know. Maybe that's why she had forgotten it.

"Mitral valve prolapse is a fairly common heart disorder and isn't usually much of a problem." The doctor glanced meaningfully at Kate. "Some patients have more severe symptoms, which require medication and can affect daily living. Of course, I can't be completely sure since there are other more precise tests required to give an accurate diagnosis. But I would hazard to guess that Kate falls into that category."

Kate swallowed tightly. Tears burned the backs of her eyes. She wanted out of here. Away from this—she didn't want to know. She knotted her hands in her lap and forced her body to stay put. She couldn't just up and run out the door. Raine would only drag her back to face this ugly reality anyway. She stole a glance in his direction. He listened quietly while the doctor spoke, his face wiped clean of emotion.

"She is physically fit. There's no reason to think she can't live a normal life as long as she takes her medication and doesn't overextend herself physically. It would be best, however, for a cardiologist to do a full evaluation."

Something indiscernible flickered across Raine's face, but he quickly banished it. "What's the medication dosage?"

"Without more in-depth testing, I would suggest one

tablet per day. And rest,'' he added quickly. ''She needs rest. From the look of her, I'd say that she is already seriously overextended physically, and possibly otherwise.'' The doctor eyed Raine for a long moment before he spoke again. ''I won't ask why she doesn't remember all this or where you got the Inderal.''

Raine met his gaze. ''It would be better if you didn't.''

''I'm going to assume that the bruise on her temple explains her lack of knowledge about her health history, and warn you again that she needs rest.'' He held Raine's gaze for a beat before continuing. ''You're welcome to stay here for the night,'' he offered hesitantly, as if he knew the answer before he spoke.

''Thanks, but we have some ground to cover before morning.'' Raine stood and reached for his wallet. ''What do I owe you, Doc?''

Kate took her cue from Raine. She shot to her feet, anxious to do anything but sit and listen to more gory details about her physical limitations. A sickening sense of dread welled inside her, making her heart flutter. Anxiety pressed down on her like a load of bricks.

The doctor pushed to his feet and extended his hand, which Raine hesitantly accepted. ''This one's on me.'' His cheeks flushed a bit. ''I haven't had this much excitement since Josh Miller shot his best friend in the foot for taking his girlfriend to the Fourth of July barn dance.''

A few minutes later, Kate exchanged goodbyes with the doctor and followed Raine into the darkness. She had a bad feeling that her heart condition played a strong role in her life. A negative role. A sob twisted deep in her throat. She didn't want to have to take these stupid blue pills. She didn't want some doctor to listen to her insides and hear unacceptable sounds. She wanted to be normal. To be a cop like her brother!

Kate jerked to a stop. She struggled to suck a breath into her seemingly too-tight chest. Her brother? She had a brother and he was a cop? The memory was there, on the tip of her consciousness but she couldn't quite grasp it.

Raine turned back to her. "You okay?"

She felt as if she might explode at any moment. An overwhelming sense of doom settled over her, pushing away rational thought. She felt the urge to run, run as fast as she could. The need consumed all other thought.

"Kate?" This time he was right beside her. "We have to go."

All but catatonic, Kate allowed Raine to guide her the rest of the way to the car. He had insisted on leaving the damn thing parked what felt like a mile from the house. So the old doc couldn't see the make and model in case he decided to call the police later. Her savior, she mused. He didn't miss a detail when it came to covering his tracks.

Kate opened the passenger-side door and plopped onto the bucket seat. She shoved her fingers through her hair and willed herself to calm, to think rationally. But it did no good. Raine worked his magic under the dash to start the engine.

The interior of the car suddenly seemed too confining for Kate to breathe. She had to get out. *Now.* Kate opened the door and bolted out. She sucked in breath after breath, but she just couldn't get enough oxygen to her lungs. Her heart pounded harder and harder. Oh, God. She was going to die. In the dark, in the middle of nowhere. Realization slammed into her like a blow to her midsection.

Panic. She was having a panic attack. She used to have them all the time.

How did she know that? She didn't want to know it! She didn't want to feel any of this.

Kate paced back and forth, alternately hugging her arms

around herself and threading her fingers through her hair. She wanted to run. Run fast. Run off all the extra adrenaline. Run until she collapsed in a pathetic heap.

Raine rounded the rear end of the car and moved toward her. "Kate."

He came too close. She felt crowded. Kate backed away, but he kept coming. A cold sweat broke out on her forehead. Her hands were clammy. God, she needed to run. But she couldn't. She had nowhere to go. She couldn't escape this reality. It was hers. She was defective, less than acceptable.

"Kate, it's okay," he said in a soothing voice.

"It's not okay!" she shouted, backing up another step. Kate closed her eyes and let the uncontrollable emotion have its way with her. "It's definitely not okay," she muttered. The open car door halted her backward movement. Frustrated and very near tears, she snapped her eyes open and banged her chest with her fist. "I don't want to have this." She surveyed her dark surroundings. "I don't want to be here." God, she needed more air. "And I don't want to know anything else about my past."

Raine braced one arm on top of the car and the other on the open door, then leaned in close, forcing her to look at him, to listen to him, crowding her with his nearness. "Kate, it's not the end of the world."

"How do you know what constitutes the beginning or the end of *my* world?" She glared at him, wishing with all her might that she could make him feel what she felt at this moment. He was perfect. What would he know about not measuring up? "Just go away and leave me alone!"

"Look," he said more sternly. "We don't have time for you to fall apart right now. We have to get the hell out of here. In case you've forgotten, we both almost met our maker tonight. Dillon and his men are out there right now trying to figure out which way we went. So if you're through feeling sorry for yourself, I'd like to get on the road.''

Anger flared inside Kate, devouring her anxiety in one hot flash. ''Don't you preach to me about feeling sorry for myself, you—you bastard. You're the one who got me into this mess. If anyone should be sorry it's you!'' Kate punctuated her statement by shoving against his chest. She needed some space. He was too close. Why wouldn't he just leave her alone?

Even in the waning moonlight, Kate didn't miss the irritation that flickered in Raine's eyes. ''Don't think I haven't been sorry since day one,'' he said hotly. ''But now that I'm stuck with you, I am trying to make the best of it.''

Kate crossed her arms over her chest and lifted her chin a notch. ''Ha! You call dragging me around like a rag doll and almost getting me killed making the best of it?''

''I haven't gotten you killed yet,'' he pointed out. He leaned a tad closer, close enough that his breath fanned her face. Kate shivered. ''I told you I wouldn't let anything happen to you, and I've kept my word.''

Kate trembled then, as much with awareness of the man towering over her as with delayed fear from the night's events. ''Why did you come for me?''

Raine frowned. ''What do you mean?''

''Why didn't you just take off? Why risk your life to save mine?'' She had to know. The answer was suddenly the most important bit of knowledge in the universe. If she never knew anything else, she needed to know this. Why didn't he just let her die? What good was she?

Confusion claimed his features briefly before he contained the outward display. "When I said I would keep you safe, I meant it. I'll do whatever it takes."

Kate hugged her arms more tightly around herself as a softer emotion crowded out all others. "You don't even know me, why would you die for me?"

"I've risked my life for a lot less in the past." The truth of his words burned in his eyes like an eternal flame of tribute to a past he'd just as soon not discuss.

She had to touch him. Kate lifted her hand to his face, to caress his tense jaw. The warmth of his skin felt devastatingly erotic beneath her palm. "You confuse me, Raine. I can't decide if you're a good guy or a bad guy."

He moistened his lips, placed his hand over hers, then kissed her palm. "I stopped wondering that myself a long time ago."

Kate pushed her arms around his neck and closed her eyes. She held him close. Somehow, this man, this stranger, cared about her. He might be a murderer, and he might be the worst of the bad guys, but he cared about her. Right now that's all that mattered. His lips felt firm and hot against her neck. She tilted her head and gave him full access to her throat. Heat and desire churned, warming her from the inside out. Kate tangled her fingers in his hair and pulled his mouth to hers. She wanted to taste him, to feel his lips against hers.

She gasped at the shock of his hard body pressing into hers. Instinct took control. Instead of pushing him away, she melted into the kiss, allowing him to mold her fully to him. His tongue pushed into her mouth, caressing hers. She tightened her hold, needing him closer when he was already practically a part of her. She demanded more and he gave it. His kiss deepened. He delved beneath the bulky layers of clothing with one long-fingered hand and found her breast. Kate groaned with need and arched into the thick arousal already straining against the front of his jeans.

Raine squeezed and caressed her breast. Kate's heart pounded frantically beneath his touch. Raine suddenly tensed, then broke the kiss, but kept her body trapped with his.

He slowly removed the hand that covered her breast and softly touched her cheek with his fingertips as he smiled, but the surface convention was strained. "We have to go."

Before she could protest, he stepped away and waited for her to get back into the car. Kate took a deep breath to steady herself and climbed inside without looking back. If she'd had any doubts about what was happening between them, none existed now. This relationship was no longer one of captor and hostage. And he didn't seem to mind at all that she wasn't perfect. Of course, he probably didn't have his mind on her heart, she admitted ruefully.

"Where are we going?" she asked when Raine had gotten behind the wheel and started down the long, rutted side road.

"Someplace safe."

Kate swallowed. She doubted that anyplace on earth would be safe from a man like Dillon. Her gaze moved over Raine's strong profile. Or him, for that matter.

RAINE DROVE SOUTH for more than two hours before he reached the city limits of Russellville. He glanced at Kate, asleep in the seat beside him. She had slept most of the way and that was good, she needed the rest. He, on the other hand, had been awake for twenty-four hours straight, and probably would be for most of the next twenty-four. Lack of sleep didn't bother him much though. During his stint in the special forces he had learned to function for days at a time with almost no sleep at all, catching a few minutes here and there.

The sun peeked over the mountaintops just in time to highlight the carefully restored historic buildings lining both sides of the main street that divided Russellville. Banks, coffee shops and other businesses occupied the federalist-style structures. Just before he reached the bridge that crossed the river, Raine turned left onto a narrow country road. He drove parallel to the river on his right. Farmhouses dotted the landscape on the left.

He slowed for a hairpin curve, then turned left at the top of the hill onto a gravel road. Over a mile later, a two-story farmhouse came into view and Raine smiled. Although the place had never really been his home, it felt like home.

Early-morning sunlight glinted from the damp-with-dew, green metal roof. A wide porch graced the front of the house like the apron on a proud southern lady. Fresh white paint coated the century-old clapboard siding, and green louvered shutters framed each window. The house didn't have much in the way of contemporary amenities, but it belonged to Raine. And so did the land, wooded and pastured, for as far as the eye could see. Raine definitely approved of the new fence that was almost complete, acres and acres of white split-rail fencing.

No one knew about this place, not even Lucas. Raine had bought it two years ago under an assumed name. A local contractor had made the essential renovations and repairs, like central heat and air and a new roof. Raine could live without a lot of things, but efficient heat and air-conditioning were not among them.

He had only been here three times, the time he'd found the place, again to close the deal, and once more six months ago to look over the renovations. But it was home, or, at least, the closest thing to a home Raine had known since he was a child. He had lain awake many, many nights and planned a life here. A new life as far away and as different from his old one as could be found. Of course, he had always known there was a strong possibility he would never have the chance to enjoy that life. He lived each day with death just one step behind him.

He might never have the opportunity to live in this house, Raine decided, but if the place served no other purpose than to keep Kate safe then that was fine with him. He drove past the house and parked the Thunderbird in one of the open side sections of the enormous barn.

Raine turned to Kate and watched her sleep. He clenched his jaw as regret washed over him. It was a miracle he hadn't killed her on that damn mountain. Without her medication and with him pushing her to the breaking point, her heart had surely been stressed to the limit. He shook his head at the emotion twisting his insides. What a fool he was. Selfish, too. Even after the doctor had emphasized that she needed rest, Raine had kissed her. Kissed her with much more than kissing on his mind. The feel of her heart fluttering in her chest had forced him to realize what he was doing and he had stopped.

Selfish, he repeated silently.

Well, it wouldn't happen again. He would protect Kate not only from Dillon, but from himself as well. He would stay with her for a little while to make sure she was okay, and then he would go. He still couldn't be sure that someone hadn't sent her for him—that she wasn't, in effect, his enemy. If Kate was his enemy, she didn't know it, and, as far as he was concerned, that made her innocent. But what happened when she got her memory back? Time was running out for him. This last unexpected run-in with Dillon had been entirely too close for comfort.

He couldn't take anymore unnecessary risks.

"Kate." Raine gently shook her.

She jerked to attention and surveyed her surroundings like a sentry caught sleeping on his watch. "Where are we?" she asked when her gaze met his.

Instinct nagged at Raine again, an instinct he knew better than to ignore, but he ignored it all the same. More mystery definitely lay behind that pretty face, but he didn't want to analyze that right now. "My place," he told her, then smiled when confusion stole into her eyes.

Raine got out, skirted the hood and opened Kate's door. He took her by the hand and led the way to the house. He reached beneath the third rock from the bottom step and retrieved his key. Inside what had once been a back porch and was now a mudroom, Raine flipped the necessary breaker for the hot-water heater. The real estate agent who had sold him the house checked on the place monthly and maintained the utilities. Raine would need to adjust the thermostat to a higher setting, since the heat was only set at a level necessary to prevent frozen plumbing.

"You live here?" Kate asked as they entered the kitchen.

"Well, I've stayed here a total of seven nights, does that qualify?"

"I suppose so," she said distractedly as she followed him into the hallway.

He moved the thermostat to a more comfortable setting and tried to remember what canned goods, if any, he had in the pantry. Kate wandered down the hall past him, obviously ready to explore. "Make yourself at home," he told her. "I'll get our things from the car."

Kate had already disappeared into the living room before he finished speaking. It pleased him immensely to share this place with her. Raine recognized the feeling for what it was. He had grown entirely too fond of Kate in the last few days, a dangerous allowance for a man like him. Those emotions had no place in his world, but he couldn't escape them where Kate was concerned.

When he returned from the car with their purchases from the day before, Kate was upstairs checking out the second floor. Since there were only three bedrooms and one bathroom up there, it didn't take Raine long to find her. He leaned against the doorway and watched her survey a bedroom.

Kate smiled when her gaze came to rest on him. "This place is wonderful. I love all the antiques." She gestured to the sparse furnishings.

"Most of them came with the house." He straightened and scanned the room. "My real estate agent picked up the rest." Tiny bouquets of pink and blue flowers dotted the faded wallpaper. Rich mahogany flooring and white painted trim made this bedroom just like the other two, only the finish on the walls differentiated the rooms. One had yellow-and-white-striped paper, while beige paint dressed the walls of the third. Raine had decided, on his first look at the house, that he favored the painted room. Flowers and stripes just weren't to his taste. Luckily all the rooms had beds. "How about you take this room?" he suggested, bringing his gaze back to his very first houseguest. This room was the farthest from the stairs and had only one window, therefore the most secure.

A look of mild surprise clouded her expression, but she recovered quickly. "This one will be fine."

Raine's heart thumped in his chest. Had she expected to share one with him? His groin tightened at the thought. "Okay." He crossed the room and placed the shopping bag containing her new clothes on the bed. "The water should be hot in a few minutes if you'd like to have a shower or bath. I'll go see what I can find to eat.''

"Thanks," she said on a smile.

Instead of doing something completely crazy like pulling her into his arms for another kiss as he so wanted to, Raine pivoted and left the room. He strode down the hall and left his own bag on the bed in the room next to hers. He would have preferred something on the other side of the globe, but a single wall would have to suffice. He only hoped that a mere wall would prove an adequate barrier to the temptation she represented.

Raine had a bad feeling that the day and night to come were going to be the longest of his life.

Chapter Nine

Steam curled around Kate, feathering against her skin like an angel's caress. The deep, hot water eased her sore, aching muscles. She relaxed fully against the smooth porcelain surface of the old claw-footed tub. Moisture beaded on her face, and Kate brushed back a strand of freshly washed hair. How could anything else on earth feel quite this heavenly? she wondered.

Kate had to admit that Raine's kiss had been pretty heavenly as well. The memory of his kiss flooded her mind, resurrecting that intense desire. A thousand sensations bombarded her. The way he touched her, the way his hard, muscular body felt against hers. His scent, his taste. Those amazing blue eyes.

She knew that allowing herself to dwell on thoughts of Raine's mind-boggling kisses wasn't safe, but she just couldn't help herself. Had any other man ever made her feel that way? Kate searched her mind for any memory of a former boyfriend or lover, but nothing came.

She sighed and slipped farther into the water's comforting depths. Maybe if she never remembered her past it would be best. Considering what she had learned about herself so far, Kate had a feeling the rest could be devastating.

She pressed her hand next to her left breast and felt for her heartbeat. She extended one leg at a time out of the water and scrutinized its muscle tone, then looked long and hard at her arms. How could she appear to be in such good physical condition, and have something so terribly wrong with her? Anxiety shuddered through her at the thought of just how wrong her problem was.

Fearing another panic attack, Kate forced the troublesome thoughts away and concentrated on relaxing. Raine probably thought she was mental already. Another bout of hysteria wouldn't help. She suddenly longed for the time before the doctor had revealed her heart problem. The time in the mountains when it had been just she and Raine. When she'd been a ''normal'' person who'd bumped her head and lost her memory. For a little while she had been free of the big, ugly problem that haunted the past she couldn't remember.

Kate focused on the warmth surrounding her. She inhaled deeply of the moist, clean air. Slowly, the heat plied her exhausted body into a state just shy of sleep. Her thoughts whirled, unhampered. Snatches of short-term memory flitted through her mind in no particular order. Raine kissing her in the darkness. Dillon's evil smile. The doctor's kind voice. Raine holding her naked against him in the shower. Danny telling her how many men Raine had killed. Raine facing Dillon to save her. She examined that last bit of memory more closely. Raine could have been killed trying to save her. But he had come for her all the same. Why had he done that? Was it merely a dogmatic sense of responsibility, as he claimed? Or could there be more to it?

Sleep tugged at Kate, enticing her toward oblivion. She was so tired and so warm. There was no reason not to give in, to escape the reality of what might lay in store for

Raine, for her. Her thoughts slowed and focused inward.
A kind of calmness enveloped her. She was safe for the
moment, and so was Raine. She could rest. A sigh of surrender eased past her lips as sleep captured her in its serene
embrace...

Kate wore black....

The man next to her wore a navy blue uniform. A
policeman's uniform. Her heartbeat accelerated. Kate
peered through the haze of billowing steam to more closely
see the man sitting next to her. She couldn't make out his
features through the thick steam. No, it wasn't steam. It
was more like fog. She was dreaming, she realized. The
haze cleared then. The man beside her looked at Kate with
sad, dark eyes.

Her father. The man was her father.

An ache, soul deep, rushed through her. Kate was sitting
on a church pew with her father. She forced her gaze forward, to the man speaking from the podium. A priest. His
long, white robes and gray hair looked stark against the
darkness of her dream. Where was she?

A funeral.

A polished oak coffin stood in front of the podium. The
priest continued to chant some sort of prayer. Kate looked
to her father, who wept at her side.

"He's gone, Katie." He shook his head in resignation.
"He's gone."

"But I'm here, Daddy," Kate insisted, confused.

Her father smiled sadly. "I know. But you don't understand the special bond he and I shared." Then he began
to weep again, louder than before.

Kate frowned. She looked at the priest for answers but
he wasn't paying attention to her. A mixture of fear and
sorrow tightening her throat, Kate stood and stepped toward the open coffin. Why couldn't she reach her father?

What was it she didn't understand? Whose funeral was this?

She looked down, into the white satin interior of the beautifully crafted oak box, and saw what it was she didn't understand.

Her brother, Joseph.

Tears slid down Kate's cheeks. Joseph was as handsome as ever. His dark hair short and styled a bit more stiffly than he would have liked. His dark eyes closed in eternal sleep. His usually smiling lips, permanently drawn into a line that wasn't quite frown nor smile. His uniform crisp and decorated, a deep blue against the white satin. His hands folded beneath his policeman's cap.

Kate could never be like him. Never live up to his super-cop reputation. Never have the place in her father's heart that Joseph held, even in death.

She would never measure up. She would always fall short of the mark. Her heart would never allow her to be all that her brother had been, all her father was....

Kate sat straight up. Water sloshed around her and over the edge of the tub. Her heart pounded while she fought to catch her breath. Her brother, her only sibling, was dead. And he had been a cop. A cop like her father, and his father and grandfather before him. She could never be a cop. She had failed the required physical.

She had failed her father.

The tradition stopped with her, because she didn't measure up. And Joseph was dead. He wouldn't be able to father a son or daughter to keep the tradition alive. Tears crowded her throat. She should have been the one to die. Joseph was perfect, handsome and healthy. He should have lived. But a twelve-year-old boy on crack cocaine had killed him with a stolen handgun. Kate's heart fluttered wildly as tears slid down her cheeks. Her stupid faulty heart. She should have died in that alley, not Joe.

A loud knock on the door penetrated the fog of grief shrouding her. "Kate, what's wrong? I heard you cry out all the way downstairs."

Kate shivered as the coolness of the water penetrated her consciousness. How long had she been dozing? Why did her dream feel so real, yet make no sense at all? She swiped at her cheeks and willed her heart to calm. She could examine those new snatches of memory later, when she was calmer. "I'm...I'm fine," she managed to say, knowing if she didn't say something Raine would grow suspicious.

"You're not fine," he argued. "Now open this damned door before I break it down."

Kate splashed the cool water on her heated face before she stood on shaky legs. She pulled the plug so the tub would drain, then stepped out onto the cold tile floor. She drew in a long, deep breath and let it out slowly. She had to pull herself together before facing him.

"Open the door, Kate," he demanded impatiently.

"Give me a minute!" she snapped right back. Kate squeezed her hair dry, then quickly blotted the water from her skin. She remembered belatedly that she had forgotten to bring clean clothes into the bathroom with her. "Damn," she muttered. She snatched up her dirty sweatshirt, but it was wet from the water that had sloshed over the side of the tub. She swore again and swiped the damp hair from her face. She had to put on something.

Kate glanced at the wet towel and considered it. At least it was clean. Before she could make a decision, something draped on the pedestal mirror in the corner caught her eye. She dropped the towel and crossed to the mirror. A white dress shirt hung on one of the decorative arms that supported the full-length oval-shaped mirror. Kate picked up the shirt and examined it more closely. From all indications it had been hanging there for a while, but it appeared fairly clean. She shook it, then held the short-sleeved garment to her face and inhaled deeply. The slightest hint of Raine's unique scent lingered on the fabric. He must have left it the last time he stayed here, she decided.

"Your minute is up." The deep timbre of his voice rumbled through the closed door.

A surge of renewed warmth flowed through Kate as the sound shivered across her nerve endings, pushing aside the sadness she couldn't bear to think about. She donned the shirt, made fast work of the buttons and opened the door before he carried through with his threat to break it down.

"What the hell took you so long?" he demanded, his shoulders rigid, concern creasing his forehead.

Kate propped her hands on her hips and stared up into those fierce blue eyes. "I had to put something on, you know," she retorted, shooting for nonchalance but not quite achieving it.

His lips parted as if he might say something else, but he changed his mind when his gaze slid down her body. Kate's stomach flip-flopped when he lingered on her breasts. The shirt clung to her still-damp skin, the white material becoming transparent and revealing almost as much as if she wore nothing at all.

"I…ah…heated up some canned soup," he said distractedly.

He lifted his gaze back to hers and Kate panicked. Her heart stumbled at the longing in his eyes. "I'm not hungry," she said quickly. No way could she trust herself in the same room with the man right now. His hunger was too strong, and she was weak—and none of it had anything to do with soup. What they both needed right now was distance. At least until she could sort out all these crazy, mixed-up memories and emotions.

He blinked twice, vacating his gaze of lust. "You need to eat."

"I'll eat later." Kate manufactured a smile. "I think I'll rest for a while." She crossed her arms over her chest and prayed he would leave. He made entirely too tempting a picture in those tight-fitting jeans and faded gray T-shirt. Early-morning stubble glistened on his jaw, inviting her touch.

Raine shrugged. "Suit yourself."

Kate blew out a relieved breath when he sauntered away. She closed her eyes and shook off the desire buzzing inside her. Her situation was screwed up enough without allowing herself to fall for a man like Jack Raine.

...he's the best in the business.

If she could only remember what business.

THE IMAGES weren't clear, the voices slightly muffled, but the dream pulled Kate deeper into the abyss of nothingness. *It's your job to find out if he's turned,* the voice told her. *And to bring him in either way.* The words echoed inside her head, making her restless. She tossed and turned in the bed, lingering just the other side of consciousness. She wanted to wake up, but the dreams wouldn't release her. She relaxed when Raine's kiss replayed behind her closed lids. Warmth shimmered through her body, heating all the right spots. She wanted to hold him close, to show him he could trust her, to believe she could trust him.

...you're our best shot at getting close to this guy. Raine's image shattered in Kate's dream, replaced by the words, by sensations she couldn't quite identify and faces she didn't recognize. *Someplace safe.* Raine's voice rushed into her head. He wanted her to be safe. *Ballatore wants*

him dead. It's only a matter of time before I catch up to you again. You're a dead man walking, my friend.

Kate's eyes snapped open and the room slowly came into focus. She pushed the hair from her face and took a long, shaky breath. Dreaming. She'd only been dreaming. She quickly scanned her quiet surroundings. Raine's house. She was safe. Sunlight spilled through the window and reached across the room.

Safe. The solitary word tugged at something buried way behind all the strange images and voices in her head.

And bring him in either way. The voice was Aunt Vicky's, whoever she was.

Kate frowned and struggled to recall her mixed-up dreams. Bits and pieces of conversation, snatches of images. Her father was a cop. Her brother was a cop and had died in the line of duty. She had wanted to be a cop and couldn't because of her heart problem. She couldn't measure up.

Kate blinked back the sting of tears. Tears for a loss she couldn't quite comprehend. She had lost a brother, but didn't remember much about that brother. How could that be possible? She could remember something as life-altering as her brother's death and still the rest of her past was a black hole in her brain.

And bring him in either way. Who did she have to bring in? And why? If she wasn't a cop, why would she be bringing in anyone? None of it made sense.

She was safe.

Raine had called this someplace safe. Safe for whom? Her? Him? *Ballatore wants him dead.* Would Raine hide here for the rest of his life? She didn't think so. Raine didn't strike Kate as the type to hide from anything.

Then why come here? *Someplace safe.*

Kate sat up with a start. He had brought her here so *she*

would be safe. Jack Raine wasn't afraid of death. He had risked his life for a lot less in the past. He had told her that. He had been on his way to New York—to Ballatore. Kate knew that fact with a certainty of which she could only guess the source. Raine's only reason for this out-of-the-way stop was to tuck her away someplace safe.

"Damn!" Kate threw back the cover and shot out of bed. He planned to leave her here—someplace safe—while he finished his business with Dillon and Ballatore. Lucas Camp was probably right. Raine intended to prove his innocence before he came in. Somehow he believed the usual channels had been breached, and he intended to do things his own way.

Lucas Camp? Kate paused, her eyes rounded in bewilderment. Who the hell was Lucas Camp? Why did Raine need to prove his innocence? Innocence of what? Kate pushed her fingers through her hair. She had no idea what any of this meant. The only thing she knew with any measure of certainty was that Raine would not hide from his enemies. He would face them. He wasn't concerned about his own safety.

Kate stood absolutely still in the middle of the room and listened. Complete silence hung heavily around her. He was probably already gone. Kate dashed out of the room, checked the other bedrooms and the bathroom before taking the stairs two at a time. She searched the downstairs. Raine was nowhere in the house.

The car. If he had left, he would have taken the car. Kate flung the back door open and raced across the yard. Though the sun beat down unusually warm for a November day, the ground still felt cool beneath her bare feet, but there was no time to worry about that at the moment. She skidded to a stop next to the muddy, black Thunderbird inside its makeshift garage. The car was exactly as

Raine had left it. Even if someone drove up to the house, they would never be able to see the stolen vehicle without walking into this attached side section of the barn with a flashlight. Despite the lack of a door, it was dark as a cave this far inside.

Kate frowned. If Raine hadn't left in the car, then where the hell was he? Though she had no idea why, Kate knew that she could not allow Jack Raine to slip through her fingers....

RAINE SHOVED the oil stick back into the engine and wiped his hands on a shop cloth. Everything checked out. He would have to give the real estate agent a bonus for going above and beyond the call of duty. The man had kept Raine's house and vehicle in tiptop shape. He glanced up at the lights hanging overhead in the barn, if you didn't count the one fluorescent bulb blinking overhead, that is. Of course, the lights out here probably didn't stay on long enough for the blinking bulb to be noticed.

For the time being, Raine used the barn for a garage to store his truck. But someday soon, he hoped to fill the numerous stalls with horses. He smiled to himself. He'd always wanted to be a cowboy. His smile faded into a frown. A pipe dream, nothing more. He knew better than to expect anything beyond this minute.

Forcing his attention to the present, Raine glanced at his watch. There was still time for a quick shower before taking off. If he left now he could be in New York well before midnight. He couldn't risk waiting any longer. Raine had already stored what he would need in the vehicle. An extra clip or two for the Beretta, and the Glock, his favorite weapon next to the Beretta. He didn't like being caught without backup protection.

A low creak sounded near the front entrance, jerking

him from his unpleasant strategizing. Raine tossed aside the shop cloth and drew his Beretta. He eased around the fender and down the driver's side of his Range Rover, then scanned the front of the barn. One side of the double doors stood open. His senses moved to a higher state of alert as his gaze followed the almost imperceptible sound of fabric rustling.

He rounded the tailgate and stood column straight at the edge of the bumper. Raine braced himself, then swung around the end of the vehicle, arms extended, weapon leveled on the first thing that moved.

Kate.

Raine swore.

Kate whirled around. Raine took a breath and lowered his weapon. "What the hell are you doing sneaking up on me like that? Announce yourself when you walk into a room with an armed man," he said crossly as he shoved the Beretta into his waistband at the small of his back.

"I…I thought you left," she stammered uncertainly. She shoved a handful of sleep-mussed hair behind her ear and met his gaze. "I was afraid…you had left…" Her voice trailed off.

She didn't say the word *me*, but Raine knew that's what she meant. Her words twisted his insides. She had been afraid that he'd left her, and that's exactly what he intended. Because he couldn't trust her, and he desperately wanted to keep her safe. "I came out to check on…" He gestured toward the vehicle, but words failed him as his gaze moved over her body.

Did she have no idea how tempting she looked standing there, all innocent and vulnerable? His shirt caressed her body in ways that made Raine's mouth go dry. Barely covering the tops of her thighs and with one too many buttons left undone, the shirt revealed a great deal more than it concealed. He remembered how it had looked against her skin after her bath. Her long, mahogany hair fell around her shoulders like a waterfall of silk. The bruise on her temple had almost completely faded now. Those dark eyes were wide with worry as she braced one hand against the front fender to steady herself. Obviously he'd scared the hell out of her as well.

He frowned. "Where's your coat?" Though the temperature was unseasonably warm and he'd shed his own coat hours ago, dressed like that, she had to be cold. He allowed his gaze to sweep over her once more.

She looked down at herself as if realizing for the first time her state of undress. "I was worried. I didn't know where you were," she murmured self-consciously. She slid one bare foot behind the other, as if trying to hide its nakedness. That innocent gesture pulled at him, made him want to protect her from any and all threats.

Raine averted his gaze and plowed his fingers through his hair. There was nothing in this world he wanted more than to take her in his arms right now. To promise her that he would never leave her, that he would always protect her, but he couldn't do that. If he touched her now, there would be no turning back. He couldn't do that to himself, and he wouldn't do it to her. Raine planted his hands on his hips and leveled an indifferent gaze in her direction. "I wouldn't leave without telling you."

She moistened her lips. "So you are planning to leave."

Raine restrained the urge to shift. He'd spent a lifetime holding his reactions in check, emotional as well as physical. Nothing had changed, he told himself. The lie proved hard to swallow. "I didn't say that."

"But you are, aren't you?" She crossed her arms over her chest and lifted her chin a notch. "You have to, don't you?"

Raine ignored the alarms going off in his head and took two steps in her direction. "My plans aren't concrete yet," he hedged. He'd actually planned to spend the night, but recognized the risk that he wouldn't be able to stay away from Kate.

She choked out a laugh and shook her head slowly from side to side. "You really expect me to believe that?" Kate pinned him with a gaze that shredded several more layers of his defenses. "My long-term memory may be off-line at the moment, but don't insult my intelligence. I know why we're here, Raine. This is where I get off, right? Did you plan to just dump me, or is this where you tie up *your* loose ends? Isn't that what a professional does? I mean, you are a professional, right?"

Disregarding his better judgment, Raine allowed the anger to erupt inside him as he closed the distance between them. He needed that particular emotion right now for protection—protection against the other much more precarious emotion he refused to acknowledge. He never second-guessed himself, he wasn't about to start.

He walked right up to Kate, directly into her personal space, and gave her his most intimidating glare. "When I've made up my mind I'll let you know." He kept his tone low and purposely threatening. "Until then, I would suggest that you don't antagonize me further. I do things my way."

Kate met his glare with lead in her own. His anger seemed to strengthen her resolve. All signs of uncertainty had vanished. "I tell you what, tough guy, why don't I save you the trouble. I'll just take the T-Bird and leave now. Then you and your nice friends can play all you want without having me around to worry about."

Raine felt a muscle jerk in his jaw. "You'll do whatever I damn well tell you to do," he said quietly, coldly.

Something changed in her eyes. A subtle, impossible-to-read shift. Instinct told Raine that he wasn't going to like it.

"Just try and make me," she challenged, then brushed past him as she strode away.

Hands still jammed at his waist, Raine watched in amazement as she stormed out of the barn. No, he didn't like this at all. He didn't tolerate insubordination. Grappling for control, he stalked after her. Halfway across the yard he snagged her by the arm and swung her around. She glowered at him, those dark eyes glittering with anger.

"Don't push me, Kate," he cautioned. "I won't let you get in the way of what I have to do."

"I'd say you're a little late." She struggled to free her arm, but he tightened his hold. "What will you do now, Raine?" She stilled and stared up at him. "Shoot me?"

Raine clenched his jaw and jerked her hard against him. "Don't tempt me."

Seconds ticked by as she stared fiercely at him, unwilling to relent. Through the thin layers of clothing separating their tense bodies, Raine could feel her heat. He wanted simultaneously to kiss her and shake some sense into her, the urge to do one or the other almost overwhelming. He had spent too many endless hours denying his desire for her, denying his needs, his feelings. Years of banished emotion threatened to crash in on him, showering Kate with its fallout.

She moved first, slamming her right fist into his gut. Raine grunted in surprise at the force behind her blow. He didn't have time to consider how the hell she could pack such a powerful wallop. He manacled her wrist while deftly deflecting her knee. Kate twisted, lost her balance and pulled him down with her. Raine shifted, holding her close and allowing his shoulder to take the brunt of impact when they hit the grass.

"Let me go, you bastard!"

"Stop squirming!" Raine pinned her beneath him, holding her hands above her head and trapping her legs with his own. She fought to throw him off, her body grinding into his. "Don't move," he growled. Desire warred with his common sense. Need bordered on physical pain, gnawing at his crumbling resolve.

She glared at him, the same battle between desire and anger taking place in her own dark eyes. The sound of her short, shallow breaths played havoc with Raine's weakening control. This was wrong, a mistake. He knew it. But he couldn't keep himself from wanting her, needing her. His gaze locked on her mouth. Her tongue darted out and moistened her lips. His control vaporized.

He took her mouth with his own, forcing her to accept him. Plying her soft lips with his firmer ones. A fierce longing shuddered through Raine, followed by a tormented groan that echoed inside her mouth.

Still fighting, Kate bit his lower lip. Raine swore, but refused to retreat. The tang of his blood mixed with her warm, sweet taste. She writhed beneath him and he kissed her harder, sucked at her tongue. Kate stopped struggling then, whether with desire or defeat, he couldn't be sure. Despite the risk that she might scratch his eyes out, Raine released his brutal hold on her hands to thread his fingers into her silky hair. Her hands went immediately to his chest, but she didn't push him away. Instead, her fingers fisted in the fabric of his T-shirt and pulled him nearer. Relief washed through him, followed by a rush of desire heightened by her acceptance.

Raine rested his weight on his forearms to keep from crushing her soft body into the ground. He cradled her head and deepened the kiss, invading her mouth with his tongue, stroking hers, teasing sensitive places. She responded wildly and his body contracted with want. The fact that they were lying outside in broad daylight no longer mattered. His need to have Kate consumed all else.

Kate tugged his shirt from his jeans and slipped her hands beneath it. He groaned when her delicate fingers traced the contours of his bare chest. He had wanted to be like this with her for so damn long. Heat sizzled wherever she touched. Raine ground his hips into hers, allowing her to feel just how much he wanted her. He drew his mouth from hers and kissed the tip of her nose, her closed lids, the shell of ear, and then lower. She lay panting, her passion-clouded eyes now following his every move, her chest heaving as harshly as his own.

Kate smoothed her palms over his heated flesh, down his chest to his abdomen, then around to his back. Her every touch left a trail of fire. She squeezed his buttocks and he almost lost it. He had to close his eyes and concentrate with all his might to slow his body's plunge toward release. He needed to be inside her, *now*. Her hands moved higher, kneading, massaging, urging him against her arching hips.

Raine knew instinctively the moment her fingers curled around the butt of the Beretta. He didn't move, didn't even breathe for one long moment. He lifted his mouth from the naked flesh he was plundering at the base of her throat, his gaze meeting hers. A beat of uncertainty passed. In that split second, something distinctly adversarial flashed in her dark eyes, then it was gone. Kate extended her arm above her head and placed the Beretta on the ground in plain sight.

A look of primal intent in her eyes, she raised her mouth to his. She sucked his injured lip, moaning softly at the taste of him. Renewed desire roared through his veins, bringing the need inside him to a boiling point and hardening already tight muscles. Again and again her lips teased his until Raine took her mouth hard, thrusting his tongue inside. Her fingers labored with the snap and fly of his jeans.

She reached inside, touched him, then circled his aching flesh with her soft fingers. Raine groaned harshly, suppressing the urge to explode in her gentle caress. Crazy with want now, he wrenched his mouth from hers, ripped open the shirt she wore and covered one straining breast. Her essence filled his mouth as he sucked first one breast, and then the other. Kate screamed her pleasure. He wanted to taste her, to touch her all over, to take her. Now, right now.

His heart pounded with impatience as she struggled to shove his jeans and briefs down his hips. She whimpered her own frustration. He kneed her thighs farther apart as he glided one hand over her feminine shape. He touched her, surprised when he didn't find panties. Kate gasped as he tangled his fingers in her nest of soft curls, slid one finger along her feminine channel, then dipped inside. She was so hot. Kate moaned with pleasure, momentarily distracted from her struggle with his jeans. Raine buried that one finger deep inside her, pressing the heel of his hand hard against her swollen nub. She arched her hips, her hands suddenly frantic to push away his restraining clothes.

Raine grunted a primal sound when his shaft leaped free. There was no time for civilized foreplay, no patience for decorum. He entered her in one savage thrust. Tight and hot, she gripped him. Kate cried out his name and he soothed her mouth with his own, murmuring unintelligible sounds between kisses.

Kate clung to him, her arms around his neck, her legs locked around his as he started to move. She lifted her hips to meet each thrust and Raine slid his arms beneath her to protect her from the cold ground. Harder and harder he pounded into Kate, driving closer and closer to release. He couldn't slow the pace, couldn't draw out the pleasure for her. Giving was out of the question, he could only take. He would make this up to her if it was the last thing he did.

Heat and sensation crashed down on him, propelling him over the edge. Raine pressed his forehead to hers and thrust one last time, shuddering with the force of it. He slowed, emptying himself into her heat.

Kate groaned her protest when he would have slumped to a stop. She quivered against him and her feminine muscles clutched urgently around his shaft. Unable to form coherent thought, instinct took control. Raine clenched his jaw and drove fully into her again and again, bringing her to the completion he hadn't expected. She buried her nails in his back, a sweet pleasure-pain, as she convulsed around him.

Exhausted and sated, they lay together without speaking, their frantic breathing and the wind shifting in the trees the only sounds around them. Kate shivered. Raine realized then how cold she must be, lying in his arms against the frigid ground.

''We should go inside,'' he murmured, and brushed a strand of windblown hair from her cheek.

She silently searched his gaze. Raine hoped she couldn't see how deeply this desperate act had affected him. For the first time in his life, he couldn't push away how he felt. It threatened to burst out of him in ways and words he couldn't yet acknowledge.

He looked away, disengaged from Kate and shifted to a

kneeling position. He shouldn't be feeling any of this. He
was a fool. He righted his clothes, then offered her his
hand. She accepted it, and they stood together. Raine swallowed tightly as he quickly analyzed what had just happened between them. He'd never let anything get this far
out of bounds before. He always maintained control of a
situation—any situation.

What the hell was wrong with him? People were trying
to kill them, for Christ's sake. And what was he doing?
Having sex like a horny teenager with no consideration to
their safety or the consequences of the unprotected act.

His gaze swept over Kate as she tugged the now-
buttonless shirt around herself. He had sworn that he
wouldn't do this to her. It was bad enough that he had
endangered her life, he didn't want to hurt her emotionally
as well. She might not be totally innocent in all this, but
her amnesia had left her vulnerable. And he had taken
advantage of that vulnerability. She needed his protection,
not his barbaric abuse.

Holding the sides of the shirt together with one hand,
Kate flipped her long hair over one shoulder and leveled
her gaze on his. "Just so you know," she said with more
challenge than he would have expected. "This doesn't
change anything. I'm still not going to let you tell me what
to do."

Before Raine could respond, she gave him her back and
walked away.

Chapter Ten

Kate watched Raine pace the length of the living room once more. She shifted in her chair and waited for the inquisition to begin again. Impatient with dread, she crossed her legs, clasped her hands around her knee and tried her level best not to appear nervous. She swallowed tightly when she considered that only an hour ago she and Raine had made love outside, *on the ground*. The only evidence of that temporary lapse in sanity were the grass stains on the knees of his jeans. Kate resisted the urge to grimace at the memory of the primitive act. One minute he had been on top of her, lost to the desires of their heated bodies, the next he had grabbed back control and tucked all emotion into an iron fist of restraint.

The transition hadn't been so easy for Kate. It had taken a shower, clean clothes and several minutes of self-chastisement to shake the intensity of the emotions she had experienced. Coming back downstairs to face him had surely been one of the hardest things she had ever done. No matter how much her heart wanted to, she could not allow herself to make more of their encounter than was warranted. Sex, that's all it had been. Desperate people in desperate situations did desperate things. As if to deny that reasoning, Kate shivered when the memory of his touch flooded her being once more.

And now he wanted some answers. Answers, for the most part, she couldn't give.

"You don't remember anything else?"

Kate avoided his penetrating gaze. She wasn't nearly so good as he at masking her emotions. "No," she lied.

Raine scrubbed his hand over his jaw as he slowly turned to retrace his steps. When he stopped he ran his fingers through his blond hair and seemed to consider long and hard Kate's response. She knew he didn't quite believe her, and certainly didn't trust her. She could only hope that what she had told him would be enough. The dreams she'd had didn't make a lot of sense, but there were parts that instinct told her were accurate.

Though Kate still couldn't recall having a father, she knew she did and that he was a cop. She'd had a brother too. A brother who had been a cop and had died in the line of duty. This information she shared with Raine, but nothing more. Kate felt the need to protect the rest of the mysterious snatches of memory. The really scary part was the bad feeling she had that her instinct to conceal this information had something to do with who Raine was and all this insanity going on around them.

"Look," Raine said, breaking into her unsettling thoughts. He sat down on the edge of the coffee table in front of Kate, his forearms braced on his thighs, his wide-spread knees on either side of hers. Those clear blue eyes settled onto Kate's, sending a spear of heat through her. "It's becoming more and more apparent that your turning up at my doorstep was no accident—"

"But you said that I had wrecked my car near your driveway," she interjected quickly. She knew exactly where this was headed and somehow she had to keep him from going there.

"That's the way it appeared."

"The way it appeared?" Indignation surged through her veins. "Do you think I hit the ditch and risked killing myself on purpose? That I'm walking around here with no clue to my past because I enjoy the mystery of it?" Realization washed over Kate, leaving her weak with disbelief. Though she had her own doubts as to exactly why she showed up in Gatlinburg, the amnesia was all too real. "You think I'm faking the amnesia." She breathed that sudden awareness aloud.

It wasn't a question, she already knew the answer. Kate saw the quick flash of indecision in his eyes. The possibility had crossed his mind.

He exhaled and looked away. There was no uncertainty in his gaze when it focused again on hers. "I don't think you're faking," he said finally. His tone was reassuring but measured. "The accident and the head injury were real. The amnesia is real. I'm just not convinced that your being on that particular stretch of road was coincidental."

"What's that supposed to mean?" Kate felt her heart flutter. She frowned, trying to remember if she had taken her medication. Yes, she had. Raine had asked her that same question right after…after they'd come back into the house. Kate willed herself to relax, to pay attention to what he had to say next.

"I think maybe someone sent you there to find me," he said carefully. He watched her closely, poised to analyze any reaction, no matter how remote.

Kate shot to her feet and stepped away from him. She couldn't be sure that she could adequately shield her emotions if he probed too deeply. There were too many unanswered questions floating around in her head. Too many pieces of the puzzle that didn't quite fit together. And a whole slew of gut feelings that skirted too close to the conclusion he had verbalized. She crossed the room and stared out the window at the clear, warm day.

"My father is the cop, not me." Kate folded her arms across her middle and looked over her shoulder at him. His expression gave away nothing of what he might be thinking. "I have a bum ticker, remember?" She injected a healthy dose of sarcasm into the repetition of his own words.

Raine stood, his height alone immensely intimidating. Those long fingers sifted through his thick blond hair once more. His body language revealed as much about his own uneasiness as her eyes likely revealed about hers, Kate decided. He seemed uncomfortable with accusing her, or, distressed by the reminder of her heart condition. Kate felt certain that, whichever was true, sentiment of that nature was way out of character for a man like Jack Raine.

"I remember." He took several steps in her direction. "But that might not keep someone from using you to get to me," he said softly, as if trying to lessen the ugly meaning behind his words. He stood right beside her now, crowding her with his nearness.

…you're our best shot at getting close to this guy. The now-familiar voice mocked, the words reverberating in Kate's skull. She shuddered and shoved that foreboding intrusion away. If Raine was right, then whoever sent her could be just one step behind them, or waiting for Kate to make a move. She was still convinced that the phone call she had made had given away their location, bringing Dillon to their door. But she couldn't be working for Ballatore…could she?

And to bring him in either way.

Kate's breath caught, she blinked, then examined the

absolute finality of the mental prompting some dark recess of her mind had just given. There was no question. Raine had hit the nail square on the head. She had been sent to find him and to bring him in despite what he had or had not done. *He needs protection, Ballatore wants him dead,* the voice reminded. If she were trying to protect him from Ballatore, she couldn't be working for him.

"You're sure you didn't know me before—" Kate swallowed the constricting lump rising in her throat "—before I showed up at your door?"

Raine shook his head, then allowed one of those rare, breath-stealing smiles. "I would definitely remember if I had ever met you."

Kate braced herself against the assorted flutters and shivers his nearness evoked. She couldn't allow those feelings right now. Like him, she needed answers. "Why would anyone be after you? What did you do?" She had really wanted to ask why someone would want him dead, but hadn't been able to manage that much courage.

Raine shifted to stare out the window. "It's not what I did, it's what I didn't do."

"What didn't you do?" Anticipation pounded through her veins as she waited for his response. The answer to this one question was somehow pivotal, Kate felt it with every fiber of her being.

That disconcerting, analyzing gaze landed on hers once more. "I didn't see it coming. That's what I didn't do." He let go a heavy breath, then swallowed hard. The play of muscle beneath tanned skin momentarily distracted Kate from the question his words would have naturally prompted.

"I should have anticipated Dillon's move," he answered without her asking. Raine shook his head. "He killed Michael Ballatore right in front of me and I didn't have a clue what he was up to until it was too late."

"That's why Ballatore wants you dead," Kate realized out loud, talking more to herself than to Raine. "He thinks you killed his son." Somehow she had known that, too.

"That about sums it up," he agreed dispassionately.

"What are you going to do about it?" she prodded, suddenly overwhelmed with the urge to develop a plan to clear him. "You can't just keep running forever. He won't stop sending men after you. Even if you kill Dillon, Ballatore will just send someone else." Fear snaked around Kate's heart. She knew without a doubt that her summation was accurate. Sal Ballatore was not the kind of man who ever gave up. Raine needed a plan—she needed a plan.

"I have to set the record straight," he said in that cold, emotionless voice that sent a different kind of shiver dancing up Kate's spine. She didn't like that side of Raine. *He's spent the last twelve years of his life living on the edge...*

"How do you propose to do that?" she asked, shaking her head to clear it of the now too-familiar voice. She didn't want to remember anything else. Raine's plan wasn't exactly the kind of plan she had in mind. "It's not like you can call up his secretary and make an appointment."

One corner of his sensuous mouth kicked up into a wicked tilt. "I don't plan to make an appointment."

Kate's mouth dropped open, and she quickly snapped it shut, then made a sound of skepticism, half sigh, half chuckle. "You said yourself that Ballatore has an army of trained killers like Dillon on his side; just what do you have?"

Raine cocked his head and allowed that one-sided tilt to widen into a grin. "*I* have the element of surprise."

"I CAN'T BELIEVE you're doing this," Kate hissed. She glared at Raine through the darkness of the car's interior. A shaft of dim light from a nearby street lamp highlighted the angles of his handsome profile. She shouldn't let him do it. But how could she stop him?

"It's the only way, Kate," he told her again. The words weren't any more convincing this time than they had been the other two times he'd repeated them. A muscle twitched in his tense jaw. She knew he'd become impatient with her resistance to his strategy, but she just couldn't help protesting what could only be called suicidal. No more than she could help the way she felt…

She cared too much. And she knew deep in her heart that when this was all over—when she had her memory back—things would never be the same. He would hate her for lying to him. Trust was a matter Raine took deadly serious. Of course, none of that would matter if the damn fool got himself killed tonight.

"What I can't believe is that I let you talk me into allowing you to come along," he said incredulously.

"Like you could have stopped me," Kate retorted.

Raine tossed her a look that spoke louder than words. The real decision had been his and she knew it.

Kate exhaled a burst of helpless frustration that had been hampering her ability to take a deep breath for the last ten hours. Raine had driven nine of those hours with only one stop for refueling before they entered the city of New York. Now they sat in his black Range Rover less than a block from Sal Ballatore's East Side estate. And there was nothing, short of shooting Raine herself, that she could do to stop what was about to take place.

"Dillon was right." Kate breathed the words into the tense stillness. "You are a dead man walking. You believe you have nothing to lose, so you don't think twice about taking a risk like this.'' Ice-cold fingers of dread nudged at Kate. Raine had a death wish and he was about to make it a reality.

Raine shifted to face her, leather squeaked beneath faded denim. That glimmer of light spread across his full lips and intense blue eyes now. ''The old man won't kill me until he hears what I have to say.''

''And if he doesn't believe you?'' Kate couldn't mask the fear in her voice. She didn't want Raine to die. Damn him! He'd made her have...all these feelings, and she wasn't prepared to let him go just yet—even if they had no future together.

''Kate—''

''What if Dillon is here?'' she demanded, cutting off whatever he would have said.

''Dillon won't be here,'' Raine assured her. His voice had taken on a placating tone she'd heard only once before—when they had made love on the cold ground beneath the sun's warm kiss.

''Dillon and I were the only two people in the room when Michael died. He's as guilty as I am in Ballatore's eyes. That's why he was ordered to find me. Failure would be a death sentence. He won't come back until he eliminates the possibility that Ballatore might hear my side of the story. This is the last place Dillon will expect me to show up.''

Kate searched his eyes, hoping against hope that she might actually be able to read his true feelings. But Raine was too good at hiding things. ''Is there any chance Ballatore will believe you?''

Raine lifted one shoulder in a halfhearted shrug. ''Maybe.''

''Maybe?'' Kate shook her head. ''How can you walk

in there knowing that you'll probably never walk out again?''

''I don't have a choice.'' Raine fixed her with a gaze that chilled Kate to the bone. ''If Ballatore backs off, then it'll be just Dillon and me. Dillon has information I need.''

''Information? About the money?'' As soon as the words were out of her mouth, Kate recognized the stupidity of them. None of this was about the money.

When he didn't respond immediately, she said, ''Who are you, Raine?'' That was the missing link. Raine was the key. The realization hit Kate with sudden, amazing clarity. She needed him alive for more than one reason. She needed him to complete her *assignment*. ''You can't go in there,'' she managed to say despite the sensations and voices whirling inside her head.

''If I'm not back in one hour, drive until you find a pay phone and call Lucas.'' Raine pressed a folded piece of paper into her trembling hand. ''He's your only shot at getting out of this mess alive.''

Lucas Camp. Kate stared first at the small white square, then back at the man who had placed it in her hand. ''Do you trust Lucas?'' *There's only one person I trust, Kate, and that's me.* Raine's words joined the medley of others inside her head.

He exhaled and cast a glance in the direction of Ballatore's dark house. ''If Lucas can't be trusted, there's no one else.''

Raine didn't give her a chance to ask anything else, he slid his hand around her nape and pulled her mouth to his. Kate didn't fight him, instead she melted into his kiss. His taste filled her, sent heat straight to her center where it bloomed and spread throughout her body. She couldn't deny her need for him any more than she could deny the truth that was unfolding inside her and around them.

Though the facts were still vague, Kate knew he was right—they were enemies, or, at the very least, on opposing sides in all this insanity. But none of that mattered when he kissed her.

Raine pulled back all too soon. Before Kate could protest, he had opened the driver's-side door, gotten out and was disappearing into the darkness on the other side of the street. She strained to make out his form moving toward the iron gate that guarded the entrance to Ballatore's property. She watched for several minutes, but there was no further sign of Raine.

…he's an infiltrator. He can get in and out of places no one else can.

Right now, Kate hoped with all her heart that Raine really was the best in the business.

RAINE HAD ONLY to wait until the perimeter guard made his rounds. Twice an hour, one guard walked the grounds inside the security fence and another outside. The one outside could always be counted on to be the newest and probably the youngest member of the security staff. He would be considered the most expendable, and walking outside the fence certainly represented the greatest risk to surviving night shift.

While he waited he considered the chance he had taken bringing Kate along. But he couldn't leave her as he had planned. Though it pained him to believe that she might be working for the enemy, he had to trust his instincts. Instinct told him not to risk her alerting *anyone* to his plans. Outside locking her up or killing her—and he could not do either—he'd had no choice but to bring her. He never took that kind of risk—he wouldn't now. No matter that some small foolish part of him wanted to take Kate and run. Leave it all behind. Disappear where no one would ever find them. Raine silently laughed at himself. *Great plan.* The only problem was, what happened when she got her memory back?

Before Raine could consider the answer to that question, the guard stopped to check the side gate. Raine pressed the barrel of his Beretta against the man's temple and stepped out of the shadows. "Take me to the old man," he said quietly.

The guard tensed. Raine could imagine the man's short life was passing before his eyes at that precise moment. "I can't do that," he replied in a clipped tone. "You could blow my head off for all they care, man, and they still wouldn't let you in."

Raine clenched his jaw, then forced himself to relax. "Just tell them Jack Raine is here to see Mr. Ballatore."

A few minutes later Raine stood in Sal Ballatore's private study. No one had roughed him up as he had fully expected. The head of security had thoroughly searched him, however, and taken his Beretta, but other than that, things had gone rather smoothly. Raine was alone now. Four men waited outside the closed doors to do Ballatore's bidding. There would be others somewhere inside and at least two still patrolling the grounds. There was always a minimum of eight men on duty. The old man had grown a bit paranoid in his twilight years.

Of course, in this business, operating a crime syndicate in a city the size of New York, it paid to be a little on the paranoid side.

A sense of déjà vu shrouded Raine with memories of another night much like this one. The night he'd had to pass Ballatore's personal inspection. As sharp as the old man was, he had accepted Raine almost without question. But that was what he did best, Raine reminded himself.

He made people trust him. At one time that particular skill had meant a great deal to him. Now it only disgusted him.

Raine turned at the sound of the opening door. He felt the muscle in his jaw jump when his gaze met Ballatore's. The loss of his only son evidenced itself in every line on his face, but the eyes were the worst. Those gray eyes no longer held the spark of life, or the power that had once radiated from their world-wise depths. They were empty. Regret, unbidden, trickled through Raine. He had experienced remorse over few things in his life, but he truly regretted the senseless death of Michael Ballatore.

Sal Ballatore, clad in silk pajamas and matching robe, crossed the room to stand directly in front of Raine. He held Raine's weapon in his right hand.

"Dillon and my men have been searching for you for quite some time now." He lifted one gray eyebrow a fraction higher than the other. "How is it that in all this time they could not find you, yet you waltz into my home in the middle of the night of your own free will?"

"I didn't come here to discuss the lack of skill possessed by the men you employ," Raine told him, careful to keep his tone as unrevealing as his gaze. "I was told that you wanted to ask me a question. I've driven all night for this little tête-à-tête, so let's get on with it."

"You never were one to waste time on idle chitchat," Ballatore noted aloud, then focused his attention on the weapon in his hand. "Before I end your worthless life, I would like you to tell me why you killed my son." The old man's voice wavered slightly when he continued. "Michael was a good boy, and he did not deserve to die by your hand, Jack Raine." He lifted his gaze back to Raine, something primal shifted in those lackluster eyes.

Vengeance. Raine recognized and understood the desire for vengeance that suddenly filled that empty gaze.

"I despise killing." Ballatore grimaced. "It's so messy, especially when you shoot a man in the head with a weapon like this at close range." He glanced around the elegant study then. "But Michael was born in this room." He smiled, remembering. "His mother waited too long before she told me it was time to go. So my son took his first breath right here in this study. And you—" his gaze lit on Raine once more "—will take your last here."

"I did not kill Michael," Raine offered quietly, firmly.

Contempt stole across Ballatore's grief-stricken features. "You are a liar," he spat. "I know who you are, Jack Raine, and you killed my son. You and that bastard government you work for!"

"Dillon killed Michael for the money," Raine countered.

"*You* took the money. Danny and Vinny have attested to that fact." Rage darkened his cheeks. "*My* money."

"I took the money only to keep Dillon from taking it." Raine opened his hand and held out a small brass key. "It's in a locker at the Port Authority bus terminal."

Ballatore slapped away the key with the back of his hand. "You think you can come here and buy redemption with my own money?"

Raine allowed his hand to drop to his side. "I don't need your absolution, old man, I didn't kill your son. I only came here to set the record straight."

"You came here all those months ago," Ballatore growled, "to destroy my family. You ingratiated yourself into this household and then you destroyed my only flesh and blood." His body trembled with the rage Raine could see building in his eyes. "*You* were like a second son to me. I trusted you with my life—with Michael's life." Ballatore shook his head slowly from side to side. "First you betrayed my trust, then you killed my son."

"I came here *for you,* old man, not your son," Raine said pointedly. "The organization that hired me had no interest in Michael. Dillon killed your son. Somehow Dillon found out who I was and used that knowledge as an opportunity to make himself a couple million and to get rid of me at the same time." Raine leaned closer to the shorter man. "Think about it. With Michael and me out of the way, that puts Dillon at the top of the food chain."

Ballatore considered Raine's words for several long, tense moments before he spoke. "Why should I believe what you say?" His eyes narrowed as he scrutinized Raine's face for the truth in the response he was about to give.

"I could have taken your money and disappeared." Raine held his gaze. "And, trust me, you and your men would never have found me."

"You don't want my money and you didn't kill my son, so why are you here?" Though some of his conviction had dissolved, sarcasm still weighted Ballatore's tone.

"I want Dillon. He has information that I need."

Realization dawned in the aged gray eyes. "You want to know who sold you out?"

"That's right," Raine agreed.

Ballatore snorted his disbelief. "What does it matter? Your cover is blown for this operation. Why do you care?"

"I can't walk away knowing that someone might be selling out others like me."

The old man nodded then. "Ah, I see. You think I give one damn what happens to the others like you?"

"No, but I'm sure you want to punish the man who killed your son."

"And you want me to believe that it wasn't you?" He smirked. "Again I ask, why should I believe you?"

"Because I'm telling the truth."

Ballatore regarded Raine warily for another beat or two. His expression slowly relaxed, as did his posture, and finally he spoke again. "What do you want from me?"

"I want Dillon," Raine said simply.

The older man's chin went up a notch, unaccustomed to acquiescing to anyone's demands. "You ask a great deal for a man whose life means nothing to me, and who has less than nothing to offer in return."

Raine mentally acknowledged his new standing with Ballatore. He hadn't come here tonight to make amends. He'd come, Raine reiterated silently, to set things straight with the old man and to set up Dillon. "You asked what I wanted, that's what I want," he replied.

Ballatore lifted his silk-covered shoulders and then dropped them in a careless shrug. "That could be arranged."

A new surge of adrenaline rushed through Raine, anticipation of the hunt. "You keep this meeting quiet for the next twenty-four hours. I'll call in a location for you to pass along to Dillon. Tell him I've asked for a meet to explain what really happened. When he comes for me, I'll be ready."

The old man's gaze locked with Raine's once more. "There are two conditions."

Raine's tension escalated to a new level.

"When you have extracted your information, Dillon is mine." He paused long enough for Raine to absorb the impact of the statement. "And, you tell your people that the next man they send for me will die a slow and painful death. Salvador Ballatore doesn't make the same mistake twice."

Raine nodded, then extended his open hand. "Done."

Ballatore placed the butt of the Beretta into Raine's palm. "Good. Maria will be glad." He gave a short, wry chuckle. "There will be no mess for her to clean up in here tomorrow."

His relief near-palpable, Raine tucked the Beretta into his waistband at the small of his back. "I'll contact you in the next twenty-four hours." He gave Ballatore one final glance, then strode toward the door.

"One more thing." The voice of the man who still held Raine's life in his hands echoed across the room.

Raine paused at the door and turned back to face him.

"Find a new line of work, Jack Raine. This one will get you killed."

Chapter Eleven

Kate sat in the near darkness of the hotel room and watched Raine sleep. It was the first time she had actually seen the man with his guard down completely. She remembered thinking that maybe he was a machine and didn't have such basic needs as sleep. She smiled and hugged the cool sheet more tightly around her naked body. She definitely knew better now. Raine was all too human. He had needs. Needs so strong they were almost frightening. Like her own. She shivered at the thought of how important he had become to her in the last few days. More important to her than remembering the truth about who she was and why she had been sent to find him.

When Raine had returned to the truck, alive and unharmed, from his meeting with Ballatore, Kate had been beside herself with relief. She had no idea if in her past life she'd been a spiritual person or even attended church, but she had thanked God over and over the moment Raine had appeared out of the darkness.

Raine hadn't given any details about the meeting, only that everything was set. Whatever that meant. Then he had driven straight to a hotel in Manhattan, checked into a room and dragged her into bed before she could so much as get a good look at the place. Like the first time, their lovemaking had been hot and frantic, neither of them taking the time to undress, only pulling down or pushing aside the absolute essentials.

Kate had sensed his desperation, the same desperation she felt even now, that this might be the last time they were together. The unrestrainable instinct to celebrate life and survival when mortality threatened. She could have resisted and he would have stopped, but she hadn't. Instead, she'd urged him on with her own frenzied response.

Afterward Raine seemed to regret that he had taken her so crudely, with no pretty words or proper foreplay. As if to make up for his actions, he'd gently removed her disheveled clothing, then carried her to the bathroom, where they had showered together. Slowly, chastely, he had washed every square inch of her body. Later, when he'd tenderly tucked her into the wide, inviting bed, Kate had given in to the exhaustion almost immediately.

Surprised at finding Raine asleep when she had awakened, Kate had pulled the sheet around her and moved to a chair so she could watch him. Dawn was still hours away, but the soft glow of light from the bathroom filtered through the room's darkness and caressed his bare chest. The ivory brocade coverlet concealed his lower body, leaving the rest for her admiration. His strong arms were flung over his head and draped across the pillow. Kate's gaze slid over his handsome profile and down his tanned throat, across his muscled chest, and then down the lean terrain of his stomach. His navel peeked above the edge of the rich cloth.

Kate's insides warmed from just looking at him. She had no memory of making love before Raine, but she could not imagine anyone else making her feel quite the way he did.

But they had no future together. Though she still didn't

know all the details, Kate knew enough to be certain about where she would stand when Raine discovered the truth. Would the man, who had made love to her only a few short hours ago, kill her when he found out she had been sent to find him? To bring him in?

As she scanned his beautifully sculpted body once more, she decided that in repose he looked almost vulnerable. But Jack Raine was anything but vulnerable.

Dangerous. A man who lived by a different set of rules.

"See anything you like?"

Kate's breath caught when her errant gaze collided with eyes so blue and piercing they seemed to reach past her defenses and touch a place no one else could. Longing welled inside her, shoving away all other thoughts.

She managed a smile despite the blood roaring in her ears and the tremble of her lips. "I see a good many things I like," she told him.

Raine threw back the cover and stood in one fluid motion. Kate's heart lurched when he moved toward her. His body was already, *or still,* semi-aroused. She shivered when she considered the mild discomfort associated with his size. He was a big man, his body strong and powerful. In the brief moments required for Raine to take the three steps separating them, her body moistened in anticipation of the desire evidencing itself in his.

Raine crouched in front of her and pressed his lips to hers. The kiss was lingering, undemanding. Kate's fingers found their way into his tousled blond hair and she urged him closer. With her movement, the sheet fell away from her shoulders, freeing her breasts so that her nipples grazed his bare chest. Desire stung her core and Kate moaned low in her throat, the sound echoed between them, intensifying her need.

He broke the kiss, pulling back despite her groan of

protest. Kate frowned her frustration that their lips were no longer touching. He smiled, the expression wicked and insanely sexy. "This time's going to be different," he assured her. His deep, sensual tone raised goose bumps on Kate's skin.

Raine stood and offered his hand. When she placed her hand in his and rose, the sheet slid down her body to puddle around her ankles. His gaze followed that same route, leaving a fission of heat wherever it lingered. Kate stepped into his open arms and he pulled her against him, maintaining the contact of their bodies as he eased her down onto the bed.

"This time," he said, pausing to place a kiss along her throat between each word, "we're going to do this right." When he reached her collarbone, he lifted his head to smile down at her and repeated, "So right."

The utter sweetness of that smile touched a place deep inside her. Kate closed her eyes and absorbed the impact to her heart. She loved this man. There was no denying it now. Whether they were enemies or not, whether she lived or died come sunrise, she loved Jack Raine. No matter who she was or what he had done in the past, nothing could change how she felt.

Not even a husband.

Honey, it's Nick.

Kate tensed, her eyes flew open. That man's voice. The one who had answered when she'd called the number...he'd called her *honey*. What if she did have a husband, children?

"What's wrong?"

Only when he spoke did Kate become aware that the tantalizing movement of his lips on her skin had stopped. She blinked rapidly to mask the fear of uncertainty in her eyes as he moved back up to lie alongside her. He propped on one elbow and swept a wisp of hair back from her cheek with his fingertips.

"What's wrong?" he repeated.

Kate forced her lips into a tremulous smile, but quickly averted her eyes from the ones examining her so closely. She focused on his broad chest. "I'm fine," she said, then struggled for something else to say when he remained silent, waiting. Her attention suddenly lit on one of the thin, jagged lines marring his tanned flesh. "I…was just wondering how you got these scars."

He chuckled, a short, breathy sound, then pressed a kiss to her temple. "Talking isn't exactly what I had on my mind, but if that's what you want to do…" His words trailed off as he captured her gaze, his own full of mischief but still hot with desire. "A few of those hundred men someone told you I'd killed didn't go down without a fight," he teased.

Kate felt suddenly helpless when faced with the reality that he had likely skated close to death numerous times. Her pulse quickened at the thought, panic tightened her chest. "What you do—" with the tip of her finger she traced one pale pattern that angled downward just beneath his right nipple "—is it always this dangerous?" Kate held her breath as she waited for the answer she already knew.

"Yes." There was no humor in his tone now.

She lifted her gaze to his. "Can you stop?" A knot of fear and uncertainty, as hard and cold as a rock, settled in Kate's stomach. "Can you just walk away?"

He searched her eyes for what felt like a lifetime, then moistened his lips and drew in a heavy breath. "No." The simple, one-syllable response tightened that knot of fear growing inside Kate.

Raine snuggled closer, offering the only thing he had to give, Kate realized. His warm, muscled body fit perfectly against hers. Hard angles and lean planes in all the right places to mesh with her fuller curves and softer valleys. There was no hiding just how much he wanted her, every hardened inch of him pressed against her hip. But he waited.

Kate shuddered at the rush of renewed need that surged through her at his patience. She wanted him so very much. Surely if she had a husband she would remember something about him. She didn't wear a ring and there had been nothing in her purse to indicate she was married, she rationalized. Everything inside her resisted the notion of children. She couldn't have children and not remember. Could a mother really forget her own child?

"Kate," he whispered, the deep timbre of his voice gliding over her like silk.

She studied his face, his chiseled jaw, those full sensuous lips before allowing her gaze to meet his. Kate braced herself for the intensity she would find there, and be unable to resist. "What if there's someone else?" She felt her frown deepen at the reaction she saw in his stormy blue eyes. Some unreadable emotion flickered fiercely but briefly before he banished it. "What if I have a husband?" she clarified softly.

A beat of silence passed, then those sinfully tempting lips slid into a wicked smile. "Then he's a fool for letting you out of his sight." He nipped at her lower lip, gently suckled it, then murmured, "Tonight you're mine, Kate."

She nodded, her breath catching as his lips moved along the line of her jaw toward the supersensitive curve of her neck. She didn't want to analyze the situation anymore, she only wanted to feel. Long fingers and a roughened palm skimmed over her heated flesh, touching, torturing, taking her body to a new level of desire. Urgent and exploratory, his hungry mouth moved lower. A wave of sensations splashed through Kate's body again and again, rising and then falling like the relentless pounding of the ocean against the shore. She arched her back, thrusting her breasts forward for his attention.

When his hot, moist mouth closed over one nipple, Kate cried out, the sound a primal plea of approval as well as a demand for more. His tongue flicked over her nipple, then slowly circled the straining, swollen peak before moving to her other breast. Her fingers threaded into his golden hair and held him in place as he drew on her more strongly. Kate writhed with pleasure at the intensified assault. His hand traced a path down her rib cage and across her abdomen, his tantalizing tongue followed, hesitating briefly at her belly button to dip repeatedly inside. The cool brush of his fingertips sent pleasant jolts through Kate. Her body arched instinctively when he parted her thighs and tangled his fingers in the triangle of hair there.

"Raine," she gasped. Anything else she would have said, as well as coherent thought, evaporated when one long finger slid along the part of her feminine folds, and then slipped inside. Colored lights pulsed behind Kate's lids as he tortured her intimately with those skilled fingers. His lips caressed the curve of her hip, her mound, his tongue darting out to scorch her shivering flesh. Kate moaned her surrender to the urgent desire. Her concentration focused inward as her tremors began. The gentle quakes vibrated from her center outward. She cried his name again when the burning sweetness erupted into fullbody shudders and stole her breath.

Kate was vaguely aware of him moving over her, but the vortex of erotic sensations would not allow her to open her eyes. The scent of his clean, masculine body filled her with a sense of completeness and well-being. She reached for him, circling his lean waist with her arms and drawing him closer, until his strong body covered hers and she could feel his ragged breath on her face. "Raine," she murmured, her lips brushing whisper-soft against his. "There's no one else but you." And in that ethereal moment she knew the words were true.

His mouth claimed hers as his weight crushed down on her, pressing her into the softness of the mattress beneath them. His tongue swept into her mouth at the same instant that he entered her in one long, powerful thrust, filling her, possessing her. Her body stretched to accommodate him, her feminine muscles contracting as she exploded once more around him. She was his and he was hers in an elemental way that no power on earth could change. When he moved against her, within her, everything else ceased to exist.

Raine took her to the pinnacle yet a third time, and this time he followed her into oblivion, bursting inside her with his own hot, sweet release. Kate clung to him, stunned by the intensity of the moment, frightened by what she felt in her heart. She could feel his heart pounding against his chest, echoing hers. Had he felt it too? Tears welled in her eyes when she considered the foolishness of that thought. How could she possibly mean anything to a man like him?

Raine rested his forehead against hers. "Are you all right?"

Since she didn't trust her voice, she nodded, though she was anything but all right. He rolled to his back, pulling Kate close against him as he did. She fought the almost overwhelming urge to cry—to sob—in his arms. Oh God, how could she have fallen in love with this man? A man who would surely walk away from her if he didn't get himself killed first. As if sensing her distress, Raine's arms tightened around her and he held her that way, until her breathing slowed and sleep claimed her.

RAINE TRANSFERRED the white bag containing the coffee he'd picked up in the restaurant downstairs to his left hand and checked the Glock beneath his jacket. When the elevator doors slid open he stepped out onto the sixth floor and headed toward the room where he'd left Kate sleeping.

He had dreaded this moment for most of the night. After Kate had fallen asleep in his arms, he had spent endless hours kicking himself for allowing her so close. What he and Kate had shared had gone way beyond lust and mere physical need. He was in hazardous, uncharted territory now. Territory he'd sworn he would never allow himself to stumble into. Jack Raine didn't need anyone. He never had. He'd always done his job, taken what he wanted and walked away. Nothing more. No strings, no complications.

He couldn't change now, no matter how his insides twisted at the thought of leaving Kate behind. It was for her own good, and he had no choice in the matter. She would realize that soon enough. Taking down Dillon and revealing the mole in Lucas's organization was a mission he could not walk away from—he'd never walked away from a mission, even one he'd taken upon himself. If he survived, he would count himself lucky. The odds were stacked heavily against him, and the risk was only increased by his strong personal involvement. Though it was a risk he would have to take, there was no way in hell he would risk Kate's life.

No way, he repeated silently as he slid the key card into the slot near the door's handle. She would forget him in no time at all. And maybe there was a Mr. Roberts waiting somewhere out there for her. Someone who had a nice safe life to offer her.

Raine swallowed tightly. The idea of Kate with another man—any man—turned him inside out. If his instincts were right about her, though, the sooner they parted ways the better. He couldn't be sure who she worked for, but there was little doubt left in his mind that her appearance at his door was not coincidental.

Ignoring the lock's blinking green light, Raine clenched his jaw at the reality of his ''relationship'' with Kate. No one had ever gotten this close to him before. The fact that she had, and under increasingly suspicious circumstances, attested to his total loss of perspective. But he couldn't leave her behind until he was sure she would be safe and unable to interfere with his plans. Now was the time. In just a few hours it would all be over—one way or another. Selfishly, Raine had taken one last night with her…one final taste of her lips. He closed his eyes and remembered the smell of her hair…the sound of her voice. He would always remember.

But now he had to go.

To leave her behind, the way he should have done in the first place.

Raine reinserted the key card, pushed the door open and entered the room. Bright morning sun poured in through the open drapes. Kate was up. He hadn't wanted to wake her when he'd gone down to the parking garage. He needed to retrieve the Glock from its hiding place behind the truck's back seat. He planned to leave his Beretta with Kate. He surveyed the room. His gaze settled on the closed bathroom door as it opened and Kate stepped out.

Though she was fully clothed in jeans and a T-shirt, her hair was still damp and Raine could smell her freshly showered scent clear across the room. The sight of her shifted something entirely too close to his heart.

''Morning,'' he said, and gave her his best attempt at a smile. He wasn't very good at this sort of thing. He didn't have a lot of practice at explaining himself, or dealing with the unfamiliar compulsion to do so. He extended the bag he held in her direction. ''Coffee?''

She approached him cautiously, the expression in her dark brown eyes wary. ''Where have you been? I thought…''

She didn't have to say the rest. She thought he'd left her. Just like back at the house when she'd come out to the barn looking for him. And, just like then, leaving her was exactly what he intended to do. Only this time, he would. Raine ignored the alien sensation in the pit of his stomach that accompanied that line of thinking.

When she didn't accept the coffee, he strode across the room to the table. ''There was something I needed in the truck,'' he told her as he removed the two disposable cups from the bag. She moved to his side, his body reacted instantly to her nearness.

''I thought you'd left without saying goodbye,'' she explained softly.

He crushed the bag into a wad and tossed it aside, then held one of the cups out to her. ''I told you I wouldn't do that,'' he replied without allowing his gaze to meet hers.

Kate accepted the cup this time. She padded across the lush carpet to the other side of the table and sat down. She pretended to be relaxed, but was far from it. The rigid set of her shoulders and the overprotective way she held her cup spoke volumes. She'd weaved her long brown hair into a braid. Her T-shirt hugged her firm, round breasts. The jeans she wore were a little loose now. She'd lost a few pounds on this trip, and that bothered Raine. He should have taken better care of her. A ghost of a smile touched his lips when he considered the delicious curves and contours that lay beneath those ill-fitting jeans. Vivid images of their lovemaking had haunted him all morning. The creamy, soft feel of her skin, the way her silky hair felt

between his fingers, the way her body—snug and hot—
welcomed him so completely.

Averting his gaze, Raine forced himself to sip his coffee.
He had to think clearly this morning. He had already decided on a place right here in New York to meet Dillon,
and he had informed Ballatore. This city was as much
Raine's home turf as any other place. The memory of making love with Kate at his house in Virginia invaded his
concentration, but he quickly shut it out. He'd had high
hopes when he'd bought the place, but it didn't really seem
to matter all that much anymore. He'd always been a loner,
but now the thought of living in that house alone held no
appeal. Assuming he stayed alive beyond the next twenty-
four hours to need a place to live, he ruminated.

Raine took another long sip of the warm, dark liquid.
Right now he had to focus on the mission. Tomorrow
would take care of itself, it always had.

"You didn't say much about your meeting with Ballatore," Kate reminded him quietly.

You were like a second son to me. Raine could still hear
the hint of pain in the old man's voice, see the deep sadness in his eyes. Maybe Raine had allowed Ballatore a
little closer than he had planned as well. He shook his
head. He was definitely getting too soft for this business.
Maybe that's why he hadn't seen Dillon coming, and
hadn't been able to keep Kate at arm's length. At least the
old man had been right about one thing, this line of work
could definitely get him killed.

"Raine?"

He jerked to attention, his gaze focusing back on Kate.
She'd asked about the meeting. "I accomplished
my goal," he hedged. She already knew too much, he
wasn't about to give her anything else that could be used
against him.

Kate set her cup on the table and stood. "You told me that part already," she said impatiently. "I want to know if he believed you when you told him that you didn't kill his son."

Raine set his own cup down and leveled his gaze on hers. "If he hadn't, I'd be dead right now."

Kate flinched. "I don't understand," she murmured as she brushed a loose tendril of hair from her cheek. "Why would he believe you over Dillon?"

"Just lucky I guess," Raine retorted, aiming for flippant.

Her eyes narrowed suspiciously as she shook her head slowly from side to side. "No, I don't think so. I think there was something more to your relationship with Ballatore."

Raine rounded the table and pinned her with his most intimidating stare. Her accusation struck a little too close to home. "I get close to people, Kate. I make them trust me." He leaned nearer and her eyes widened slightly. "I infiltrated Ballatore's organization first, then his family. If Dillon hadn't blown my cover, I would have taken the old man down no matter what our relationship." He felt a muscle contract in his jaw when he paused. "That's what I do. And I'm very good at what I do."

Kate blinked, her dark eyes misty. "Is that what we've been about?" She swallowed visibly. "Getting close and making me trust you?"

The hurt in her eyes had the effect of an unexpected kick in the stomach. How could he have allowed himself to get in this deep? He'd sworn he wouldn't. Denial of her charge burned in his chest, but he ruthlessly tamped it down. This was the turning point. He recognized the necessity of what he had to do, despite the fierce desire to do just the opposite. He had lived on the edge for far too long. He had worked to gain trust and then betrayed it too many times in the name of God and country. He couldn't change now. Spend too many years with the scum of the earth and you become like them, Raine reminded himself.

He had to remember that Kate was most likely his enemy in all this. Raine just had no way of knowing which of his enemies had sent her. But he knew for certain that she was not like him. Maybe she was new to the business or maybe she was simply being used by someone to get to Raine. Whatever the case, he recognized the innocence in Kate that he had long ago lost to the world of deceit in which he lived. She would have plenty of regrets when she regained her memory. She would hate him then for taking advantage of her vulnerability. It would be better for her to believe that, he decided. Let her believe that he was the ruthless bastard of which his reputation boasted.

"Was last night just part of what you do?"

Raine struggled with his conscience—the one he hadn't even realized existed until he met Kate. "You don't want to know the answer to that," he lied, drawing the necessary line in the sand.

She quickly masked the flicker of hurt in her eyes, then lifted her chin in defiance of his indifference. "I guess that makes me as big a fool as Ballatore," she suggested, her voice lacking any kind of inflection. "I suppose that since Ballatore obviously believed you—considering you're not dead—now you have his blessings to go after Dillon?"

Raine ignored her question. He stepped past her to the bed, reached beneath the pillow he had used and removed the Beretta he'd hidden there. "Take this." He offered the weapon to Kate, but she only glared at him. Raine captured her hand and forced her to take the weapon. "You'll be safe here. The room is guaranteed with a credit card that can't be traced back to me." He held her wrist tighter when she would have jerked away. "Don't go out for anything. Use room service for whatever you need."

"How long do you expect me to stay here?"

"As long as it takes," he said, impatient with her resistance, as well as with his own ridiculous emotions.

"Once you walk out that door, what's to keep me from doing the same?" she retorted hotly.

Raine yanked her closer, anger overriding all else. "If you want to stay alive, you'll stay put until this is over."

"Dillon will do whatever it takes to kill you, you know that, don't you?" The hurt was back in her eyes now. She was afraid for him—another unfamiliar and unexpected glitch.

"I know," Raine replied quietly. He released her, then blew out a disgusted breath. He was a fool. He had swallowed the bait, hook, line and sinker. Kate's inadvertent amnesia only made her more effective against him. No one had ever held this much power over him. Raine swallowed, hard. But that wouldn't stop him from doing what he had to do.

"And that doesn't matter? Why can't you let Ballatore settle the score with Dillon? The mission you were assigned is over!"

"You don't know all there is to know," he argued in spite of himself. Why didn't he just leave?

"Well, fill me in," she demanded. She braced one hand on her hip, the Beretta hanging loosely at her side from the other.

Raine closed his mind, his heart, to what she wanted from him. She was hurt and confused. She wanted him to tell her everything would be all right, but he couldn't. And he shouldn't care, but, damn him, he did. "I can't do that," he said simply, allowing the coldness of his tone to speak for itself.

"Can't or won't?" she countered.

"Take your pick." Raine plowed his fingers through his hair and looked away. He didn't have time for this, and he sure as hell couldn't bear to watch the hurt in her eyes a moment longer. "I have to go now. If you'll follow my instructions you'll be safe." He turned and started toward the door, a sick feeling eating at his gut despite the knowledge that he was doing the right thing—taking the steps necessary to ensure her safety as well as the success of his mission.

"You're not coming back, are you?"

The faint glimmer of desperate hope in her voice stopped him halfway to his destination. He closed his eyes and willed away the emotions twisting inside him. He shouldn't feel any of this. "No," he admitted, brutally squashing that tiny seed of hope to which he knew she still clung.

"And if I try to stop you?"

Raine turned around slowly to face her. Her grip tightened on the Beretta, but she made no move to take aim. *Don't do this, Kate.* No way could he bring himself to hurt her. Pushing aside the unfamiliar emotions that bound him to Kate, he reached deep inside until he found that desolate place where he felt nothing at all. "Attempting to stop me would be a mistake."

Silence screamed around them for several tense seconds before she spoke again. "I can't let you go."

Despite having fully anticipated this possibility, betrayal stung Raine. He almost laughed out loud. The great Jack Raine, who made a career out of betrayal, had just gotten his in spades. What a fool he was.

Kate lifted her right arm, holding the Beretta like a practiced professional. A cold emptiness stealing through him,

Raine watched her determined stride as she moved toward him.

She stopped directly in front of him, a bead dead center of his chest, her gaze locked on his. "I won't let you go."

"Don't leave the room," he told her again, as if she'd said nothing at all, as if the weapon were not in her hand and aimed at his heart. "I'll call to let you know when it's safe to leave. Don't believe anything until you hear it from me."

"I said," she repeated, "I'm not letting you walk out that door."

"Then shoot me." Raine turned his back on her, took the final steps to the door and walked out without looking back.

Chapter Twelve

Kate stood in the middle of the hotel room with nothing but the echo of the closing door to break the absolute silence. He was gone. Her entire body shook from the receding fear and adrenaline. She glanced at the gun in her hand. Could she have stopped him? No, not without using the gun, and she knew she couldn't and wouldn't have done that. Would she? Fear and confusion twisted inside her. She blinked, feeling as if she was coming out of some sort of trance. Why did she draw the weapon on him in the first place? Is that what she was supposed to do? Stop him? She frowned, trying with all her might to remember.

What did it matter now anyway? He was gone.

Kate blinked again, then slowly surveyed the luxurious room. Without Raine's presence, previously insignificant details seemed to rush in on her all at once. The crystal chandelier hanging overhead. The lavish arrangement of fresh-cut flowers setting on the mantel above the marble fireplace. The lush burgundy carpet and drapes with gold intricately woven throughout. The perfectly coordinated French provincial furniture. And the wide inviting bed with its ivory brocade coverlet and tangled sheets still scented with their lovemaking.

…he needs protection.

Kate drew in a shuddering breath. She had to go after him. *The assignment.* She had to salvage this assignment. …*to bring him in either way.* Kate raced across the room and fumbled with the lock on the door.

Don't go out for anything. Raine's words slammed into her head, stilling her trembling fingers on the ornate gold lever that would disengage the dead bolt. Kate squeezed her eyes shut against the confusion, against the words and voices churning in her head.

What should she do?

She pressed her forehead to the door's cool surface and willed herself to relax, willed the panic rising inside her to retreat. Her heart thumped frantically in her rib cage, ignoring the command to slow.

Her medicine, she needed her medicine. With all that had happened since their arrival at the hotel, Kate had forgotten to take the little blue pill that kept her heart condition under control. Her condition—the bane of her existence. Kate opened her eyes and exhaled shakily. She straightened and pushed away from the door.

Smooth move, Robertson, she chastised as she retraced her steps across the room and located her purse. Kate froze, the prescription bottle in her hand.

Robertson? Kate frowned as the name whirled around her like a tiny tornado. Katherine Robertson. Katherine. Katie. Her father called her Katie. But she preferred to go by Katherine, it sounded more professional.

Adrenaline rushing through her, Kate set the pills aside and dug through the purse until she came up with her driver's license. Anticipation pulling at her, she studied the picture, then the name listed. Why would she be using the name Kate Roberts if her real name was Katherine Robertson?

That wouldn't keep someone from using you to get to

me. Raine was right. Her own suspicions were right on the mark. She had been sent to find him…to get close to him. And to bring him in. That was her assignment. But she'd failed. Though she had no idea who had sent her, the fact that she had failed—failed miserably—resurrected a pain that was all too familiar. It squeezed at her already tight chest. Tears stung her eyes. She was a failure. *Again.*

Kate clenched her jaw against the self-pity that threatened. Her inability to get the job done didn't matter right now. What mattered was that Raine was about to get himself killed while she stood around feeling sorry for herself.

"Damn," she hissed, throwing the bottle against the wall. Kate closed her eyes and rubbed at her forehead with the heels of both hands. Losing it wasn't going to help. Reaching for calm, she crossed the room and snatched up the bottle and twisted off the cap. Pill in hand, she trudged to the sideboard and poured water from the crystal decanter into a matching goblet. After taking her medication, Kate stared into the large, gilt-framed mirror hanging on the wall.

"Who the hell are you?" she muttered to the familiar yet strangely alien woman staring back at her. Kate placed the ornate goblet on the silver tray and turned her back to the puzzling reflection that seemed to mock her.

To her way of thinking she had two options. She could stay put as Raine had instructed or she could call for help. *Call in,* the voice she recognized as Aunt Vicky's urged. Kate concentrated hard on the voice of the woman who identified herself as Kate's aunt, but no further recognition came. Aunt Vicky was probably an alias. Maybe this Vicky person had hired Kate to find Raine. She couldn't take the chance that whoever sent her might be out to hurt Raine. Dillon and Vicky could be partners. Kate hadn't forgotten that Dillon had shown up at their motel in Charlottesville only hours after her call to *Aunt* Vicky.

No, Kate had to call someone Raine trusted. *If Lucas can't be trusted, there's no one else,* he'd said. Kate reached into her jeans pocket and withdrew the slip of paper that contained Lucas's number. Fear welled inside her again as she studied the bold handwriting that belonged to the man she loved. No matter that he would never want to see her again, and certainly would never trust her again. Somehow she had to help Raine. Lucas Camp was her only hope.

TWO GUT-WRENCHING, hand-twisting hours passed before the expected knock came. The gun in hand and her purse strap looped over her shoulder, Kate jumped from her seat and rushed to the door. She peered through the peephole at the man standing on the other side. He was tall, dark-haired, and he wore a suit. Kate frowned at his spit-and-polished appearance. She'd somehow expected Lucas Camp to be a little older, and a lot less stiff-looking. His phone voice in no way matched his image.

When the man knocked again, Kate swallowed back her indecision and summoned a businesslike tone. ''Yes?''

''Miss Roberts, I'm Agent Hanson. Lucas sent me here to see that you're escorted to a safe house,'' he said with a definite air of authority.

Kate moistened her lips as she mulled over his voice. He sounded trustworthy enough. ''I need to see some ID,'' she told him, adhering to the side of caution.

''Of course.'' He reached inside his jacket and removed the leather case containing a picture ID, which he held in front of the peephole for her perusal.

Hanson, Zachary P., Agent, Special Operations. The ID looked authentic enough, Kate decided. She had no choice but to take the chance. It was the only shot she had at helping Raine. With a deep bolstering breath she opened the door, the gun still gripped firmly in her right hand. Agent Hanson surveyed the room before stepping inside.

He turned to Kate and smiled. "You'll need your coat, Miss Roberts."

Kate nodded and started to turn away.

"I'll have to take that for you," he offered kindly as he reached for the gun she held. "Regulations," he explained when she hesitated.

For a moment Kate considered refusing to release the weapon, but what choice did she have? In his eyes she was an unknown factor, a loose cannon, she supposed. He probably didn't relish the idea of riding in a confined automobile with an armed woman. She would do the same if the situation were reversed. Kate allowed Agent Hanson to take Raine's Beretta, then retrieved her coat and preceded him out the door.

The trip to the lobby was made in silence. They stepped off the elevator and onto the white mosaic tile that stretched across the elegant lobby. A towering vase of fresh-cut flowers sat atop a pedestal table beneath a huge crystal chandelier that sprinkled shards of light over the shiny floor. Kate managed a smile for the blue-jacketed clerk as she passed the mahogany-paneled registration desk. A lush red runner carpeted the foyer and led the way past a security guard and through the brass revolving doors.

"This way, Miss Roberts," Agent Hanson said as he paused beneath the canopied marquee.

With another friendly smile, he led Kate to a dark sedan parked at the curb. The windows were tinted, making it impossible to see anyone who might be inside. Reminding herself that she was doing the right thing, Kate thanked him when he opened the door. She had just taken her seat and reached for the seat belt when someone spoke.

"Nice to see you again, Kate."

The air in her lungs evaporated as her senses absorbed, analyzed and recognized the voice of the man who had spoken.

Dillon.

DUSK HAD ALREADY SETTLED before Raine entered the deserted warehouse. The place hadn't been used in years, and time and the elements were wearing on the huge structure. At one time the warehouses on this dock had been in high demand. But not so much anymore. Like several others along this stretch of waterfront, the one Raine had selected for his meeting with Dillon now amounted to nothing more than a crumbling relic of a different time and way of life.

Raine took up a position inside that would give him an unobstructed view of the entrance. A streetlight provided just enough illumination for him to see any comings and goings near the open door leading into the building. He checked the Glock under his jacket, then the cellular phone in his right pocket. The old man had insisted that Raine contact him immediately after his business with Dillon was complete, and since there were no working phones in the vicinity, Ballatore had provided a means of communication as well.

Raine never allowed himself to develop any sort of attachment to his assignments. He shook his head when he considered the strange relationship that had evolved between him and Sal Ballatore. Maybe it was because Raine had never known his own parents, and had spent his juvenile years in one foster home after the other. He and the old man'd had that in common.

Distrustful of relationships, just like Raine, Ballatore

hadn't married until well past middle age. He was pushing seventy now, and his twenty-year-old son had been the light of his life. Raine supposed that being thirty-four, he had served somewhat as a generational bridge between the old man and his son. Michael had taken to Raine from the start. Raine almost smiled as he recalled the serious case of hero worship the kid had had. The reputation the agency had set up for Raine, too realistic and ruthless, had intrigued Michael.

Raine shifted against the cold invading his body. He pushed away any further thoughts of Ballatore or his son. That mission was over, and once Dillon had been taken care of, Raine and Ballatore would never have contact again. That was the way it was supposed to be—the way it had always been.

Permanent ties weren't a part of Raine's life, professional or personal. The only long-lasting relationship he had allowed was the one with Lucas, and it only bordered on friendship, staying for the most part a professional relationship. That suited Raine just fine. He'd never had any desire for long-term on a personal level.

As if to refute the thought, Kate's image filled his mind. Raine blinked to dispel the vivid mental picture, but she refused to go away. Those dark eyes, going even darker with desire for him. Those tempting lips that made him ache for another taste of her. And all that long, silky hair begging for his touch. No one had ever made him feel the way Kate did. The range of emotions that tightened his chest were so foreign, he felt at a complete loss to try to sort the tangle. How one woman could hold this kind of power over him baffled Raine.

He had never been in love with anyone, and he assured himself that he wasn't in love now. But the denial sat like a stone in his gut, and that annoyed him beyond reason.

He felt responsible for Kate, protective even. But he didn't love her—he couldn't love her. Surely some skill was involved in an emotion that strong, and Raine had never mastered any such talents. This thing between him and Kate was nothing more than physical attraction complicated by her vulnerability. It just couldn't be anything else.

Besides, what kind of life could he offer a woman like her? She had a family somewhere, one that loved her like he wouldn't begin to know how to. She might already have a husband or boyfriend. His jaw tightened at the notion. He didn't want to think about that part of Kate's life. He would never see her again anyway. Like Ballatore, she would be just another part of Raine's murky past.

Kate didn't need a man like him anyway. He didn't know the first thing about family or any of those other forever kind of things. He lived from one mission to the next. Hell, he didn't even know if he could survive retirement. He had lived on the edge so long with nothing but adrenaline for a companion, that he wasn't even sure he could pull off a "normal" life.

Raine folded his arms over his chest to ward off the increasing chill that seemed to come more from inside him than from around him. Kate would be much better off without him. He knew it, and deep down she knew it or, at least, would come to realize it later. He hadn't intended to let their relationship go so far. She would have enough regrets when her memory returned. She would regret letting him walk out of that hotel room alive. Whether she had a boyfriend or husband or not, she would regret sleeping with Raine. He closed his eyes to block out that image.

Kate was better off without him.

He was better off without her.

Especially considering their entire relationship was built

on lies. Nothing had been what it seemed. Raine laughed at himself. Was it ever?

The almost imperceptible squeak of leather drew Raine's full attention back to the door. Tension and adrenaline did their job as he reached for his Glock. Two seconds later a dark silhouette moved in the shadows just outside the circle of light bathing the entrance. Raine clenched his jaw when Dillon stepped into the light and proceeded through the open door as confidently as one who had already decided that this battle belonged to him.

Dillon was alone and that didn't sit well with Raine. Danny and Vinny were probably right outside, but Dillon wasn't a man who took unnecessary risks. And Dillon had a lot riding on this little showdown. Something didn't add up.

As though he owned the place and had absolutely nothing to fear, Dillon walked just beyond the reach of the light and waited, facing the entrance, his back to anything that might be lurking in the dark warehouse. Sensing a setup, Raine silently made his way to the right until he stood directly behind Dillon's position. Less than a dozen soundless steps later, Raine had the barrel of his weapon nestled at the base of Dillon's skull.

Dillon turned around slowly, his hands held high in a gesture of surrender, a sadistic smile curving his thin lips. "I told you it'd only be a matter of time until we met again."

"Too bad I'm the one with the bead between your eyes," Raine returned, carefully diverting the rage building too quickly inside him to something more appropriate for the moment—revenge.

Dillon shrugged. "You know, it doesn't have to be this way. We could split the money. With your expertise, Ballatore would never find you, and, of course, I'll be long gone.''

"I don't think so, Dillon.'' Raine felt one corner of his own mouth lift into a satisfied tilt. Was that desperation he heard in Dillon's voice? Good, Raine mused, he liked to see that in an adversary. For all his cockiness, maybe Dillon wasn't quite as sure of himself as he pretended to be. "I don't want to make a deal, *amigo.*''

Dillon shook his head, frowning dramatically. "Gee, Raine, that's too bad. I guess that leaves us with nothing to talk about.''

"Not quite.'' Raine snugged his finger around the trigger. The line of sweat on Dillon's upper lip provided instant gratification. "We still have to discuss that little detail of who dropped the dime on me.''

Dillon's smile returned. "You don't really expect me to reveal my sources, now, do you? Especially since you're so unwilling to share the spoils of victory. And surely you've been in the spook business long enough to know what happens to those who kiss and tell.''

"In that case—'' Raine leaned closer, dropping his voice to a deadly level "—I'm afraid you don't have an option. Fact is, if you don't start singing the tune I requested, I'm going to hand you over to the old man. And he knows you killed his son.''

Dillon didn't flinch. Raine's gaze narrowed. *He knew.* Somehow Dillon already knew.

Wariness, much stronger than before, gnawed at his gut as Raine continued, "But if you give me what I want, I'll put you out of your misery right now.''

"Oh, that's a tough one.'' Dillon pursed his lips in exaggerated indecision. "I can either die now, or later—after endless hours of less than imaginative torture.''

Raine nodded succinctly. "That's pretty much the bottom line."

Dillon leveled his evil gaze on Raine's. "I think I'll take door number three, Monty."

Anger seared through Raine's control. "There is no door number three, you low-life scumbag. Now tell me the name of your source." Raine pressed the barrel of the Glock to Dillon's forehead. "I'm fresh out of patience."

Dillon smirked. "Oh, but you don't understand, my friend. This is my game and I set the rules."

"Say good night, Dillon," Raine warned.

"Rule number one," Dillon continued despite Raine's warning. "If you kill me, Kate dies."

Raine blinked, his heart skipped one beat, then another. That satanic smile spread across Dillon's face once more. "Ah, I thought that would get your attention."

"Go to hell," Raine snarled.

"Been there, and it wasn't half as much fun as being here with you. Or being with sweet little Kate."

"You're a liar."

"When it suits my purpose," Dillon agreed.

"Kate's safe." Raine could feel the muscle in his jaw jerking rhythmically. "And you're dead." Raine tightened his grip on the butt of the Glock in anticipation of the recoil.

"For the moment, she's safe." Dillon knitted his eyebrows as if trying to remember some important detail. "What was it she said?" He hummed a note of irritation, ignoring Raine's mushrooming agitation. "Oh yes. She shouldn't have believed anything until she heard from you."

Dillon's words stabbed into Raine's chest and cut right through his heart. He'd warned Kate not to believe anything until she heard it from him. How could Dillon know that? He couldn't possibly know where Kate was. She was safe.

"You lying son of a bitch," Raine muttered as he refocused his attention on putting a bullet between Dillon's eyes.

"She should have trusted you, Raine." Dillon shook his head. "But she didn't. She shouldn't have believed anything until she heard it from you, but *she did.*"

"What do you want?" Raine demanded, barely able to restrain the rage trembling inside him.

"The same thing I've wanted all along. I want you." Dillon lifted one dark eyebrow. "And the money, of course."

Chapter Thirteen

Raine sat in a chair next to the telephone in the hotel room he had shared with Kate less than twenty-four hours ago. Housekeeping had changed the sheets and made the bed, and left clean towels sometime since he'd left. But nothing could erase the memory of her sweet scent from his mind. The taste of her skin and the feel of her welcoming body around him was imprinted forever in his soul. But she was gone.

He'd walked out on her.

It shouldn't have mattered how she'd wound up on his doorstep or who had sent her. He should not have allowed anything to come between them—not her true identity or this mission.

But he had.

Raine drew in a harsh breath and set his jaw against the pain that shuddered through him at the thought of Dillon touching Kate. Raine had suffered death a thousand times over during the seemingly endless hours since his meeting with Dillon. And now, as the lighted display on the clock blinked from 2:00 to 2:01 a.m., Raine still waited for Dillon's call.

Ballatore hadn't been too happy about Raine letting Dillon walk out of that warehouse alive, but the old man had been willing to back off and let Raine handle Dillon. "As long as he dies," Ballatore had said when he'd given Raine the case containing the bait.

Oh, he would die. Raine intended to watch Dillon die. At the moment, that single goal was all that kept Raine from losing his mind. He just didn't know if he'd be able to live with himself afterward if the bastard had hurt Kate.

The telephone rang and Raine snatched it up before the first ring ended. "Yeah," he rasped, his voice rusty from the long hours of disuse.

"Take a walk in the park. Head in the direction of the zoo. We'll be waiting."

A click ended the brief call. Raine placed the receiver back in its cradle and stood. He bent to pick up the leather case that held Ballatore's money. The bag actually contained only a quarter of a million. The rest of the bulk was plain paper cut and banded into stacks. Dillon wouldn't know the difference until it was too late.

Raine mentally reviewed the vague orders as he crossed the room. The hotel overlooked Central Park, but there was a hell of a lot of territory between it and the zoo. Raine recognized the strategy. Dillon would be watching, and when Raine was where he wanted him, Dillon would make his move.

And Raine would be ready.

AT THIS TIME OF NIGHT, not much moved in the park, and what did should be avoided if possible. The idea of Kate somewhere in this asphalt and foliage jungle urged Raine forward. He hunched his shoulders against the cold, his leather jacket proving less than adequate against the coldest night New York had seen this season.

The occasional antique-reproduction street lamp didn't help much in the way of visibility. Trees, shrubbery and benches provided ample cover for anyone who didn't want to be seen, yet allowed for freedom of movement. Dillon definitely had the advantage.

Dillon had selected a location that would provide him with the best cover, as well as numerous routes of escape. If anything went wrong, disappearing into the shadows would be simple. Why not stack the deck in his favor? It was Dillon's favorite way to play the game—a win-win situation.

Raine moved quietly past an artfully designed wall of boulders, his gaze shifting quickly from left to right. Nothing moved. The zoo entrance loomed in the distance. It wouldn't be long now. Raine's tension escalated, sharpening his senses.

Ten minutes later and midway between street lamps, Dillon stepped out of the shadows, Kate at his side. Raine stopped several feet away. His gaze slid swiftly over Kate and found no indication that Dillon had harmed her, at least as best Raine could see in the faint light.

"Nothing like a stroll in the moonlight," Dillon taunted as he pulled Kate closer.

Kate struggled against his hold but Dillon only laughed at her attempts to free herself. Raine willed himself not to react. Any reaction would be just that much more ammunition for Dillon. Raine needed distance. He had to separate himself from his emotions. To think, not feel.

"Did you come here to talk, Dillon, or did you come to deal?" Raine asked curtly.

"Is that the money?" Dillon gestured toward the bag Raine held.

Raine nodded and tossed the bag on the ground in front of Dillon. "You have your money, now let Kate go."

"Lose the piece." Dillon gestured to his left. Raine

drew the Glock from beneath his jacket, reached down and placed it on the ground, then kicked it away.

"Nothing up your sleeve?" Dillon asked sardonically.

Raine shouldered out of his jacket and dropped it to the ground. The night air's bite made his muscles contract as he held his arms high in the air and turned slowly around, allowing Dillon to see that he wasn't hiding anything. Saving Kate was too important. Raine wouldn't risk her life by pulling any fast ones this time. Dillon was hovering too close to the edge. Raine would just have to fly this one by the seat of his pants.

"Good." Dillon smiled his approval, then pulled the bag containing the money a little closer with one booted foot. "Just to prove what a good sport I am, I'm going to give you two things, my friend, *before* I kill you."

"I thought we agreed that I would take him down."

Raine snapped his gaze in the direction of the familiar sound of a male voice. Raymond Cuddahy, director of Special Operations for the past two years, stepped out of the shadows to stand next to Dillon. Shock vibrated through Raine as he mentally acknowledged the seriousness of the situation. No one—at any level—was safe with a man like this at the top of the heap. For about two seconds Raine felt some sense of relief at having been right about Lucas, then the graveness of the situation hit him all over again.

Cuddahy smiled, seeming to enjoy Raine's surprise. Raine had always despised the man's cocky attitude. Short and stubby, Cuddahy had a major Napoleon complex.

As if reading Raine's mind, Dillon laughed and cut Director Cuddahy a glance. "That's one." Dillon pushed Kate away from him. She hit the ground hard. "That's the other."

Kate scrambled to stand, but froze when Dillon trained

his Ruger in her direction. "Stay," he commanded roughly.

Kate's frightened gaze jerked from Dillon to Raine. Raine nodded once, willing her to stay put with his eyes.

Raine suffered a twinge of panic when Cuddahy picked up the leather case, but relaxed when he didn't seem inclined to open it just yet.

"Why?" Raine heard himself ask.

It was Cuddahy's turn to laugh this time. "For the money, what else?" He shrugged. "I've taken advantage of my *position* on several occasions. The opportunity is always there. Especially with a sting this big. What's a couple mil to a man like Ballatore? You just have to find the right man for the job. One who's willing to take the ultimate risk and end up with nothing."

Before the meaning behind the words could penetrate Dillon's thick skull, Cuddahy had turned his weapon on him and pumped two silenced shots into the center of his chest. Dillon dropped like a rock, a look of disbelief permanently etched on his thin face. Kate screamed her horror, but to her credit, she quickly composed herself.

"Of course, killing Michael Ballatore wasn't part of the deal." Cuddahy shrugged. "It's hard to find good help these days." He glanced down at Dillon and shook his head. "Oh, well, there's plenty more where he came from." He smiled then. "One down, and two to go."

Raine heard the depth of the breath Kate took. Her heart condition flitted across his mind, and he wondered briefly if she had taken her medication. Of course, there was a good possibility that in a few minutes it wouldn't matter one way or the other.

Cuddahy shook his head, his dislike for Raine obvious. "You and your glorious reputation. Well, you sure as hell slithered into the wrong den of snakes this time, hotshot."

"I did what I was contracted to do," Raine replied evenly.

"But you still screwed up, didn't you? You had no idea Dillon was on to you until it was too late." He smirked. "No going out in a blaze of glory for Jack Raine. Hell, you even let *her* pull the wool over your eyes."

Raine looked from Cuddahy to Kate and back, waiting for the other shoe to drop. Could Kate be working for Cuddahy? Raine couldn't bring himself to believe that.

"Your old friend Lucas hired some big-time private agency to find you when you disappeared," he explained, his hatred for Lucas as evident as his distaste for Raine.

"You mean, when your people couldn't?" Raine suggested, purposely antagonizing him.

Cuddahy glared at Raine. "Well, she found you." He stepped closer to Raine. "It was her call that alerted us to your whereabouts in Gatlinburg, and then in Charlottesville," he sneered, leaning nearer.

Cuddahy's words only confirmed what Raine had already figured out. His instincts were seldom wrong. But now wasn't the time to dwell on that. "Where's Lucas?" he asked. If Lucas had caught on to Cuddahy's extracurricular activities...

"He had himself a little accident," Cuddahy said glibly. "Your little friend here called to let him know what was going on with you, and, like any good deputy, Lucas passed the information on to me. Unfortunately, he had himself an accident on his way here. He'll be out of commission for quite some time I'd say."

"Lucas is no fool. He'll figure out what went down eventually." Raine saw the flash of insanity in Cuddahy's eyes. Power and greed had done their work. He also saw in his peripheral vision, to his extreme horror, Kate inching her way toward the weapon on the ground. Raine clenched his jaw and forced his attention to stay on Cuddahy.

"Maybe, maybe not," Cuddahy jeered. "I'm not opposed to recruiting myself another deputy. Maybe I'll just drop by Bethesda on my way home and make sure that Lucas stays permanently out of commission."

"The only place you're going, you sleazy bastard, is the county morgue if you make one wrong move," Kate countered in a tone so ruthless that Raine barely recognized the voice as hers.

Raine glanced over Cuddahy's shoulder and saw Kate with the Glock pressed against the back of his head. Raine smiled and shifted his gaze back to Cuddahy. The mild surprise that registered in the man's expression was swiftly replaced by insolence.

"Now, now, Miss Robertson. Lucas told me how this was your first field assignment. Are you sure you know how to handle a precision piece of weaponry like that." Cuddahy laughed, then added, "Are you sure you know how to take it off safety?"

Even in the dim light, Raine saw the killer instinct glaze Kate's eyes before she spoke. "I'll tell you what I know, Director Cuddahy," she said coldly, calculatingly. "I know this is a Glock 19 nine millimeter with a barrel length of a hundred and two millimeters, a magazine capacity of fifteen plus two, and if my impression of Raine so far is accurate, it probably has a modified hair trigger." She paused, Cuddahy's mouth sagged open in disbelief. "And just so *you* know," she continued. "I took it off safety when I picked it up. Now, if you don't drop your weapon, I will pull this trigger."

Several charged seconds passed before Cuddahy, his eyes wild and his chest heaving frantically with fear, reacted. He leveled his silenced weapon on Raine's chest.

Less than three feet separated them. "I'll kill him," he barked, all signs of his previous cockiness gone now.

"I can't stop you from pulling that trigger, Cuddahy, but considering the trajectory and range of my weapon, you'll die first."

A split second before he fired, Raine saw the decision in Cuddahy's cold eyes. Raine moved, pitching himself to the right, but he wasn't quite fast enough. By the time the hissing puff of the silencer reached his ears, the burn of metal had seared into his flesh. Raine hit the ground and rolled, momentarily dazed.

Two more quick, thudding pops sounded in the cold night air. Cuddahy crumpled to the ground. Kate stared at the downed man, then at the weapon in her hand. The shots hadn't come from the Glock. Raine hadn't bothered with a silencer. If Kate had fired, everyone in Central Park would have known it.

Groaning at the pain shooting through his side, Raine pushed to a kneeling position and turned to see who had put Cuddahy down.

Ballatore.

Raine shook his head and muttered, "Stupid old bastard."

Kate dropped to her knees next to Raine and laid the weapon aside. "Where are you hit?" she demanded, hysteria rising in her voice.

"I'm fine." Raine struggled to his feet, his left hand not quite stemming the flow of blood leaking from his side. He didn't miss the hurt that marred her expression at his rebuff.

"I believe this belongs to me," Ballatore said as he nodded to one of his men who immediately snatched up the leather case containing the money.

"I thought I told you to stay the hell out of this," Raine growled.

Ballatore shrugged carelessly. "I've never taken orders well, and I'm too old to change now," he countered, then smiled. "That's why I'm the boss."

"How did you find us?" Raine had to ask, he knew he hadn't been followed.

Ballatore smiled, some of the old shine back in his eyes. "I knew you'd spot a tail in a heartbeat, so I put one on Dillon when he left the warehouse last night," he said proudly. "The stupid bastard couldn't spot a tail if he tripped over it."

Raine frowned. "You were at the warehouse last night?"

"Did you expect me to pretend it wasn't happening?" He pinned Raine with a steely gaze. "This is my city, Jack Raine, don't forget that."

"Get the hell out of here, old man, you just killed a government agent." Raine fought the vertigo interfering with his ability to remain standing.

"I just did the feds a favor, and saved your pathetic excuse for a life in the process," Ballatore challenged.

"Go," Raine repeated harshly.

Ballatore hesitated as if he might say something else, but thought better of it. He and his four henchmen disappeared into the shadows.

"We have to get you to a hospital." Kate tried to visually assess his condition in the near darkness. Raine's shirtfront was soaked with blood and he could still feel the warm, sticky stuff seeping between his fingers.

"You should go, too, Kate," he suggested.

"I won't leave you," she argued, concern tightening her voice and evidencing itself on her sweet face.

Raine bit down on his lower lip, but couldn't stifle a

groan of pain. He dropped to his knees. He wouldn't be able to hang on to consciousness much longer. "Well, you're in for a hell of a cold night, because I can't walk out of here." Why hadn't he kept that damn cell phone?

Kate draped his jacket around his shoulders, then reached for the Glock. To put him out of his misery? Raine wondered through the fog filling his head. He jerked when the loud, repeated report of the weapon sounded into the quiet night. After firing several shots into the ground, Kate returned to his side.

"There," she said, obviously pleased with her ingenuity. "That ought to get us some attention.

Raine attempted a smile. "Creative, Kate," he mumbled. "Very creative." Pain ripped through his side. He squeezed his eyes shut and doubled over with the intensity of it.

"Don't you dare die on me, Jack Raine," she pleaded, but her voice sounded oddly distorted and far away.

Don't worry, I won't, he wanted to say, but his lips wouldn't form the words. *I won't ever leave you again. I love you, Kate.* A sense of relief and calm came with the realization.

And then her sweet face blurred out and the world faded into oblivion.

Chapter Fourteen

Katherine sat on the front pew in the deserted hospital chapel. The room was lit by what looked like, in her opinion, upside-down seashells posing as wall sconces. They didn't provide much in the way of illumination, but she supposed that they had been selected for the ambience they provided rather than the candlepower. An elaborate crucifix overwhelmed the front of the room, but its presence was somehow comforting.

She'd spent several hours in the waiting room, but felt restless, and she'd eventually found herself here. Katherine shifted on the hard bench and surveyed the chapel once more. Did being in a place like this put you any closer to God? she wondered. She frowned, trying to remember the last time she'd been in church. Too long ago to recall, she decided. Or lost forever thanks to the amnesia she'd suffered. Was this confusion and uncertainty residual effects of her slowly returning memory?

But not being able to remember her spirituality or lack thereof didn't stop her from reaching to that higher power now in her time of despair. Katherine had prayed, pleaded with God to spare Raine's life. She closed her eyes and fought the hot sting of tears. She should probably go back to the waiting room, but she felt too numb to move, and too dazed to deal with the police and the other assorted agents and investigators lurking there.

She clasped her hands in her lap. Her skin felt unnaturally cold and more than a little clammy. She needed to sleep, but couldn't. The very thought of food sickened her. Raine was still in surgery and no one would tell her anything. The only thing anybody wanted to do was ask questions. She shuddered when her last images of him replayed before her eyes. So much blood. Raine had been unconscious for several minutes before help had arrived. And the paramedics wouldn't have arrived then—even before the police—had it not been for an anonymous tip called in on a cellular phone.

Ballatore no doubt.

When they had arrived at the emergency-room entrance, Raine had looked so pale. Katherine swallowed tightly at the memory of the hospital staff wheeling him away from her. He had to make it, he just had to.

And then what?

He had told her that he wasn't coming back. Raine had intended to walk away and never look back. How could she possibly believe that he had changed his mind? If she hadn't made that call to Lucas, there would have been no reason for him to see her again. It was only his sense of responsibility to save her from Dillon that had brought him to that park, she felt sure. Even then, after he'd been shot, he had told her to go. Her heart squeezed painfully at the memory. He knew now that she had been sent to find him. That made her his enemy—a traitor. He would probably never forgive her, amnesia or not. But she just couldn't think about that right now. She had to concentrate on willing him to live.

She was so very tired. Her eyes closed in exhaustion. Maybe if she could marshal the strength to walk back to the waiting room, some of the vultures would have gone by now. She shook her head at the improbability of it. Would her life ever be normal again?

Normal? Ha! Had it ever been normal? On cue, her heart fluttered in her chest. Hardly, she admitted ruefully.

"Katie?"

Recognition washed over her, bringing with it a sense of having come home. She turned around slowly, her gaze lifting to meet the man who had spoken.

"Daddy." She breathed the word, her head whirling from sensory overload. Images, voices, sped across the landscape of her mind, too fast to analyze fully, and all belonging to the past she had forgotten. With warp speed, she was back. Her life, her family, the fact that she loved pepperoni pizza and chocolate ice cream, it was all there!

Before Katherine realized she'd moved, she had rushed into her father's arms. He held her tightly, his arms strong and reassuring. The tang of Old Spice as familiar as the man himself. How could she have forgotten this man? The man who'd been both mother and father since she was eight years old.

He drew back to look down at her, cradling her face in his big hands. "Little girl, you gave me a hell of a scare," he said gently.

Everything hit her at once, the good as well as the bad. The old doubts and fears, the overwhelming sense of not quite measuring up flooded her. Katherine wilted in her father's arms, giving in to the tears she had managed to hold at bay for the last few hours.

She had failed. She'd had such high hopes for her career at the Colby Agency. Now she would lose the man she loved as well as her job. A heart-wrenching sob tore past her lips.

"Shh now, Katie." Her father held her tighter. "Everything's going to be fine."

"It's not ever...going to be fine," she stammered. "I really screwed up this time. And Raine...Raine's..." She couldn't say her worst fears out loud. She just couldn't.

"Don't say it, Katie." He patted her back as he gently rocked her from side to side. "From what I hear, you did a tremendous job and that fella you brought in is going to be just fine."

...and bring him in either way. Victoria's words rushed into Katherine's head, pushing aside all else.

She drew back and swiped at the tears streaming down her cheeks. "How do you know he's going to be fine? And I didn't do a good job. I blew it," she blurted, her words tumbling out over each other. "I failed. I'll never be like Joe." She shook her head. "Never."

A deep frown marred her father's features and sadness filled his coffee-colored eyes. "Katie, I don't want you to be like Joe. I want you to be yourself." He smiled, and some of the sadness disappeared. "I love you just like you are. I always have. Don't you know that?"

Kate realized then that he did love her. Her father hadn't held Joe as a measuring stick of success, she had. She threw her arms around his neck and hugged him close. "I love you, Daddy." Just as abruptly, Katherine pulled away. "How did you know I was here? So much has happened, I didn't even think to call you."

"That's what I was about to tell you." He glanced back over his shoulder. "Nick brought me here."

Katherine followed her father's gaze to the tall black-haired man who stood waiting at the back of the chapel. "Nick?"

A wide smile broke across Nick's handsome face as he slowly closed the distance between them, his limp a bit more pronounced than usual. "Hey, gorgeous," he said as he pulled her into his strong embrace.

Katherine hugged him back. Nick Foster was a good friend, as well as her co-worker at the Colby Agency. "Thank you for coming," she managed to say past the lump rising in her throat. He wasn't her husband or her boyfriend. He was simply Nick, her friend. And he had given her the book of matches. *You never know when you'll need 'em, he'd said.* The man always carried matches, despite having quit smoking more than two years ago.

Katherine frowned as she remembered that Nick hadn't been the same since a job he'd taken around that time, in Mississippi. She didn't know the details, but she sensed something bad had happened, and it was still eating away at him.

Nick held Katherine at arm's length and gave her a slow once-over with those assessing green eyes of his. "Technically I'm here on business." He smiled when he had completed his visual survey and seemed satisfied with Katherine's well-being. "But you know I would have come anyway."

Katherine moistened her dry lips. "Victoria knows, doesn't she? I'm surprised she didn't come herself." Katherine knew her voice sounded stilted, but it was the best she could do under the circumstances. She had worked so hard to make a place for herself at the Colby Agency. How had she managed to screw up so badly?

"She's at Bethesda checking up on Lucas," Nick explained. "And, yes," he added quietly. "She does know. I had to tell her. When I arrived at the rendezvous point to find you and the target gone, and your car in a ditch, we knew the assignment had gone sour. I couldn't risk not telling her."

Katherine nodded numbly. "Do I still have a job?"

Nick chuckled. "Are you kidding? The whole agency is talking about how you tracked down some big-time secret-agent guy. You'll have to tell me the whole story one of these days." He playfully chucked her under the chin. "Hell, Katherine, you're a regular celebrity back in Chicago. I plan to throw you a victory party when you get home."

Home. Katherine frowned at the emptiness that word suddenly conjured. What good was home or a career without the man she loved? How could she go back to her old life and just forget about Raine? "I should get back to the waiting room. There may be news about Raine by now."

"He's doing great. They moved him to recovery," Nick told her. "When I stopped in the waiting room looking for you, I heard the doctor giving the detective in charge an update."

Katherine closed her eyes and breathed a heartfelt sigh of relief. *Thank you, God.* Raine was going to be all right and that was all that mattered. She would learn to accept and live with her heart condition—but she wasn't sure she could live without Raine.

RAINE FOUGHT the thick blackness that surrounded him. He could hear someone calling his name, but he couldn't quite rise to the surface of the overwhelming darkness. He couldn't wake up. He tried, God knows he tried. But he just couldn't. Sleep, like a millstone around his neck, kept dragging him back into the abyss of nothing.

Later, a lifetime later it seemed, he struggled again to find his way to the surface, to break through that inky veil that hung between him and consciousness.

Finally, by slow degrees, his eyes opened. At first he squeezed them shut again, the light was too bright. But he couldn't find Kate if he didn't wake up. And he had to find Kate. He had to tell her that he'd been wrong to walk out on her. That she meant the world to him. That the past didn't matter. *That he loved her.* That realization still shook him, but there was no denying it any longer. He would tell her. He doubted it would change anything, but he had to say the words just the same.

But what if she'd already left?

He opened his eyes again. He blinked until his vision adjusted to the sterile, white brightness of the room. He moved his right arm and grimaced. Tubes from a nearby IV were attached to that arm. So he moved his left instead. He touched his parched lips with his fingers. Man, he could use a drink of anything wet.

Raine turned to his right to look at the array of beeping machines next to his bed. Pain speared through him, almost sending him back into the blackness. Frowning and confused, the fingers of his left hand found the bandage wrapped tightly around his midsection. Oh, yeah. He remembered now. Cuddahy, the son of a bitch, had shot him.

Gingerly, he looked to his left, making sure that nothing below his neck moved. His heart bumped into overdrive when he found Kate sleeping in a chair beside his bed. Her long hair fell around her shoulders. Those wide, expressive eyes were closed in what he felt sure was much-needed sleep. Had she been with him all this time?

Raine's frown deepened. Hell, he didn't even know how long he'd been here. Had it been days, or only hours? Lucas? He needed to find out about Lucas.

Raine licked his dry lips again. A water pitcher was on the table next to his bed. Maybe he could reach it. He cautiously stretched his left arm in that direction and the room spun wildly. A groan escaped when pain seared through him again. Raine swore under his breath, gritted his teeth and tried a second time.

"Raine." Kate moved to his side. "Don't try to move," She filled the cup sitting next to the pitcher with water, and peeled the wrapper off a bendable straw. "Here." She placed the straw against his lips and Raine took a small sip.

"Thanks," he said, feeling tremendously better just knowing she was nearby.

"If you want me to leave now I will," she said hesitantly. "I just wanted to make sure you were all right."

He frowned. "I don't want you to leave."

"Good." Kate smiled down at him then. She looked nervous and tired and more beautiful than any woman he had ever seen in his entire life. "You're going to be fine," she assured him.

"Lucas?" He had to know about Lucas.

"Lucas is fine. Victoria, my boss, called this afternoon. He has a concussion and a few cracked ribs, but he'll be out of the hospital in a couple of days."

Raine nodded. "Good." His gaze focused on hers. Had she only stayed to make sure he was all right? Would she go now? Now that she'd done what Lucas had hired her to do?

Kate averted her gaze for a long moment before she met his once more. Her eyes were suspiciously bright then. Raine saw the tremendous effort it took for her to gather her courage. He waited. This was the part when she would tell him that her job was done and she had to go back to wherever she'd come from. She was safe now, and he should be pleased that Kate could get back to her life. But he wasn't.

"I've done a lot of thinking during the last twenty-four hours," she finally said. She smiled crookedly and Raine's heart ached with the thought of never seeing that smile again. "I made a little list." She retrieved a small, wrinkled piece of paper from her jeans' pocket. She studied it a moment. "First I wanted to thank you for saving my life—more than once. And I want to apologize for not telling you the whole truth. I mean, as it came to me. I didn't tell you everything and I should have. I was afraid—"

"Kate, you don't have to do this." He couldn't bear the hurt on her face or the pain in her voice.

"Just let me finish, okay?"

"Okay," he relented.

"Second, I want to properly introduce myself." She essayed another tremulous smile. "I'm Katherine Robertson. My dad calls me Katie, but you can still call me Kate. I lived my whole life in Arlington, Virginia, until I moved out to Chicago to join the Colby Agency. I wanted to be a police officer, like my dad, but my 'bum ticker' got in the way." She released a shaky breath. "I'm a private investigator, and I'm pretty good, despite my physical shortcomings, if I do say so myself."

Raine felt his lips spread into a grin. "Pretty damn good," he agreed.

"Lucas hired the Colby Agency to find you because he wanted to help you. He didn't fully trust anyone in his own organization. He wanted to know the truth about what really happened." She smiled. "Finding you wasn't so difficult since you called and left that telephone number on Lucas's voice mail." Kate looked away a moment then. "I know I betrayed you, but I was only—"

"Kate," he interrupted.

"I'm almost finished," she insisted, then glanced nervously at her paper. "Third." Kate wet her lips and swallowed visibly. "Could I just do one thing before I tell you number three?"

A mixture of worry and uncertainty tugged at Raine. "Sure."

Kate leaned forward slightly, hesitated, her gaze locked with his. Her own uncertainty flickered in those deep brown eyes. She inhaled sharply, parted her lips as if she might say something, but closed her eyes and pressed her lips to his instead.

She kissed him softly, sweetly, the essence of hot chocolate lingering on her lips. Raine threaded the fingers of his left hand into her silky hair and pulled her mouth more firmly against his. He traced the seam of her lips with his tongue and she opened, inviting him inside. He stroked her tongue and all those other sensitive spots inside her soft, warm mouth until they both struggled for breath.

"Raine," she breathed. "Can I…is it okay if I touch you?"

Nipping her lower lip to draw her mouth back to his, Raine responded by taking her hand and placing it on his jaw. He groaned with pleasure when her soft palm stroked his beard-roughened skin. Her answering moan sent heat straight to his groin.

When she broke the contact of their lips again, Raine swore, caught her chin and pulled her mouth back to his.

"Wait," she protested, flicking a concerned glance at the quickening staccato of the monitor that tracked his heart rate. "We shouldn't be doing this, you're hurt." She licked her lips, no doubt tasting their kiss. "Besides, if I don't finish this now, I might just lose my nerve."

Raine exhaled in frustration, but relented. "For the record," he rasped. "I'd have to be dead not to want you to kiss me." Despite having just had major surgery, his loins were tight with desire. No one had ever shattered his control the way Kate did.

"Just be quiet and listen," she scolded gently.

He gave her his full attention and kept his mouth shut.

"Okay," she said, more to assure herself than him, he decided. "I hadn't anticipated this happening anytime soon in my life, but that's beside the point. It did and...and I'm glad." She leveled her gaze on his. "I love you, Jack Raine."

He felt stunned. He couldn't have uttered one word had his life depended on it. Could this woman—the kind of woman he'd never dreamed of having—really love him? Even knowing what she must know about his past?

"I...I know our lives are worlds apart and that it might never work even if you forgive me for not being completely honest with you." She fiddled with the edge of the white sheet covering him, her attention concentrated there for a time. Raine waited, he had to know what else she had to say, what *she* wanted.

"And I know that my heart condition is considerably less than appealing, but I..." She looked up then. "I just wanted you to know that I'll never, ever forget you and—" she swallowed "—that I'll always love you."

Raine searched her face, unsure what to say. No one had ever told him that before. No one. He had known that Kate had feelings for him, but he'd never expected her to love him.

She forced a smile. "That's all I wanted to say." She looked anywhere but at him. "I should go. You need your rest." She shoved a handful of hair behind her ear. "Goodbye, Raine." Kate wheeled away from him. Her movements jerky, she grabbed her purse and coat and headed to the door.

She was almost there before Raine found his voice. "Don't go, Kate."

She hesitated but didn't turn around.

Unsure of himself in this emotional territory, he plodded ahead, "I didn't get my chance."

She turned around slowly, her expression as uncertain as his own must surely be.

Raine attempted a shrug, but wound up grimacing. "I mean, I don't have a list or anything, but I do have some things to say."

Kate took two hesitant steps in his direction. "I'm listening."

He took a deep breath for courage and went for broke. "First, I want to apologize for being so rough on you." Fear of what could have happened plagued him again. Without her medication and with a concussion, anything could have happened in those damn mountains. His gut knotted at the thought.

She smiled hesitantly. "It's okay. I'm tougher than I look."

That was true, he knew, but he'd been a real ass. Admitting that to himself hadn't been so bad, but saying it out loud to Kate was another story. Raine cringed inwardly. This touchy-feely stuff would take some getting used to. But Kate was worth every moment of discomfort. "Second, I thought you'd want to be the first to know that I plan to officially inform Lucas that I'm out of the business as soon as he's back on the job."

"I'm glad for you," she said quietly.

Her reaction was entirely too reserved. He'd hoped for something more, like maybe her throwing her arms around his neck and then begging him to take her with him. I'm glad *for you*, she'd said. He wanted her ecstatic for both of them.

"The downside is, I don't know what I'm going to do with myself." He frowned in speculation, then chuckled wryly. "I'm not sure my particular skills are in high demand in the private sector."

A full-fledged smile spread across her sweet face with that remark. "I'm sure you'll find something to do."

Now for the serious stuff. Raine swallowed tightly at the lump swelling in his throat. This was where he had to climb out on that flimsy emotional limb. And damned if he didn't suddenly feel afraid of heights. "Well, I have that place in Virginia and I was kind of thinking of horses," he ventured cautiously.

"Horses?" Her eyes lit up. "Oh, that'd be great." She took the final steps that separated her from his side. "I love horses." A hint of hopeful expectation joined that twinkle in her eyes.

"It would only be great if you shared it with me."

Her eyes rounded in what looked like surprise. "We really don't know each other that well, Raine. Most of what we do know is half truths and speculation. You might change your mind when you get to know me better."

Raine resisted the urge to cut his losses before taking the next step. "I love you, Kate." He took her hand in his and laced their fingers. "That's all that matters."

"But you said you weren't coming back," she argued, obviously still not ready to believe him. "You intended to walk away."

"I was afraid to trust you with my heart." He heard the slight tremor in his own voice, but he didn't care. Stretching the IV tubes and earning himself another stab of pain, he reached up and touched her soft cheek with the fingertips of his right hand. "But it's too late. You already own my heart. You have almost since the moment we met. And now I have to trust you. I do trust you," he added firmly. "I hope you can find it in your heart to trust me."

"So, it all comes down to a matter of trust," she suggested carefully.

"Can you trust me, Kate? Trust me with the rest of your life?" His breath stalled as he waited for her reaction.

Her lips quivered into a smile. "Oh, yes. I've trusted you this far, why change now?" Kate leaned forward and kissed him thoroughly, with all the love Raine knew was in her heart.

Epilogue

"The Colby Agency cost me the best contract agent I had."

Victoria lifted a speculative eyebrow at the man sitting on the other side of her immense oak desk. "The way I see it, *you* cost my agency one of our best trackers."

Lucas Camp sighed, then twisted his lips into that one-sided smile that Victoria found entirely too charming. "Touché, Victoria," he admitted.

"It is nice to see two people so much in love," she said wistfully. She and Lucas had attended the private ceremony for Katherine and Raine, which had been held in a tiny wedding chapel in the Smoky Mountains. Victoria felt a pang of regret at the reminder that she would never again share that special bond with a man.

Lucas nodded his agreement, his silvery gaze too knowing.

"Well," Victoria began, pushing the matters of the heart aside. "Nick tells me that you were rather impressed with his final report."

"Very impressed. And not just with the report." Lucas sat a little straighter and pulled a businesslike face. "I could use a man like Nick on my team."

"Don't even think about it, Lucas. Nick is too valuable

to this agency. Don't you dare try to recruit him. I won't stand for it.''

''Okay, okay,'' Lucas placated. ''Nick's a hell of a guy, but I would never recruit him behind your back. It was just a thought. It never happened,'' he offered by way of apology.

''I'll hold you to that,'' Victoria stated pointedly, giving him notice.

Lucas got to his feet. ''I should be going.''

Victoria stood, feeling oddly reluctant to let him go. ''When is your flight back to D.C.?''

''Tomorrow morning.'' Lucas reached for his cane propped against the nearby table. ''If you don't have any plans,'' he said slowly, ''perhaps you'd like to join me for dinner tonight.''

Victoria swallowed at the tight little lump that had lodged in her throat the moment Lucas entered her office. ''I thought you never mixed business with pleasure.''

That crooked smile tilted his lips once more. ''There's a first time for everything,'' he suggested. ''Of course, we could talk shop if you prefer.''

Victoria surveyed the tall, distinguished man before her for a long moment. The gray peppering his coal-black hair hadn't detracted from his good looks. Nor had the passing of nearly half a century since his birth softened his rugged frame. He still commanded a presence that made a woman breathless. When Victoria's gaze settled back on his, she noted the uncertainty her scrutiny had generated.

''Dinner would be lovely, Lucas.'' Victoria smiled and the doubt in his eyes vanished. ''And I would prefer to discuss anything but shop.''

''I'll call for you at seven then,'' he said before he turned toward the door.

Victoria nodded and then watched his slow, labored

progress as he crossed the room. Her attention riveted to his right leg. She knew that beneath the classic wool slacks he wore a prosthesis. Tears stung her eyes as memories flooded her mind. In that cage, all those years ago, during a war that no one wanted to remember, the price of one young lieutenant's life had been the right leg of another.

And Victoria would always owe Lucas for that.

* * * * *

HARLEQUIN®
INTRIGUE®

Elevates breathtaking romantic suspense to a whole new level!

When all else fails, the most highly trained, covert agents are called in to "recover" the mission. This elite group is known as

THE SPECIALISTS

Nothing is too dangerous for them...
except falling in love.

DEBRA WEBB

does it again with an explosive new trilogy for Harlequin Intrigue. You'll recognize some of the names from her popular COLBY AGENCY series, but hang on to your hats this time out. Because THE SPECIALISTS are more dangerous, more daring...and more deadly than any agents you've ever seen!

UNDERCOVER WIFE
January

HER HIDDEN TRUTH
February

GUARDIAN OF THE NIGHT
March

Look for them wherever Harlequin books are sold!

HARLEQUIN®
Makes any time special ®

Two women in jeopardy...
Two shattering secrets...
Two dramatic stories...

VEILS OF DECEIT

USA TODAY bestselling author

JASMINE CRESSWELL

B.J. DANIELS

A riveting volume of scandalous secrets, political intrigue and
unforgettable passion that you will not want to miss!

*Look for VEILS OF DECEIT in April 2003
at your favorite retail outlet.*

HARLEQUIN®
Makes any time special ®

Visit us at www.eHarlequin.com

PHVOD

HARLEQUIN®
INTRIGUE®

Receive 75¢ off your next Harlequin Intrigue® book purchase.

75¢ OFF!

Your next Harlequin Intrigue® book purchase.

RETAILER: Harlequin Enterprises Ltd. will pay the face value of this coupon plus 8¢ if submitted by customer for this product only. Any other use constitutes fraud. Coupon is nonassignable. Void if taxed, prohibited or restricted by law. Void if copied. Consumer must pay any government taxes. For reimbursement submit coupons and proof of sales to: Harlequin Enterprises Ltd., P.O. Box 880478, El Paso, TX 88588-0478, U.S.A. Cash value 1/100¢. Valid in the U.S. only.

Coupon expires July 31, 2003.
Redeemable at participating retail outlets in the U.S. only.
Limit one coupon per purchase.

110447

5 65373 00075 5   (8100)0 11044

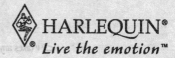

HARLEQUIN®
Live the emotion™

HARLEQUIN®
INTRIGUE®

Receive 75¢ off your next Harlequin Intrigue® book purchase.

75¢ OFF!

Your next Harlequin Intrigue®
book purchase.

52604515

Visit us at www.eHarlequin.com
NCP03HI-CANCPN
© 2003 Harlequin Enterprises Ltd.

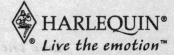

HARLEQUIN®
Live the emotion™

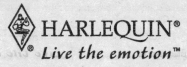

FTD.COM

SHOP ONLINE OR DIAL 1-800-SEND-FTD

$10.⁰⁰ OFF

COUPON

Expiration Date: April 30, 2003

To redeem your coupon:

**Log on to www.ftd.com/harlequin
and give promo code 2199 at checkout.**

Or

**Call 1-800-SEND-FTD
and give promo code 2194.**

Terms and conditions:

NCP2199